WICCA CODEX

RAYMOND NIEDOWSKI

The Wicca Codex is a work of fiction. Any similarity to names or events is unintentional.

Copyright© 2025 by Marion Niedowski

First printing

All rights reserved. No part of this book may be reproduced, stored in a retrieval system, or transmitted in any form or by any means without the prior written permission of the publisher, except by a reviewer who may quote brief passages to be printed in a newspaper, magazine, or journal.

Published in the United States by Riverhaven Books

www.RiverhavenBooks.com

ISBN: 978-1-951854-43-0

Printed in the United States of America

Book and cover design by Stephanie Lynn Blackman

Whitman, MA

In Memoriam

The Wicca Codex is being published in Raymond Niedowski's memory as his attempts were not successful in the mid-1990s when the final manuscript was generated. Having retired at the early age of 53 to write his novel, he finally accepted that his effort was going to be delegated to the "curiosity" rather than the "Great American Novel" category. Better late than never, it is now available for all to enjoy.

Ray travelled to more than 85 countries for which he did a personal write-up for each visit, in addition to writing many travel articles for various publications and short stories as well. A gifted photographer, he spent time during his retirement years pursuing that and many other varied and creative interests.

This book stands as a tribute and recognition for all that he accomplished over the course of his lifetime!

— Marion Niedowski,

his loving wife for 57 years

Chapter 1

Friedrich and Ilsa Grundig leaned into the stiff wind swirling through the central German countryside. It was just past noon on the last day of October. The year was 1490. The couple's ragged clothing was ill-suited to the autumn chill, made even more penetrating by the low, slate-gray clouds hovering overhead. They had left their village of Hockenberg a day and a half ago and now struggled along the rough path that had long since degenerated into a rocky trail as it entered the foothills of the Harz Mountains. They were cold, weary, footsore, and hungry, having already eaten the few items they could carry. Despite these hardships, they expressed little complaint. They knew this was part of the price to be paid for the special powers they possessed.

"Hurry, wife," extolled Friedrich, as Ilsa lagged behind. He had stopped and turned toward his mate so she could better hear his plea. His six-foot frame, shortened by a stoop incurred through decades of labor with the land, had been bent further by the strenuous journey. He leaned heavily on a staff fashioned from a fallen branch many miles back. Impatience was etched into his dusty face, which also bore the rough features of forty hard years of life. Nevertheless, his words were not spoken in an unkind way. "There are still several hours of travel before we reach the Sabbat, and we must be there by dark. You know how unforgiving the leaders are with latecomers. It will not do to test the good will of Bentar and the council. We must make haste."

"Yes, you are right," replied Ilsa, struggling to catch her breath. "I am coming."

In most things, Ilsa was the opposite of her spouse of twenty years. She was short—only two inches beyond five feet—but stood erect even when the weight of travel tried to arch her back. Friedrich's words were typically muted; hers were always direct and confident and sent on their way with a volume that dominated most conversations. If he sometimes lacked wisdom, she exhibited an uncanny knowledge of many things.

Wicca Codex

Where he displayed the unmistakable evidence of years of toil, she showed a smoothness in her features that belied the wearying work she engaged in. Ilsa realized she was stronger in some ways than her husband but knew her role was one of subservience to him. He had the physical strength to endure; she the mental toughness to survive. Each was the perfect complement to the other. It was why their partnership had lasted through the years, even in times so often marked by treachery and tribulation.

"I remember the unfortunates who were tardy last Walpurgis Night," said Ilsa. "I've no wish to experience the same fate." She recalled the grisly scene from half a year ago, when the leaders of the Sabbat took their anger out on several late arrivals, who were made sacrificial examples in lieu of the usual animal offerings. Shuddering from the thought and shivering from the chill, Ilsa wrapped her scraggly shawl more tightly around her neck and shoulders and dug deeper for the strength to proceed.

The Grundigs' destination was Brocken, the highest mountain in the Harz range. Just shy of 4,000 feet, it was not among Europe's most imposing peaks. It did, however, have a reputation larger, perhaps, than its modest size might normally engender. For one thing, the surrounding area had been mined since the tenth century for its silver, gold, and other valuable elements. But this particular locale also produced a phenomenon called the Specter of the Brocken, known as *Brockengespenst* to the German countryfolk. This involved an optical illusion in which a vast ghost-like shadow was projected on the mountain's mists under certain atmospheric conditions. The effect was so real and so terrifying that it invariably sent waves of trepidation through any unfortunate enough to experience the effect. Observing the Specter was considered an evil omen of the highest order by the local populace. This circumstance was almost certainly a factor in selecting Brocken for one of its most important—and infamous—uses. It was the gathering site for the region's practitioners of witchcraft. This was the purpose the mountain would serve this night. It would host The Great Sabbat of All Hallow's Eve.

Brocken held several advantages for such meetings. Perhaps most important, it was sufficiently remote to discourage unwanted attention, particularly from the prying eyes of the Papal Inquisitors. It was within reasonable travel time of much of Germany and even its surrounding countries, drawing large numbers of attendees—up to several hundred at the most important meetings—which further discouraged interference from civil and religious authorities. Also, the omen of the Specter produced just the right sense of awe and fear among the attendees. Finally, the abundant forests and pasturelands of the region afforded ample supplies of food, wood, and other materials needed for large gatherings.

This particular meeting, or Sabbat, was the most significant of the annual events held at Brocken, and indeed throughout the pagan world. Because of its importance, Friedrich and Ilsa had attended each of the past dozen years. All Hallow's Eve, also known by some as Samhain, was the feast of the dead, the one night during the year when the non-living could return to do their work—good or ill—among those who still inhabited the earth. The Grundigs were also faithful attendees of Roodmas, or Walpurgis Night, every April 30. And when they could, they participated in the lesser ceremonies held here on Candlemas—February 1—as well as Lammas—July 31, but they were not always able to get away for these. But tonight was to be special, and they would not have missed it for anything. After the initiation of new members, which occurred at the beginning of each meeting, Friedrich and Ilsa were finally to be elevated in status and made leaders of their own coven. Actually, it would be Friedrich who would officially assume the title of coven leader, since this honor was almost always conferred on a male. In reality, however, Friedrich knew he would be most ably assisted by Ilsa and would consider her their group's co-leader. They had aspired to be leaders for some time and had recruited several new members in their village, situated to the southwest in the Vogelsberg area of Hessen. Their goal would be achieved in just a few hours, and on the year's most important night. If they needed motivation to proceed with their journey, they had it.

The couple continued to strain along the rugged route. Eventually, they diverted onto an even narrower and more torturous side path, one that twisted away from the main trail and climbed through rocks, boulders, and the gnarled branches of old trees. Mercifully, after a hard half-hour trek, it widened and broke out into the Brocken meeting site, a large clearing about two-thirds of the way up the mountain. Twilight had started to settle into the deeper recesses of the surrounding hills, but Friedrich and Ilsa saw, thankfully, that they were not late. The ceremonies would not start until well after dark, with the most important event, The Black Mass, scheduled for midnight. A large group had already gathered, and others were continuing to come in from the surrounding area, including many from a considerable distance. Most traveled alone or with but one or two companions, not wishing to attract the attention that might come to a larger group.

Ilsa, regaining some of her stamina, took pleasure as she always did in the beauty of the setting, now bathed in the last of the day's rapidly dwindling light. Another observer might ponder the irony of choosing so picturesque a location for the activities that were about to take place. Ilsa gave it no thought. In fact, she would say, if asked, that the site was in harmony with the proceedings, which comprised such an important component of her religion—connected to nature and to the natural progression of the seasons.

Friedrich and Ilsa sought out Bentar to pay their respects. He was the highest-ranking Chief at the Sabbat. As such, the Grundigs thought it best to pay him his due. They also met as many of the lesser regional leaders as they could. It never hurt to spread homage around, they knew. With these necessities out of the way, they filled their near-empty stomachs on the food and drink the meeting organizers had arranged to be provided. Although the main feasting would await the conclusion of the festivities, it was learned a long time ago that things went better if at least the worst of the hunger was taken care of in advance. They chatted with a few acquaintances they recognized among the throng and warmed themselves at the large fires built at several locations in the clearing to provide both light and heat.

In wandering about, they happened on a small boy, about ten years of age in appearance, ill-clothed, tousle-haired, and rough-bred. His features were dark, some would say even menacing, yet there was a brightness in his eyes and an unmistakable air of authority draped about him. They inquired of him and learned he was a German lad—Johann Faust by name—from a village not far removed from their own. At the moment he stood in the center of a group of ten or fifteen people conversing on many topics. He was apparently unaccompanied and spoke in words well beyond his years. His knowledge of the world in general, and the upcoming rites and rituals in particular, was remarkable. To Friedrich, and Ilsa especially, there was something strangely troubling about the boy. He commanded respect and attention, yet there was a certain unease that settled over those who entered his circle. Perhaps it was his young age, perhaps his learned words, or his confidence, or his disturbing mien. Most likely it was all of these. Ilsa and Friedrich could not quite identify or explain it, but it was there nonetheless. They listened to the discourse for several minutes, not taking part in any of the discussion, then forced themselves to break away and move on.

As night crept in and enveloped the clearing, the couple selected a place at the edge of the encampment to await the proceedings, which began shortly after the last light had withered away. The darkness, lessened only by the flames from the surrounding fires, served to enhance the eeriness of the ceremonies and the feeling of apprehension generated by the Specter. As the attendees became aware that the first activities were about to begin, a heavy silence descended on the space. The quiet was broken only by the crackling of the flames and the cries of the various animals assembled in pens at the edge of the clearing. Somehow these creatures sensed that these were their last moments of life, brought to this spot to serve as food, or as sacrifices. To them the reason mattered little, the end result being the same.

All activities of the Sabbat were to take place in the center of the

Wicca Codex

open area, now inhabited exclusively by Bentar, as the regional Chief, and six councilor assistants. All sat at an altar-like table constructed from Brocken's ample supply of stones and boulders. A Chief such as Bentar was considered the devil's actual representative and was thus accorded honor and respect as though he were Satan himself. Many of his underlings believed, with no doubt whatsoever, that he was. His appearance—tall and ominous, dark and foreboding, an aspect he took pains to produce and project—gave every indication that he was The Black Prince. If any thought otherwise, they would not dare question it. He was an effective leader—bold in judgment, ruthless in executing decisions, impatient with weakness, merciless to any perceived offender. He demanded homage and respect, and he received it. It would take an extraordinarily courageous—and foolhardy—individual to challenge his authority. None had done so during the ten years since he had wrested control from his predecessor, an impotent individual who had little chance against the likes of Bentar. He quickly inserted his strongest and most trusted followers on the council. Before anyone knew what had occurred or could object, he had usurped unerring control of the German region. There was every indication the situation would remain thus for a long time to come.

For tonight's celebration, Bentar was covered in goatskins, denoting his association with the underworld. He stood solemnly and began by invoking the demon spirits—the incubi, the succubi, and the imps—to guard the site and the proceedings. He exhorted them to bring down suitable catastrophes on the enemies of Satan. Having set the appropriate tone, Bentar then asked for the initiates to be assembled. The continued life of the group was dependent on expanding the membership, so it was considered extremely important to bring fresh blood, so to speak, into the organization. On this day there were to be thirteen new members—a propitious number. Each initiate was brought before the council, still seated at the altar-table, and made to listen to a long series of ritualistic incantations recited by each council member in turn. Afterwards the newcomers took a blood oath, on pain of death, to accept the absolute authority of Bentar and the council—represented locally by their coven leaders, show unswerving loyalty to the cause of the black arts, maintain absolute secrecy about these proceedings, and work untiringly to destroy Pope Innocent VIII and his lackeys, the abhorred Papal Inquisitors.

After each initiate swore allegiance, several of the animals were sacrificed and the initiates made to drink their blood. A lock of hair and a nail paring were taken from each person, since it was known that he or she could be manipulated by the possessor of these items. The candidates were then stripped naked and, as a final act of humility and obeisance, made to kiss Bentar's buttocks. They were cut on the finger with a sharp fragment of bone to procure several drops of blood, which were co-mingled with a drop taken earlier from Bentar. The blood specimen was hurled into the fire as a final act of purification and bondage. The initiate was then clothed in a black robe and declared a full-fledged witch, then led off to the wild cheers of the congregation.

With this phase complete, Bentar called on those who were to be elevated to leadership of a coven. There were four such individuals on this night—all males, as expected—including Friedrich. Along with the others, he took his place, sitting on one of the low stones set up in the center of the clearing, immediately in front of Bentar and the council. Ilsa looked on from the edge of the gathering encircling the central area. There was a touch of pride, but a larger dose of wariness, despite her having witnessed this ceremony many times before. One never knew what whim of Bentar or some council member would cause the rite to be changed unexpectedly. The leaders knew that unpredictability was often the most effective means to foster the proper spirit of obedience—and fear.

One of the council members, an ancient specimen with shriveled hands and face, rose with an exaggerated stoop. He reached into a cloth bag and extracted what looked to Friedrich to be a very old book. He did not open it but merely laid it solemnly on the altar-table, as if to give authority to his words, which were slowly spoken to the coven-leader candidates in a voice as gnarled as his skin.

"You have been chosen," creaked the old man, speaking from the memory of countless similar past ceremonies, "for a most significant task: to help fulfill the mission set upon us by The Black Prince. You have no more important purpose than to see that his will is carried out. He has already provided you with extraordinary powers in the pursuit of that cause and, by this elevation, you will take on even greater abilities, which he has given us the means to confer on you." He cast a glance toward the book lying on the altar. "You must see to it that you dedicate your lives to the fulfillment of his objective. Your own lives are important only in so far as they can be used to attain the goals that have been established by The Great One."

The old man paused, leaning lightly on the altar. He continued after a moment or two. "These include, first and foremost, the acknowledgment of his supreme authority and the worship of his being. Second, the growth of the body of members serving his cause. This you have already demonstrated an ability to accomplish with your recruitment of new members. Third, the dissemination of his words and ideas to all with whom you come in contact. Fourth, the exercise of your powers to the enhancement of his cause. Finally, the destruction of all that is anti-black and pro-Christian; in particular, the one most opposed to his goal, the lecherous and barbarous Roman Pope, Innocent VIII,"—the words had become biting, venomous, surprisingly robust for one of so many years—"his treacherous *Summis Desiderantibus*, the murdering Inquisitors whom he has sent into our midst these last six years to destroy us and our cause, particularly the zealots Kramer and Sprenger and their malicious *Malleus Malificarum*, and all others who follow the tyrant Pope. There can be no higher achievement than the fulfillment of these ends. You are truly honored to be selected for this task."

The speaker halted again. Friedrich was not certain if it was done for dramatic impact or if the effort required to deliver the scathing dissertation had taken its toll on the old man. Apparently, it was the former, as the councilor then asked the four candidates to stand before retreating to his own seat once again. Friedrich could hear only the crackling of the fire and the pounding of his heart. He rose from the cold stone seat and faced the council and Bentar, who walked slowly from behind the altar-table to stand in front of them. Those in the rear of the large throng were spared his scowling visage by virtue of distance. The ones in front, particularly Friedrich and his three companions, had to endure it. For a long time Bentar said nothing. Then he began.

"You may be tempted to think," said Bentar, excruciatingly slowly, unbelievably quietly, while thrusting his stiletto gaze into the face of each candidate in turn, "that you are something special by this elevation to coven leader." Bentar paced from one man to the other as he spoke, his hands buried in the folds of his robe's oversized sleeves. "You may perhaps think this makes you better than the rest of the membership, entitled to certain privileges and honors. You may also think that hearing our council call you 'honored' to help us do the work of our Prince places you above those whom you would lead. If this is what you think, YOU...ARE...MISTAKEN!"

These last words thundered from Bentar's lips so that they reverberated from the surrounding mountains and echoed into the ears of the recipients again and again. His years of leading the group had turned him into a skilled orator. He gestured effectively and inflected his voice upwards or downwards to achieve its desired purpose. A pause from Bentar could be as biting as a shouted epithet. He continued, his voice only slightly less voluminous. "You are to remember that you are miserable creatures, worth nothing other than to do what must be done. You have no value but to serve this membership and the purpose for which we are assembled here in this Sabbat. You will go forth and do our bidding, then return at the next convocation and report your successes and failures. It is expected that there will be many of the former and none of the latter. If that is not the case, you may be tempted to remove yourself from our midst before the next meeting. But consider: where would you go? To what realm do you think you could take yourself that you would be beyond our reach? You know it is not possible. You must remember that we have effects from your miserable bodies. These will be used to call on The Prince's demons to exact retribution if the need arises. So, leaders-to-be, do not tolerate failure. Accept only unqualified success. You will be the happier for it, to be sure."

Bentar paused to let his carefully chosen phrases work their intended purpose on these men. With few exceptions over the years, they served him well. Having fulfilled their initial intent, his words turned in a different direction. His demeanor softened, his eyes grew less intense, his tone lightened, his hands emerged from their hiding place and were clasped in front of him in as conciliatory a gesture as he could muster.

"But now, my friends, be not dismayed. You must rejoice in the moment at hand. You have achieved success in the past, so there is no reason to believe you will not continue to attain it. You will go forth and gather about you twelve others of like mind so that our Prince may someday take his rightful place among all those who walk the earth. For ours is the one true religion, and our noble goal is to bring it to all others, without exception."

The use of the term "religion" in Bentar's diatribe-turned-congratulatory monologue might have seemed curious to most persons living in the late fifteenth century, but not to certain scholars of the period who had studied the evolution of witchcraft. They surmised that its roots lay in the religious practices of an ancient people, one based on fertility rites and principles, and that its followers enjoyed a certain pre-eminence well before the seeds of Christianity were planted in the Middle East. As the latter gained ascendancy, however, the old religion waned until it could exist only as it did under Bentar: clandestinely and furtively. During Christianity's early period, the Popes dealt relatively mildly with adherents of the old ways. But as the new religion grew in power and extent, pagan practitioners were considered to be more of a threat. Some cults gravitated toward the supernatural and the occult, magic and witchcraft, sorcery and Satanism. After a time, it was easy, or convenient, for the Church to blur the distinction between sects. All who were thought to deal in the old rites were said to have evil powers and were labeled witches. These "heretics" were dealt with ever more harshly, including torture and death. The most recent authority for doing so had been emphatically promulgated just six years earlier in Pope Innocent VIII's Bull *Summis Desiderantibus*. The grisly methods and rules for doing so came shortly thereafter from Henry Kramer and James Sprenger, Professors of Theology and members of the Order of Friars Preachers, in their *Malleus Malificarum*. Both documents and their authors were anathema to all those assembled this night at Brocken.

Now, having set the candidates' minds somewhat at ease, there was only one more thing to be done. Bentar turned to the council member who had spoken earlier and retrieved from him the old book that had been placed on the table. He lifted it above his head for all to see. "Behold The Great Book," he said reverently. "Mark it well, for within lies the source of all that is of meaning to us. It has journeyed from the dim shadows of the past so that we may continue our struggle. With it, we will prevail. Without it, we are nothing. Look upon it and rejoice that it has been provided to us." Bentar placed the book on the near edge of the altar-table, opened it to the appropriate page, then turned to face the four men. He spoke once more. "By the power of the Great One who has given us the means to pursue his cause, I confer on each of you the special powers to which you are entitled as leader of a coven. You will approach the altar now and place both hands on the pages of The Great Book opened before you."

Each man did as instructed. At Friedrich's turn, he approached earnestly after first glancing in Ilsa's direction. He noticed a thin smile on her lips and was heartened by it, although he dared show no emotion. Friedrich raised both hands before him, palms down, and placed them as directed on the pages of the open book. Even in the flickering firelight he noted that it contained various markings and symbols with which he was unfamiliar. He had seen few books in his years. Nonetheless, he was somewhat acquainted with writing but had seen nothing before that resembled this. A peculiar sensation came over him as he felt something flow from the book into his hands, then his arms, and finally his entire body. It was not particularly painful, but neither was it pleasant. He tried to withdraw his hands but found that he could not. They remained on the book for what seemed like an eternity before Friedrich was able to remove them and swagger back to his position. He was lightheaded, though his arms felt as heavy as tree trunks. He could barely move them.

Friedrich was fascinated with this thing Bentar had called The Great Book. The volume held an unexplainable link to...something. What was it that made him want to take it up and wrap himself around it, feel the pages again, learn about the exotic symbols that had the power to make him feel this way, despite the discomforting physical sensation? It was beyond his understanding. He knew only that he could not take his eyes off it, even as Bentar spoke the final words of the ceremony.

"You have now been invested," bellowed Bentar, "into the company of leadership for The Great One's purposes. Go forth and do his work. But for now, enjoy this moment. Remember it, savor it. We congratulate you on your achievement. Now, take part with us in celebrating your good fortune." With these words, he turned to the throng and bade them raise their voices in cheer for the four new leaders. Friedrich accepted the accolades with gratitude, then strutted to where Ilsa stood. She threw her arms around him. He tried to acknowledge the gesture, but his limbs still felt like stone. The sensation lasted for quite some time before gradually declining.

The induction ceremony, important though it was, ranked below the main business of the evening, which was a celebration of the Black Mass. This was a mocking parody of the Catholic Mass, characterized by various sacrilegious acts, the more irreverent the better. These included such profanities as trampling on a Crucifix and desecrating a blessed communion wafer, illicitly obtained. As strongly as the Church held the Mass to be its most sacred rite—the veritable transformation of bread and wine into Christ's body and blood—Satanists saw it as its most malevolent, an outrageous representation of everything they stood against. Whatever could be done to mock it, deride it, pervert it, was done with vigor.

When the ritual was concluded, it was time for what most in the assemblage considered the real attraction: a frenzy of dancing, feasting, and drug-induced revelry, building in intensity until concluding with a sexual orgy. The debauchery extended through the early hours of the following morning, brought to an end only by extreme exhaustion and drunkenness. Despite the importance of this Sabbat in the annual cycle, it was no different in this respect from any other. The council knew that fear tactics were useful, but only up to a point. They were most effective if accompanied by satisfaction of the animal appetites of the membership.

Friedrich and Ilsa took part in these activities with enthusiasm before collapsing into a drunken stupor. When they next awoke, they found themselves lying in a dank, squalid, foul-smelling cell, not knowing where they were, and unaware as to how they came to be there.

Chapter 2

Maximilian Antares was a member of the Roman Catholic clergy in Germany. He was also a large, brutish man, well-endowed for his role as one of Pope Innocent VIII's Regional Inquisitors. All belonged to the religious community, specially chosen for their fervor in defending the ideals and principles of The Church. They were sent out among the populace to seek out heretics, witches, and others who might inflict harm against the true teachings of Christ.

Not only did Maximilian possess the physical resources necessary for the job, but he truly enjoyed his work, and there was a lot to be said for that. He was recruited by the papal legation sent to Germany shortly after the promulgation of the Pope's bull against witchcraft. He knew what the bull was intended to do: the complete and utter extermination of this heretical doctrine and those who practiced its black arts. The Pope's words imbued Maximilian with the spirit to do that which was required to safeguard The Church and its adherents:

"Desiring with the most heartfelt anxiety, even as Our Apostleship requires, that the Catholic Faith should especially in this Our day increase and flourish everywhere, and that all heretical depravity should be driven far from the frontiers and bournes of the Faithful, We very gladly proclaim and even restate those particular means and methods whereby Our pious desire may obtain its wished effect, since when all errors are uprooted by Our diligent avocation as by the hoe of a provident husbandman, a zeal for, and the regular observance of, Our holy Faith will be all the more strongly impressed upon the hearts of the faithful.

"It has indeed lately come to Our ears, not without afflicting Us with bitter sorrow, that in some parts of Northern Germany, as well as in the provinces, townships, territories, districts and dioceses of Mainz,

Cologne, Treves, Salzburg, and Bremen, many persons of both sexes, unmindful of their own salvation and straying from the Catholic Faith, have abandoned themselves to devils, incubi and succubi, and by their incantations, spells, conjurations, and other accursed charms and crafts, enormities and horrid offences, have slain infants yet in the mother's womb, as also the offspring of cattle, have blasted the produce of the earth, the grapes of the vine, the fruits of the trees...; these wretches furthermore afflict and torment men and women, beasts of burthen, as well as animals of other kinds, with terrible and piteous pains from performing the sexual act and women from conceiving, whence husbands cannot know their wives or wives receive their husbands; over and above this, they blasphemously renounce that Faith which is theirs by the Sacrament of Baptism, and at the instigation of The Enemy of Mankind they do not shrink from committing and perpetrating the foulest abominations and filthiest excesses to the deadly peril of their own souls, whereby they outrage the Divine Majesty and are a cause of scandal and danger to very many."

Maximilian had memorized these words and took them into his heart as no others he had yet heard. He yearned for the opportunity to expunge the vileness afflicting the purity of The Church and the "scandal and danger" tormenting those who would adhere to the holy doctrines defining the one true path to The Creator.

Equally inspiring to Maximilian were the precepts set forth in the *Malleus Malificarum*, which provided specific guidance for enforcing the Pope's call-to-arms. Maximilian knew it as well as the matins and lauds he prayed daily. He especially admired the title: "Hammer of Witches." It had a simple, yet forcefully elegant, quality that emphasized his own philosophy toward these heretics. Beat them down into submission. No quarter given.

As a Regional Inquisitor, Maximilian had the power to do just about anything necessary to accomplish his mission. For one, he had at his disposal at each place of inquisition—generally one of the larger towns where an abbey was located, a town such as Hockenberg—a "staff" of several enforcers ready, willing, and quite able to do God's work. For another, each town—typically the civil authorities but sometimes the abbey itself—usually had the equipment required to loosen a recalcitrant's tongue and pry the necessary confession from the poor unfortunate. In Hockenberg, this function was housed in a separate building located a short distance from the Abbey St. Bertholde, a kind of annex. The upper levels of the annex held offices and living quarters for an Inquisitor and his assistants. The lower levels, of which there were several, held prisoners' cells, interrogation rooms, and, of course, the torture chambers. The layout of this particular complex was most considerate of those staying at the abbey itself, in that these sometimes-annoying functions were kept discreetly separate so as not to disturb the solitude of the holy residents. The lower levels were also quite well equipped for their macabre purpose. No effort or expense was too great. Maximilian appreciated this, because he knew how to employ each and every device to its full advantage. He was very good at what he did.

Maximilian was a Dominican monk, and it was that order of saintly men that had been selected for the special task of dealing with heretics, witches, and similar deviants from the accepted orthodoxy. He had learned that this charge came from Pope Gregory IX in 1232, who was unsatisfied with the work of the bishops in conducting the "inquisitio"—the inquiry. To accomplish the grizzly work that had to be done, they were simply too timid for the Pope's liking. That year was now considered the official start of the Inquisition, although the repressive measures employed by Gregory had been conducted on and off by his predecessors against practitioners of the old religion for hundreds of years. From that point, however, the Dominicans handled the task so well that they came to be called "Domini canes," Latin for "hounds of the Lord." Maximilian was not offended in the slightest by this play on words. He rather fancied it and thought it did the order justice.

Maximilian had heard of another Dominican, one Tomás de Torquemada, who, as Grand Inquisitor for all of Spain these last three years, had developed a reputation far and wide for his extraordinary success in administering the Inquisition in that country. This success was brought about, in Tomás' view, due to his absolute devotion, in the view of many others, his absolute ruthlessness. It was a reputation Maximilian desperately aspired to attain. He had also learned of another monk—closer to home but further back in time—by the name of Conrad of Marburg, who had been among the first Inquisitors assigned by Gregory IX in the thirteenth century. His tactics were so ghastly he was ultimately assassinated by the populace. In general, Inquisitors were not well loved by the local gentry, even under the best of circumstances. They received little support and cooperation. This was inherent in the function of the office. These facts, however, deterred Maximilian not one iota. Indeed, they spurred him on to emulate Conrad and Tomás or even surpass them if possible.

And so it was that on a cold morning in early November 1490, Maximilian stood at the window of his quarters in the annex of the Abbey St. Bertholde and looked out at the gray clouds scudding across the angry sky. He rubbed his burly hands together as he looked forward with particular eagerness to the duties of the day. In some respects, it would be typical, in that he would have to deal with the usual collection of minor infractions allegedly perpetrated by the otherwise inconsequential peasantry. Nothing exciting there. He would dole out a few penances and fines and that would be the end of it. Today, however, there was to be something different, something that promised to provide more than the usual sport for Maximilian and his dedicated crew. Two individuals—a man and a woman—had been apprehended the day before on the road from Brocken. It was known that strange goings-on took place there, particularly on certain days of the year associated with old pagan events such as All Hallow's Eve, which had just passed but two days hence. Consequently, Maximilian had directed his chief assistant—Igor by name—and several others to station themselves along the route on the chance they would run into a careless evildoer or two.

Maximilian admired Igor greatly and appreciated his competence. He was an uncommonly small man, no more than five feet tall, and overly conscious of his diminutive stature. He made up for his lack of inches with a fierce determination to prove his virility whenever possible. The man could hold his own against anyone and thus had proven himself invaluable to Maximilian and various other Inquisitors who ventured into the region from time to time. Igor was especially adept at tracking down and capturing heretics for his superiors. He was clever, resourceful, loyal, and, above all, ruthless in his work, traits that endeared him to Church authorities. He was hoping this would be another successful venture. It was to be his lucky day.

The couple in question had for some time been suspected by Maximilian's local assistants of involvement with sinister groups, possibly even to the extent of being witches themselves, so it was quite fortuitous to come upon them staggering along the trail. Not only that, they were in such a dazed condition that they had put up absolutely no resistance. Indeed, they appeared to have no realization as to what was taking place, unable even to respond to any of the questions put to them. There was certainly no need for the weapons with which Igor and the others had equipped themselves, ready for, and in fact expecting, a fight. But there was to be none on this day, a disappointment for the men, Igor in particular. They had to content themselves with loading the prisoners unceremoniously onto a straw- and dung-filled wagon brought along for the purpose, whereupon the couple promptly collapsed into a deep sleep for the journey back to the village.

Maximilian's cohort also threw into the crude vehicle an object that had been carried by the man. It had slipped from his grasp when Igor and company had grabbed the couple rudely. The object was wrapped in rough cloth. Igor gave it a quick glance but decided against a close inspection. It was best just to get back to Hockenberg for now, he surmised. He would let Maximilian deal with these scoundrels—and whatever was wrapped in the cloth—in his own way.

Neither Igor nor any of his men noticed the single pair of eyes—

belonging to a small boy—that took in these proceedings from a concealed position a short distance back along the trail. The boy was particularly interested in the cloth-covered object and followed its departure with the most earnest attention.

And so, Igor delivered these prizes to his superior who, noting their trance-like state and unresponsiveness to his inquiries, directed that they be thrown into one of the underground cells. Maximilian personally took possession of the cloth-wrapped article. For now, he was content to place it in an out-of-the-way location within his spartan quarters. There being no discernible change in the condition of the man and woman for the rest of the day, he reluctantly decided to let them be and tend to other business. There was no paucity of other criminals requiring his attention.

At the end of the long day, Maximilian returned to his rooms to rest—and to eat. Extracting confessions out of heretics could work up quite an appetite in a man, after all. He called for some food and drink and was about to devour the meal—he could hardly believe how ravenous he was—when he remembered the item brought in with the suspected Grundig witches earlier that day. He retrieved it from where he had hidden it for safe-keeping and placed it on the table. Removing it from its cloth covering, he gazed at what appeared to be an ancient tome.

Maximilian had seen books before, of course, particularly during his studies for entry into the Dominican order. He even had several in his possession. This one, however, seemed different. He took it into his hands and examined it more closely. Its top, bottom, and back spine coverings were comprised of wooden plates clad in leather, with a flap made of similar material pulled over the front edge to protect the contents. A metal clasp secured the flap, permanently attached at the bottom plate, to the top cover. Unlike other books Maximilian had seen, there was no title on the top cover or back spine, nor did it have markings of any kind. Though not particularly large, it was heavy, and a somewhat strange, musty odor emanated from it.

Maximilian replaced the book on the table and undid the clasp. He opened it to the first leaf, whereon he saw, not words, but various symbols in faded black ink on graying, well-worn parchment. This document had surely been produced an extraordinarily long time ago, he guessed. The symbols were arranged in neat rows but were unfamiliar to Maximilian, who had seen nothing similar to them previously. He turned to the next leaf and saw more symbols, row upon row, presenting no more meaning to him than if the page had been completely bare. He turned again, with the same result. Once more. And again. All the same. Incomprehensible markings.

Maximilian knew Latin and German, and some Greek as well. He also knew there were other languages and writings with which he was unfamiliar, including the strange symbols of mathematics and hieroglyphics, but there was nothing he recognized. Absolutely nothing. Of what use could this have other than for perfidious purposes? Why would a mere peasant have such a volume in his possession? It seemed to be irrefutable evidence of nefarious doings, especially since it had been found in the possession of a man and woman strongly suspected of witchery. What stronger case could there be against these two?

During these ponderings, Maximilian's hands had come to rest on the document's pages. He noticed a tingling sensation developing in his fingers, also a heaviness in his hands. It was most unpleasant. He quickly removed his hands and pulled back away from the book as though it were cursed. He became uneasy over this. Uncharacteristically so. He was not one to succumb to worry about strange and unfamiliar things, but there was something exceedingly peculiar and unsettling about this book, if that is what it could be called. He decided that he had had enough of it for this evening, so he closed it—touching it carefully, slowly, reluctantly—clasped it, replaced it in its cloth covering, and returned it to its hiding place. He would deal with all this on the morrow.

Maximilian decided to retire for the night, his food uneaten. He had lost his appetite completely.

Chapter 3

Friedrich was the first to awaken from the long sleep that had overtaken both him and Ilsa. Consciousness returned only grudgingly. When enough of it had been restored, he sensed that something was very wrong. The only thing that registered any familiarity was a figure lying beside him. He supposed it was Ilsa but could not be sure. Everything else—the murky light, the abysmally foul smell hanging in the fetid air, the chilly dampness, the faintly distant cries of...what? human beings in anguish? — all were totally foreign. Where were they? Why were they here? Who had brought them to this despicable place? Why were they not at their home in Hockenberg? The questions assaulted his head as he lay on the cold and clammy ground. The only thing movable were his eyelids, and even that took considerable effort.

Friedrich tried to think about the events of the past several days. He struggled to bring his mind into the present and tear it away from whatever powerful forces had hold of it. The image of a meeting—the one at Brocken—coalesced briefly, faded, and then reappeared. He recalled a ceremony, something having to do with being made coven leader, and celebrating afterwards with Ilsa and the others, and...and... Beyond that, nothing.

He was still lying on his side. It occurred to him that he should try rising to a sitting position and take further inventory of the situation. He did not feel any shackles on his hands or feet—probably no need for them in here, he guessed, wherever "here" was—so he should be able to move freely. Friedrich tried lifting himself with his hands and was gratified he could do so without any serious physical pain. Even in the gloomy light he noted there was no one else in the room other than the adjacent figure. On closer inspection, he confirmed that it was indeed Ilsa. In his groggy state, he did not have the presence of mind to check that she was all right, or even alive. He was too curious about the dreadful surroundings. His eyes continued to explore.

Their "room" was indeed a cell, a small one, barely ten feet square. The walls and ceiling were of stone, the floor of dirt. There were no windows. In the center of one wall was a door of heavy wood, its only opening a minuscule one near the top, protected by a criss-crossing of iron bars. The cell's sole light was that which managed to slither in through the grating, probably from a torch somewhere outside. The only sounds were those that had penetrated Friedrich's consciousness—almost imperceptible, a mixture of shouts and cries, from men or women, he thought, yet more animal than human. He shivered. There did not appear to be anyone outside the cell, though he could not be certain of that without crawling to the door and peering through the bars. He decided that could wait.

Friedrich's thoughts turned to Ilsa. He leaned over and touched her shoulder gently. "Ilsa," he whispered. "Ilsa. Wake up. You've got to get up." No movement. Friedrich shook harder, his eyes widening, his breath emerging in short, raspy bursts. Gradually, Ilsa stirred slightly and opened her eyes, struggling to lift her head from the dirt floor and prop herself on an elbow. She rubbed the drowsiness from her eyes and slurred, "Friedrich? Is that you? Where are we? What's happened?"

Friedrich managed a brief smile. "Yes, Ilsa," he mumbled weakly. "It's me." His mouth and lips were dry, and he longed for water to quench his fierce thirst. He found it difficult to speak, almost painful. "I don't know where we are, nor how we got here, but it seems we have gotten ourselves into much trouble. How do you feel?"

Ilsa managed to sit up and take stock of her situation. She too was thirsty, but found her speech not as adversely affected as her husband's. "My head is pounding," said Ilsa, raising a hand to ease the hammer blows, though unsuccessfully, "but I seem to be all right otherwise. And you?"

"I'm fine, for the most part. I mean, nothing hurts much, but I can't remember anything after the ceremonies at Brocken. Do you recall what happened there?"

Ilsa thought for a moment. "I remember very little," she said. "Just that after you and the others were made coven leaders, there was much celebrating. Everyone was drinking and dancing and having a good time. We were doing the same, to be sure." The haziness kept flickering in and out, so she closed her eyes to force further recollection. "You expressed awe for The Great Book used by Bentar and the council during the ceremony. You complained how your hands felt heavy after touching it, but you wanted to see the book again and talk to Bentar about it. I think I remember that you wandered off toward the center of the clearing where Bentar and the council members had performed the ceremonies."

"You say I went off on my own?" said Friedrich. "Toward Bentar? I don't remember it at all."

"I am reasonably sure of that part, but all is dark afterwards. I must have passed out." Another dim spark rose in Ilsa. "Wait. There is one more thing. I seem to remember seeing that boy...the one called Faust, I think...near you as you went off. I..." There were sounds outside the cell—the trampling of boots, voices, a key turning in a lock. Friedrich motioned for Ilsa to be silent.

The door to the cell flew open and several men entered with torches. The sudden light caused Friedrich and Ilsa to shield their eyes, which had known only darkness for...how long? Hours? A day? Two? There was no way to tell. The torchlight also served to verify how unsuitable the cell was for human habitation. A slimy mold hung from every surface. Filthy water oozed from the walls and ceiling and ponded in small pools at several locations on the dirt floor, forming muddy depressions. Mounds of what appeared to be dried human feces occupied two of the cell's corners, those furthest from the door. Remnants, no doubt, left by prior occupants. This accounted for the horrible odor of the place, which, it was clear, had not been cleaned in quite some time. All was worsened by the cold, made visible now in the wispy breaths issuing from each of the cell's occupants.

One of the men, a small fellow, directed the others to lift "the

Wicca Codex

heretics" to their feet and have them follow him out of the cell. The men appeared to be repulsed by the figures of Friedrich and Ilsa but did as they were told. Friedrich heard one of them call the leader Igor.

Friedrich and Ilsa were half dragged, half carried on wobbly legs down a long, dank corridor, lined with what appeared to be other cells similar to their own along both sides. They came to a stone stairway, which they were made to climb. It led up to a large room with a high ceiling. It seemed that everything in this horrid structure was windowless. The sun never penetrated the bowels of this place, thought Friedrich. Smoky torches along the walls provided the only light. Friedrich noted that the room's center was empty except for a rough wooden table and several chairs, also of wood and poorly made. The table was bare save for something on it covered in cloth.

The figure of a large man stood next to the table. Friedrich and Ilsa, each propped up by two of Igor's underlings, were delivered to face the man. Friedrich noticed his exceedingly large frame, his air of unquestioned authority, the menacing scowl, and finally the hatred that poured from his eyes. It did not appear that this was going to be a pleasant encounter.

Friedrich managed with some difficulty to tear his gaze from the man to see what else he and Ilsa would have to contend with. Lining the walls of the room were various devices made of wood, metal, and rope, the purpose of which was only too clear to Friedrich. The sounds he had heard earlier were louder now. They seemed to be coming from somewhere nearby, although he still could not make out anything distinctly. They carried the same unearthly quality as before, much like moaning.

The large man motioned to the leader of the band sent to get them—the short one they had called Igor—to have Friedrich and Ilsa seated at one end of the table. This done, Igor and the others retreated to the edge of the room, there to await further orders. The glint in their eyes betrayed that each savored the anticipation of a good morning's sport, but whether this came to pass would be up to the Inquisitor—as well as the two whom he would now interrogate.

For a long while, the large man studied the two figures seated before him. He walked slowly around them, gazing from one to the other, studying them, analyzing their demeanor, saying nothing. Friedrich and Ilsa sat stoically, hands in their laps, looking only at the tabletop, with an occasional glance at the cloth-wrapped thing at its other end. They had not fully recovered from their earlier stupor, though their minds had cleared sufficiently for each to guess what these proceedings were about.

Finally, after some minutes, the figure looming above them spoke. "I am Father Maximilian Antares, Regional Inquisitor appointed by His Holiness Pope Innocent VIII of Rome, representative of Our Lord Jesus Christ in heaven." Maximilian's words boomed off the stone walls into the ears of their intended recipients. "As charged by His Holiness, my responsibility is to seek out and punish all those who, through their words or deeds, profess opposition to the teachings of the one true Church." He paused, waiting for some reaction, but received none. "What are your names?"

Friedrich and Ilsa, despite the dryness in their mouths and an ever-increasing fear, managed to croak out a meek response. Maximilian continued.

"You are accused, Friedrich and Ilsa Grundig, of heretical teachings against The Church, in particular the practice of witchcraft. You are accused of taking part in covens with heathens of like mind. You have recruited others to the cause of your Black Prince, the antithesis of Christ and the Christian religion, and have corrupted the minds of those whom you would seek to bring into your fold. You have been seen to cast spells against others, acts which have caused harm to those persons or their property. You have been observed returning from the vicinity of Brocken, which is the site of evildoings at various Sabbats held there throughout the year, most recently on All Hallow's Eve. At these and other gatherings you have worshipped Satan, cast aspersions on Christ and His Holiness the Pope, and taken part in blood sacrifices. What say you to these charges?"

Ilsa was so shocked she could say nothing. Friedrich, his hands gripping the edges of the table, tried to gather his thoughts, but could only say, "No, no, Lord Antares. These accusations are not true. My wife and I are simple peasants. We work the land and know of no such things. Who is it that accuses us?"

"Silence, heretic," shouted Maximilian. "Who accuses you is not your concern. You are not the one to ask questions at these proceedings. You are only to answer."

The Inquisitor's outrage was not surprising, given that it was customary for those bearing witness against others to remain anonymous. Such persons had only to step forward and profess knowledge of improper acts or writings or preachings. Accusations from at least two persons were considered sufficient for the establishment of guilt, conviction, and punishment. Maximilian had taken the opportunity during the Grundigs' confinement to acquire such accounts, which were usually given freely lest the interviewee be considered uncooperative and, thereby, in league with the heretics. At times the merest suspicion of wrongdoing was accepted in lieu of eyewitness proof. In the case of Friedrich and Ilsa, however, their strange activities over the years had roused suspicion in many of their neighbors, so it was not difficult to establish a case. They did, after all, consort with others of questionable character, Maximilian was told unhesitatingly. They did wander off at planting or harvesting time to who knows where, leaving pastures and animals untended. They were suspected of conjuring evil deeds against those with whom they quarreled—the cattle and chickens of their enemies turned up dead in too many instances for it to be mere coincidence. They appeared to want for nothing, belying their hard existence.

Despite the seriousness of these and other claims, there was no opportunity on the part of any accused to confront those making allegations against them, nor to have any representation on their behalf. Once apprehended and charged, acquittal was exceedingly rare. However, it was considered essential that loose ends, so to speak, be avoided. This required that a confession of guilt be obtained. Because these types of crimes were viewed by the Church as a very serious threat to its viability, the Popes had come to sanction the use of extraordinary means to obtain such a confession. This included, since the time of Gregory IX more than 250 years before, the use of torture. To root out heretics, witches, and others opposed to the Christian religion, an official system of accusation, inquiry, confession, trial, and punishment was established in many European countries, all administered by the roving Inquisitors.

Maximilian continued. "It will be better for both of you to confess your crimes without delay and accept just punishment, which is death by means of burning. Forcing us to extract the truth from you will be most painful, I can assure you. You undoubtedly have heard the sorry pleadings of others in this...establishment to be certain of that point. The result will be the same, of course, but with needless suffering on your part. And much wasted effort on ours."

Maximilian did not actually believe that extracting confessions by means of torture was as much a waste of time as he professed. There was some considerable pleasure and proficiency involved in inflicting pain without causing death, and one must keep in practice for these skills to remain sharp. The death of an accused heretic prior to having an acceptable confession was, after all, an annoyance best avoided.

Friedrich's mind raced in an effort to refute the charges. "Father Antares," he said, trying to summon up as convincing a voice as possible under the circumstances, "I implore you to listen. The activities you have mentioned can be explained. It is true we have just returned from Brocken, but we were there only to visit relatives of my wife, Ilsa. We visit there regularly and know of no such proceedings taking place of the type you describe. The gatherings you refer to at our home involve friends who have common interests, nothing more. We have no desire to undermine the teachings of The Church. You must believe me."

Maximilian laughed mockingly. He grabbed the table with both hands and leaned forward so that his face was but inches from Friedrich's. "You must take me for a fool, Herr Grundig. Do you not think we have checked on you and your wife? We know that Frau Grundig was born a short distance from here and that her relations reside in this area. And peasants meeting to discuss—what?—affairs of state? Not likely, I think."

Maximilian paused for effect, then pushed back from the table and said, "And what of this?" He bounded to the other end of the table, reached for his prize—the cloth-covered object—and slid it in front of him. He unwrapped it and, overcoming his antipathy toward the book, pushed it closer to Friedrich, but well beyond his reach.

"What of it, Lord Antares?" answered Friedrich, who gazed at the object displayed before him. It was clearly a book of some kind, and there was something vaguely familiar about it. He scoured his mind for anything that might let him identify it, to no avail. "I have no knowledge about what you place before me," he said cautiously, trying not to betray his emotions, his unease, the feeling that he had seen this thing somewhere before. "May I see it more closely?"

"You may not," shouted Maximilian. "Your attempts to deceive us are hollow. You will have no opportunity to lay your hands on this vile abomination and use its evil powers to cast spells, I can assure you. This codex was in your possession when you were apprehended. It will do you no good to deny knowledge of it. The facts are clear." Maximilian opened the book to a random leaf and spun it around to face Friedrich. The Inquisitor found himself grabbing at his hands, trying to dampen the tingling sensation that started to gnaw at the tips of his fingers. He rubbed first one hand, then the other. "What is the meaning of these symbols, heretic?"

Friedrich glanced at the markings on the page. Suddenly, he knew where he had seen this manuscript. He struggled to keep from bolting out of the chair, grabbing the document, and running from the room. This was the very same book—or codex, as Antares had called it—used by Bentar in the ceremonies at Brocken! He tried to remember when that took place. The recollection of it was still unclear to him, although it did not seem that long ago. Even more uncertain, however, was how this Great Book, as it had been referred to by Bentar—so important to their cause—had come to be here in the possession of the representative of their most despised enemies. Friedrich could not believe he had had it on his person, as the Inquisitor said. But if he did not, how did it come to be here? Friedrich hoped his face displayed neither his knowledge of this object nor his shock at seeing it on the table before him.

"I have seen nothing like this before, Lord Antares. I am but a poor peasant and have no familiarity with such things. I am able to read but little; my ability is most limited. These markings are not known to me."

Maximilian held his anger at these denials, permitting himself only a guttural noise to indicate his disgust. He turned quickly to Ilsa, who had remained silent to this point, staring only at the tabletop's rough surface. "And you, madam witch, I suppose you, too, know nothing of this," he yelled.

Ilsa struggled to stay calm and alert, since the effects of whatever had caused her long sleep had not fully dissipated. "That is so, Father Antares. My husband speaks the truth. I—we—have not seen this thing before, nor do I know the events of which you speak. We eke out a meager living as we can and have not much education. I know nothing of such things, my lord."

Despite her pleadings to Maximilian, Ilsa suddenly felt—no, knew, without a doubt—that Friedrich was the one who had brought this book here. Did he not have something in his possession when they finally left Brocken? The image was fleeting, fuzzy. She remembered nothing about the trip back from the mountain, and she had only the vaguest recollection of being apprehended by the Inquisitor's henchmen outside the village. But she was now certain that Friedrich had—somehow—taken the book during the revelries at the Sabbat, most likely when he wandered off in the direction of Bentar and the council members.

It seemed inconceivable to her that a document of such importance would have been left unprotected, but then, no one was immune from the animal frenzies of the Sabbats, including its leaders. In his dazed condition, Friedrich must have stumbled aimlessly to the altar-table in the center of the clearing, whereon he saw what had caused such strange sensations in him just hours earlier. There being no one to stop him, he picked up the book, covering it with some coarse fabric he found nearby. Not to hide it, really, since he was not even cognizant of his actions. The purpose was simply protection, since he had a vague awareness, even in his state, that this was something that required safekeeping, even if only by means of a rough, tattered cloth. And so, it must have been that Friedrich came into possession of this object, simultaneously most sacred—to Friedrich and Ilsa—and most profane—to Maximilian and The Church.

The clarity of this knowledge cut into Ilsa as a knife. She was unaware of how to accomplish the task, but she knew a way had to be found to keep this Great Book from remaining in the hands of these murdering Papists. If possible, it had to be returned to Bentar. She suddenly recognized its importance in fulfilling the purpose to which she and Friedrich had devoted their lives. As it had been spoken at Brocken, they were unimportant as individuals, except to the extent they could serve The Black Prince.

Ilsa was forced out of her reverie by the calculated words of Maximilian: "I can see that your stubbornness will require the use of extraordinary means to encourage your confession of evil deeds and sorcery." He half turned and spat out with relish, "Igor, make ready the rack. Let us see if that will assist in changing the minds of these apostates."

There is some irony in the fact that otherwise sincere and compassionate members of The Church, those who aspired to the Christian theme that every human being was worthy of love, could devise such inhuman—and inhumane—instruments of agony and torture. Instruments such as the one for stretching the body beyond the limits of all endurance, as the rack was designed to do. As well as others for gouging, impaling, cutting, burning, crushing, drowning. Ingenious devices, most effective for their intended purpose, as Maximilian was now prepared to demonstrate to these heretics.

The rack was a simple wooden frame onto which a human body was placed. The hands were secured above the head by means of a rope and pulley system. The same held true for the feet at the opposite end. A turn on the levers extended the arms and legs further and further from the body, causing excruciating pain. That was the idea, after all. When the pain became sufficiently intolerable, the prisoner usually chose to relieve it by telling his or her tormentors whatever they wanted to hear. In cases where the victim somehow survived the early stages of this torture and neither fainted nor confessed, continued application of outward pressure resulted in complete separation of the arms and legs from their sockets.

Although some who operated the mechanism relished this level, the Inquisitors generally did not, since this inevitably resulted in death without the desired confession. This was bad form and was to be avoided. Rather, pain was applied, then relieved to give the heretic an opportunity to consider the agony of the next application. This was usually sufficient to obtain the desired result—an unequivocal and emphatic admission of guilt.

Maximilian faced Friedrich and blurted, "We will deal first with you, Herr Grundig. Then with your wife, if you are uncooperative. Are you prepared to confess your abominations and blasphemies?"

Friedrich's left eye began twitching uncontrollably and he felt a slight tremor in his bound hands as he responded, "There is nothing to confess."

"Very well, then." Maximilian directed Igor and two others to lead Friedrich to the rack. Two other men were to remain with the woman. As this was being done, Friedrich glanced at Ilsa, whose gaze conveyed to him an understanding that he should not have fear in his heart. He took solace in the conviction emanating from her eyes and the knowing smile displayed on her lips. He silently acknowledged Ilsa's unspoken communication and accompanied Igor and the others, showing no apprehension as they proceeded to attach him to the dreaded frame. He offered no resistance.

Suddenly, Ilsa bounded from her chair, sending it careening backward. Her two guards were so taken aback by this audacity that they merely stood at their positions, shocked into inaction. Ilsa raised an arm and pointed it toward Maximilian as though it were a sword. Never before had she felt imbued with such strength, such rock-solid determination. Her brow was furrowed with hatred, her face red with rage. The words that roared from her twisted mouth reflected fierce conviction. "Lord Antares, I warn you not to do this to my husband. You are unaware of the forces that can be brought to oppose you and your murdering Pope. The consequences will be dire." Ilsa heard herself speaking, but what forces she was referring to escaped her. She had absolutely no idea what consequences she would—or could—bring into play to back up her words. Still, she sensed a supreme confidence in what she was doing.

Maximilian was stunned, but only momentarily. He recovered quickly and wheeled around to face Ilsa squarely, thundering, "Silence, woman! You will soon be made to see that true power lies in The Church and in the word of The Almighty Spirit. In Him lies the might to break your resistance and bring down those who oppose His word." Maximilian turned once more toward Igor and said, "Proceed."

Igor gleefully started turning the wheel that began the stretching process. The ropes tightened slowly; the frame creaked.

Ilsa had to do something. But what? What? There were things she could do as a witch, but these were quite limited in scope. Things such as causing the loss of cherished or essential objects for daily living, bringing dry conditions to the farms of her enemies when life-sustaining moisture was critical, even inducing human or animal illness. But this situation called for a higher level of ability—much higher. A level, she felt, even greater than the enhanced powers just conferred on Friedrich as coven leader.

Then it struck her, as a lightning bolt strikes the highest ground in a tempest. The answer was in The Great Book! She was unfamiliar with the specific capabilities it endowed, but sensed the great powers contained within it. She had seen the effect the book had on Friedrich and the others at Brocken. She hoped—somehow—to summon its energy and channel it toward her ends. Was this not why they—and the book—had been brought here? To counter the enemies of The Prince? These thoughts crystallized in her mind. All was suddenly clear.

She turned. There it was. So close. She took advantage of Maximilian's momentary inattention and lunged for the manuscript. Before anyone could stop her, Ilsa grabbed it. She instinctively shouted, "Assist me, Oh Great One, in this hour of need."

Maximilian reacted to Ilsa's movement a moment too late. He reached for the book in Ilsa's grasp but found he was being repelled from it by a tremendously hot wind, a wind emanating from Ilsa's open mouth. Had he been able to see, Maximilian would have been horrified by the grotesque creature standing before him. Ilsa's face and hands had been transformed into a gnarled mass of wrinkles and red, oozing sores. Her bulbous eyes glared hatred. But he could not see. The heat seared Maximilian's eyeballs and the skin on his face and hands. It caused his clothing to burst into flames.

The fiery, swirling mass flung Maximilian across the room, impaling him on an iron pike used to suspend prisoners in certain forms of torture. His body hung there, twelve feet above the others, strips of burnt clothing and seared flesh falling to the floor below.

Igor and the others knew they could do nothing but look on in sheer horror. They were immovable—for a moment, that is. Shortly after Maximilian's body was hurled onto the pike, the scorching wind swept through the room as a maelstrom, only made so much more terrible because of the incredible heat of it. The men became tormented by it. They were transformed into flying objects, slamming against walls and columns and torture devices and each other. As with Maximilian, they—or what was left of them—were quickly consumed by the flames, which now engulfed the entire space and all within it. All save

Wicca Codex

Friedrich and Ilsa, who felt the terrible heat but found that they somehow had remained unscathed.

Ilsa, still the source of the conflagration, stood as a monolith in the center of the room. If human ears had still been present, and if those ears could have heard above the deafening roar of the cataclysm, they would have heard these words shouted through the firestorm: "You have chosen not to heed the warnings given to you. Now you have seen and felt the power of The Prince of Darkness. You have tasted the flames you hurled against so many others. They have cleansed you of your crimes. My purpose has been accomplished." The words did not issue from Ilsa, but from some unknown, unseen source. From her came only the terrible wind and fire, from every orifice of her body.

As suddenly as they had begun, the destructive elements ceased flowing from Ilsa, though they continued unabated through the room. She regained her former features and slumped to the floor, exhausted and debilitated but still alive. She sensed that Friedrich remained unharmed, though still fastened to what remained of the rack. The heat was now so intense that even the iron components of the machine and all other devices of torture in the room were melting. Even the building's stonework was crumbling from massive internal forces. The entire room was engulfed in a gargantuan conflagration, all except tiny islands of safety surrounding Ilsa and Friedrich. Their powers were formidable, and so they were able to fend off the flames for a time, but the clear area around them became smaller with each passing moment.

Though a curtain of flame separated them, Ilsa lifted herself and turned in Friedrich's direction. "Dearest husband," she said with great difficulty, but yet with a calm experienced never before. She knew the end was near for them, but there was no sadness in her words. "The power to destroy our enemies has been granted to us by The Black Prince we have worshipped these many years, but I know now we cannot save ourselves. We have accomplished what had to be done, and so our lives have run their course. Though I regret we will not be able to continue our work in this life, I approach with joy the opportunity to be with you in another form to help fulfill our mission. It matters not whether it be accomplished in life, or in death. I thank you for your companionship and for your dedication and loyalty through the years." She paused briefly, then said, "Farewell, Friedrich. For now."

The same flames shrouded Ilsa from Friedrich's view, but he was able to hear her words, just as Ilsa was now able to hear his. "Yes, Ilsa, I understand, and I take comfort in the knowledge that we have done a most notable thing. The struggle will surely continue, though we have contributed our small part toward this noble cause. I don't fear these cleansing flames about to consume us, dear wife. I, too, look with joy toward the next phase of our existence. I will meet you there shortly. I take my leave now. Goodbye, Ilsa."

The flames slowly closed in on Ilsa and Friedrich and consumed them. Indeed, the entire building collapsed onto itself and filled the lowest levels of the annex of the Abbey St. Bertholde, as an avalanche falls into the valley below. No one in the village of Hockenberg—nor anyone else who came to view the surreal firescape—had ever seen such total destruction. Compounding the tragedy were those unable to escape. This included many innocent victims—no one knew how many for sure—prisoners held there for questioning to extract confessions of heresy, or witchcraft, or some other alleged offense against The Church. But for these, the flames were a welcome relief from the unbearable tortures inflicted on them. Those flames carried them to a meeting with their God, just as they carried Friedrich and Ilsa to a meeting with theirs.

And so it was that little remained of this place of The Inquisition. Little, that is, save for one item. Beneath the smoke and charred debris lay The Great Book, still intact, no trace of the swirling flames having marred its smooth surface, or even its cloth covering.

Chapter 4

It was several days before the smoky ruins of the Dominican annex had cooled sufficiently to allow town officials and residents to approach the place and pick over its sparse remnants. These included little more than the incredibly charred bone fragments of those unfortunate enough to be caught in the conflagration. Identification was impossible, given the complete and utter destruction of the building, its contents and occupants. It was believed the Inquisitor Maximilian Antares was among the victims, since he made his headquarters in the annex during these Inquisition periods, and no one had seen him since the fire. Several of Maximilian's assistants were also missing and presumed dead, but there could be no absolute confirmation of any of this. There was sorrow over the lost villagers, but little for the Inquisitor. His reputation for brutality, as well as the inordinate pleasure he took in the conduct of his duties, particularly in the afflictions of his victims, stirred up feelings of hatred in the community, although any outward expression of that sentiment was considered unwise. Even now. Antares may have died, but the power of fear engendered by the Inquisition was as intense as the flames that had destroyed the scene of its tortures.

The lack of salvageable items in the ruins created considerable disappointment on the part of the townspeople. However, there was one who did not come away from the wreckage empty-handed. The person was not a town resident, nor was he among those who scoured the debris days after the fire. He was a boy of perhaps ten years. Anyone who might have taken note of him, although none did, would have said he looked no different in manner and dress than other German urchins of similar age—just another lad among the curious at a village fire, taken in by the excitement. He was among those who had witnessed the fire and had remained at the site long after most of the others had returned to their homes. Although no one noticed it, the boy appeared to be strangely drawn to the scene, almost as though he was seeking something in the swirling flames. Eventually he did leave, but only so as not to draw undue attention to himself.

But the boy returned after dark, when the fire site was illuminated by an eerie light from the dying embers. He surveyed the scene to confirm that no one else was there. No one was. Without hesitation, he walked into the still-hot ruins. He was unaffected by the heat and the glowing coals scattered among the debris, as well as the pungent smoke that curled skyward. He moved sure-footedly toward the center of the steamy mass and into the large pit created when the structure's upper stories collapsed into its lower levels—the cells and torture chambers located below ground.

He continued inward and downward, eventually reaching the core's heart, where he stopped and stood silently. Glancing around, he saw nothing unusual. After a moment, he noted a faint glow, different in color from the orange of the smoldering coals, perhaps greenish-purple in character. It was a mere two or three steps away and just below the surface of the debris. The boy moved toward it and squatted so he could dig through the hot rubble with his hands—hands that would surely have been burned had they not been protected by some unseen force—to uncover the source of the glow. A minute or two was all the boy needed to retrieve something covered in cloth, which was unscorched by the fierce flames, as was the object itself. He took no time to inspect his find, turning instead to retrace his route out of the hole and back to ground level.

Before emerging from the depression, he checked the area for intruders. Seeing none, he crept toward the safety of the surrounding brush. Only then did he turn and look back over the fire scene for a brief moment. He cast his eyes downward to what he held so lovingly in his small hands. A satisfied smile came to his lips as he whispered, "Thank you, my Prince. I shall use this well." He then turned his back to the village and stole away into the night.

WICCA CODEX

* * *

Almost one hundred years later, in the year 1587, a remarkable book was published in Frankfurt, Germany. Its title was *Historia von Dr. Johann Fausten*. It told the strange tale of a boy named Faust who grew to manhood in Germany and led a wondrous life as a scholar and schoolteacher. His powers and abilities in magic and the supernatural were legendary. The narrative claimed that Doctor Faust, as he came to be called, was born around 1480 and died about 60 years later in central Germany.

The *Historia* maintained that Faust derived his extraordinary powers by means of a compact made with Satan. This may have come about as a result of the many stories and legends attached to the man. Some who knew him, or of him, claimed he was a charlatan—a mere trickster. Others said he derived his skills from a secret book acquired under mysterious circumstances while still a young lad. It was also said that no one ever saw such a book, although others remarked that he boasted of it on the rare occasion when he had imbibed an excess of ale. No volume of this sort—if, indeed, there ever was such a thing—was ever found in his possession, not in life nor at the time of his death. Many sought it, to be sure, for it promised a life of fame and fortune, as it presumably had done for Doctor Faust.

After his passing, Faust's legend grew to astonishing proportions. He became the subject of many strange tales of literature and music. All who heard or read them took pleasure in their fantastical nature and reveled in the creator's genius for storytelling. No one could ever know how the now-tormented Faust writhed in agony each time his tale was told, for the good Doctor had secured his eternal place in hell for the few years of pleasure and power he had acquired during his lifetime. His fabulous skills and abilities had indeed been derived from a book, though not an ordinary one. It was a codex with strange markings whose meaning was revealed only to those willing to pay the ultimate price. The book's secrets were so terrible that Faust felt compelled to conceal it against accidental discovery during his lifetime. He did this so successfully that *The Codex*—and its power—lay hidden for four hundred years.

Chapter 5

Monday, October 16

The young man sitting at Table 3 slouched in his chair and fought back a yawn. He didn't have to work nearly as hard to continue with his daydreaming. Stephen Blake couldn't believe most of the year was already long gone. Why, before you knew it, the '90s would be history and we'd be staring a new century in the face. *Time flies when you're having fun*, he thought, derisively. Stephen couldn't wait to escape his increasing boredom and flee outside into Boston's crisp mid-October air. He would give anything right now to clear out his tormented brain. At the moment, though, he was captive at one of those dreary industry functions designed, he was convinced, to suck the very life out of the sane. Drinks at six. Inane conversation until dinner at seven. More chatter as each of several bland courses was served by disinterested waiters in a drab function room. Finally, three-quarters of an hour—if he was lucky—of listening to some self-proclaimed expert drone on about the evening's topic. What was it tonight? He was listening only half-heartedly, and realized he didn't even know. Soon, thank God, he'd be able to say his goodbyes, extract himself from the depressing surroundings, and get out. He'd give anything right now to be somewhere else—anywhere else. It didn't matter.

Stephen was awakened from his distraction by polite applause. He gleefully realized the event was over and joined the throng evacuating the room to blitzkrieg the coat-check girl. "Good night, Stephen. See you tomorrow." The words registered only faintly as he snatched his coat and dropped a dollar bill into the tray. The voice was familiar, but for some reason he was having a difficult time associating it with a name or a face. He made the connection just in time to avoid seeming uncivil. He turned to see John Demming, one of his company's suppliers, extending a plump hand in his direction.

"Right, John," said Stephen, sleepily. "Tomorrow it is. I'll look over your proposal and we'll hash it out over lunch at Locke-Ober. See you there at noon."

"You bet," said Demming, a knowing smile on his lips. He was a veteran of these same wars. "Looking forward to it. Best get home and get some rest. Looks like you need it."

Stephen managed a weak smile. "Yeah, I guess. It's been a long day. 'Night, John." Then he was out the door, walking briskly, thankful for the unseasonable chill and the relative quiet of Boston's downtown streets. Unlike New York City, with which he was all too familiar from numerous business trips, nightlife in downtown Boston was negligible, especially at this time of year and in this kind of weather. He hoped this wasn't a portent of another lousy winter. Last year was easy, but the two before were bears, he remembered. And things had a nasty habit of averaging out.

Stephen Blake was in publishing, Manager of Procurement and Inventory for the city's second largest firm, HubBooks, Inc. It was his job to arrange for whatever supplies and materials the firm needed. Paper, equipment, whatever. All at the best possible price. Margins were minimal these days, and it took lots of hard-edged negotiation to eke out even the slimmest of profits. He liked his work and was good at it, rising from junior executive to his present position in a little over five years. He made enough to be comfortable, though he didn't chase after a particularly extravagant lifestyle. The firm's modern offices were in the heart of downtown, near the financial district. They occupied several floors of one of Boston's post-war-vintage gray granite structures that had been elegantly restored during the real estate boom of the 1980s. Stephen's office overlooked the Central Artery, that dinosaur of an urban expressway. The road rose phoenix-like from subterranean depths to perch on ponderous green stilts above the city, severing it in the process and mocking the history that enveloped it like a blanket. Every time Stephen looked out at it he thanked God they planned to push it back into the earth where it belonged. Right now, he felt as though that's where he'd just been. Buried.

"Well, we survived another one, kiddo, but just barely," he whispered, to no one in particular. He had a habit of doing that, even when other people were around. At the moment he honestly didn't know if he could go to one of these things again—ever. But he also knew his job would require him to endure many more similar evenings—about once a week, on average. The thought made him wince. A quick glance at his digital watch informed him he had about three quarters of an hour before the Ten O'Clock News came on. He had an apartment over on Marlborough Street in Back Bay, so he didn't have far to walk. At least this dinner had been downtown rather than at one of those highway hotels scattered around the metro area, so he could walk over after work, then stroll home afterwards.

He lived alone. Had for five years now. No wife, no kids, no companion, no roommate. Didn't have to rush home to anyone. Not that he was overly concerned even when he *was* married, which hadn't been that long ago, it seemed. It had lasted only about three years. Just didn't work out. No one's fault, really. That's the way it goes sometimes. He had his career, Janet had hers. She found someone else who could give her what she wanted and needed: conversation, companionship, a zestful spree through life. He put in too many hours at the office, liked to read, wasn't much of a talker, hated to party. To him, zest was a bar of soap. She called him dull. He was hurt by that and protested, but not too strenuously. She was probably right. It had been a clean break at the end, leaving him with no commitments or interferences on his neat, thirtysomething existence. He was thankful for that.

Being outside energized him, so he decided to kill a little time by taking the long route home. He wasn't cold at all. In fact, he suddenly felt great. His blue eyes reacquired their usual sparkle, shedding the stodginess that had clouded them at dinner. The curls of his healthy crop of black hair seemed to spring back to life with each step. They were unfettered by a hat, typical even on the coldest of days. It was amazing what a little air—and a sense of freedom—could do for one's psyche. Stephen buried his hands deep into the pockets of his gray overcoat—it was part of the executive's uniform he was starting to despise more and more—and followed familiar streets for a while. Congress, State, Devonshire, Washington, School, Tremont. He looked down at the red stripe of the Freedom Trail embedded in the sidewalk along part of the route. 'Got to get out one of these days and do the trail,' he thought.

Stephen admired Boston for its history and appreciated its importance. He grew up in a western suburb in a household that instilled the benefits of such things—his mother and father had both been teachers in the same school system. His had been a fairly typical middle-class existence, except for having had two working parents and no brothers and sisters. All the other kids he knew seemed to have a mom constantly at home, taking care of two point four kids each. Stephen was alone most of the time. Even when his parents were home, they always seemed to be marking papers or preparing lessons or whatever. They were loving and caring, it's just that they were...well... busy. He had a few friends, but they were more in the way of casual acquaintances, really, not strong "best buddy" relationships. He got along reasonably well with his peers but didn't go out of his way to cultivate connections with anyone. He enjoyed studying and learning, and he always did well in school. These traits stuck to Stephen like Velcro through grammar school, high school, and college. They were part of his makeup even now as he walked along the city's brick and concrete sidewalks.

Stephen admired the well-lit, marbled atriums in the steel and glass towers he passed. He thought it was interesting that you could live in a city for so many years, walking its streets day in, day out, never noticing the details of urban life. You could sleepwalk the same routes over and over and never find out what lay beyond the familiar path. A fragment of something he recalled hearing or reading a while back snapped into his head, something about taking a road less traveled. He made a spur-of-the-moment decision to do something about it. 'No time like the present to try Route B. Maybe this'll be the start of the new me I've been promising myself.' Excited by his newfound boldness, he wandered off into unknown territory.

Route B turned out to be Park and Beacon streets next to Boston Common—familiar enough, all right—then a detour into the innards of Beacon Hill, that patchwork-quilt of streets lying across from the Common and Public Garden, sliding down from the State House to the Charles River. Odd as it may seem, in all these years, he'd never ventured in. Stephen found it to be a different environment altogether—narrow, tree-lined, residential byways, old gas-style lamps casting a dim glow on brick sidewalks and cobblestone pavements, quaint houses sporting brick facades, multicolored doors, ivy climbing heavenward. It reminded him of an arboretum. The names of the streets added to the effect—Walnut, Spruce, Chestnut, Branch, Myrtle, Grove, Garden, Cedar.

Stephen felt mesmerized by the place. He wandered around for some time before deciding to head for home. He was walking south in the "flats"—the section between Charles Street and the river—so he turned east at the next corner to make his way over to Charles, which would take him back to Beacon. He was proceeding briskly now, not wanting to miss the news. A block short of Charles, he noticed a small shop on the corner. The light spilling from its hodgepodge window display yellowed the sidewalk and welcomed passing strangers, despite the late hour. This was confirmed by a crudely lettered "Open" sign dangling inside the glass door. The few other shops in the vicinity were dark, having long since shut up tight for the night. Stephen noted a weathered wooden plaque above the door, silently proclaiming the place to be "Ye Olde Booke Nooke." Yet another sign in the window stated, "Where History Comes Alive." Written right under this were the words, "G. Ernst, Proprietor."

Stephen loved books. He could hardly bear passing up any bookshop. His favorites were old, historical texts, and this shop seemed to exude mustiness. Through the window, Stephen could see piles of old books stacked everywhere. He glanced at his watch: nine fifty-two. If he left right now and hurried, he could just about make it home for the news. Then again, how often does one have a chance to explore a potential find like this? The tug of war waged for several moments. The Booke Nooke won.

Stephen tried the door and found it to be open as advertised. He entered the shop as a tiny bell tinkled merrily above his head. He couldn't help but smile at the quaintness of it. If Beacon Hill was a new experience for him, this was another world entirely. The place was a book-lover's paradise. It wasn't where you'd come to buy the latest bestseller, to be sure. There were no glitzy displays of the latest hot reads. The walls were plainly painted, peeling here and there. The floor was old wood planking and would have been nice if properly maintained, but the effect of years of neglect was evident. A small counter occupied the rear wall, just to the right of a faded lace curtain that led to the back of the shop. An old-style cash register sat stoically on the counter, the kind with metallic press-down keys and pop-up numbers. Stephen hadn't seen one of those in years. Running into a computer in here, it seemed, was not likely. That was okay with him. However, for anyone interested in old atlases, first or limited editions, almanacs, back issues of long-defunct magazines, or just old books not likely to be found at the mega-emporiums, this was the place. But it was also not for the impatient. Although bookcases lined the walls and tables cluttered the floor, there didn't seem to be much in the way of logical order to the displays. And, as Stephen had noted while still outside, there were countless piles of books. On tables, on chairs, even on the floor. The place may have been a treasure trove, but finding one's particular gem could take some time.

Given the hour, Stephen was not surprised to find the shop deserted. In fact, not only were there no patrons lurking about, there was no

Wicca Codex

evidence of any salesperson, either. Apparently, the muted sound produced by the tiny bell on Stephen's entry either couldn't be heard in the back room or was being ignored by whoever was in charge. This wasn't a problem, though. Stephen just wanted to look around and was content to do so in solitude. He didn't know quite where to begin, so he walked over to the nearest pile and started examining titles on the spines. He picked one that appeared worthy of closer scrutiny.

He was leafing through it when the first sign of human habitation came through the curtain. It was an old man, perhaps seventy-five or eighty years of age, with silver hair, matching close-cut beard and mustache, wrinkled skin, and slightly bent shoulders, but with eyes that were alive and sparkling. Stephen could make out their vibrancy even through the wiry spectacles—the kind with tiny rectangular lenses—balanced on the end of his pockmarked nose. His clothes matched his features—old and wrinkled—with a blue vest covering a red flannel shirt, tucked haphazardly into gray chino slacks.

The old man approached and addressed Stephen in a stiff, somewhat raspy, but otherwise vigorous voice. "Good evening, sir. I am sorry I did not come right out when you entered. I heard the bell but was engaged in a matter that could not be left untended. My apologies."

Stephen detected a hint of an accent. Probably German, he surmised, assuming this was the Hurst— no, Ernst, wasn't it?—stenciled on the window. It was charming. "No problem," said Stephen. He assumed he was talking to the owner. Who else would be here at this hour of the night? "I was just out walking and noticed the light was on, so I thought I'd check you out. Actually, I was kind of surprised to find a place like this still open this late."

"Yes, it is late, I suppose, but I do not have much else to do and I live just above the store, so I do not have much of a commute, you know." There was a slight chuckle. Stephen smiled, admiring the old man's sense of humor. "I enjoy being here, so it is not a burden to stay open," said the man. He paused briefly, wondering if this explanation made sense to his customer, then added, "Is there something in particular you were looking for, young man?"

"Not really. As I said, I was just wandering around on my way home. I like books, and it's always nice to find a new place to explore." Stephen's eyes wandered over the shelves' contents and the innumerable stacks rising from tables and floor like stalagmites. "You have quite a collection of old stuff here. Where'd you get all this?" inquired Stephen, genuinely interested in what could turn out to be quite a find for a bibliophile like him.

"Oh, here and there." The owner was pleased at the interest shown by his visitor, whose enthusiasm seemed genuine. Perhaps he really was who he said, just someone out for a stroll who literally stumbled in. It could be true. Probably was. "I keep my eyes and ears open," continued the old man. "Sometimes I travel a little to buy collections when people pass on or no longer want them. Or old acquaintances may come in and donate items. Or sell me things for a few dollars. You would be surprised how much is available if you know what to look for—and where."

Stephen loved the way the man spoke, especially the way he refrained from using any contractions. Every word was pronounced to its fullest and enunciated impeccably. Sort of like an intellectual version of Arnold Schwarzenegger. Or maybe Doctor Ruth, but not as accenty. A lightly rolled "r." "v"s where "w"s should be. Stephen picked up the thread. "I'm surprised, actually, there's enough of a market in stuff like this for you to make any money at it. Aside from me, I know maybe one or two other people who like old books. And I'm in the publishing business."

The old man's bushy eyebrows lifted slightly at this news, unnoticed by Stephen. The man laughed again and said, "Oh, there are a few others besides yourself who would find my inventory interesting. There are many collectors, of course, looking for something they cannot find elsewhere. And there are those who are looking for a different kind of gift for someone. There are even some who buy because they like the special look and feel—even the smell—of an old book, something they cannot get at Barnes and Noble or Brentano's. Then again, even if there were few buyers, I would still remain open. I do not need the money any longer, you see. I have enough to live on. I simply like the company of my old friends, as I call my inventory." The man extended his arms and made a half circle to indicate his "friends."

"Well, I can think of worse companions to have than these, that's for sure," said Stephen, chuckling once again at the old man's wit. "There *is* something very comforting about an old book."

Stephen wasn't just making conversation with this last statement. He found much pleasure in reading and in the bookmaker's craft. He could spend hours engrossed in an old historic text as easily as the latest spy thriller. He wouldn't admit it as readily as the old man, but these were his friends as well. They helped fill his hours when he wasn't working. He didn't feel alone in their presence, as he did sometimes with people. He found he didn't need lots of human interaction to survive, but he did need his books. Maybe that had something to do with why his marriage had gone down the tubes.

"We agree on that point, young man. By the way, my name is Gustav Ernst." The old man offered a handshake. "May I ask yours?"

Stephen took the old man's hand and was surprised by his strong grip. "Stephen Blake. Pleased to meet you. As a matter of fact, I'm sorry I didn't run into you sooner. I feel as though I've missed out on something special here."

"Well, better late than never, as they say. Please consider my friends to be yours, too. The best part is, they do not have any egos to bruise." This precipitated another snicker. Stephen joined in, finding Ernst's philosophy remarkably in tune with his own. He was drawn to the old codger.

Ernst said, "Here I am going on about this and that when you came in to look at books. Please walk around." Ernst gave a half bow and invited Stephen to browse with a wave of his arm. "I will be in the back. Just let me know if you see anything interesting or have any questions. Stay as long as you like. No hurry."

"Will do, thanks," said Stephen, who proceeded to get lost in the many old and interesting offerings of this jewel of a bookstore. He had forgotten completely about the dreadful meeting earlier that evening, the Ten O'Clock News, and everything else, for that matter. When he glanced at his watch, he was startled to find that it read ten forty-five. It seemed as though he had just wandered in a few minutes ago. He felt a bit guilty about keeping the old man up so long. Stephen called out, "Mr. Ernst? Are you there?"

The old man came out from behind the curtain. "How do you like my collection?" he asked. "Did you find anything of interest?"

"I sure did. There are lots of things I'd like to have. But I think I'll limit myself to this one for now." Stephen placed one of the two books he was holding on the counter. He handed the other to Ernst, along with a twenty-dollar bill to cover the price. The spine's title read, "Essays of Eliah," authored by Charles Lamb. It was a small text, only four inches by six, with the brownness of age marring the book's edges. Stephen had checked for a date. There was none on the title page, but a personal bookplate attached to the back of the front cover provided a clue. A hand notation was penned within its black border in faded blue ink: "Mabel Bowdoin, 1898."

Ernst looked at the book and said, "Yes, I am familiar with this one. You will have many pleasant hours of enjoyment with it." He saw that the book Stephen had returned to the counter was a Modern Library version of Dostoyevsky's *The Brothers Karamazov*. "You prefer Lamb to Dostoyevsky?" he asked.

"Not necessarily," replied Stephen. "I'd like to have them both. It's just that...well, to be honest, my wallet's a little light at the moment, and I see you don't take plastic. Let's just say it's an excuse to come back another time."

Ernst said, "I would love to have you return." He paused, contemplating something. "Since you seem to feel as I do about fine old books, perhaps you would like to see some of my better items. I keep my most prized possessions out back. I would be happy to show them to you."

"You mean now?" asked Stephen, incredulous at Ernst's stamina. Was he being a super salesman, just being hospitable, or what?

"Certainly, if you can spare the time," replied Ernst.

Stephen made a show of looking at this watch again, which indicated a time only three minutes later than his last check. "Gee, I don't know. It really is getting late, and I do have to work tomorrow, as much as I'd like to play hooky and spend the next couple of days and nights in here. Maybe I'd better take a rain check."

"It is up to you, of course. But I think I can assure you that you will be very interested in my special items. How about just five minutes to see what I am talking about. Then you can decide if you want to see more or not. I promise not to pressure you. What do you say?"

Stephen resisted the urge to steal one more look at his watch, then succumbed. His curiosity had won out over the fatigue that was starting to wash over his body, as well as his mind. "Well, okay. A few minutes more can't hurt, I guess. Let's see what you've got back there."

"Excellent, Mr. Blake. I know you will be pleased. Come take a look." He started toward the back. "By the way, why not take off your coat and leave it here. You will be more comfortable. I think it will be safe at this time of night." Another chuckle from Ernst. Stephen complied and left his coat lying on the counter next to the cash register.

The old man walked to the cheap curtain, held it aside, and invited Stephen with a sweep of his arm to enter the back part of the shop. Stephen stepped into a narrow corridor, dimly lit. Immediately on the left was a set of stairs leading up to what Stephen guessed was Ernst's living area. Beyond that, also on the left, was a door, perhaps fifteen feet from the curtain. Directly opposite on the right wall was another door, with a third at the far end of the corridor, about twenty feet away. Although Stephen's eyes had not yet become accustomed to the faint light, there did not appear to be markings on any of the doors to indicate what lay beyond. Ernst walked to the door along the right wall, unlocked and opened it, and led Stephen inside.

If the shop out front was a throwback to the early twentieth century, this room seemed to predate that by fifty years, maybe more. It was a small space, about twelve feet square, resembling a comfortable den one would find in an old home. There was only the one door, and no windows. Two overstuffed armchairs dominated the space on either side of a small coffee table. There were also a couple of old floor lamps with faded, tasseled shades, now more orangy brown than their original white. A thick floral-pattern rug softened the floor, and several dark pictures hung in heavy wooden frames on the door wall and the one opposite. Each of the other two walls was lined with floor-to-ceiling bookcases, beautifully made of dark, shiny cherrywood, with lockable glass doors to display and protect the contents. Stephen wasn't an expert in these matters, but everything looked Victorian to him. In addition to the old electric floor lamps, which Ernst illuminated by means of a wall switch as they entered, casting a soft glow on the scene, there were candles and one or two kerosene lamps for added illumination, if needed. The only "modern" convenience Stephen saw in the room was a black, rotary-dial telephone sitting on a small table along the far wall. Like everything else in the place, it looked as though it had been there for a very long time.

Stephen stepped into the room and started to examine the contents of the bookcases. Through the glass he saw volumes worthy of a museum, many with fine leather bindings and gold leaf printing. Some had wonderfully illuminated pages. Some were hand-lettered. Stephen was awestruck. "These are incredible," he said. "I've never seen anything like this before. How could you possibly assemble such an extraordinary collection?"

Ernst laughed. "As I said, I have connections. Please feel free to select something and have a closer look. Sit down and relax while you examine it. I can even get you a small libation if you like."

Stephen longed to take each one into his hands and hold it, feel its fine craftsmanship, admire its exquisite printing, read the words on each wonderful page. He was sorely tempted to take Ernst up on his offer, but knew if he did so, it would be extremely difficult to break away. Presented with a bag of superbly tasty potato chips, it was impossible to eat just one, he knew. With great reluctance, he said, "Thanks anyway, but I think I'll pass on the drink. I had my fill at dinner. You know, I'm afraid I could never afford to buy even one of these beautiful books. They're works of art and have got to be way beyond my price range. You'd only be wasting your time showing them to me."

"There is no such thing as a waste of time when it comes to books," replied Ernst, sincerely. He was heartened to confirm his initial feeling about this Mr. Blake. He truly loved books. It was in his eyes, and in his voice. He surely wasn't faking any of it. And his being in publishing: could there be anything more appropriate? Wasn't it fate that brought him to the shop tonight? "Whether you buy anything or not is inconsequential," said Ernst, happily. "Consider this as your personal library. It gives me pleasure just showing them to someone who appreciates them as I do. Do not feel as though you have to buy anything to be welcome here."

"Well, that's an extraordinary offer. I don't know what to say, except thank you." Despite this wonderful discovery and Ernst's kind invitation, Stephen felt he really had overstayed and should be getting home. "I'm afraid I really have to be going," he said. "I certainly would like to take you up on your offer and come back, if you're serious. I'd love to spend some time here and see what else you have. That'd be quite an experience." Stephen meant every word of it, too. He was dazzled by what he saw, and he truly liked this old man, who somehow had acquired this magnificent collection. Yet there was something disturbing about it all. It was certainly true that these treasures didn't exactly fit this odd little shop. But they were irresistible. Perhaps he would have the chance to dig into it and really find out how all this came to be. Perhaps he could... His thoughts trailed away as he heard Ernst speaking again.

"Do not mention it," said Ernst. "And yes, I did mean it. As I said, it is my pleasure. Come anytime."

They left the back room and returned to the shop, where Stephen found *Essays of Elia* sitting on the counter, next to *The Brothers Karamazov*. Ernst rang up the sale while Stephen retrieved his coat and put it on. As he took the bag from Ernst, the old man said, "Now do not forget. Anytime."

Stephen laughed, "Okay, okay. I promise to be back. How can I turn down such hospitality? Good night, now."

"Good night, Mr. Blake."

Stephen heard the tinkle of the bell as Ernst closed the door behind him. He walked over to Charles Street and made the turn south toward Beacon. He had gone only a block or two when he noticed the bag he was holding seemed to be kind of heavy and bulky for one book. He opened it and found that it contained two: the Lamb, which he had bought, and the Dostoyevsky, which he had decided not to buy. He knew he had paid only for the first. Ernst had made a mistake. 'Forgetful old geezer,' he thought. Then, he looked more closely at the second book and saw a note stuck to the front cover. Stephen was able to make out the writing in the shimmering light of a streetlamp: "Mr. Blake—Permit me to make a gift of this to you. G. Ernst." Stephen was somewhat taken aback and decided that he should return it. After a moment he surmised that doing so would probably be an insult to Ernst, so he rationalized that he should keep it. He felt, though, that he should at least go back and thank him for it, especially since he had only walked a short distance from the shop. He wasn't sure if it was still open, but it was worth a try.

Stephen retraced his steps. About a block before he got to the store, he saw that its lights were still on. 'The old guy's still awake. At least it gives me a chance to....' He stopped abruptly when he noticed several people entering. Maybe four or five. Instinctively, Stephen took a step back into the shadow of a tree. He didn't quite know why he did that. It was just that...well...he hadn't expected to see anyone. Stephen saw Ernst admit the group and close the door behind them. He even heard the tinny bell. It also looked as though Ernst locked the door after they

Wicca Codex

were in. The "Open" sign had been turned to read "Closed." Stephen didn't know quite what to do. He still felt the urge to thank Ernst for the gift but didn't know what to make of the people he had just seen. Maybe it was a party. After a moment or two, Stephen saw another two or three people come down the street and tap lightly on the shop's door. Stephen remained hidden by the darkness as he watched Ernst let the new arrivals in.

Stephen was perplexed. What was happening here? Whatever it was, he guessed it must be something with a logical explanation, something Ernst would not have minded Stephen seeing if he had decided to stay longer, as he had been invited to do. Maybe these were other bibliophiles come to talk about books—a kind of club. Maybe it was a reading. Bookstores did readings every so often, didn't they? That was probably it. But why so late? Maybe these were just busy people, and this was the only time they could get together. Whatever. Why worry about it?

Stephen decided against returning to the shop. He didn't want to disturb the party, or the reading, or whatever it was. He spun around, walked to his apartment on Marlborough Street, and went to bed. The activities of the day—and night—had finally caught up with him.

Chapter 6

Tuesday, October 17

Lieutenant Vincent Mulcahy of the Boston Police Department motioned for Sergeant Patrick Johnson to come into his office.

"Hi, Vinnie," said the Sergeant. "What's new in the homicide business?"

"Very funny, Pat. Get a load of this, will you?"

"They found another one last night, Pat," droned Mulcahy, his blue eyes peering straight into his friend's. "Over on Boylston. Broken neck. No fuss, no muss. Stockbroker this time." Mulcahy unwound himself and sat upright, temporarily unwrinkling his light blue shirt. A red rep tie was knotted jauntily around his ample neck. Ample as in athletic, not couch potato. Mulcahy, unlike his partner, had never lost that sports-jock look from his high school days. He made sure not to.

Despite the difference in rank, the friendly banter was understandable to all who knew the two officers. They went back years, having attended the same high school, played the same sports, dated the same girls. Both had wanted to be cops for as long as they could remember. They graduated from the Academy about a dozen years ago and had spent parallel lives on the force in the same precinct house on Berkeley Street. Each lived in the same Boston neighborhood, only a couple of blocks apart. Both had married their high school sweethearts and were working on families.

"Vee and Pee," as they were called by just about everyone, including their wives, had partnered during their early years on the beat. They did everything together. Each had made sergeant at the same time, then split up to team with other guys, usually rookies. They did vice, drugs, robbery, then eventually landed in homicide. It was where they wanted

Wicca Codex

to be. They couldn't exactly explain it when asked. They just thought it was the glamour thing to do. Maybe it was the macho-ness of it. Dirty Harry. Sergeant Friday. Starsky and Hutch. Whatever the reason, they got what they wanted. Now they knew better. There was nothing glamorous about murder. It was gritty work. Still, there was some distinction attached to it, and they wouldn't have traded places with anyone else on the force. Then, just last year, Mulcahy earned his lieutenant's badge. Johnson did not. Although this could have driven a wedge between the two, it didn't. The ties went back too far. The friendship was too strong. There wasn't the slightest trace of jealousy on Johnson's part. If anything, he was proud of his friend Vinnie. Johnson knew his turn would come someday, preferably soon. He also knew Vinnie was rooting for him to make it. He'd just beaten him to it by a year or two, is all. It didn't interfere with their ability to collaborate, either. In fact, they had worked several cases together over the last year, earning a couple of commendations.

Mulcahy was leaning back in his swivel chair, hands cupped behind his head. He was self-conscious about his thinning brown hair and growing bald spot and tried to hide these deficiencies whenever he could. He balanced a long, gray-slacked leg on the edge of his tan metal desk, which occupied a disproportionately large part of the tiny, institutional looking room. A navy-blue sport jacket with cheap gold-plated buttons was draped sloppily over a file cabinet behind the desk. The only things that humanized the place were a couple of photos of the wife and kids—two girls, three and five—and several police-league softball trophies and caps scattered about. Everything else was stacks of paper, file cabinets, bookcases, styrofoam coffee cups, and old newspapers.

Johnson sauntered over to Mulcahy's desk and plopped his squat shape down into one of the heavy wooden chairs. If Mulcahy represented Union blue and Confederate gray, Johnson could easily be mistaken for a UPS trainee. Everything on him was brown or tan or beige or ecru—slacks, shirt, tie, shoes, socks, everything. He loved brownish and rarely sported anything else. Probably because it coordinated nicely with his eyes. Once a match for Mulcahy's athletic ability, Johnson had let himself go just a tad. It looked worse than it was, though, because he was only about five feet eight. "Jeez, Vin. That makes...what?...four in two months? Who's on this one?"

"Strickland, for now. But I just came from the Superintendent's office. He's getting major heat from the higher-ups, not to mention the press. And when he gets hot, the temperature goes up all around." He tugged at the knot of his tie and loosened it a bit. "Wants me and you to take this one, buddy. Somebody's gotta pull this together, now that it looks like we may have a serial situation on our hands. The news guys are starting to ask a bunch of questions, especially about the way these people died. There's lots of speculating going on, and the Super doesn't want this thing to drag out for too long before he feeds 'em something. He's talking about a press conference in a couple days, with the Commissioner taking the lead, no less." Mulcahy found it hard to sit still. He got up and stuffed his hands in his trousers, doing a slow pace behind the desk. His six feet one made the room seem even smaller.

Johnson noticed his partner's unease. He felt the same himself. "A couple days? Christ, Vin. What about my other cases? I've got the Martinez thing, and we haven't tied up Frazier yet, and..."

"Yeah, yeah. I know. Not to worry, pal. We're shifting them to another lucky soul. This one becomes your top priority...and mine."

Johnson smiled as he scratched an eyebrow. "Well, okay, then. Why didn't ya say so in the first place? Let's get on it. What've we got?"

Mulcahy continued his back-and-forth stroll as he reviewed the facts of each death. Four since the middle of August. All presumed homicides, and probably related, but in a strange sort of way. In each case the victim was very dead, but there was no evidence of blood or gore. None. The crime scenes were neat and clean. As Mulcahy had said, "No fuss, no muss." Each victim had died of a broken neck—two probably from falling down stairs, two from no identifiable cause. Each had apparently been alone. There were no witnesses attesting to visits by others or claiming to have heard voices or noises just before the estimated time of death. Last night's victim—the stockbroker—had died in his downtown office building, the others at their Boston apartments or condos. The victims included two men and two women. Two were professional types: a female advertising executive and the stockbroker—a male. The others included an older gentleman—retired—and a young housewife. All the victims were white. Aside from the cause of death, the only other common threads among these cases were time of death—all were estimated to have occurred between midnight and three A.M.—and a small mark found on the back of the neck of each victim. The mark was coal black, almost perfectly round, about the size of a dime, and, according to the medical examiner, appeared to have been burnt into the skin by an intense heat source. There was nothing else remotely resembling physical evidence. Nothing indicated that race or drugs or theft or anything else, for that matter, was involved in any way. None of the victims had a criminal record. There were no weapons found at the scene, no notes, no motives—as far as they could tell—and no witnesses. There were no suspects. There was nothing. Just an annoying puzzle, with pressure building for a solution.

    Johnson listened to Mulcahy's presentation with great interest. It struck him that there were enough unusual elements here to make it more appealing than the standard stuff they dealt with day in and day out. It seemed like quite a challenge. "That's great, Vin," he complained. "We sure don't have a helluva lot to go on here, do we?"

    "You've got that right. I figure we've gotta get out and talk to the victims' families, friends, acquaintances, fellow employees, whoever. Starting right now. I know it's been done already, but nothing's turned up so far. It's worth another go; especially since we don't have any other choices, as far as I can see. Why don't you take the first two—Clark and Walters. Here're the files. I'll do the last two—Bates and…let's see, what's the stock guy's name?" He shuffled through some papers littering his desk. "Here it is—Crandall."

Johnson took the files and tucked them under his arm. He couldn't help wondering, though. "Hey, Vinnie. I know we're a boffo team, but why do ya suppose the Super tabbed us for this one? Is he payin' off a bet or somethin'? Or are you?"

Mulcahy knew he wasn't going to be able to avoid the issue for long. He decided to plunge right in. "Nothing like that, Pat. He didn't say exactly, but I think it might have something to do with that course we both took last year. You remember the one I mean? The one on ritualistic killings? With an occult twist?"

Johnson's eyes narrowed. "I was afraid you were gonna say somethin' like that," he said, lowering his voice a notch. "That was a real hair raiser, and..."

"Hey, Pat?" said Mulcahy, mostly good-naturedly. He had a knack for saying things that got results but left no nasty recriminations. "It's almost Thursday. Why're you still here?"

Johnson leapt from the chair. You didn't have to bang *him* over the head with a hammer. "On my way, Vinnie," he said, bounding from the office.

Chapter 7

Tuesday, October 17

Like most big cities, Boston had a slew of daily newspapers in the old days. But, like other urban areas, most had been lost through competition and the hard realities of modern economics. The Hub of the Universe, as Boston liked to call itself, was down to its last two—*The Boston Globe* and the *Boston Herald*. The Globe was the city's Hertz, The Herald its Avis. The latter was forever trying harder, but was destined to be Number Two, it seemed.

The Herald's operations were housed in a nondescript red-brick structure. Its two-story squatness dominated one corner of the intersection between the Southeast Expressway and the Massachusetts Turnpike Extension. Its main entrance fronted Herald Square, a rather elegant appellation for the rather mundane intersection of Herald Street and Harrison Avenue. The site was on the edge of downtown, whose affluent skyscrapers seemed to resist leapfrogging the Turnpike into this area of blue-collar ambiance.

Jason Burgholz—called Jay just about everywhere except his birth certificate—sat in one of The Herald's beehive cells, otherwise known as an office. He was its metro news chief and had just come from the morning editors' meeting, where they had discussed the news stories for tomorrow's first edition. Today's three were already closed out, of course, had been since the morning's wee hours. One of Burgholz's responsibilities for the day was to produce an article on a murder in downtown Boston last night. Normally, one more wipeout wouldn't have ranked high on the list for a feature. The city usually produced a hundred or more killings a year. Maybe not up there with the likes of New York or Chicago or L. A. But just enough to take the sensationalism out of all but the most spectacular or lurid cases. Last night's crime didn't really appear, at first glance, to fit that category—a stockbroker dying in his office sometime after midnight. Still, there seemed to be some similarity here to several other deaths over the last couple of months. Deaths so far unexplained satisfactorily by the police, the media, or anyone. Not only that. There was a twist of the macabre to them. All broken-neck cases. It was weird, all right. Just the sort of thing worth a little effort to flesh out and see if it might develop into something newsworthy. But it needed someone to take hold and run. Maybe "run" wasn't exactly the right word. There was a lot of dirty dog work involved in hacking out a good story before you could get any speed on it. First you had to crawl, then walk, then maybe came the running part. If you were lucky.

Burgholz thought this might be just the thing for that young up-and-comer, Alison Simmons. Hadn't she been nipping at his heels to let her do something with "potential?" She was talented, all right, and incredibly ambitious. Quite a mix. It was all he could do to keep her under wraps sometimes. Well, this had potential, didn't it? Then again, there could be nothing here at all. He didn't want to waste one of his middle-aged superstars on something that could be a dead end. Alison seemed like the right choice for this one.

Burgholz was a sixtyish, old-style news junkie who had been around the block a few times. He was starting to think about retirement in a few years, looking to mentor an up-and-coming dynamo with printer's ink in his or her veins. He hadn't found anyone sufficiently worthy to this point, but thought this young girl Simmons might have what it takes. He liked Alison for her competence and enthusiasm and admired her work ethic but wanted to bring her along slowly. She was doing fine, but he didn't want to put undue pressure on her to produce a "scoop," despite her ability. All in due course. Burgholz convinced himself one last time, then phoned out to her desk in the newsroom and asked that she come in.

"Hi, Jay. What's up?" warbled Alison, as she breezed into

Burgholz's office. She had made the mistake of calling him "Mr. Burgholz" only once, during their first meeting. Please don't, he had said. There was no need for such formality, despite the difference in their ages and experience levels. It was more fun, and usually more productive, to be collaborators rather than general versus private. Life was too short, or something like that. Especially in journalism. She came to accept that philosophy eventually, and, in fact, found that it suited her to a tee. She was fun-loving and generally preferred the unstructured approach to things, finding that she flourished under loose reins rather than a tight yoke. She knew Burgholz had seen that in her early on, and she appreciated it.

Alison had known forever that she wanted to work for a newspaper. Some said it was a blessing, others a curse. Even as a young girl she was fascinated by the tabloids her father brought home. Who did these stories? she wanted to know. How did they get done? Who put the paper together? Her questions were endless. She organized a group of kids in grammar school and put out a newsletter for the sixth grade. She was editor-in-chief, of course. It fell apart after a few weeks, but she loved it while it lasted. It confirmed her life's ambition. Her feelings stayed with her through high school, where she joined the school newspaper as a freshman and rose through the ranks to became Numero Uno in her junior year. Her chosen course of study for college was a foregone conclusion.

She was a moderately good student academically, achieving success more through effort than natural talent. She strained and struggled to achieve what she wanted, and she almost always got it. She applied for and managed to get accepted at several good colleges, choosing Ohio State University and graduating five years ago with above-average grades and a degree in English. She stayed on and earned a master's in journalism, doing so in only eighteen months. The next couple of years were spent paying dues at two small, local weeklies out west. Working in her chosen field—finally—was heady stuff, but she soon learned the bottom-line mentality of the real world. The almighty deadline became king, stress replaced the relatively easy-going atmosphere of academia, and all for next-to-nothing in monetary compensation.

She loved every minute of it, but felt it was time to start making her mark on a big-city daily. Resumes went out to her three first-choice papers around the country: *The Washington Post*, *New York Times*, and *Boston Globe*. To her dismay, all three rejected her. They weren't looking for young staff writers at the moment, so they said. Undaunted, she sprayed another batch of resumes around to several second-choice papers—the Number Twos of the profession in their respective cities. They included The Herald. She was asked to interview there and at one other paper in the mid-west. She decided to go for broke at The Herald, mainly because she was from the Boston area and was hoping to "come home" after trying out her wings elsewhere. The interview worked out and she was offered a job.

Since coming on board she had built up a large file of clips, including some features, lots of politics (it was one of Boston's favorite sports, on a par with the Celtics, Bruins, Red Sox, and Patriots), a little of this, a little of that. She got to know her way around and developed a useful list of contacts and sources. She loved her work, but was forever bugging her editor to let her do the next "big story," whatever that turned out to be.

"You've called me in to give me the story of the century, right?" Alison had a bubbly personality that made it clear to everyone she was not being sarcastic when she spoke this way, just enjoying life. This trait complemented her physical features perfectly: a perky five feet four, bouncy blond shoulder length hair, pretty face—though not of the cover-girl variety—and large, absolutely sparkling green eyes that had the capacity to melt anything they set their sights on. Or turn into a block of ice just as easily. She and Burgholz had developed an excellent working relationship. It allowed Alison to kid around while still maintaining a professional attitude the editor liked to see in his employees. Burgholz considered Alison a real professional, despite her youth. More so than some of the old guys who had been around forever.

That was worth a lot in Burgholz's book. Despite his ability to lighten up when required, he was still an old-fashioned type when it came to getting the job done. Levity was okay to a certain extent, but when the chips were down, you either performed or you were out. Alison understood this. It bought her lots of slack.

"Absolutely," squealed Burgholz, adjusting his wire-rimmed glasses and banging a fist on the desk. "This is the big one, Ali."

"Well, it's about time, is all I have to say," said Alison, hurrying over to Burgholz's desk and flopping into one of the two less-than-comfortable chairs he provided. In fact, "less-than-comfortable" is being kind. To say they were instruments of torture would be perhaps going too far, but only slightly. Their wooden hardness was unsoftened by even the most meager of cushions and exacerbated by the numerous nicks and gouges that dug into one's clothing and skin at back and bottom. Burgholz's philosophy was simple: The More Comfy the Chair, The Longer the Meeting. And Burgholz didn't like long meetings. He was a busy man. "I hope it was worth waiting for," continued Alison. "What've you got that's gonna win me the Pulitzer?"

Burgholz chose not to sit behind the desk. This was another effective way to expedite a meeting, he found. Instead, he planted his five-foot, ten-inch height in front of a window that overlooked Herald Street and on into downtown Boston beyond. His back was to Alison and the rest of the office, which was in a mild form of disarray. Controlled chaos. Moderate messiness. Grizzled grittiness. Call it what you will, it was his home-away-from-home, and it suited him just fine, thank you. All the kids and grandkids were there under a smallish brass table lamp, arrayed in frames and designed to bring a smile to his lips when things got particularly low. The walls were covered with pictures of boats and waves and beaches and sunsets, reminiscences of vacations and long weekends aboard the 30-foot ketch he and his wife had bought second-hand many years ago and restored lovingly. A couple of dark-stained bookcases held his business life: copies of books on journalism, novels by journalists, dozens of manila file folders that never seemed to make it into his small two-level filing cabinet, a 12-inch black-and-white TV to scan CNN or C-SPAN or the networks for breaking news stories, plus assorted knick-knacks and memorabilia accumulated over a lifetime in the news business.

Burgholz glanced at the cumulus puffs drifting lazily over the city, then said, "Remember that article I had you do last month on the Clark murder? The lady who fell down the stairs and broke her neck?"

Alison searched her mental databank, faltered, then made the connection. "Oh, yeah. I remember. Tragic story."

"Yeah," agreed Burgholz. "Well, there've been three other broken-neck deaths in the city over the last two months or so, including one just last night. In one of those office towers." Burgholz waved his finger toward the scene framed by the window. He turned toward Alison. "Now, there may be nothing to this other than just a series of coincidences, but it's worth a shot poking around to see what you can come up with. I've got to have an article on last night's incident for tomorrow, so you'll need to get on it right away and get me something. Unfortunately, it didn't come in on the police wire in time to make today's late edition. The Globe missed it too, but you can bet they're gonna have something on it tomorrow morning." He pushed at the nosebridge of his glasses with his left hand, as he did several hundred times a day. They were forever sliding down his ski slope of a nose. He was always too busy to have them adjusted. "It's not page-one stuff just yet, but it's got the editorial staff's attention. First, do me the blurb for today. I'll reserve two columns for it—half page. The TV guys'll be all over this one today. We can't beat 'em to the punch, so we'll need a little different angle. Mention the similarity to the other deaths, but don't make anything big out of it for the moment. Afterwards, you can spend some time nosing around and see where this thing leads, if anywhere. Talk to the boys who did the stories on the other victims to get started, then check out the police. You know the drill. If the trail gets warm, follow up. Not that you have any choice, but how does that grab you?"

Alison normally had a smile on her face. It just got bigger than normal when something struck her fancy. Her smile got a lot bigger. "It grabs me. It grabs me." She could hardly contain herself. She couldn't stay seated, almost leaping out of the chair and gushing, "Now that's definitely something. I'm on it already. Three columns, you said?"

Burgholz laughed. "Two, Alison. Let's start with two and see where it goes."

She saluted playfully. "Oui, mon capitain. Two it is."

Alison thought about running over to Burgholz and planting a little kiss on his cheek, but knew he'd be self-conscious about it. After all, there was only a glass wall separating his office from the crazy world of reporters out on the floor, and prying eyes were everywhere. She decided against it, opting merely to glide over to the door that opened onto that weird world and make a quick exit before he changed his mind. Before leaving, she turned toward Burgholz and tossed a merry "Thanks" his way.

Burgholz's gaze followed her out as a smile came to his lips. "You're welcome," he said to the door. He walked over to his desk and sat down slowly, then said, "Go get 'em, tiger."

Chapter 8

Tuesday, October 17

Locke-Ober is one of Boston's dining institutions. It seems as though the place has been around for centuries, but it's actually "only" been since 1875. One of its ads encourages the reader to "Learn from History," providing an impressive list of well-known patrons from years gone by. Among the enlightened who have supped within its walls, apparently, are the likes of Theodore Roosevelt, Enrico Caruso, John Maynard Keynes, John F. Kennedy, Jack Benny, Sarah Bernhardt, and Marilyn Monroe. It's curious that females are included among this elite, since it took a lawsuit some years ago to bring the restaurant into the twentieth century and finally force admission of women to the main dining room. As recently as 1970, they were relegated to taking their meals upstairs. Until then, it had adamantly resisted giving up its place as one of the last male bastions in the state, if not the entire country. The establishment sits right in the heart of downtown, and so is popular with well-heeled office workers, politicos, and assorted movers and shakers. Or wannabees for all of the above. It has a rather heavy atmosphere that extols its single-sex days: lots of dark wood paneling, stained glass, long Dominican mahogany wraparound bar, ponderous objets d'art. Waitresses? Forget it. Black-suited waiters rule the roost. Overlooking all is the nearly in-the-buff image of Yvonne, casting flirtatious glances from her perch high up one wall. The menu is not exactly on the cutting edge, although some changes have been made in deference to the lite-and-lively crowd. Despite the forced accommodation to today's new society, its male clientele can still come and sit at the same tables, eat the same platters of meat and potatoes and gravy, served by the same waiters, several of whom had been there

WICCA CODEX

for decades. It has a certain charisma, if not a five-star culinary rating.

Stephen Blake sat at one of the downstairs tables, nursing a Heineken and waiting for John Demming, his lunch appointment. Stephen didn't always have a drink at lunch, but Locke-Ober wasn't the kind of place where you ordered a Diet Coke or a lemonade. At least the guys didn't. Besides, Demming was already fashionably late by ten minutes for their noon appointment, and Stephen didn't want to just sit there. He was perusing the late-morning edition of The Globe he'd just bought. There was the usual: the latest on the mess in Bosnia, a story on the mean-spirited politics characteristic of the Republican Congress and the Clinton administration, speculation on when the Arabs and the Israelis would finally decide that peace was better than killing each other, an article declaiming Boston's lack of a world-class convention center, and the latest misadventures of the local sports teams. Nothing new today. It was always the same.

"Hey, Stephen, how're you doing?" John Demming materialized and glided onto the red leather chair opposite his business acquaintance. "Sorry I'm late. Got caught on the phone just as I was leaving. Have you ordered yet?"

"No. Just the beer. Thought I'd wait for you to get here. Let's grab the waiter. I've got to get back for a one-thirty meeting."

They ordered, then got on with the business of talking business, which was successfully conducted during the meal. Stephen managed to extract from Demming a favorable price for paper and ink to cover the first quarter of next year. Both men could live with the deal. It was fair to both sides, which is how their business discussions generally ended up, usually without undue acrimony or posturing. It was the main reason they respected each other and enjoyed doing business together. They also liked each other personally, although they didn't socialize much outside their mutual business circles.

Stephen passed on dessert, but Demming couldn't resist the heavy chocolate layer cake, washed down with black coffee. From Demming's rotund appearance, Stephen judged that his dining companion didn't take a rain check on dessert too often.

"This is pretty good stuff, Stephen. You should give it a try," said Demming, as he aimed another forkful of dark brown cake and icing toward his gaping mouth. He was obviously having a great time.

"No thanks," chuckled Stephen. "I'm stuffed. You go ahead and enjoy it, though."

"I will indeed. May even have seconds. Actually, I'm just trying to keep from going back to the office, if you want to know the truth." He took a slug of coffee and wiped some that dribbled down his chin and spotted his tie. "Had some excitement in the building last night—a murder, apparently. Place was crawling with cops this morning. Asking all kinds of questions. Couldn't hardly get any work done."

Stephen's eyebrows lifted. "A murder? In your office?"

"Not my company, but yeah, in the same building," offered Demming, playing up his semi-celebrity status, now that he was involved in a murder investigation, however remotely. "I'm not really sure it's a murder, actually, although the homicide cops are the ones doing all the asking. Seems they found this stockbroker guy with a broken neck, from what I understand. Guess he was working real late. Security guard found a light on and went to investigate, but he was gonzo. Still sitting at his desk. That's all I know." Demming pointed to the paper folded at Stephen's elbow. "Didn't you read about it? Bet it's right there in The Globe."

Stephen glanced at the paper but didn't open it. "I didn't see anything like that, but I could've missed it, I suppose. Then again, I'd be surprised if they had anything on it. Don't the papers have early morning deadlines?"

"Yeah, I guess," said Demming, scanning the room for their waiter. He had finished his dessert and was looking for a reprise. No luck.

"Broken neck, huh?" repeated Stephen. "A guy is working at his desk and ends up dead with a broken neck? That's a little weird, don't you think, John?"

"I suppose, now that you mention it." Demming wagged a fat finger.

A waiter emerged and took his order for another slice of cake. He provided coffee refills before heading off toward Yvonne.

Stephen glanced at his Seiko and thought he could spare another few minutes before getting back to the office. He decided to ask Demming about the bookstore. If anyone could tell him anything about the place, it was Demming. He was even more of an aficionado of good books than Stephen, especially old ones. And, being in the business, he knew pretty much everything there was to know about them, including where they were sold, by whom, for how much. Everything.

"John, I want to find out about something, and you should be the one to know," began Stephen, somewhat tentatively. "On my way home last night, I took a little detour and came across this great old bookstore. It's in the Beacon Hill area, a block or so off Charles Street. It's called...let's see,"—he dug a business card out of his wallet, one that Ernst had stuck into one of the books he bought—"yeah, here it is...Ye Olde Booke Nooke. It was packed with goodies you wouldn't believe. Ever hear of it?"

Demming took the card and eyed it curiously. "Ye Olde what? Never seen so many words ending in 'e' before. On Beacon Hill, huh? Thought I was familiar with all the bookstores in the area, but I have to admit I don't know that one. Must be fairly new."

"I don't think so," said Stephen, shaking his head. "At least not by the looks of it. It seemed as though some of those books have been in the same piles for decades. And the owner looked like he'd been around even longer. Guy named Ernst. Ring a bell?"

"Ernst?" Pause. "Nope. Can't say as I know the gent." The waiter arrived with the second wedge of cake for Demming, who proceeded to attack it with gusto. Stephen waved off more coffee. Demming accepted.

"A real nice fellow," explained Stephen, who did his best to avoid watching his friend eat. It was becoming a bit disconcerting. "I bought a book and he threw in another one I'd shown an interest in. A surprise freebie. Didn't find out about it 'til later. Which reminds me. I still owe the guy a thank-you call." Stephen made a mental note to do that. "Seems quite knowledgeable, too. Really knows his stuff."

"Izzatso," mumbled Demming, getting interested.

"Yeah. Has rooms in the back of the shop where he keeps the really good material. Invited me into one of 'em. I was amazed at his collection. Wished I could've stayed longer, but it was getting late. He said I could come back anytime and use the place as a library if I wanted. I'll probably take him up on it. You might want to check it out, too. He really had some treasures in there I think you'd be interested in."

"Sounds like it might be worth a trip. Lemme take down the info." Demming copied the shop's name and address, along with the owner's name, into the back of a pocket calendar he used to keep track of his appointments. "If it's half as great as you say, maybe it'll serve as another good source for my collecting habit. Maybe I won't have to rely so much on the Antiquarian Book Fair anymore."

Demming was referring to the Boston event held every November for the last two decades or so. This year it was to be at the Hynes Convention Center. It dealt in rare, collectible books, modern first editions, letters, maps, autographs, and the like. It served a wide swath of the industry, including dealers from across the country and internationally. But, as its ads liked to say, it also catered to "the serious collector and the curious browser." And the serious and curious did come, apparently. Attendance was up to about six thousand and growing. Demming attended religiously and was enthusiastically looking forward to next month's event. Stephen had been to one or two himself, but he wasn't quite as fanatical as Demming.

"Well, John, I do have to get back. I'm glad we could do business. I'll finalize the arrangement we agreed on and get the paperwork done in the next couple of days. I'll give you a call when it's ready."

"Okay, Stephen. A pleasure, as always. And thanks for the tip on that bookstore. Sounds like a real winner. I'll check it out, first chance."

"No problem. Maybe I'll run into you there one of these days. I'm definitely going back myself."

Stephen called for the check and paid. It was his turn. As they left the restaurant and parted company on Winter Street, Stephen said, "Hey, John, let me know what happens on that murder thing in your building. It sounds like an interesting case."

"Will do, Stephen. See ya."

Chapter 9

Tuesday, October 17

The phone rattled in Ye Olde Booke Nooke. The older of the two men sitting in overstuffed chairs in one of the shop's back rooms said to the other, "Excuse me, Lariakin. Let me answer. This is, after all, still a business establishment."

The man called Lariakin merely said, "As you wish."

The old man walked to the back table, picked up the receiver and said matter-of-factly, "Booke Nooke. Gustav Ernst speaking. May I help you?"

"Good afternoon, Mr. Ernst. This is Stephen Blake. You may remember me from last night. I was in fairly late and bought a book. You also invited me to see your special collection in the back of the shop."

Ernst's eyes became livelier. His voice sounded more animated. He turned toward his companion and gave him a thin smile and a brief nod, as though indicating this call was a welcome one. "Yes, Mr. Blake. I remember. How are you?"

"I'm fine. I wanted to say thanks for your hospitality last night, and also for your generous gift of that second book I considered buying. I was really surprised when I opened the bag and found it, along with your note. I was only a couple of blocks away at the time, so I actually started back to the shop to thank you, on the chance you'd still be open. I decided not to bother you when I, uh, noticed several people entering your shop. I figured you were having some kind of special get-together and I..."

"Oh, that was just a gathering of some friends with common interests, Mr. Blake," said Ernst, lightly. He had detected a hint of something unnatural in Stephen's voice, something that hadn't been there the night before, and wanted to snuff out any unnecessary speculation on his part. He didn't want any questions. Not at this point. "We do that fairly regularly, as frequently as two times a week, actually. We discuss different things, sometimes books, sometimes politics, whatever strikes our fancy. I was actually going to ask you to stay last night and join us, but you seemed insistent on returning home, and I did not want to inconvenience you."

This seemed like a reasonable explanation to Stephen. It was probably why Ernst hadn't been in any hurry to whisk him out. "I thought it might be something like that, only it seemed so late. I wasn't sure what it was, actually."

Ernst sensed Stephen's relief through the line. "Yes, we usually get together during the late hours. We are all—what is the expression?—night owls." Ernst couldn't suppress the urge to laugh, nor could Stephen. The phrase seemed especially humorous coming from the old man. "Most of the members have rather busy schedules. Except for myself, of course. My general lack of customers means I could do it anytime." More laughter.

"Well, anyway, I just wanted to thank you," said Stephen. "And to be honest, to see if you were serious about that offer to explore the treasures in the back of your shop. I admit to being awed by your collection and would love the chance to spend more time there. I just couldn't do it justice last night. Too worn out. So, if you meant what you said, I'd like to do it again sometime."

Ernst could hardly contain himself. He wished he could slither through the wire, grab Blake by the hand, and bring him over right now. "I am very glad to hear that, Mr. Blake. I can assure you I meant it when I asked you to return anytime. We...I would love to have you." Ernst recognized his slip and hoped that Blake wouldn't. He glanced at Lariakin, who was paying the utmost attention to the conversation, but otherwise gave no hint of the faux pas. Ernst continued: "It is not often one finds someone such as yourself who appreciates fine books like these." Pause. "As a matter of fact, why not drop in on Friday evening? My friends will be coming again, and I would like you to meet them. I know they would enjoy meeting you, too. You could come early, and we could spend some time looking at books and talking. Maybe even have that drink you passed up last night. What do you say?"

"Well, let's see," pondered Stephen, checking his mental appointment calendar and finding it available for Friday the twentieth. "I've got nothing planned that I know of, so I guess I could do that. And I won't have to work the following day, so staying late won't be a problem. Fine, let's plan on it, then."

"Wonderful," said Ernst. "Can you make it about nine o'clock? That will give us some time together before my friends arrive. How does that sound?"

"Sounds fine. I'll look forward to it."

"As will I. Until Friday then."

"Thanks again. Goodbye."

Ernst gleefully placed the telephone back in its cradle and turned to his companion. "That, by a most fortunate coincidence, was the gentleman I was telling you about. The one in the publishing business. It may be that our leader is arranging for these events to occur at just the right moment. Now we will not have to hope for Mr. Blake to return to the shop at some uncertain time. As you heard, he will be here on Friday night, along with the others, at which time we can pursue what we discussed about him. Is that satisfactory?"

"Yes, most satisfactory," said Lariakin. His gravelly voice was flat and monotonous, lacking any of Ernst's emotion or effusiveness, nor was there any change to his dour expression. His only movement was a slight shifting of position in the chair. His gray eyes were dark, lifeless. "For the moment, that is. There is still the matter of convincing him to join us and assist with implementation of the next phase of our work. Do you think you will be able to do that?"

There was no hesitation from the old man. "I am confident it can be done according to the preferred method. The alternative is always available, if he finds out too much."

"Yes, that is always possible, although it would be better to keep him...with us...to serve in other ways as well."

"Of course. That is the goal. But the most important priority must be given to completing this part of the work, would you not agree?" Lariakin was about to answer, but Ernst continued. "Which makes him, along with everyone else involved, expendable. Is that not so?"

"Yes, it is so," said Lariakin, as he bored deep into the old man's eyes. "Everyone is...quite expendable."

Chapter 10

Wednesday, October 18

Alison Simmons was perplexed as she sat in a standard-issue swivel chair at the *Herald* and leaned back from her desk. The long day of research on the broken-neck murder cases had taken its toll. She raised her arms over her head to stretch away the fatigue that had set in, then rubbed her eyes. If anything, there were more questions now than when she started.

When she had left Jay Burgholz's office the day before, she was walking on air. She was energized, ready to get on with her exciting task. In no time at all, Alison had checked her files on the case she herself had handled about a month ago—the one involving the young housewife—and talked to a couple of other *Herald* staffers who did similar stories on the other two cases. She also gave the Boston police a buzz. They provided some basic information on the stockbroker incident from Monday night—early Tuesday morning, really—enough to let her do the story Burgholz needed for today's first edition. Anything more substantive would have to wait, they said. Pieces of the puzzle were still being pulled together. More information would be forthcoming at a press conference scheduled for Thursday morning at ten o'clock. They suggested she attend, where they would make available whatever they had. She learned that a police team had been assigned to investigate the killings. *Their names?* Mulcahy and Johnson. *Any particular reason why them?* They're experienced and have a good track record together, as well as certain, uh, special qualifications. *What special qualifications?* They'd get into that at the news conference. *What about the similarities in the four deaths?* Sorry, nothing more could be said at the moment. They were still investigating. Further information would be provided on Thursday. There wasn't anything more they could tell her at this juncture.

At this juncture. Alison wondered why police personnel were so fond of using fractured phrases like that. The alleged perpetrator of the crime...The occupants of the aforementioned vehicle...At which time the weapon was discharged. It sounded as though all of them were made to take a course in Cop Talk 101 before they were allowed to leave the Academy and hit the streets. It seemed to be a requirement for membership in their special club.

Alison had pumped the police spokesman for a few more quotes, then visited the scene and did interviews with the stockbroker's boss and a couple of his colleagues. She took a photographer along to add a visual touch. With the information she was able to scrounge together, Alison had drafted a two-column article for Burgholz's review. He had seemed pretty pleased with it, making only a few relatively minor changes. He even gave the piece a headline she could live with, not that she had a choice. It read, "Stockbroker murdered—one in a series?" Alison actually preferred a jazzier style of headline, but this wasn't too bad, considering. The story had progressed through the whirlwind chain of events that constitutes a production run for a big-city daily. It had emerged from the tornado and been disseminated into the early morning chill hovering over the Boston metro area.

Now it was a day later—Wednesday afternoon—and Alison had spent the better part of it following up on the fragments she had accumulated the day before. She managed to find out quite a bit more over the phone, although not from the police. She reached the head of the investigative team assigned to the murders—Lieutenant Mulcahy—but he was totally non-committal, saying only that their investigation was continuing, and they would have more to say about the whole thing at tomorrow's scheduled news conference.

"Yes, but what about..."

"Sorry, Ms. Simmons, but that's really all I can say for now. You'll have to come to the news conference."

"Okay, okay. I get the picture."

Alison's information came from extensive phone research involving key people in the four incidents. Friends, relatives, colleagues, anyone who might have something to say about the perplexing series of cases. Her head was becoming cluttered with bits and pieces of information, mostly disjointed. She was filling a small notebook with facts acquired from various sources, including the police, her own files from the earlier investigation of the first murder, the Herald reporters who did the other broken-neck stories. Names, dates, phone numbers, questions, factoids, doodles—a conglomeration of ballpoint-penned scratchings. Most anyone else would have found it as incomprehensible as a foreign language. It was Alison's own brand of cryptography, but even she was having a hard time making sense of it. She felt the need to take a step back and sort through everything, maybe over a beer with Jay after work. He was "amenable" to that, he said.

'Amenable. That's a good word,' thought Alison. It was added to the notebook for future reference. She was always willing to learn something new, and use it in a later article, too.

At the end of the workday, Alison, Burgholz, and three or four other reporters strolled over to one of several watering holes frequented by the Fourth Estate crowd. Since it was the one they most often visited it had come to be known unofficially as "Herald's Hellhole," a more or less apt description of the place. Alison, and Burgholz for that matter, wasn't exactly a regular at this scene, but they both enjoyed an occasional evening-out-with-the-guys thing just to maintain their social integrity. They left their companions at the long, wooden bar, found an open booth and slid onto the torn leather bench seats. Between the loud conversations cascading through the place and the even louder music blaring from the speakers scattered around the room, it was all they could do to hear one another. A wall-mounted TV at the end of the bar cast ESPN to the crowd below, but no one was watching. You couldn't hear it anyway. Waves of sound assaulted the senses, but no one seemed to mind. It was part of the ambiance of the place.

"The beer's on me, Alison," yelled Burgholz above the din. "Or anything else your little heart desires. Just a little something for yesterday's good work."

"Why, thanks, Mr. B," smiled Alison. "That's mighty kind. But I'll stick with the beer. Anything stronger and I start to lose it. I'm not much of a hard drinkin' gal, I'm afraid."

They each ordered a draft beer when the young, slinky, gum-chewing waitress appeared a couple of minutes later. Jay leaned over the table to make himself heard. "By the way, not being a hard-liquor type is nothing to apologize for, Ali. Or to be ashamed of either. In fact, it's rather refreshing to find someone who admits to that these days. As of a couple of years ago, I myself have taken to restricting alcoholic intake to beer and wine."

"Why the change of heart?" asked Alison.

"I guess I was convinced by a saying I came across. It went something like, 'One reason I don't drink is because I wish to know when I am having a good time.' It's one of those celebrity quotations they're fond of putting on desk calendars, but I forget whose name is associated with that one. It did make an impression on me, though."

"That's a good one, Jay," laughed Alison. "I'll have to remember it." Slinky delivered the beers. The raucous hilarity of the place seemed to abate somewhat, making conversation a little easier. Or maybe they were just getting used to it. "But really," continued Alison, grabbing an icy mug and lifting it in a silent toast, "it's me who should be buying you a drink for giving me that vote of confidence. I appreciate that, even though I've been bugging you about it for a while. I won't let you down."

"I know you won't, Ali," said Burgholz, watching the head on his beer disintegrate. "Actually, you've already shown me what you're capable of doing with yesterday's story, especially the angle about starting to tie the four cases together. You didn't make too much of what we had, yet you planted a seed to make people think about the possibilities. That was a nice piece of work on a tight deadline. Then again, I knew you had it in you."

"Well, aren't we the mutual admiration society. I think maybe we'd better stop this before it gets too mushy. Is it a deal?"

"Deal."

"Good."

They both laughed. Alison sipped her beer and watched Wayne Gretzky doing an unheard interview on the tube. She tried to find the right words for what she wanted to say next. Burgholz sensed her mood change and gave her a lead. "What's on your mind, Ali?"

Alison wrapped both hands around her mug. Her perpetual smile was still in place, but the gaiety of it was down a notch. "You know, Jay, I'll be the first to admit I haven't gotten into it that deeply yet, but this whole broken-neck thing is odd. I have this gut feeling there's something strange going on with these murders. I can't quite put my finger on it yet, but I'd be willing to bet there's a story here. Maybe a big one."

"I'm all ears."

"You don't mind talking shop?"

"I'm afraid we in the business are doomed to talk shop until relieved of the responsibility by death. Even then, we might find a way around the inconvenience."

This brought back Alison's toothy grin, but only for an instant. She extracted the notebook from her handbag and thumbed through it, summarizing the highlights. "Okay. Here's what we've got. The first victim was the housewife, the one I did my story on. Name was Mary Clark. Twenty-eight. Two young daughters. Happily married. Strictly a carpool and PTA type. Wasn't into anything on the side that anyone knew about. Ended up with a broken neck from a fall down the stairs in her downtown apartment."

Alison glanced up at Burgholz, who merely nodded at her to keep going. "Number Two was the ad exec—Elizabeth Walters. Owned her own agency, a small one. Kind of aggressive in her business dealings, and apparently successful at it. Had a few dollars saved but put most of

Wicca Codex

it back into the agency. Unmarried. No one could tell me anything bad about her, except maybe she liked to play around some. But there were no stories about any jealous lovers. Found at her desk one morning with a broken neck."

Alison came up for air and slurped at her beer before continuing. "Next came that retired electrician, Harold Bates. Lived with his wife, married thirty-five years. Came into a small inheritance a while back. The money was nothing substantial, just enough to allow him and the wife to relocate to the city from the suburbs. Kind of backwards, I suppose, but they wanted to be closer to the amenities of urban living, she said. Like Number One, he died from a fall at his home. Broke his neck. The last one you know about, for the most part. Ben Crandall. Downtown stockbroker. Probably had the most money of the four. Successful wife with her own professional career. No children. Found at his desk, after hours. Way after hours. Like the ad exec, no known reason for the broken neck."

Alison snapped the notebook shut. "That's basically it, Jay. If you see connections in any of this, please let me know."

"I see what you mean. Not exactly the kind of people who'd make an enemies' list, are they?" He sipped his brew, thinking. "How about money?" he offered. "You said two of 'em made pretty good bucks. And the retiree came into some dough a few years back. What about the housewife?"

Alison shook her head. "Didn't have any of her own, but her husband did fairly well. A lawyer. Enough to be comfy living in downtown Boston, but not enough to take out a membership at the Fort Knox Country Club. Not yet anyway. I just don't see money as the issue here, Jay. According to the police, there was no robbery at the crime scenes, and there were no big withdrawals from any of these people's accounts. I don't think that's the angle."

"Maybe that's the problem. Maybe they were supposed to pay someone but didn't. How about failed blackmail schemes? Could there be anything to that?"

Another head shake from Alison. "Not likely, according to the info. We seem to be dealing with squeaky clean individuals here, or at least reasonable facsimiles thereof. No one mentioned anything during any of these investigations that points in that direction."

The raucous music turned more melodious and less ear-splitting. The sweet sounds of Bonnie Raitt wafted overhead. Burgholz and Alison were both grateful for the respite.

"Okay, no blackmail," said Burgholz. "What about drugs? We have been known to have that kind of problem here in Boston." Burgholz caught the eye of the waitress and waved her over. "Want another beer?" he asked Alison, after ordering another for himself.

"No thanks. All set here," said Alison. The waitress slithered off toward the bar. "You're right about the drug thing, but again, there's no evidence on the record of anything like that in these cases. Try again, Mr. B."

"I'm starting to run out of reasons. Let's see. How about revenge? That's always a good one."

"Not bad. Maybe there's something there, but right now it's nothing more than a remote possibility. No one offered anything like that as a motive during the investigations done by the police. Or those of our own guys while they were doing their stories, for that matter. But who knows? Maybe it's worth another shot. I'll put a check mark next to that one."

"Please do. Especially since we've eliminated everything else so far. What about gambling? Any of these people run up unpayable debts?"

"Don't know. All I can say is, nothing led in that direction when the cops were checking on the money angle. I suppose it's possible, but none of the victims had any known history of gambling, so that seems like a bit of a stretch."

"I agree. It's probably not a hot-ticket item." Burgholz paused. He didn't know where to head next. "I'm getting to the bottom of the barrel here, I know, but what about wealthy relatives? Could the murderees possibly have had some connection with another family member who maybe had some money the victims needed or wanted? Could be the reverse of the usual blackmail thing. Maybe it was the victims blackmailing someone else. How about that?"

Alison looked forlorn. Everything was coming up empty. "I'm not real strong on that one, Jay. And what about the fact that every one of these people was killed in the same way? And had the same little black mark on the back of the neck? If any of these reasons had any credibility, why didn't they die in different ways? It doesn't make any sense. But who knows? As far as I can tell, no one has really checked into family connections all that deeply. Maybe there *is* something to it. I guess it won't hurt to keep that one on the list, if for no other reason than we'd only have one checked item otherwise."

"Well, if you want another, one that fits the M.O.'s, check this out." Burgholz warmed to the task, talking as much with his hands as vocally. "It's possible we're dealing with a certifiable nutcase here. Someone who doesn't need a reason to destroy a life, other than the sheer fun of it. Or maybe the challenge of it. Or maybe this guy is hearing voices from somewhere, telling him these people are bad guys and gals and it's his moral duty to eliminate them from continued membership in the human race. Maybe it's all of the above. And if it's one weirdo, that accounts for the similarity in methods, right? The serial angle. And if he's a kook, he wouldn't be doing it for the money. Ergo, no robberies. Whadaya think?"

"Well, I have to admit that might make some sense. Except for one thing."

"What's that?"

"This guy would have to be as slithery as a cat, and maybe as small. So far, no one's seen any evidence of human activity at the scenes. Absolutely zero. And remember, he would've had to gain access to two homes and a couple of offices without leaving any trace of a forced entry. Only trouble is, everything was clean. Nothing broken or disturbed. No voices heard. No evidence anywhere. That's downright remarkable, don't you think?"

"A good point, but not necessarily a fatal flaw in my theory. There've been other killers, or thieves, or criminals in general, who've been very adept at unforced entries and who've left little if any evidence. It may not be a common thing, I'll grant you, but it *is* possible."

"Maybe," said Alison. "But I still have one more problem with it."

"I'm listening."

Alison tried to organize her thoughts. It was her nature to play devil's advocate, to question, to probe. This often led somewhere, even if it wasn't exactly where she might have guessed. Better to think out loud and move along than sit in the breakdown lane. "Why was there no sign of a struggle at any of these places, Jay? If these were murders, as the police seem to suspect, why was each victim found without the slightest trace of them trying to stop, or at least fight off, the person or persons about to do this terrible thing? Maybe it's possible that that could happen in one, maybe two of these cases, say the ones involving falls down stairs. But what about the two where the victims were found at their office desks? If you're one of those people, don't you think you'd confront the killer? Maybe he's a strong guy, so you end up losing the battle. But do you really see yourself just sitting there while someone walks up, wraps his hands around your skull, and snaps your neck in two? And why does he leave that mark on your neck? And how's it done? Is it some kind of calling card? It just doesn't seem to fit, Jay. I can't buy into that."

"Well, I admit there may be a couple holes to work out. But, after all, that's why you're on the case, right? Ready for another beer yet?"

"Thanks, but I think I'll pass," said Alison. She still had that serious look on. Burgholz could see she was really into this. "Actually, you got me thinking," she said. "Maybe there's something there after all, but with a different kind of angle. I want to go home and get started on a little research. Sorry to be a party pooper, but I don't want to lose my train of thinking here."

"What're you up to, Ali? This can't wait 'til morning? You're gonna leave me here to drink with those other news freaks at the bar? Ugh."

That broke the tension. Alison snickered. "Sorry, Jay, but I think you'll survive just fine without me. I'd like to check something out before tomorrow morning's press conference at police headquarters. For the moment, I want to keep it to myself. It's kind of far-fetched and may not lead to anything. In fact, I'm almost sure it won't, and don't want to be embarrassed when it flops. If something develops out of it, though, you'll be the first to know."

"Why, thank you, Ali girl," said Jay, playfully. "I will count on that. I surely will."

Alison slipped out of the booth, offered goodbyes to Burgholz and the others, then escaped the din of the "Hellhole" for the walk to her South End apartment. The quiet of Boston's streets was a welcome respite. The talk with Burgholz had been worthwhile, as she knew it would. It dredged up possibilities, dashed others. But now she needed to zone in. If there was anything to what was in her head at the moment, this was going to be the most interesting assignment she had gotten herself into. Absolutely.

Chapter 11

Thursday, October 19

The only thing Sergeant Patrick Johnson hated more than getting up at six o'clock in the morning was getting up at six o'clock in the morning after he had gone to bed at two. It was a fate no human being deserved to experience, he would tell you, if you bothered to ask. He would also tell you this didn't apply in his case because he wasn't necessarily a human being, just a Boston cop. The two were mutually exclusive, as far as he was concerned.

Johnson wished the alarm clock clanging next to his head would vaporize. When it didn't, he decided he'd better turn off the jarring sound of it before it drove him insane—and before it fully woke his wife Fran, who mumbled and turned over about three feet away. Somehow, he knew he'd get through this. Always did. The only consolation he could think of at the moment was that his friend and partner, Vinnie Mulcahy—excuse me, make that Lieutenant Vinnie Mulcahy—was experiencing the same unearthly event right this very second just a couple of Dorchester streets away. Vee and Pee had both worked on the broken-neck murder cases the night before until the wee hours. It wasn't much of a consolation when you came right down to it, but it was better than nothing.

Johnson grumbled his way out of bed, being careful not to disturb Fran. She and the kids—Jamie, four, and Mark, two—didn't need to get started for another forty-five minutes or so, so he reset the alarm for a quarter to seven. He was thoughtful that way. He normally wouldn't have been up and around until then himself, but he and Mulcahy had to brief no less than the Police Commissioner in advance of this morning's scheduled press conference.

This was getting to be big. It had been decided a couple of days ago that the Top Cop would lead the conference due to the growing interest in the murder cases, particularly their serial nature. Also, the calls for action were becoming more strident, both in the press and out on the street. One, in fact, usually led to the other—a chicken-and-egg kind of thing. The commissioner felt the need to demonstrate the department's concern over these cases and the commitment of its top leadership in finding a solution. Mulcahy wanted to leave enough time to get the briefing done right, not to mention answer—or at least try to—the inevitable questions from the brass. Questions for which, if the truth be told, there were still lots of non-answers. That was why they were up until all hours going over everything. When the Commish was involved, you did these kinds of things.

Johnson stumbled through his morning routine, then got picked up by Mulcahy at six forty for the ride downtown. By seven, they were at headquarters, where there seemed to be more than the usual pandemonium. Not only were morning assignments being arranged and details sent off, but preparations were simultaneously underway for the upcoming news shindig. The joint, as they say, was jumping.

Mulcahy and Johnson spent the next couple of hours sorting through the facts of the four murder cases with the higher-ups, excluding the Commissioner. He was scheduled to be briefed at nine thirty, which should leave enough time to get updated for the ten o'clock conclave. For now, there was a ton of information to slog through, especially all the new stuff acquired over the last couple of days. This included the results of a second round of interviews with those involved in each case, follow-up info from the detectives who did the earlier investigations, review of photos and other crime lab forensics. It went on and on.

At nine thirty-five, Commissioner Dominic Rizzotto called Mulcahy and Johnson into his spacious office, abounding in wood, leather, and brass. Assistant Commissioner Bob Westerman, who had taken part in some of the earlier discussion with the two investigators, was already there, seated in front of the large oak desk. Behind it, Rizzotto was all suit, wire-frame glasses, and slicked-down hair. If not for "Police Commissioner" on the walnut-and-gold nameplate fronting his desk, one could not be faulted for mistaking him as a mafioso don. Despite his spit-shine facade, he had a rather pleasant voice and manner. Part policeman and part politician, he slithered between the dual roles, adroitly handling the inevitable conflicts that cropped up. He was generally well-liked and respected by the men on the force, as well as their supervisors.

Mulcahy, Johnson, and Westerman went over everything again, boiling it down in summary fashion for the Commissioner's quick mind. Before long, there were two sharp raps on the door. A head emerged from behind it and said, "They're all here, Commissioner. Whenever you're ready." To which Rizzotto replied, "Tell 'em we're on our way, Jerry." Jerry was the department's PR guy.

At five minutes past ten, Rizzotto, Westerman, Mulcahy, and Johnson made their way to a room normally reserved for meetings with the outside world, including the press. As soon as they entered, it was obvious they could have used a much larger facility for this one. It was stuffed to overflowing with representatives from the print, radio, and television media, as well as other members of the police department. A dozen microphones were spliced in their usual jumble at the podium. Faces and notebooks filled every nook and cranny, along with a phalanx of dazzling TV lights and bug-eyed cameras. Johnson looked around and was glad he had worn his best sport jacket, button-down shirt, and paisley tie for this one—all brownish, of course.

Jerry, who was doing his best PR thing at the mikes when they came in, quickly switched gears and said, "Okay, folks, we're ready to begin. Commissioner Rizzotto will make a brief statement, then take questions. Also in attendance for Q and A are Assistant Commissioner Bob Westerman and the two investigating officers, Lieutenant Vincent Mulcahy and Sergeant Patrick Johnson." Each man gave a quick wave or nod as Jerry pointed them out. "Here's the Commissioner."

Wicca Codex

Rizzotto walked swiftly and confidently to the podium. He knew it was going to take some doing to get through this one, at least in the way they hoped. Maybe a little luck wouldn't hurt either. "Good morning, ladies and gentlemen," he began, slowly and calmly and in a strong voice, white teeth showing. The cameras were rolling. This was his element. "Thank you all for coming. I'll try to fill you in on where we are in our investigation. Then we'll get into your specific questions. As you know, we've had several—four, in fact, as of this past Tuesday—murders of a similar nature over the last two months or so. It appears they're related in several ways. First, of course, is the cause of death. The victims all died in the same way—from a broken neck. Second, the time of death in each case has been ascertained to be somewhere during the early morning hours—generally in the midnight to three A. M. range." He leaned over the podium slightly, eyes moving from side to side, sizing up the crowd. He wanted everyone to get a good view. "Third, each scene was free of any disturbance or sign of struggle. There was, for all intents and purposes, no indication of anyone else having been there, except for item number four, which is that each victim had a small mark on the back of the neck. This is the only thing that could really be called evidence in each case. The mark was identified at the autopsies as an intense burn, very localized. Fifth, extensive investigation of the victims' families, friends, work colleagues, or whoever else may've had any association with them, revealed no unusual activity on the part of the victims that might indicate foul play. That is, there doesn't appear to be any motive for any of these killings at this time."

Commissioner Rizzotto stopped briefly and looked around the room. Despite the cramped quarters, there was an unusual silence. No one took advantage of his pause, as they sometimes did, to break in with questions. Everyone was listening intently, taking pictures, writing. He felt the hot lights burning into his face but resisted the temptation to wipe a bead of perspiration from his brow.

Alison Simmons was one of those who had barely managed to

wedge herself into the back of the room. She was taking notes as the Commissioner spoke, but so far, he hadn't said anything she didn't already know. She hoped that would come next. She looked up during Rizzotto's momentary break, then gazed back down to her notebook as he continued, ready to record the rest of his statement.

"The victims," continued the Commissioner, "seem to have no connection to each other, at least that we can identify right now. There also doesn't appear to be any pattern to the identity or characteristics of the victims. There are two males and two females. They span a rather wide age range, as well as social status. That is, there're two career professionals, one housewife, and a retiree. On the face of it, there's nothing remarkable there. None of the four had ever been arrested or had anything in their past to indicate any kind of criminal connection. None was what you would call a social or political activist. At the moment we have no new leads, but we're working on some things." Rizzotto was still hopeful he wouldn't have to get into what one of those things was. "We're asking for information from the public. Anyone who may have knowledge about any or all of these incidents. A special toll-free phone number has been established for that purpose. We're also planning on doing follow-up interviews with the families and acquaintances of the victims to make sure nothing's been missed."

Mulcahy and Johnson exchanged discreet glances as they sat at the table adjoining the podium. This follow-up business was news to them. They never talked about doing that at the earlier briefing. The Commissioner was winging it. They had told him about the exhaustive series of interviews already conducted, ending up just last night. He was groping to give these leeches something—anything. It was all they could do to keep from rolling their eyes.

Rizzotto was hitting his stride but fought against getting carried away. "Less Is More" was his motto. Besides, he really didn't have a heck of a lot beyond what he'd already thrown out to the dogs. He was ready to wrap it up. "Also, we'll be expanding our liaison with other police departments to see if anything of a similar nature has occurred recently or in the past, here in New England as well as other areas of the country. We'll be putting out descriptions of each incident and disseminating them to the authorities. Our preliminary research in this area hasn't turned up anything so far, but we'll be continuing and expanding that effort." Another brief pause. "That's what we know so far, ladies and gentlemen. At this point, I'll throw it open to questions."

A chorus of voices rose in a cacophony of sound as soon as the Commissioner finished. He couldn't understand anything being said. He raised both hands and shouted, "One at a time please. One at a time." He picked out a large hand being thrust in his direction. It belonged to one of the somewhat familiar faces from a local TV station. The name escaped him. He hated it when he couldn't remember things like that.

"From what you've told us, Commissioner," said the face, "it doesn't seem as though you've got an awful lot to go on. Is there a suspect—or suspects—in any of these cases?"

Commissioner Rizzotto cleared his throat but hid his unease remarkably well. "No. There are no suspects at this time. Our feeling is that the same individual or individuals are involved in each case, however, due to the similarities I outlined earlier. In particular, the burn mark on the neck indicates a serial-type situation."

"What about those marks, Commissioner?" asked another reporter. "What can you tell us about them?"

"Not much more than I already have. The marks were all small and neat. Their centers were almost like pin pricks, although the surrounding area was indicative of a very intense burn. Aside from these marks, the autopsies revealed no other adverse medical conditions on the part of any of the victims."

The press was really into it now, scrambling for anything that would give them the next big headline. "Commissioner, what assurance can you give the victims' families and the public that the killer or killers will be apprehended before there are any more of these incidents? It appears as though you're not that close to finding answers in any of these cases."

Rizzotto kept his cool nicely. He'd been through too many of these things to let himself get flustered by this crowd. "I can assure you—and them—that we're doing everything possible to solve these crimes. I've already indicated some things currently underway and planned. We've assembled a top-notch team of investigators—they're sitting right over there—who are committed to these cases full time and who will be giving top priority to resolving them as soon as possible." The politician in him was taking over with a vengeance. Flim-flam-speak was bubbling to the surface. "I myself have directed that the full resources of this department be made available to the effort and will put at their disposal whatever is needed to bring this to a successful conclusion."

At that point the Commissioner discovered, to his chagrin, that they were not about to "get lucky" in avoiding what they were all hoping to avoid. He selected another hand, one way at the back of the room, for the next question. It belonged to Alison Simmons.

"Commissioner Rizzotto," said Alison, "a police department spokesperson indicated to me in an earlier telephone interview that the investigating team was selected because they had so-called 'special qualifications' to handle these cases. Can you elaborate on that? What kind of special qualifications was he talking about?"

The Commissioner had to restrain himself from asking Alison who the hell had told her that—she either wouldn't know the name or wouldn't say anyway—but made a mental note to find out who they had manning the phones over the last couple of days. Whoever spilled the beans was in deep doodoo. "Why, uh, yes, I think we can get into that, in a preliminary way. It's something that's just developing, so there isn't a whole lot to tell you at the moment." The Commissioner waved for Mulcahy to come up to the podium. "I'll ask the head of our investigating team, Lieutenant Vincent Mulcahy, to talk about that. Lieutenant, why don't you come up here." Rizzotto moved aside, but did not sit down. He wanted to be within striking position to regain control in a hurry, if necessary.

Mulcahy made his way to the podium while trying to stay calm. He

Wicca Codex

had started to formulate a way to get into this area on the short walk over to the press conference and during the Commissioner's remarks, just in case, but whatever he had come up with was melting like butter in the searing lights of the cameras. All of a sudden, they seemed much more intense than they had just a moment ago.

Mulcahy adjusted his jacket and jabbed at his tie as he tried to compose himself. "Let me reiterate," he began, "that we will be continuing our investigation over the coming days as outlined by Commissioner Rizzotto. As he said, everyone is committed." He could almost hear brows wrinkling in the first couple of rows. Mulcahy sensed the weakness of his opening. 'They're right,' he thought. 'They don't need another politician up here. They want something concrete.' He cleared his throat, hunched himself up, and began anew. "In the past, various police departments across the country have had cases kind of like this one. I don't mean in terms of the exact same circumstances, but rather in terms of there being certain unexplainable aspects. Over time, the knowledge gained in these cases was pooled and discussed with certain professional members of the community. Psychologists, psychiatrists, religious leaders, people like that." Mulcahy knew this was the tricky part. But, dammit, full speed ahead. "From those efforts came special courses on factors that could be involved in these types of cases. Those courses have been refined over the years and have become quite sophisticated. They're given routinely to several members of each department from time to time. My partner Sergeant Johnson and I have taken such a course, and, so, have a certain expertise not normally associated with routine cases."

Mulcahy didn't really know where he was going with this, but the problem was solved by Alison, who asked, "So what exactly are you saying, Lieutenant? What kind of course are you talking about?"

"I was getting to that," squirmed Mulcahy. "What I'm talking about is something called 'Investigating the Occult in Crime.' We went through it about a year ago and've had a couple of update seminars since."

Despite the blinding lights, Mulcahy could see a number of heads lift. Everything seemed to stop at once. Suspended animation. Mulcahy wanted to keep moving and give a little more explanation before things got out of hand. He felt the presence of Commissioner Rizzotto somewhere behind him.

"I want to emphasize," continued Mulcahy, "that this is but one additional avenue we in the law-enforcement profession have at our disposal." 'God, I sound just like the Commissioner. But at least I didn't say "lore-enforcement."' "When we're confronted with circumstances that may not be explainable for the usual reasons, we think it prudent to consider other approaches. Due to the facts of the four cases, we have at hand, it appears as though that angle needs to be more closely examined. That's not to say anything will come of it, just that we need to look under every stone, so to speak."

Before her stunned colleagues extricated themselves from their uncharacteristic silence, Alison took advantage and got in one last question. "Lieutenant Mulcahy, you said 'more closely examined.' Does that mean you've been looking into that aspect before today, on the earlier cases?"

Mulcahy grabbed the sides of the podium. He apparently wasn't being yanked yet by Rizzotto, so he plunged forward. "Well, sure. Of course. When you have cases like these that don't fit the normal mold, you've got to look at something else. It hasn't necessarily been high on the priority list until now, but yes, the thought has occurred to us previously."

Now the questions were coming fast and furious again. The impact of Mulcahy's statement had registered with the reporters, and they were warming to the task. One of the TV people asked, "Lieutenant, what exactly do they tell you in that course you took? The one on the occult in crime. Have there been any actual incidents of that sort here in Boston, or anywhere else, that've been documented? What more can you tell us about that?"

Rizzotto had heard enough. Before Mulcahy could answer, the

Commissioner gently nudged the Lieutenant away and reclaimed center stage. He thanked Mulcahy for his remarks, then turned to the glaring newspeople. "I'm sorry, ladies and gentlemen, but that's really all we can say at this time. We're only just starting to get into that part of it. We'll be continuing our investigation and will keep you informed of progress. I'm sure you won't let us forget to do that." He smirked as he delivered the last remark. "Thank you all for coming." He walked quickly to the door, followed closely by Mulcahy, Johnson, and Westerman, despite the fury of questions hurled in their direction.

Alison smiled and said "I knew it" under her breath. As everyone piled out of the room, she added one final thought: 'And you're absolutely right about one thing, Commissioner. We won't let you forget. No way.'

Chapter 12

Friday, October 20

It looked and felt like snow as Alison Simmons emerged from her car in The Herald's parking lot, ready for another exciting day in the world of print journalism. The sky was slate and the air raw, with a chilling wind that stabbed icicles through layers of clothing with ease. Even though it was only October, she remembered back to the same month a couple of years ago when Boston's streets were whitened by several inches of snow on its tenth day. It was the earliest measurable snow in the city since they had started keeping weather records. She recalled the date because it was easy to remember—the tenth day of the tenth month. Ten ten. Snow wasn't in today's forecast, but you could never be sure in New England. There were too many occasions when people ended up shoveling six inches of "partly cloudy." She hoped the weather gurus were right this time, though. She just wasn't quite ready for winter.

When Alison arrived at her desk, she found a copy of this morning's edition of the paper sitting there. It was folded to an article on the first page. The headline jumped out at her: "Police see occult ties in murder investigation." Right below was the best part: "by Alison Simmons." It was her first page-one story, so Burgholz had left it for her with one of those little yellow stick-on notes saying, "Nice goin.' Let's talk when you get in." She had to smile at his thoughtfulness. Not to mention the nice addition she'd be making to her personal clip file, which was growing by leaps and bounds. 'If it wasn't morning,' she exulted, 'I'd head right on over to the Hellhole and hoist a cold one. Maybe tonight.'

Alison noticed no one in Burgholz's office. She wandered over and stuck her head in, rapping her knuckles on the jamb a couple of times. "Hi, Mr. B," she said jovially. "Got your note. Thanks. Is now a good time?"

"Sure, Ali. Come on in." Burgholz was sitting at his cluttered desk. He waved at one of the chairs in front. "Make yourself at home," he said.

Alison started to settle into one of the wooden chairs, then thought better of it, not wanting to torture herself so early in the morning. She ambled over to one of the bookcases lining the walls and leaned against it. "What's on the agenda?" she asked.

"Just wanted to touch base with you on those murder cases again, especially in light of yesterday's bombshell at police headquarters." Burgholz frowned and shook his head. "The occult, of all things," he said emphatically. "I can't believe it. Jesus. They couldn't have come up with a better one if they tried. Whadaya think about that?"

Allison almost burst out laughing. "What's the matter, Jay? Where's your sense of adventure and enthusiasm for the mysterious? I'm really surprised at you. Wasn't it just a couple of days ago you were talking about some whacko hearing voices from on high?"

"Hearing voices isn't exactly the same thing. And anyway, I was just making conversation. As for buying into the weirdo world, I do not. Do you? Tell me it isn't so. I can't believe you think we've got another *Exorcist* situation on our hands here."

"Well, not quite that, I don't think." Alison reflected back to the scary book and movie set in Washington, D.C. She had to suppress a shiver just thinking about it. "That involved demonic possession, if you recall. The devil invaded the body of a young girl to claim her for his own. She didn't die. In fact, she was given some rather remarkable powers by old Mr. Beelzebub. She could rotate her head 360 degrees. Our four victims couldn't quite make it that far around before their necks snapped like matchsticks."

Burgholz leaned back in his chair and put his hands behind his head. "Yeah, and now you're willing to believe that some cosmic force comes down from who knows where and does the snapping? Come on. Where did a nice girl like you get ideas like that?"

Alison could see that this was going to take a little time, so she sucked it up and dragged herself over to Burgholz's desk. 'To hell with the pain, she thought. She sat down as delicately as she could, as though trying to avoid significant contact. She would have hovered there if she could, much like the girl in one of the hairy scenes from *The Exorcist*.

"Well, to tell you the truth," explained Alison, "I've always been a little interested in the supernatural. I read a book on it back in high school. I kind of got hooked on it, I guess, maybe because girls weren't supposed to be interested in such things. I don't like being predictable."

"You, predictable? That's a laugh," squealed Burgholz.

Alison ignored the taunt. "And besides," said Alison, "I've been doing some research."

Burgholz's eyes widened. "What kind of research?" he asked.

"You know about the Internet, right? And the World Wide Web?"

"Sure. I *am* an ancient old curmudgeon, but I do know a smidgin' about the modern world. They're only the biggest craze in the computer industry at the moment." Burgholz pointed to the relic of a computer poised on the edge of his desk. They hadn't quite gotten around to upgrading him yet, and he wasn't pressing. "It seems as though there're only two kinds of people: those who are already on the 'Net, and those who want to be. I'm not exactly a devotee myself yet, so I guess I'm in Category Number Two."

"I confess to being a Number One myself," said Alison. "I've got a computer at home that's set up for cruising around the Information Superhighway, and I like to dabble in it. When you allow me a moment or two away from the office, that is." Alison smiled, just to make sure Burgholz knew she was kidding.

"Hardy har har," retorted Burgholz.

"There's a lot of junk out there," continued Alison. "But there's also some fascinating stuff, too. I came across a few interesting tidbits after our beers at the Hellhole the other night."

"So that's what you were in such a hurry to get to. You left me flat to surf the 'Net? I had hoped I was more interesting than that." Burgholz spread both hands out on the desk and let his chin drop onto

Wicca Codex

his chest. "I'm smitten, shocked, and embarrassed."

Alison laughed at Burgholz's mock put-down of himself. "No need to worry, Jay. I still find you more interesting than, oh, twenty-five, maybe thirty percent of what's on the Web."

"Ah, I'm relieved. I thought I was dirt. Thanks for that," said Burgholz, rather sanctimoniously.

Alison laughed again, then got serious. "Want to hear more?"

Burgholz caught Alison's mood change. "Shoot," he said.

Alison inched her chair closer to the desk. "Well, for starters, this occult thing is more than just a word in the dictionary, or a device used by writers in horror stories. There's an awful lot of interest in this kind of thing in the real world. The number of people associated with what you could call the occult is surprising, judging by what I came across. There're all sorts of unusual types out there—people that aren't exactly in the mainstream of things, to say the least. Look at this." Alison pulled several folded sheets out of the notebook she instinctively carried everywhere and spread them on the desk.

"What's all this?" asked Burgholz.

"A list I wrote out summarizing different groups I came across in just one quick session on the Web." It showed the name of each group, its purpose, where it was based, and various other facts Alison had found interesting enough to record. She slid even closer to the desk and laid her elbows on its edge. She recognized enough of her handwriting to go over the items while reading upside down. "Exhibit Number One is Satanism, or devil worship. They've got an FAQ section on the Web, and..."

"Whoa. Slow down, pardner," exclaimed Burgholz, a puzzled look on his face. "Why don't you run that by me again. F...A...what?"

"FAQ. That's 'Netspeak for 'Frequently Asked Questions.' It's usually where you go first to find out the basics about something, instead of asking the same old, stupid questions that have to be answered over and over by those on the receiving end. It works pretty well. If you want to know more than what's in the FAQ, you can follow up. At least that way you don't make an asshole of yourself. Excuse the expression."

"Okay," said Burgholz, haughtily. "You may continue, now that I am suitably informed."

Alison's gaze alternated between her notes and Burgholz, who could see she was really into this occult business. For the moment, she was the teacher, he, the pupil. "As I started to say, it seems Satanism is big all over. Here in the States, in England, even in places like New Zealand. Everywhere, really. There're all kinds of spinoffs, too. Each group is organized to do its own thing, but each adheres to certain common elements. Look at the list." Alison directed Burgholz to the appropriate column. "There's the Church of Satan, the Ordo Sinistra Vivendi, the Order of Nine Angles, Ordo Templi Satanis, the Black Order, the Temple of Set, Fraternity of the Jarls of Balder, just to name a few. There's even a Satanic Bible, and you can find out about Satanic Ethics, the Satanic Credo, the Twenty-one Satanic Points. It goes on and on."

Despite Alison's obvious seriousness, Burgholz couldn't repress a laugh. "Satanic ethics, huh? Now there's an oxymoron if I ever heard one. That's in the same category as 'military intelligence,' or 'political correctness,' wouldn't you say?"

Alison smiled. "Yeah, I guess that's right," she said. "And you can add 'rapid transit' to the list, at least here in Boston."

Burgholz, a word freak of sorts, couldn't resist keeping the game going. "Especially during the 'commuter rush hour,' which is another good one."

Alison playfully tapped her fingers on Burgholz's desk. "Would you like to get back to business, Mr. B? Or shall I see if I can top that one?"

"Okay. Okay. I get the message." Burgholz put on his dourest look.

Alison paused before continuing. "Then you have your basic witchcraft groups, and again they're all over the place. Non-western societies have their witch doctors, medicine men, shamans, what have you. Many Asian cultures resort to witches and sorcerers, and witchcraft is widespread in Africa. Latin America and Haiti have voodoo, which is a form of witchcraft. Closer to home, we've got our own practitioners in the U. S., and not just out in the boondocks, either. Big cities, too. Most of us've heard about the infamous witch trials in Salem—right in our own backyard. Quite a few people were tortured and killed. Even though it happened three hundred years ago, I can assure you from what I've been reading that witchcraft is very much alive and well. Maybe not with the same degree of fanaticism, but it's there, nonetheless."

"Cool it, Alison. You're starting to scare me a little." Burgholz said this with a happy face, but Alison thought she read something behind the smile. She wasn't quite sure whether he was kidding or not.

"Well, there's lots more," said Alison, "but I can stop. I think I've made my point, anyway. You may think the occult is balderdash, and you may even be right. But you can't ignore the fact that there're an awful lot of people who take these things very seriously. Right now, in fact, they're talking to each other on the Internet about the devil, and magic, and sorcery, and spells, and other sinister things. Not to mention those who go beyond the talking stage. They've found like-minded people and have organized into cults and covens and who knows what else." Alison waited, mostly to let Burgholz break in, if he wanted. But he was listening intently and said nothing. She went on. "Most of 'em may be harmless. But some may not be. And it only takes a few, or even one, for that matter, to cause big-time trouble. You've been around long enough—no offense, Mr. B—to know there're things that happen for no apparent reason. They have no rational explanation. I'm sure you've heard about people who have extraordinary powers of mind or body. I've read about a few who can move objects without physically touching them. Even seen them on TV." She wasn't sure these demonstrations were always on the up and up, but that was a separate issue. No sense complicating things. "Others seem to have strong advance sensations about significant events about to happen to others—members of their family, maybe, or even complete strangers. And there's lots more, if you take the time and trouble to look into it. The mind is a powerful thing, Jay. Homo Sapiens have come a long way from the ape, but who knows what we're really capable of. Maybe some of us are way ahead of the others. Or maybe some of us have some kind of advantage over the rest. With a little help from outside sources."

"Maybe this, maybe that," said the editor. His voice reflected his skepticism. "There are too many maybes. Let's just say I'm not one hundred percent convinced."

"That's okay, Jay. All I ask is that you keep an open mind."

"It's a deal." Burgholz had his own idea what to do next but refrained from dictating his preferred course of action to Alison. He wanted to see what her thoughts were. "So where do we go from here?" he asked.

Alison's eyes brightened by several watts. He was giving her rope to play with. Or maybe hang herself. "Well, at least you didn't say the whole thing's off. I take that as a sign you still think there's a story here. And I agree with that, especially after yesterday's news conference at police headquarters. I'd like to do some more research on the victims, their families, friends, and so forth. There may be something we're overlooking, or sometimes things come out the second or third time around. We've got to keep digging. I also want to stay in touch with the police. Maybe ferret out some more info on the occult angle, not to mention doing a bit more Web surfing to follow up on my preliminary wanderings. How does that sound?"

Alison had carved out territory that was acceptable to Burgholz. "Well, given the police business yesterday, and the strangeness of these cases, I think we can afford to keep you freelancing. For a while longer, anyway. If nothing develops, we'll have to pull in the reins and get you back to being a productive journalist again. So, with that qualifier, let's keep going."

"Good decision, Mr. B. You won't regret it."

Alison extricated herself from the cruel and unusual punishment of Burgholz's visitor chair and ambled toward the door. Before leaving, she turned and said, "And remember. No one ever won the Pulitzer

Prize by covering dog shows and beauty pageants. See ya."

Burgholz could do nothing but smile at Alison's back as she pirouetted out the door.

Chapter 13

Friday, October 20

It was lunchtime, and Stephen Blake was brown-bagging it today. Sometimes he just felt like holing up in his office and not fighting the noontime crowds in the Financial District. He liked to nibble at his lunch and read the newspaper, only he hadn't bought one this morning. He decided to wander around to see if anyone else had a paper he could borrow. After a couple of minutes, he hit paydirt. He noticed *The Boston Herald* on Freddie Jorgensen's desk. He preferred The Globe, himself, but he was in no position to be choosy. He was thankful to have anything. Jorgensen was at his desk, apparently crunching away to meet some Friday deadline.

"Hi, Freddie," said Stephen, trying to be as jovial as possible. "Slaving away through lunch again?"

Jorgensen barely glanced up from his work. "Oh, hi Stephen. Yeah. Got to get this damn project done and out the door by five. It's gonna be tight. No rest for the weary, as they say."

"I know the feeling." said Stephen, truthfully. He'd been in this position many times himself. "Sorry you're stuck. But since you are, mind if I borrow your paper? I'm eating in and forgot to get my own this morning. It'll help pass the time."

"Sure, go right ahead," said Jorgensen, as he handed the paper to Stephen. "As a matter of fact, you can keep it. I've already seen it. Be my guest."

"Thanks, Freddie. Appreciate it. Good luck on your project."

Stephen retreated to his office and read the headlines on page one as he bit into his sandwich. He noticed one that said, "Police see occult ties in murder investigation." He decided to read that first since it seemed to be a bit out of the ordinary. And indeed it was. The writer—Alison Simmons, he noted—described the continuing investigation being conducted by the Boston Police Department into a series of murders occurring over the last several weeks, all involving a bizarre feature: each victim had died of a broken neck.

'A broken neck?' thought Stephen. 'That sounds familiar. Where've I heard that before?' He remembered. It was earlier this week, when he met John Demming for lunch at Locke-Ober. Demming had told him about a murder—a stockbroker, wasn't it?—that happened right in Demming's building. There was an article about it in Wednesday's Globe that Stephen had read after Demming told him about it, but he didn't recall many of the details. Stephen's curiosity was aroused. He wanted to find out more about the murders. He wondered if Jorgensen might have kept any of the papers from earlier in the week. He went back to see Jorgensen.

"Sorry to bother you again, Freddie," explained Stephen, "but I was wondering if you have any of your Heralds from earlier in the week. There's an article I wanted to check up on, and I think it might be in one of those editions."

Freddie looked up from the disaster on his desk and said, "You're in luck. I usually hang onto 'em for a while before I get overwhelmed and go on a clean-out binge. I probably have what you need. Which one're you lookin' for?"

"Let's see," pondered Stephen. "It was the day I went to lunch with John Demming. That would've been Tuesday. No, wait. It had to be Wednesday, the day after our meeting. Yeah, that's it. Wednesday."

"Well, all of this week's papers are over there," said Freddie without looking up, whipping a thumb over his shoulder at the table behind him. "Help yourself." Stephen rummaged through the pile, found Wednesday's edition, and thanked Jorgensen.

Back in his own office, Stephen flipped rapidly through the paper. Bingo—there it was. A blurb on page four by Alison Simmons: "Stockbroker murdered—one in a series?" He read the article, which portrayed the basic facts about the murder, much as he now remembered reading in The Globe. More importantly, it went beyond the latest case and tried linking it to the ones preceding it. There were some insights in it that forced one to speculate and ask questions. Stephen found it to be an interesting piece of writing.

Stephen finished his lunch and managed to make it through the rest of the afternoon, although he found it hard to concentrate. He kept thinking about what he had read at lunch. Also, he was looking forward to tonight. He had been invited back to that neat little bookstore on Beacon Hill and was anticipating doing some serious browsing through Ernst's back-of-the-shop collection of old treasures. Then there was the matter of the meeting with Ernst's friends. Stephen had consented to go to the meeting because he didn't want to hurt the old guy's feelings. Not only that, it might possibly jeopardize seeing more of his collection. In all honesty, though, he would just as soon forgo the get-together. Especially at that late hour. He was planning on going over at nine, as Ernst had suggested, stay a couple of hours, maybe, then find some suitable excuse to leave before the meeting got going. Maybe a headache. Used to work for Janet. In any event, he would think of something when the time came. An odd mixture of excitement, anticipation, and a little guilt created a troubling brew inside him.

At four forty-five, Stephen couldn't take it anymore. He said goodbye to Connie, his secretary, and wished her a good weekend. He waited impatiently for the elevator, then bolted through the marbled lobby of the office tower and out the front door for the walk to his Back Bay apartment. He went there directly, got comfortable, prepared a simple dinner, and downed it indifferently with a cold beer while watching the evening news.

Afterwards, he caught the first period and a half of the Bruins game at the FleetCenter. Tonight's opponent was the New Jersey Devils. Stephen thought that was appropriate, given the possible occult connection in the murder cases he had read about that afternoon. It looked like the Bs would get whacked again tonight. It was not starting out to be an auspicious year for the local hockey entry. He started to feel a certain melancholy come over him, not only for the fact that the once mighty Bruins were only a shadow of their former gritty selves, but also by the fact that the old Boston Garden was gone forever. It had been an anachronism, sure, but it was a great old building, nonetheless, full of history and memories. You didn't even have to be a native Bostonian to appreciate the place. It transcended geography and was home to some of the greatest sports teams of all time. And now it was gone. And they didn't even have the smarts to call the replacement arena the New Boston Garden. He was willing to bet that most folks, even those who didn't want to see the old Garden go, would have bought into that name after a while. But the FleetCenter? No way. It oozed money and yuppiness. 'Some people may call it that,' he thought. 'But not me.' And not any of those whose sports memories are full of the glory days.

Stephen snapped out of his funk and saw it was time to leave for the bookstore. He went out into the cool night and made the ten-minute walk briskly over to Beacon Hill, arriving at just about nine o'clock. Stephen liked to be punctual when it came to meetings, invitations, and the like. He considered it a sign of interest and courtesy. Janet had always kidded him about it, she being more of a free-wheeler in that regard.

The lights of the bookstore were inviting as he turned the corner, and it came into view. He opened the door and heard the melodious tinkle of the little bell above his head—a friendly, thanks-for-coming sound. Ernst was at the cash register with a customer, who appeared to be about to purchase a book and leave. Ernst turned toward the door at the sound of the bell. He recognized Stephen immediately, and said merrily, "Good evening, Mr. Blake. Come in, come in. I will be with you in just one moment."

Stephen nodded, taking pleasure in hearing the lilting German accent once again. He busied himself by browsing through one of the myriad piles of books on a nearby table. Ernst concluded his transaction, thanked the patron for the sale, and ushered him out the door, locking it when the man had left. He also changed the "Open" sign to "Closed," but left the lights on in the shop, presumably for those who would be coming to the meeting later. Returning his attention to Stephen, Ernst said, "So, Mr. Blake, it is indeed good to see you again. I am so pleased you were able to accept my invitation for this evening. I told my friends about you—and this time I mean my *human* friends rather than my *book* friends..." Ernst really enjoyed his little joke and started laughing profusely, which was contagious and got Stephen laughing as well.

When Ernst regained his composure a bit, he continued with his interrupted thought. "As I was saying, they are most anxious to meet you. I am sure you will like them. But before they come, I want you to see more of my collection. And maybe we can talk about a few things before my friends arrive." Ernst waited briefly, then resumed. "Would it be presumptuous of me to say my *other* friends? Even though we have just recently met, I feel as though I can call you my friend already. Anyone who likes books as much as I do cannot be all bad, is that not so?" Ernst laughed again.

"Well, I guess that's true," said Stephen. "And no, I don't think it's presumptuous. Actually, I'm rather flattered you feel that way. So, let's consider this the official start of a brand-new friendship."

"Wonderful, Mr. Blake," said Ernst, animatedly. Stephen could see the old man was genuinely pleased. Must be kind of lonely running this place all by himself, thought Stephen. Not too many people to talk to, probably. "I suppose," continued Ernst, "now that we are friends—officially, as you say—we should call each other by our first names. I would be very pleased if you called me Gustav. And, if I may, I will call you Stephen. Did I remember it correctly?"

"You certainly did," said Stephen, somewhat amazed that Ernst had remembered. "I'm rather impressed with your memory, for...for so many days having passed since we met. And after only the briefest of introductions."

"What you really meant to say, I will wager, is that you are impressed with my memory, for an old man. Is that not right?" Ernst held up a comforting hand to Stephen, indicating that no reply was necessary. "Please do not worry," he continued, soothingly, "I am not offended in the slightest. After all, I *am* an old man. But I have always prided myself on my ability to recall names, dates, and other facts. It is probably my strongest quality." Ernst paused momentarily. "But enough of this chatter. I would like to propose that we celebrate our newfound friendship with a small toast. If you will accompany me to the back of the shop, I have some wine that I think you will enjoy. Do you like wine, Stephen?"

"As a matter of fact, I do. And I'm not too fussy about what kind, either." Stephen was starting to forget about the cares of the day and the past week. He really liked this Ernst fellow quite a bit. The more you got to know him, the more congenial he was. Stephen liked the way he felt in his presence. He knew he was going to enjoy the evening immensely. Or at least the first part of it with Ernst and the book collection. He still didn't want to stay for the meeting and was planning on finding a way to avoid it. But that was a problem for later. Right now, he just wanted to enjoy the company of Ernst and his books.

"In that case," said the old man, "let us proceed to the back, my friend. I think I can assure you that you will not have to settle for the bottom of the barrel. I have a fine German Riesling I think you will like." Ernst led Stephen to the same room he had visited on Monday night. As then, Ernst had to unlock it first. Stephen thought that was a reasonable precaution to take, given the value of the rare books he had seen. Stephen took off his coat and settled into one of the soft chairs. Ernst opened the wine, eased into the other chair, and poured two glasses. They toasted each other and their newfound friendship. Stephen enjoyed the coolness of the liquid as it slid down his throat. He said, "You were right about the wine, Mr....I mean, Gustav. It's excellent."

They finished the first glass together as they talked and as Ernst showed Stephen many of the manuscripts displayed in the cases lining the walls. After an hour or so, the bottle was empty, and Stephen was enjoying himself beyond his expectations. He had not only examined many wonderful old texts and maps, but also heard stories about them from his host, who was a treasure trove of knowledge on each item. There were incunabula—books from the earliest days of printing—in elegant bindings, including products from the presses of the likes of William Caxton, Johann Gutenberg, Nicholas Jenson, and Aldus Manutius. There was an album amicorum of Johannes Franck from the late sixteenth century, a Book of Hours printed in Bruges in 1494, and works by Jacobus de Theramo, Giovanni Boccaccio, Constantijn Huygens, Roemer Visscher, and many other ancients. Not to mention more modern works—just as exquisite—from Ashendene Press, the Bibliophile Society, Bird and Bull Press. Also, autographed letters from Samuel Pepys, Aubrey Beardsley, Wilkie Collins, Alfred Sisley, Lord Byron, and a host of others. Each was magnificent in its own right. Taken together, the collection was beyond description. 'How could any one individual amass such a set of museum-quality antiquities?' wondered Stephen.

"So, Stephen," said Ernst, "what do you say? Are you glad you came?"

"Am I ever!" answered Stephen, truthfully. "This has got to be one of the most incredible experiences I've had. For someone in publishing, this is an extraordinary opportunity to see some of the best documents from the past. The workmanship on these volumes is incredible. Just gorgeous. And your knowledge of them matches their beauty. I can see you have a real love for your possessions. It's a real privilege to be here. What more can I say?"

Ernst's eyes sparkled. "I knew you would feel that way, Stephen. And yes, I do love them. But love is something to be shared, is it not? That only serves to increase its intensity. So, I am very happy to have you share in my amorous relationships with my 'friends'." Ernst's sweep of his hand around the room indicated he was speaking of the

Wicca Codex

'friends' now in their presence rather than those coming later.

Ernst sensed the time was right to discuss with Stephen something of great importance. Something that was the real reason for inviting him back to the shop, and especially the meeting to follow. Something he and Lariakin had talked about several days ago right in this very room. Something critical to the success of their work. But he must broach the subject in the right way. Slowly. Carefully. Cautiously. "If you like what you have seen so far, Stephen, I think you will be even more impressed with another document I have. It is quite old and extremely valuable, and so I have to keep it even more secure than these volumes. It is in the room across the hall. Would you like to see it?"

Stephen noticed that Ernst, though still smiling, seemed to take on an air of seriousness beneath the outward mask of jollity. It was a quality he had not seen in the old man before. He wondered what this was all about. His curiosity was aroused, as Ernst knew it would be. "Well, Gustav, you certainly have managed to awaken my sense of intrigue. How can I possibly turn down something that mysterious? Of course I'd like to see it. What is it?"

Ernst laughed. "Patience, my friend. I will explain all in due time. For now, I must ask that you will not reveal anything about what you see here tonight. To anyone. Can you agree to that, Stephen?"

"Why...sure. If you insist. No problem. Now I'm even more curious."

"Fine, then. I know that your word is good. Come, let us go see it. Please follow me."

Ernst led Stephen out of the room and to the door directly across the narrow hallway. Not surprisingly, it had to be unlocked. Ernst did so, then reached in to switch on the light. The old man stepped aside and invited Stephen to enter. In appearance, this room was much like the one they had just left. Perhaps slightly smaller, but with similar furnishings. The main difference was the lack of bookcases along the walls. In fact, Stephen couldn't see any books at all. It also had what looked to be a small closet.

Ernst motioned for Stephen to sit in one of the two comfortable-looking chairs straddling a small table. "Let me retrieve what I was telling you about," said Ernst. "I keep it locked up for safe-keeping. One moment please." He went over to a table against the wall and bent low to reach the knob of a small safe sitting inconspicuously below. Stephen hadn't noticed it when he came in. Ernst twirled the tumblers several times and popped open the safe's heavy door. He removed an object that appeared to Stephen to be wrapped in brown cloth. The fabric was quite tattered and worn. It seemed older than anything he had ever seen before. Stephen noticed that Ernst locked the safe right after removing the object. 'Why would he do that?' wondered Stephen. 'Must be other valuables in there.'

Ernst brought the object, still wrapped in its covering, to where Stephen was sitting and set it on the small table. The yellow light from a single old lamp cast a soft glow. Ernst sat in the chair on the other side of the table. He carefully undraped the folds of the cloth until the item beneath was revealed. Stephen saw that it was, as Ernst had said, an ancient book. It was bound in leather with a protective flap over the front edge, secured by a metal clasp. There were no markings on the front cover. Stephen couldn't see the back spine from his position, and so didn't know if there was any writing there that might identify it.

Ernst maintained the silence for a while, then said somewhat reverently, "This, my friend, is what I was telling you about. For the moment, I would advise you not to touch it. This is not because I am concerned that you will damage it, but rather because it has been known to cause, let us say, certain unpleasant sensations in those who have not become accustomed to it. It seems to have a certain energy about it, particularly for the...uninitiated."

Stephen had a strong urge to ask what Ernst meant by "sensation" and "energy" and "uninitiated," but decided not to break the mood. He merely sat quietly and kept his eyes on the book while listening to Ernst continue his monologue.

"Before I open this, Stephen, let me give you some of the history of the manuscript, and an explanation as to what it is. That will allow you to have more of an appreciation of it. Since you are in the publishing business, you may recognize this as a codex—a very early book. Everything, of course, is done by hand. The binding is leather over wooden boards, which is typical of the medieval period. This particular binding has been dated to about the tenth or eleventh century. Fibers from its cloth wrapping were analyzed and found to be from the fifteenth century. However, the parchment leaves and writing, in my estimation, come from a much earlier period. I believe that the leaves pre-date their binding by at least fifteen hundred years." Stephen did the math in his head: 500 BC, give or take a few years. He whistled in awe. Ernst continued. "They were preserved by the first owners—perhaps 'keepers' would be a better word—as best as they could be and handed down over time, probably in an original binding long since disintegrated. It is likely that one of its subsequent users had the leaves mounted in the binding you see before you, which remains remarkably well-preserved for its age. You will notice when I open *The Codex* in a moment that there is no writing in the traditional sense. That is, there is no alphabetic script, only symbols."

Ernst felt he was getting close to the limit as to how much explanation was required. He reminded himself that he needed to be very careful what should be revealed and what should remain unknown. He went on: "It is believed the symbols represent some ancient system of wizardry whose meaning has been lost. For this reason, I have come to call this manuscript "The Wicca Codex." 'Wicca' is an Old English word meaning 'wizard.' Now, let me show you the inside."

Ernst undid the metal clasp and turned back the top cover to reveal the first leaf and its assortment of strange signs and symbols. Stephen recognized some as being familiar geometrical shapes, but, for the most part, they were incomprehensible to him. As other leaves were turned to show their markings, the same type of symbol pattern was revealed. Stephen was mesmerized by the whole experience, and for a while could do nothing but run his eyes over *The Codex* and its contents. He longed to touch it, to let his fingers feel the texture of the old leather and the graying parchment, but he heeded Ernst's warning not to. He had so many questions, he hardly knew where to start.

Ernst saw the wonderment etched on Stephen's face and said, "I can see you are as taken by this volume as I was when I first saw it. I am sure you would like to know more about it. I will do my best to confer what knowledge I have of it to you."

Stephen took a deep breath and managed to gather himself sufficiently to make his first remark since seeing *The Codex*. "I must admit I'm rather stunned by this. I've never seen anything like it before. And you're quite right; I have at least a million questions." Stephen paused briefly to try to inventory the swirlings in his mind. "I guess the first thing I'd like to know is how it came into your possession. Where did you find it?"

"That is a very fair question," said Ernst. He was willing to disclose the answer, at least up to a point. "Let me begin my response by saying that I am originally from Germany, as I am sure you have concluded by now from my name and accent. Perhaps even my choice of wines." Ernst chuckled. "Well, I have had the fortune to return to my native land from time to time, mostly to visit relatives, or to see familiar sights, or sometimes just to explore places I did not have the chance to see as a child. I left Germany with my mother and father when I was quite young. They wanted to start a new life in America soon after World War One. In any event, on one of my return trips, I wanted to do some research on where we used to live, where my relatives were located, that sort of thing. The search took me to a small village in central Germany that was said to be the home of some of my ancestors." Ernst shifted in his chair. He noticed that Stephen sat immobile, absorbed by the tale.

"By checking land ownership records," continued Ernst, "I was able to locate where they were supposed to have lived. Most of the houses were no longer there, of course. Some fell apart over time from age. Others were destroyed in the war—World War Two, that is.

Wicca Codex

Nevertheless, I was able to locate one building that remained. It was deep in the countryside and so had not been taken over for city development. It was in ruins, but was not in anyone's way, so it was left alone all these years. I found it fascinating to explore the site. In doing so, I happened on a hidden entrance to a small room below the cellar. It was evidently used to store perishable food items and keep them cool. Although it was severely damaged, I was able to make my way into this room. One of its stone walls was shattered, and I noticed something protruding from the dirt and rock. It turned out to be *The Codex* you see here. I managed to extract it from its resting place and return with it to Boston. Since then, I have been doing further research to try to find out anything I can about it. What you yourself now know is what I have been able to find out, or at least surmise. There is no telling how long the document had lain hidden away in its dark home, or how it came to be there. That may be the most fascinating story of all, but we may never know it."

Ernst had related this to Stephen truthfully, for the most part. He *had* gone to Germany, and he *had* found the ruined house and Codex, and he *had* returned with it to the United States. However, there were a few unmentioned details that were somewhat fundamental to the story. Ernst did not say he was drawn back to Germany by a strange force that he could neither explain nor control. He simply was compelled to go. He also did not relate that, once in his native land, there was no need to check land records to locate this particular house. Whatever elements were at work directed him to the correct town, then down the right road into the countryside, then to the remains of the house. Finally, the hidden entrance to the room below the cellar was revealed to him as he explored the site, without any effort on his part. And, once inside the secret room, the way to *The Codex* was illuminated by an eerie green-purple glow that filtered through the darkness. These were the facts, but there was no need to confuse Stephen Blake with them. For Ernst's purposes, there was enough truth in what he had said to make the story plausible without muddling it with complications. At least for now.

Perhaps there would be a time to come when the rest of the tale could be told. But not now, not today.

"So, Stephen, there you have it," said Ernst. "That is how the manuscript came into my possession. I consider myself extremely fortunate to have stumbled on it the way I did."

It took some moments for Stephen to disengage from Ernst's narrative. During its telling, he shifted his gaze between Ernst and *The Codex* many times. He didn't know which was more fascinating—the look of delight on the old man's face as he told his tale, or the mysterious volume sitting on the table within an arm's length. "That's some story," exclaimed Stephen limply. He was still under the spell woven by Ernst's words. "What a piece of detective work on your part. With maybe a little bit of luck thrown in."

"Yes," agreed Ernst, "there was most definitely some measure of good fortune involved in finding it. I am honest enough to admit it. It would be foolish to do otherwise."

Stephen had wondered about something throughout most of Ernst's story. He decided to ask him about it. "After you found *The Codex*, did you take it to anyone and let them know what you found? You know, experts in the field of old books, people like that. Or have them do research to find out something about it?"

Ernst had to be careful. Stephen was in publishing and had an affinity for old books, so he might know more than he was letting on. He didn't think there was an ulterior motive for the question, however. Just curiosity, most likely. Nevertheless, a truthful response was simply not possible. It would reveal everything. "Yes, of course," said Ernst. "I did seek out one or two people who were said to know of such matters. And they did indeed help me identify some things about the book, things I have already related to you. Other facts I discovered on my own. As you may suspect, I was somewhat reluctant to give undue publicity to my find, given its historic value, and probably its monetary one. The fewer persons who knew about this, the better, I felt."

Stephen thought that made sense. "That probably explains why I never heard of anything about this before. Some of the people I deal with in the industry are a lot more knowledgeable than me about things like this, but I don't recall anyone ever mentioning anything about it."

"That is not surprising," said Ernst. "Frankly, I am glad to hear you say that. I insisted that anyone I contacted about this pledged to keep it to themselves. No one was to discuss it with colleagues, or write papers about it, or give out any information whatsoever. That was the most important condition for my allowing them to work on it." Such was Ernst's explanation to Stephen, but, as before, it was just not possible for him to be truthful. If that were the case, he would have to say that everything known about *The Codex* was revealed to him by the one who imparted the power inherent in its strange symbols. Ernst simply absorbed such knowledge through contact with the manuscript over time. At first, he knew nothing of it. Gradually, he came to know more and more. This transference of knowledge convinced him he was to be an instrument, a vehicle, a catalyst driving a more complex reaction. It became his purpose in life to discover his reason for being. He would learn of it after his first meeting with Lariakin. He finally knew who he was and why he was here.

"How long have you had *The Codex*?" inquired Stephen.

"My last trip to Germany was in 1988. That is when I found it. I have not been back since."

Stephen couldn't resist any longer asking what was really on his mind. "You said earlier there was some sort of energy in it that made it inadvisable for me to touch it. That's kind of creepy. What did you mean by that?"

Ernst anticipated he would have to deal with this and was ready for it. If Blake was going to assist in their endeavor, he must be given information. Enough to feel at ease, willing to work with them, even eager. Ernst approached it delicately. "I was actually considering whether to even mention it. I decided to do so, more out of concern for your personal comfort than anything else. What I meant is that some people seem to be affected by contact with *The Codex*. It makes them feel uncomfortable. This first became apparent when I had it investigated by those I have already mentioned—the experts you asked about. It also seemed to be the case in the years since, whenever I invited others to see it—people such as yourself. It may have something to do with its apparent connection with wizardry, magic, and sorcery. It plays on the mind. Whether the feeling is real or not, I do not know. I myself am not affected. But who is to say what the mind considers to be real? Perhaps it is just that some people think too much about it and believe they feel something when they touch it. As I said, I do not really know the answer to this with any degree of assurance."

Once again, Ernst knew the answer. Once again, he could not relate it. His experiments so far had indicated that no one except himself—and Lariakin, of course—could touch *The Codex* without experiencing a rather unpleasant sensation in the hands and arms. Over time, the one whose power was in the book had permitted him to understand that no one other than the chosen instruments of the cause were to have any physical contact with it, without suffering the consequences, that is. He accepted this as irrefutable evidence that he was destined to perform the work identified to him by Lariakin.

"If you wish," said Ernst, "you may do a little experiment and see if *The Codex* affects you as it seems to affect others. Go ahead and place your hand upon the book."

Stephen felt a real sense of excitement surge through him at this invitation. But after Ernst's story, he wasn't sure if he wanted to or not. He certainly didn't want to seem cowardly about it. And when you came right down to it, he didn't really believe in anything like this, despite his having heard about baffling things that couldn't be explained. It's all in the mind, he kept telling himself. Now was his chance to test this out. "I want to," said Stephen, uneasily, "but at the same time I don't, if you know what I mean."

"Yes, I know exactly what you mean," Ernst replied. "It is up to you. Either way, I will understand."

Even though Ernst expressed no interest in the course Stephen

Wicca Codex

decided to pursue, Ernst was, in fact, quite interested. It was important to know whether Stephen was a risk-taker, willing to go out on a limb and make a decision to try something not only new, but with a little danger inherent in it. This would be useful in deciding if Stephen really was right for Ernst's continuing work.

"Well, which way will it be, my friend?" asked Ernst.

Stephen sat perfectly still for a moment. He gazed at Ernst, then at the book sitting on the table next to him. He recalled his vow of a few days ago to start remaking his dull existence and try new things. Put your money where your mouth is, right? Time to make like Nike-man and Just Do It. Slowly, he raised his right hand and extended it toward *The Codex*. With a slight hesitation before it reached the manuscript, he placed his hand lightly on the book, keeping it there for several seconds before hurriedly lifting it off. He could not be entirely sure, but he detected what he thought was the onset of a pins-and-needles sensation in his hand. "You've probably got me thinking about it, all right, but I do seem to feel something." He flexed his fingers several times. "It's only a slight tingle, nothing extraordinary. If it's there at all, it isn't particularly a good or a bad feeling. I'd give it a longer try, I guess, but I think that's all I want to do for now. Sorry, Gustav."

"No apology needed, Stephen. I am impressed that you would try it at all, given my mysterious tale. You were able to overcome the uncertainty in your mind and try something that was potentially unpleasant, just to see if it was true. Your experience may not have been conclusive, but at least you ventured forward. I applaud you for it."

"Thanks, I think." After a moment, Stephen added, "There's one other thing I wanted to ask you. I was curious why you keep *The Codex* locked up in the safe. I heard what you said earlier, but some of your other old treasures next door are probably just as valuable. Why not keep it with the other manuscripts? It'd still be behind the locked doors of your bookcases."

Ernst hesitated only for the very briefest of moments before responding. Stephen didn't even catch it. "Oh, you are probably right about that, but I suppose I have a special feeling about this one. Perhaps it has something to do with its age, particularly the parchment leaves. Perhaps its strange symbols are part of it. Maybe even the mysterious feeling that some people seemingly have about it, as you experienced a moment ago. As I said, it could be worth the most of all my possessions, although I have not bothered to get it appraised." Ernst's eyes wandered off their target and onto *The Codex*. Until now, he had made it a point to maintain steady contact with Blake's. This would build his confidence, which was important in increasing the chance of him coming on board. Ernst reestablished the connection, then continued. "In any event, appraisals of historic objects do not really have that much meaning. Their valuation extends beyond mere economic principles of supply and demand, would you not say?" Stephen knew the question was rhetorical. He merely gave a slight nod, then let Ernst go on. "So, for all these reasons, and perhaps others I cannot even begin to understand, I have not come to be comfortable in exposing *The Codex* as I do the other manuscripts, at least not yet. Perhaps, with time, I will be able to do so. For the moment, however, I feel compelled to protect it as I do. The only times I remove it from its sanctuary are to show it off to a few trusted friends, as tonight. You may think it odd, I suppose, that I have put you in that category after less than one week of our becoming acquainted, but I feel I am a good judge of character, and I have developed a feeling of trust about you, even in this short time. I would not have shown this to you otherwise."

Stephen was genuinely pleased that Ernst felt this way. He had come to admire the old man and wanted him to return the sentiment. "Thanks for the vote of confidence," said Stephen. "As much as I'd love to tell my publishing colleagues about this, I can assure you I'll keep it confidential. But if you ever change your mind," laughed Stephen, "I'd surely like to be the first to know."

"That is...how do you say it?...a deal," said Ernst, returning the laugh. He wondered if this might be an opportune moment to raise the next important issue. He decided it was. "Oddly enough," said Ernst,

Wicca Codex

"that time may be closer than you might think. I was going to discuss something related to it at tonight's meeting, which I see is quickly approaching." Ernst glanced at an old clock sitting on one of the bookcase shelves. "It is already after eleven o'clock, and the first of my compatriots will be starting to arrive soon. I..."

"Let me say something about that before you go on." Stephen hadn't realized how late it had become. He had to interrupt Ernst and broach the idea of not attending the meeting. It was now or never. "I know this will disappoint you, Gustav, but I don't think I can stay. As much as I'd like to, I think I should take a rain check on it for tonight. I'm afraid the wine and the excitement of learning about *The Codex*—and maybe my own poor dinner selection—have conspired to give me a bit of indigestion, not to mention the beginnings of a headache. I really don't think I'd be able to last, and I know I wouldn't be very good company. I'd prefer that your friends see me at my best."

Ernst let out an audible sigh, and the smile he had worn most of the evening vanished for a moment. "You are correct, Stephen. That is most disappointing news. I was so looking forward to having you join our little group tonight. I know they will be saddened as well. Are you certain you cannot attend? Perhaps you will feel better if you sit quietly for a few minutes. I can..."

"I really think it best if I go home," said Stephen, calmly yet firmly. He had to nip this in the bud, or he'd be stuck. "I know once I start to feel this way it's gonna be a long and uncomfortable night. I should've laid off the wine, I guess, but I thought I could handle it. I'm sorry, Gustav. I hope you'll give me another opportunity, though. Maybe at your next meeting, whenever that might be. I do want to meet your friends. Really. It's just that trying to force it tonight wouldn't be a good idea."

"As you wish, Stephen," said Ernst, whose congenial demeanor had returned. "I certainly do not want to compel you to do something you feel is not wise. I will explain your indisposition to the group. And, of course, you are welcome to attend our next get-together, which is already scheduled for next Tuesday night. In fact, most of our meetings take place on Tuesdays and Fridays. We were not able to meet this past Tuesday due to a conflict, so we scheduled it for Monday instead. That's why you saw my friends entering the shop on your first visit this past Monday night—after you left and returned. In a normal week, you would have missed them entirely."

"Okay, then," said Stephen, grasping at the chance to make amends, "let's make it next Tuesday." He pushed himself up out of the chair and started walking slowly to the door. "I want to let you know I had a wonderful time tonight, Gustav. I enjoyed your company immensely. Not to mention seeing more of your collection. And seeing *The Codex* and hearing your story about it was the highlight of the evening. What did you call it, again? The Wicker Codex?"

Ernst laughed. "That is close, but not quite right, Stephen. The correct name is Wicca, w-i-c-c-a."

"Oops. Sorry about that. I guess I was thinking of the wicker chair I have in my apartment." This precipitated another round of chuckles. Stephen cast one last glance at *The Codex*. "Do you want to lock it up again before we go next door?"

"I will take care of that after you go. Come, let me not keep you any longer. You should return home and get well." Ernst led Stephen across the dim hallway into the room where they had started the evening—the collection room, as Stephen started calling it in his mind. He wanted to retrieve his coat and be gone before Ernst's guests started filtering in, which could happen any minute now. He didn't want anything to interfere with his leaving.

Stephen donned the coat and offered a hand to Ernst, who pumped it enthusiastically several times. "Well, thanks again, Gustav. I really did have a great time. And I promise to make the next meeting." Stephen went out into the hallway and through the curtain to the front of the shop.

Ernst trailed behind, saying, "Now, do not forget, Stephen. Next Tuesday night. I will insist that you attend that one. No more procrastination." Ernst laughed as he said this to hide the seriousness he attached to it. "Please come early again if you like. You can spend more time looking through the shop. There are still many things you have not seen."

"Don't worry. I definitely promise to be here. And I'll try to come early, if I can. Goodnight, Gustav. And thanks again." As Stephen left, he heard Ernst lock the door behind him. He waved a final good night to the old man through the window, who returned the gesture.

After Stephen had gone, Ernst was quite troubled. He was upset that Stephen was not to be at tonight's meeting. There were things he had planned that were dependent on his being there. Lariakin would not be pleased by this turn of events, but there was nothing that could be done about it now. He would have to make the best of it.

Ernst went back to the collection room and locked it in anticipation of the upcoming meeting. Even with trusted coven members coming, he took no chances. There was no such thing as being too careful where his beloved books were concerned. He then went to *The Codex* room and removed the old manuscript from the table. He did not, however, return it to the safe. Instead, he carried it out of the room and down the narrow hallway to the door located at its far end, the third of the three lining the corridor. He unlocked it and entered the room to which it led.

He snapped on the light switch, illuminating the space with the stingy light from four minuscule sconces, one on each wall. This chamber was larger than *The Codex* and collection rooms to which it adjoined—perhaps thirty feet square, with a high ceiling. It was permanently arranged to accommodate the semi-weekly meetings attended by Ernst and his companions. In its center sat a small circular wooden table, covered with a dark cloth. It was perched on a slightly elevated platform, about six inches high, also circular and near eight feet in diameter. Two single candles graced opposite ends of the table, whose perimeter held several objects and implements to be used at the meeting—fetishes of wands, dishes, and stones. There was also a ceremonial double-edged knife—an athame. Twelve metal folding chairs were arrayed concentrically around the central platform, about three feet from its edge. Several tables lined the walls around the room, each completely covered with candles of all shapes and sizes. These were typically the room's main illumination during meetings but were as yet unlit. There were also incense censers, ready for use.

Aside from the main entry door, there was only one other. It opened to a closet occupying the far-left corner. There were no windows. Except for the room's spartan furniture and its creaky wood-slat floor, the entire interior was painted black, even the ceiling. This perhaps explained why the rays from the wall lamps reached only reluctantly into the room, just barely enough to be useful. They waged a constant battle for life, as if trying to escape from a black hole. The walls were bare except for several Latin inscriptions painted in red and yellow, as well as several pentacles—five-sided star-shaped objects—in the same colors.

There was also a single large painting hanging directly opposite the entry door. It was a hideous likeness of Satan, done mostly in black and gray and mounted in a heavy dark wooden frame. Its location ensured that it was the first thing visible on entering the room. The object was easily its most prominent feature. There was no special light source for it, yet it appeared not to require any. The image stood out clearly, almost eerily three dimensional. Its own blackness seemed to transcend that of the surrounding wall and flatten it, subdue it, crush it. Then there were the eyes. Hideous, penetrating eyes. They were the epitome of evil, casting their ghastly gaze down upon all who occupied this space, with a hellish redness that could not be duplicated by any artist's palette. Those who dared look up into them could bear to do so only for the briefest of moments. They were pervasive. They were menacing. They were deadly. They were real.

Ernst walked to the platform, stepped onto it and placed *The Codex* directly in the center of the table. He returned to *The Codex* room to await his friends, who would start arriving shortly. He spent the next few minutes thinking. The evening had gone exceedingly well, up until

Blake's decision to forego the meeting, that is. That was a most unfortunate circumstance. Now he had to formulate another approach, something that would preclude the possibility of further delay. There was no telling when Lariakin would return. He didn't think it would be tonight. Lariakin rarely attended routine coven meetings. But whenever it was to be, Ernst must prepare an explanation, as well as a feasible plan.

But for now, that would have to wait. It was about eleven forty-five, and Ernst heard the ring of the doorbell. He had had a particularly loud one installed so he could hear it out back. He pushed the curtain aside and saw the first arrivals outside in the shop's light. He let them in, offered greetings, and directed them to proceed to the meeting room and start setting up while he waited for the others. The instruction was unnecessary, since all members were familiar with the routine. They knew the first to come were expected to get things ready. After several more minutes, the rest arrived. Most were regularly punctual, not wishing to incur Ernst's anger. Meetings started promptly at midnight, and woe to those who dared to be late.

When the full complement of attendees had assembled in the meeting room—except for Lariakin, who, it seemed, would not be there tonight—Ernst turned off the lights in the front of the shop. There was no reason to arouse suspicion at this late hour. He went to *The Codex* room and pulled a black robe from the closet. He donned it and slipped the hood up over his head. He went to the safe, opened it, and removed a small notebook. It was plain, but quite important, and extremely sensitive. This last characteristic is what had compelled Ernst to lock the safe after removing *The Codex* from Blake's presence a short time ago. He was not ready to share that. Not just yet. He inserted the notebook into one of the robe's pockets, then went into the meeting room.

Several members had prepared the room by lighting the two candles on the center table, as well as scores more around the periphery. Their flames danced gently in the air currents. Others activated the incense trays. A pungent, intoxicating fragrance wafted through the room. The wall lights, puny though they were, had been turned off to enhance the effect. For tonight's meeting, someone had placed a small table—a stand, really—eighteen inches on a side, next to the main table on the platform. For the moment, its pockmarked wooden surface remained empty. All was ready.

Ernst glided into the room, creaking across the wooden floorboards to the center platform. He stepped up and dug his hands into the deep pockets of his robe. He said nothing, merely gazing down on the audience surrounding him. It consisted of twelve individuals—one in each chair circling the platform—fiercely loyal to their leader and willing to do whatever was required to attain their common objective. Ernst had recruited them to do no less, and he had chosen wisely. The members were mostly men, although there were several women as well. Each was dressed in a black, hooded robe—similar to Ernst's—secured from the corner closet. Each held a lit candle. Ernst paced around the edge of the platform, peering out at those in the circle around him. He relished being its epicenter and indulged himself these few moments to revel in it.

Finally, after some time, he began speaking in a slow, deliberate, almost melancholy tone. "Welcome, brothers and sisters. I am sorry to have to report that we have a shortened agenda tonight. The guest I mentioned to you at our last meeting, and who I had expected would be here, was not able to come. I did meet with him earlier this evening, however, and managed to accomplish a few preliminary tasks. I feel it went very well. Although I was not able to broach the subject we discussed earlier this week, I have reason to believe he will be useful to us in our work. He has promised to attend our next meeting without fail, and I will endeavor to ensure that he does so. As you are aware, scheduling is very important to our cause, and we must prepare for the next phase. Further delay is not acceptable. I am confident, however, we will be able to do that which must be done. Now, with your permission, we will proceed to our main business."

Wicca Codex

There was a slight rustling of feet and squeaking noises from the chairs as their occupants repositioned themselves. Otherwise, there was only a heavy silence and the flickering of shadows in the candlelight.

"You are all aware," continued Ernst, "that this first phase of our work has gone very well to this point. Very well, indeed. We began slowly but have accelerated our pace of late. We propose to continue in that manner, if we are all in agreement. Is there any objection?" There was none. No one among the membership had any doubt as to who was in charge of the group. It was not a democratic institution. "Very well, then," said Ernst. "Let us make the selection."

Ernst extracted the small notebook he had taken from the safe and put in his pocket before entering the meeting room. He opened it and said, "As we discussed last time, the next name on the list is Peter Markis. Is there any disagreement on the selection?"

Silence.

"As you wish, then. Let the Proclaimer make the pronouncement."

One of those seated around the platform stood and raised a sheet of paper that had been prepared in advance. He read its contents in the dim candlelight. "By unanimous decision of the membership, it is hereby declared that Peter Markis has been chosen for cleansing. There being no objection amongst the members, the judgment will be carried out immediately." The reader strode over to the small stand next to Ernst, placed the sheet on it, and returned to his seat.

Ernst then said, "Is the Procurer ready?"

Another member rose and said, "The Procurer is ready."

Ernst asked, "Were you able to secure the necessary object?"

Since everything had been arranged in advance, the Procurer was able to reply, "I was."

"Very well. Bring the object to the table and place it on the proclamation," ordered Ernst.

The Procurer carried a single rumpled sheet of paper to the small table and put in on top of the declaration just placed there by the Proclaimer. He returned to his seat.

Ernst walked to the main table, in the center of which lay *The Codex*, surrounded by the other implements. He took the wand and recited some incomprehensible phrases while waving it slowly over the manuscript. He then touched several of the stones scattered across the table, solemnly uttering further incantations. He grabbed the athame and raised it toward the Satanic image on the far wall, as if offering it to The Dark Prince. The little light there was glinted off its hard steel edges before he placed it back on the table. Finally, he opened *The Codex* to a specific pre-selected leaf, then asked the members to stand. He let things settle into absolute stillness, then placed both hands on the book, closed his eyes, and waited for the familiar sensation to course through his body. Although partially hidden by his robe's hood and obscured by the weak candlelight, his facial expressions were visible to those seated in front of him. They could discern contortions and twitchings in response to invisible currents of energy. After a minute or so, Ernst said in a strong voice, "O Black One, you who have guided us in this endeavor, we ask that you send your power through this manuscript to carry out that which you have directed us to do in your name. Send the force of your spirit to the one who has been designated on this night, that your power may be demonstrated and that your work may be done. We implore you to let us serve you in this way."

Ernst remained motionless, his eyes still closed and hands placed firmly on *The Codex*. The members encircling him were immovable objects. Save for the occasional blink of an eye or the flicker of a candle flame, there was neither movement nor sound of any kind in the room for several moments. It was a scene frozen in time.

Then, suddenly, a spark-like trail of faint silvery light emerged from the top surface of *The Codex*. It coursed through Ernst's fingers, brightened, then arced silently over to the small table holding the proclamation and the rumpled paper, both of which glowed briefly. The spark trail hovered there for several seconds, doing its deadly dance. After a brief moment, it rose slowly to a height of perhaps seven feet above the floor. It remained there for an instant, then exploded as a rifle shot toward the far wall of the room. Its trajectory took it straight toward the center of the framed Satanic image, whose blackness watched over the proceedings. Just before penetrating the picture and the wall, it reverted to an invisible beam of incredibly intense energy. It emerged in that form into the Boston night and sped on toward its destination, unseen by any who might still be awake at that hour.

Inside the room, Ernst remained in contact with *The Codex* for several moments. Gradually, he begin to recover from the experience. He felt no pain, but the intensity of the ritual was sufficient to keep him in a trance-like state for a minute or two before fully regaining his faculties. When he had recovered, he removed his hands from the manuscript, opened his eyes, and said to the members, "As you have seen once again, brothers and sisters, our leader has demonstrated his might and authority over the evil forces that would deter him from his objective. We are indeed fortunate to be able to participate in these mysteries. I am thankful to be chosen as his instrument in helping to right the heinous wrongs of the past."

Ernst raised a hand and, with some effort, slowly pushed back the hood from his head. He appeared to have emerged from the special state that had overtaken him. He steadied himself by grasping the edge of the table. "Thank you for attending tonight," he said, somewhat unsteadily. "As I said earlier, we are certain that next Tuesday's meeting will be of special interest. We look forward to seeing you then."

With the meeting over, the members blew out their candles and deposited them into a box at the door. The wall lights were turned on while several people helped extinguish candles on the surrounding tables and generally got things back in order. There was little milling about. This was not a social gathering, but strictly business. And that business was too important to cheapen in any way. Ernst had made that abundantly clear early on in the group's existence, reinforced every so often as the need arose. And so everyone quickly removed their robes, returned them to the closet, gathered up coats and hats, and left the shop as directed.

Ernst removed his own robe and redeposited *The Codex* and the notebook with the names back in the safe. He finished cleaning up the meeting room and checked to see that the premises were secure. Satisfied that they were, he slowly climbed the stairs to his apartment over the shop. Only now did he feel the first fatigue set in from the long day. He undressed and prepared to retire. As he lay on his bed, he thought about the events of the day—the dullness of the long daytime hours as he tended the shop; the pleasure of his evening with Blake, whom he genuinely liked as a fellow book-lover; the disappointment of Blake's announcement that he would not attend the meeting; the joy of the meeting itself, always a delight as they did the work of their leader. But the best of all, by far, was the extraordinary excitement of his contact with *The Codex*, which he felt was no less than a union with the dark force of the devil himself. Ernst reveled once again in the energy of the book as it had flowed through his body and emerged into the room, then floated above them and sped on to do its awful work. He could conceive of no greater feeling in the world. In the galaxy. In the entire universe, even. This was the ultimate experience, and it had been granted to him. And all for his allegiance to the one he revered so fully. If the truth be known, he would have offered himself up to his idol without benefit to himself. Or rather, just for the chance to be with him in eternity. But to be given this authority, this power, this feeling of invincibility. It was beyond belief.

Ernst turned on his side and let sleep overtake him as he smiled his last smile of the day.

Chapter 14

Saturday, October 21

The final moments of Friday night gave way to the first ones of Saturday morning. High school daters were trying to decide whether to heed curfews imposed by usually well-meaning but nonetheless intrusive parents. The option was to defy the establishment, at least for a little while, and prolong an evening of fun that helped them forget another boring school week. This was the predicament faced by Peter Markis and his girlfriend, Jennifer Cullinan, as they drove east along Day Boulevard in South Boston.

Peter had borrowed his father's Corolla for the evening and promised to be home by one o'clock. Jenny's folks wanted her back by twelve thirty, so they didn't have much time left before she was officially overdue. They had seen a movie earlier that evening—the latest in high-tech explosions with an incalculable body count—then went bowling at the Morrissey Boulevard lanes, just a short distance away. They capped off the night with burgers and sodas at their favorite eatery near the bowling center.

Pete and Jenny were seniors at South Boston High. They had started going together early in their junior year when he made the varsity basketball team, and she joined the cheerleading squad. In fact, the couple was celebrating their first anniversary tonight. One year together already. The best year of their young lives, each would have said. Peter had boyish good looks and was athletic without being a flamboyant jock type. This appealed to Jenny. She was pretty, but in a subdued way. Both were okay students, generally in the B range, with an occasional A thrown in when they really liked a subject and were willing to apply their talents. There were also Cs now and then, especially when they were turned off by the course, or the teacher, or both. Each had lots of friends, but neither tolerated anyone who was into the drug scene. They were too smart for that. Everyone said they made the perfect couple. They liked each other a lot and got along exceptionally well. They hoped to continue their relationship, which they considered to be super special, after graduation next year. Both planned on attending the same college just so they could be near one another. Jenny's parents liked and respected Peter, and Peter's folks thought the world of Jenny. The kids themselves didn't mind the adults either. They were okay—for parents. It seemed as though Pete and Jenny were destined for each other.

The night was brilliantly moonlit, lending a surreal quality to Carson Beach and the waters of Dorchester Bay, with the JFK Library silhouetted in the distance. It was a romantic scene that tempted the youngsters to head out to one of their favorite haunts—Castle Island, about a mile up the road. You could drive out there over a causeway built in the 1920s. It didn't seem much like an island anymore, since the road joined it to the mainland and made the whole thing look like a bird's beak on a map. Once there, they could look out at the stone walls of old Fort Independence and across the Inner Harbor to Logan Airport. There might even be a late-night plane or two swooping in over the fort on final approach, if the wind was right. Not to mention the possibility of a few romantic maneuverings in the car as it sat at the end of the road. The couple had been known in the past to express their feelings for each other in this way.

And so, all of these things conspired to lure the young couple out to the "island" on this particular night, despite the lateness of the hour and the closeness of Jenny's personal curfew. It was a chance they were willing to take. Besides, they didn't plan on staying too long, and they were only a few minutes from Jenny's home in the nearby residential area of South Boston. They would make it back it time. No problem.

Pete cruised past the L and M street beaches and the metallic likeness of Admiral Farragut, who stared wistfully out to the sea he loved. Then it was around Fitzgerald Circle and out past the yacht club to seek out a suitable parking spot, one that maximized the views but minimized the ambient light, which was difficult to do on such a bright night. He found a good location, cut the engine, and cuddled up with Jenny.

"I had a really fun time tonight, Pete," sighed Jenny. "The movie was great, and bowling my personal best helped a lot, too." She couldn't help giggling at the thought of her "personal best" high game of 125. That was for the ten-pin variety, not New England's famed candlepins.

"Yeah, me too, Jen," agreed Pete. "Maybe next time you'll remember not to throw the ball in the gutter so much. You might even break 130."

Pete said this somberly, but Jenny knew he was kidding, so she made a fist and hit him hard in the arm. She immediately regretted her act of barbarism and started rubbing the stricken spot. "Oh, Pete, I'm sorry," she apologized. "I didn't mean that. Does it hurt?"

"I think I'll survive," retorted Pete, "but don't do it again. I'm delicate." He couldn't help himself and broke out into loud laughter. Jenny joined him, then laid her head on Pete's shoulder and took one of his hands in both of hers.

"Oh, Pete," she said softly, burying herself deeper into his embrace. "I love you so much. I wish we could figure out a way to grow up quicker so we can be with each other. Just like this."

Pete stroked Jenny's hair with his free hand and said, "I feel the same way, Jen." He paused, thinking about what she had said. They didn't call him "Practical Pete" for nothing. "But I don't know any short cuts. I think we'll just have to abide by the rules a while longer, much as we don't want to. And besides, high school and college aren't that bad, really. Beats working, from what I can see." They both laughed.

Jenny looked up at Pete, who lowered his head slowly to plant a delicate kiss on her lips. The gentle nature of the act was an indication of the love and respect shared by the couple. Passion had a place in their young lives, but they often found that the tender moments were more memorable, more lasting, more expressive of their true feelings for each other. They sat huddled together in this way for several minutes, quietly enjoying each other's company and the surroundings, finding the need for further words unnecessary. For each of them, it was as close to heaven as they could get. The force of their love was stronger than anything they could have imagined at that moment.

Also at that moment, high above Castle Island and the streets of South Boston, a force of another kind was wending its way across the night sky, unseen by any below who might happen to glance toward the heavens. It had started its journey on Beacon Hill but a short time ago, and had taken a direct path across approximately three miles of terrain to this spot, guided by the words of Gustav Ernst, bookstore owner, and the power inherent in his most prized possession, the manuscript he called The Wicca Codex. The invisible beam had made the journey in the twinkling of an eye, defying the laws of gravity and physics and, perhaps, logic. Its purpose was to defy another law, the law of God and man against the taking of a human life. It had been programmed to seek out a specific member of the human species and do its evil work. The powers that had sent it on its way had indicated its goal by means of a name—Peter Markis—as well as an article that had been associated with the target in some way. In this case the appropriate information had been transferred through a scrap of paper that had been handled by the quarry and subsequently discarded by him. It had ultimately been retrieved by one of Ernst's compatriots, the one he called the Procurer, an agent of the one who served as the instrument of the dark side—the unexplained elements of the universe.

The purpose of the unseen force was neither retributive nor vindictive, but rather restorative. That is, its mission was to help reclaim the balance of nature and justice that had been thrown out of equilibrium so long ago. What had occurred during those ancient times was an abomination that must be addressed, and cleansed, and healed. The gaping wound that had been left open to fester must be cauterized. The putrescent infection must not be permitted to continue untreated.

And so the silent force sensed the proximity of its prey and began a swift descent over Castle Island. It sought out the vehicle inhabited by Peter Markis and Jenny Cullinan, much as a plane would approach the airport across the harbor on its final glide path. It passed through the frame of the vehicle, entered the interior space—still unseen and unheard—and stopped above the rear seat. It validated that a target consistent with its programmed information was indeed inside. This allowed the invisible force to materialize into the same spark-like trail of light that had left the meeting room in the bookstore on Beacon Hill just a short time ago.

It was Jenny who first sensed something unusual. Something that gave her a feeling of unease. She opened her eyes as her head rested on Pete's shoulder. It looked brighter than she had remembered it being a moment ago. Not remarkably so, but brighter nonetheless. She raised her head slightly and said, "Pete, where's that light coming from?"

"What light?" said Pete, who still had his eyes closed, enjoying Jenny's presence, the feel of her body next to his, the smell of her hair. "I think you're seeing the moon, Jen."

Jenny bolted up from her comfortable position next to Pete and started to swing her head around toward the back seat. She couldn't be sure but thought there was something back there, something that might have to do with the brightness. She didn't think it was the moon. It was only a fleeting glimpse, but as Jenny turned to look toward the back of the car, she saw it. The light force had detected its target and had intensified into a pencil-thin, extremely high-energy beam that zeroed in on the back of Pete's neck. In a split second it penetrated the skin, searing the flesh as it entered and leaving a small, neat burn mark. It continued on its mortal journey and, once inside the target, caused the head of the victim to rotate on its axis. The movement was swift, sure, and fatal. In an instant Pete's neck snapped around and severed the spinal column. He had no time to react to the attack, nor even to realize that anything momentous had occurred. He felt nothing. He was gone before anything registered in his brain, which had ceased to function.

Death was instantaneous. All of the terror and the screaming and the pain would be left for Jenny to endure.

She had seen the rotation of Pete's head next to hers and didn't understand how that could happen. She still couldn't respond even as she saw his head slump—lifeless—onto hers. Only then did the sense of terror consume her. She started yelling uncontrollably, struggling to wrench herself away from the dead weight that pressed itself against her. The deadness that was a breathing, loving being just a moment ago. She grabbed Pete by the shoulders and shook him violently, as though that could be the mechanism to restore him, to wake him—and her—from this horrible, tormenting nightmare. Her shouts turned to sobs. "Oh my God! Pete! What's wrong? Wake up! What's happening, Pete? Please get up. Please."

Pete was unable to respond to Jenny's sorrowful pleas. This was beyond her comprehension, certainly at that moment, and most likely for a long time to come, if ever. All she could do was continue crying and screaming in the moonlight.

Chapter 15

Saturday, October 21

The early light blushed red and bright and sparkling in Boston. It was one of those absolutely glorious New England mornings that promised brilliant blue skies and dazzling sunshine. The spectacle enhanced the vibrant foliage that graced the scenery in this corner of the world, even in its urban concentrations. It was so enticing that John Demming decided to use part of the day, at least, to do something for himself. He had been intrigued by Stephen Blake's description of that old bookstore at Locke-Ober the other day, so he thought this might be a good time to check it out.

Demming had to go into the office for a couple of hours anyway to take care of a problem that had cropped up. He could never get away from work completely, it seemed. But he would try to make a day of it in the city and accomplish some of the things he'd been wanting to do for a while. Pare down that to-do list a bit. Maybe some shopping in Downtown Crossing, or along Boylston Street. Or maybe he'd take in the current Imax theater show at the Museum of Science—he had heard it was a good one. He loved sitting inside that huge dome and letting the oversized images and thunderous audio surround him. Or perhaps he would drive over to the Cambridgeside Galleria or maybe see a movie at the Nickelodeon in Kenmore Square. Anything was possible.

He and Arlene used to do things like that, but she had succumbed to breast cancer about five years ago. He still thought of her every day. She had been vivacious and outgoing, the driving force behind many of their fun times. He had cut back considerably on outside activities after her death. Occasionally, though, he would get out of the house for something other than his usual work-related routine, and this day promised to be a good one for that. His plan was to get to the office fairly early, around eight o'clock or so, take care of his business problem in a couple of hours—if he was lucky—then head over to the bookstore, which should certainly be open by then. After that he would wing it.

Demming drove downtown from his home in Winchester, just north of Boston, and parked in the recently renovated garage below Boston Common. It was convenient to his Tremont Street office and the bookstore, as well as some of the other places he might want to go afterwards. He made it into work a little later than he had hoped, about eight fifteen or so, and did what he needed to do. Fortunately, everything seemed to come together without any of the usual disasters, so he was still able to finish up by about ten o'clock. This put him in good spirits, especially since he saw from his office window that the day had indeed fulfilled its early-morning promise. He wanted to follow through on his desire to find that little bookstore—what was it called again? The Booke Nooke, or something like that?—so he dug out the pocket calendar where he had written down the address given to him by Stephen Blake. He knew it was on Beacon Hill but wanted to make sure he could home in on the right street when he got in the vicinity. Luckily, he was able to locate the address without difficulty. Actually, luck had little to do with it, since he carried his little booklet with him everywhere. He was forever writing down names, addresses, phone numbers, tidbits of information, whatever. Meticulous, to a fault. No telling when they might come in handy. He checked out the street in a metro Boston atlas kept around the office and found what he was looking for.

Demming left the confines of his office tower and enjoyed the warm rays of the October sun as they caressed his face. It felt super. Especially since he had left his suit and tie at home. It was quite uncharacteristic, but he was feeling daring today. It was a treat hacking around in casual slacks, shirt, and cardigan. His one concession to conformity was a sport jacket over the sweater. He didn't want to be

Wicca Codex

totally rad. Besides, he needed the jacket to carry his cell phone. He didn't like the bulge it made in his pants pocket. All in all, though, he was pleased with himself.

He made up his mind to do this more often. And to melt away those excess pounds his doctor kept clamoring about. For now, though, he decided to cross the Common rather than climb the hill up Park Street and slip past the State House and its golden dome. The old girl's bonnet was particularly sparkling today, belying the sometimes-somber activity that took place below its stately elegance. He couldn't help grinning at the irony of it.

Demming emerged from the colorful leafiness of the Common, crossed Beacon Street, made his way to where the bookstore should be, and—voila—there it was. It looked to be as quaint as Stephen Blake had described. He wondered again why he hadn't heard about the place. He knew them all, or so he thought. In his business, he had to. No matter, he said to himself, better late than never.

He approached the store and saw the same signs Stephen had seen. "Ye Olde Booke Nooke." "G. Ernst, Proprietor." "Where History Comes Alive." 'Well,' thought Demming, 'let's go see what this is all about.' He didn't see any business hours posted on the door but noticed lights on inside, so he assumed it was open. He swung the door aside and heard the tinkling of the bell. 'Nice touch,' he thought. 'Seems to fit this place perfectly.' Demming saw there was no one in the store, so he stood at the entrance and took in the scene in his typically businesslike way. 'Lots of inventory, but not much organization.' In fact, there was none that he could see. 'Great place if you like dust. Pretty small, too. And there's no one even here to greet the customers. Come to think of it, what customers?' And marketing? This guy had evidently never heard of that new-fangled concept. Demming realized maybe it wasn't all that surprising he had never heard of this establishment. It looked like a real disaster. But he was here, so why not give it a chance? After all, Stephen seemed to like it, and he knew something about books, didn't he?

As Demming was about to start wandering around to scrutinize the piles of books lying about, Gustav Ernst stepped from behind the curtain separating the front of the shop from the back. He was typically attired: baggy gray pants, blue checked shirt, gray vest. The nouveau rumpled look. "Good morning, sir," said Ernst. "So sorry to keep you waiting. My hearing is not as good as it used to be, and I am afraid the little bell above the door does not always fulfill its intended purpose. I have a buzzer out back that usually alerts me when the front door is opened, but it has been having a little problem. I was in the process of fixing it when you came in." The device Ernst referred to was in addition to the doorbell provided for his late-night visitors. He thought it wise to know when someone came through the door during business hours. Not so much to service his customers better. He wasn't overly concerned about that. It was, well, precautionary. "Please forgive me," said Ernst. "How can I help you, sir?"

"Please don't concern yourself about it," said Demming. "I was just...admiring your little place here. Mind if I look around?"

"Well, considering that this *is* a place of business, I would be very happy if you did," laughed Ernst. "Please feel free to browse. Take as much time as you like."

'This must be the old guy Stephen told me about,' thought Demming. 'Seems jovial enough, just like Stephen said he was.' "Actually," he said, deciding to plunge right in, "I'm here on the tip of a friend who stumbled on your shop earlier this week. He spoke very highly of the place, and of you, I might add, so I thought I'd come by and see for myself. My friend and I are both in the publishing business, so we're always looking out for..."

Ernst made the connection instantly. "Why, you must be speaking of Stephen. Stephen Blake. He came in last...Monday, I think it was. We had a very nice time looking over some of my older manuscripts. He's a fine person, and seems to know a lot about books, too."

"That's him. He said you had a wonderful collection, especially in the back of the shop. Actually, I was hoping you might let me see it. By the way, name's John Demming." He offered a business card with his left hand and a handshake with his right. Ernst accepted both. Demming smiled and said, "Glad to meet you."

"And I you, sir," said Ernst as he perused the card quickly. "I am Gustav Ernst. I own the shop, and am its only employee, as well. It keeps down my payroll, you know." Ernst laughed at his little joke. Demming didn't. "But of course I will let you see my collection, if you like. Especially if you were sent by Stephen. I take great pride in showing off my books to anyone who is interested. I keep the best ones in the back, for security. There is some irony in the fact that the more historically interesting a book or manuscript or map might be, the more one finds the need to keep it hidden away for fear that someone might want to, let us say, appropriate it, perhaps mischievously. Some can only see the monetary value in these things, while others can appreciate their other qualities. I do not mean any offense, Mr. Demming, but which are you interested in?"

"No offense taken, Mr. Ernst," said Demming, probing the old man's capabilities, as well as his defenses. Demming's antennae were up. He didn't know why, exactly, but he suspected that Ernst fostered the appearance, outwardly at least, of being a bit of a country bumpkin. What with his disheveled clothes, tousled hair, funny little witticisms, and all. Not to mention this little dustbin of a store. It might all be deliberate, to throw people off guard. Demming was used to this type in the business world: posturing one way while being something else, to their advantage. These were the most dangerous of men. It was easy to be led astray by them. They made you susceptible.

"I can honestly say I'm interested in all aspects," said Demming, truthfully. "This is my business, after all, so I can't ignore the money angle. But I enjoy fine old treasures, too. Not so much for what they're worth, but for the sheer beauty and art in 'em. Been doing it now for a long time, so I've picked up a fair number of items myself. I love old books for their aesthetic qualities, but if they increase in value over time, so much the better. That's as honest an answer to your question as I can give. Hope you understand what I mean."

"I do indeed," said Ernst, as he in turn tried to assess the character of the man who stood before him. Misplaced trust could be a dangerous thing, he knew. "And I appreciate your candor, sir," Ernst continued. "I must tell you that I myself might have been more interested in monetary value at a younger age, but that aspect is almost totally suppressed now in favor of other things. I find I am not as interested in what something is worth any longer as much as in what a beautiful creation it is. As I mentioned to Stephen, I do not keep the shop to make money. Not any longer. I have made more than enough to live on. It pleases me to keep the store open for the occasional collector. And for others who may be interested in old books, for whatever reason. People such as Stephen. And yourself. It helps an old man pass the time away. I do not know what I would do otherwise."

"How long you had this place?" inquired Demming, still puzzled by his ignorance of the shop's existence. "I was surprised when Stephen told me about it, actually. Thought I knew all the book outlets in Boston, especially those dealing in the rarer items. The kind you apparently have, according to Stephen."

Ernst didn't like the way this was going. Demming's tone was a little too...probing. Not antagonistic, really, but...aggressive. He started to see his visitor as a potential complication, something that was definitely not needed at this particular point in time. He was probably more curious than anything else, but Ernst thought he detected a certain misgiving on the man's part. A small doubt could blossom into something larger, something that posed more of a threat. Not only that, but this fellow apparently was a top dealer in the business. He could start asking embarrassing questions about how, when, why, and from whom Ernst had acquired many of the items he had in the back of the shop. Questions Ernst was not prepared to answer. Also, Demming and Blake were colleagues, maybe even good friends, with a common interest. They might end up comparing notes on what Ernst told each of them. That could be a problem. Now that he—and Lariakin—had

Wicca Codex

decided to recruit Blake to assist in their work, Blake's connection to Demming could be touchy. Perhaps even downright disastrous.

Ernst was in a quandary as to how best to handle the situation. Perhaps his offer to let Demming see what he had out back had been premature, but he felt he had to follow through on it. In fact, he didn't know how he could possibly refuse to let this man see what Stephen had already told him about. But he had to be careful. Extremely careful. He decided to see if he could get away with being as vague as possible.

"I have been in business for several years," explained Ernst, "but not all at this location, or even in Boston. I had been interested in old books for a long time and had collected many items over the years. I acquired so many things, I decided to open a store to help rid myself of some of the less interesting volumes. I have had this particular shop for only a few years."

"A few years? Really? Still don't know how I could've missed finding out about you." Demming was trying hard to be light, just make conversation, but it wasn't his nature to speak differently than he felt. He had always been a lousy liar.

"Well, as I said, I am not in it as a serious business venture. More as a hobby to amuse myself and help pass the time. I do not find the need to advertise. I am happy only to serve the occasional customer who might wander in. It does not surprise me that you did not know anything about me." Ernst said this with a smile on his face, but he didn't know if he was being convincing. He was having trouble reading Demming. "But enough of this talk. Let me show you what I have out back."

Ernst took Demming to the same room where he had first taken Stephen Blake earlier in the week. He unlocked the door and invited Demming to view his collection, opening several of the bookcases so he could experience some of the best items up close. This elicited from Demming the same amazed reaction Stephen Blake had. He was taken aback by the quality, as well as the number of high-end items that one individual had been able to assemble. He examined many of the volumes carefully and concluded they were genuine. Or at least appeared to be. If not, they were remarkably competent counterfeits, undetectable to his trained eye. He talked to Ernst about some of the technical aspects of how a few of the volumes were produced, as well as various production techniques used at different times in the past. Demming concluded that Ernst knew what he was talking about. His knowledge, in fact, was prodigious.

Demming leaned back in one of the room's inviting chairs as he balanced an old manuscript on his lap. "Well, I don't often admit it, but I'm overwhelmed. If anything, Stephen understated what you have here. Isn't often I see such quality—and quantity—in an individual collection like this, and I've been around over the years." He could see his effusiveness pleased Ernst greatly. The old man was genuinely proud of what he had. Demming wanted desperately to find out more about how Ernst had come to acquire these works, but something inside told him not to pursue it. Not right now, anyway. He didn't quite know why, but he still had that uncomfortable feeling about all this. He thought it best not to dig too deeply, at least not directly. He chose a different approach. "I bet you've broken a lot of hearts with these at the Antiquarian, huh? I know there're an awful lot of people over there who'd kill to get their hands on these."

Ernst was becoming a bit flustered, and he didn't like the feeling. He stroked his beard, trying to ward it off. "I...I am afraid I do not know what you are referring to, Mr. Demming. What is the Antiquarian?"

Demming couldn't believe Ernst didn't know about this. Or maybe he could. "Why, only the biggest, most impressive old book fair in New England, if not the entire country. Surely you must've heard of it—a dealer like yourself in old books. It's held every year, in the fall. In fact, this year's version is coming up in just a couple of weeks. Thought you might be going." Demming tried something else. "How about the ABAA? Didn't see you listed with 'em. I checked after Stephen told me about you."

"Once again, I show my lack of knowledge. Please enlighten me."

"ABAA. The Antiquarian Booksellers' Association of America.

Wicca Codex

Virtually all dealers in old books and manuscripts are listed in a national directory." Demming was sorry now he had brought all of this up. Why did he have to make the old man feel bad? It was obvious Ernst wasn't a mainstream kind of guy. Not everyone follows the norm. He could be legitimate and not be familiar with these things. Couldn't he?

Ernst was quite troubled now but managed to avoid showing it. He didn't know whether Demming was innocently pursuing this line of questioning or playing some dangerous game of cat and mouse. If the latter, Ernst felt he had to control who was the cat and who the mouse. "I must confess to a certain embarrassment over this, Mr. Demming. It may seem odd to you that I am not familiar with such an event, or an important group such as you mentioned. But, as I said, I have never thought of this as a serious business. My interest has always been merely a personal one, so I have never found the need to do anything in a public way. I collect only for the pleasure it brings me, and perhaps a few of my closest friends. For that I do not need to attend book fairs, or advertise, or keep detailed financial records, or any of the other things you might expect. I hope you can understand that, Mr. Demming."

"Uh, yeah, I think I see the logic in that. No matter, really. To each his own, as they say." Demming knew this sounded awkward, but he couldn't think of anything else to say. He suddenly felt he had seen and heard enough. His sense of unease kept increasing. He just wanted to get out of there as soon as possible. He still didn't really know why. It was just a feeling he had. "Well," said Demming, checking his wristwatch, "Gotta be going. Wish I could see more of your collection, but I'm supposed to meet someone for lunch. Probably gonna be late as it is. Thanks much for giving me the tour. Enjoyed it." He laid the book he had been examining on the table and rose from the chair.

"You are most welcome," said Ernst, rising also. "As I said, friends of Stephen are mine as well. If you would like to stop in again, please do."

"Yeah, I will. Thanks for the invite."

They left the room, which Demming noticed Ernst locked again, and returned to the front of the shop. Ernst offered one of his business cards, which Demming saw was the same one Stephen Blake had shown him at Locke-Ober. He took it, thanked Ernst again, said his goodbyes, and left.

Demming walked back to the Common, where he plunked himself down on a park bench in the late-morning sunshine. Bicyclists, skaters, and walkers were out in droves, enjoying the beauty of the day and the season. But Demming was oblivious to it. He was thinking about what had just occurred. He didn't really know what to make of Gustav Ernst and his odd little bookshop, neither of which he had ever heard of until a few days ago. Why hadn't Ernst known about the Antiquarian book fair? Or the ABAA? How does someone in the business make it this far without knowing those things? It could be like the guy says, he supposed. Ernst was really just an old man who couldn't care less about making a buck anymore. Probably had his run years ago and didn't need the dough any longer. Maybe the guy was even an eccentric old gazillionaire. Stranger things have happened, for sure. And maybe Ernst really didn't give a damn about the historic value of what he owned. Maybe he really did just like having them. Bringing them out every once in a blue moon to admire, and feel, and smell, and talk about. Maybe...yeah, just maybe.

Then again, what was it about the guy that gave him the heebie-jeebies? Oh, he was personable enough, all right. And he had that quaint little accent. And he sure did know a lot about his books. He'd give him that much. It was easy to understand why Stephen raved about the guy. But, deep down, Demming was uneasy. Uneasy for himself, but more so for Stephen. Demming didn't intend to have anything more to do with Ernst, books or no books. But Stephen was hooked on the guy, or so it seemed from their lunch the other day. 'Everything was probably okay,' he told himself. 'You're making a mountain out of you know what. Just being a paranoid jerk.' Then again, why did he feel this way? He couldn't shake it.

On the spur of the moment, he decided to call Stephen. He took out his cell phone and flipped the mouthpiece open. He had Stephen's business number programmed, but not his home number. He knew Stephen lived on Marlborough Street in Boston, so he got it from the operator and punched it in. Stephen's phone rang a few times before the answering machine kicked in. Demming was going to hang up, then elected to leave a brief message. He waited for the beep, then said, "Hiya, Stephen. It's John Demming. It's Saturday morning, about eleven thirty. Just came from your friend Ernst's bookstore. A most interesting fellow, and a little strange too, from what I can tell. I'd like to talk to you about him, but it can wait 'til Monday, I guess. Gimme a call at the office when you get a sec. Thanks. 'Bye."

Demming soaked up the sun for another minute or two. It really was a one-in-a-million kind of day. He thought he might do some shopping along Boylston Street. Afterwards, he could stroll over to Newbury, just a block away. He would probably just look rather than buy, though. It was one of Boston's toniest retail streets, and he wasn't on that kind of budget. But it was a great day for walking around, no matter what direction he took, so he quickly forgot about Gustav Ernst and Ye Olde Booke Nooke. He left the park bench behind, dodged a couple of skateboarders, and charted a course for Boylston Street.

* * *

Gustav Ernst wasn't feeling particularly well. It wasn't anything physical, as far as he could tell, although he was unusually tired for some reason. And anyway, he wasn't supposed to be burdened with things like that. That was part of the deal with Lariakin. No, it was more of an ill-at-ease feeling. Ernst didn't know, of course, but it was much the same thing being experienced at that very moment by John Demming as he sat on a bench in Boston Common. Ernst decided to close the shop and go up to his apartment to rest—and to think. He turned the sign to "Closed" at the front door, turned out the lights, went upstairs to his rooms, and laid down on the bed.

What should he make of this fellow Demming? At best, merely a complication. At worst, however, a downright danger to the accomplishment of Ernst's well-structured and long-standing plans. There was no way to be sure which was more accurate. He brainstormed on it for a long time, but always came to the same conclusion, which was that he didn't think he could afford to take any chances. They were at a critical crossroad. All the work and planning—was it perhaps in jeopardy?

He decided the situation was serious enough that it required further consultation. Immediately. He sprang from the bed and swaggered over to the telephone. He dialed a number, heard it ring once, then said to the voice at the other end of the line, "Lariakin. I believe we have a problem."

Chapter 16

Sunday, October 22

John Demming had spent a most enjoyable Saturday in Boston—after he left the bookstore, that is. So much so that he completely forgot about his experience with Gustav Ernst and the resulting mixed bag of feelings he had about the visit. He ended up having such a good time that he wanted to continue his do-something-nice-for-yourself weekend on Sunday. It was another fine day—maybe a little cooler, but still A-okay—so he thought he'd take advantage of it to see some foliage. The best part was, he wouldn't have to go too far. It was past peak up north but the color line had fallen southward into Massachusetts. 'Fallen like a leaf from a tree,' he thought, waxing poetic. It might even be a little late down here in spots, but a drive along Route 2, which crossed the northern part of the state, should still provide some nice views. He might even stop at a farm stand and get some apple cider. The alternative was football on TV, and it was much too nice a day to waste indoors. Yes, he decided after a leisurely breakfast—low cholesterol, he was proud to say—that's what he would do today. He was well on the way to expunging all those bad habits from his life. Turning a new leaf, you might say. 'Hey, that's good. Turning a new leaf, during foliage season. Feeling better already.'

He hopped in the car and headed south on Route 3, then cut across 60 to pick up 2. He turned west and drove through Arlington, Lexington, Lincoln, and on into Concord. He knew he wasn't too far from the Minuteman Monument and Old North Bridge where the Revolutionary War had started over two hundred years ago. Oddly enough, as many years as he had lived in the Boston area, he had never visited these historic sites. Probably like a New Yorker avoiding the

Empire State Building or the Statue of Liberty. He made a mental note to come back some time, hopefully sooner rather than later, and walk the same paths trod by the rebels and the Redcoats.

It was out somewhere near Walden Pond that Demming started to notice the problem. Not with the car, but with his head. He had slapped at a pinprick of pain on the back of his neck, thought it was a leftover mosquito from the summer season. Then he started experiencing episodes of lightheadedness. He didn't think anything of it at first. It was just one of those things that happen for no apparent reason, he told himself. Nothing to worry about. But after three or four minutes the feeling was still there. If anything, it was worse. Now he was starting to feel downright dizzy. He thought about pulling over to the side of the road until the sensation passed, but then there was somewhat of a lull, and he continued driving. Traffic was still fairly light in the area. It was well before noon and most folks had not yet gotten out on the road. He didn't feel he was a threat to anyone.

He drove slowly for another half mile and started to feel better. 'I'm okay,' he thought. 'Just a little indisposition. Probably not used to all that healthy food in one sitting, that's all.' Encouraged, he gradually picked up speed until he was back up to a little over the legal limit, which was 45 miles per hour along that particular stretch of road. He continued for another mile or so.

Suddenly, Demming felt a tremendous jolting pain in his head. He instinctively raised his left hand to the affected area while keeping his right hand on the steering wheel. The car wandered across the centerline. He was on the wrong side of the road. He struggled to pull back to the right, but he overcompensated. The pain increased to an intolerable level, so much so that he had to grasp his head with both hands. Unfortunately for John Demming, he no longer had the presence of mind to step on the brake as he released his grip on the wheel. His foot increased its pressure on the accelerator as the car swerved sharply onto the bumpy dirt shoulder and wrapped itself around a utility pole at 57 miles an hour. The impact was sufficient to thrust the pole into approximately the same position Demming had occupied a moment earlier. Since his vehicle was not a late-model car, it was not equipped with an air bag. He died instantly, skull crushed by the pole, hands still wrapped around his head.

Two Concord police officers arrived on the scene in a cruiser shortly thereafter in response to the call of a motorist who had seen the crash. They were surprised to find no skid marks on the pavement. They couldn't tell if the victim had been drunk. There was no discernible smell of alcohol, nor did there seem to be any bottles or cans lying around inside the vehicle. They were willing to bet, though, that this guy had been out on an all-night binge and was just now getting around to finding his way home. On the other hand, it did seem awfully late in the morning for something like that. In any event, that was for the medical examiner to determine.

One of the officers was about to call the accident in when the other motioned for him to come over to the mangled car. The one who had been inspecting the wreckage said, "What do you make of that, Mike?"

"What do I make of what?" said Mike to his partner Ed.

Officer Ed pointed out the peculiarity. "On his head, toward the back. That black mark. And his hair. It's crazy but...it almost looks like the guy's hair's been burning. You can still see it smoldering. What do you suppose that's from? The car sure didn't catch on fire."

Officer Mike leaned into the car as best he could and viewed the remains of John Demming's crushed and bloodied head. All he could say was, "I'll be damned."

Chapter 17

Monday, October 23

Stephen Blake saw the piece in The Globe's Metro Region section. It was just a short writeup under "New England News Briefs" on the last page, but it hit him with the force of a jackhammer as he was eating breakfast and trying to gear up for the first day of the new workweek.

> Motorist dies in
> unexplained accident

Concord, Mass.—Concord police were called to investigate an automobile accident along Route 2 on Sunday morning just before noon. Found dead at the scene was John J. Demming of Winchester, age 52. There were no passengers in the car and no other vehicles were involved. Mr. Demming's car hit a utility pole at a high rate of speed, according to a witness, although the lack of skid marks made it apparent that the victim did not try to avoid the collision. He died of massive head injuries sustained in the accident. Driving conditions were reported to be excellent at the time of the crash. Preliminary findings indicate that alcohol was not a factor. Police are continuing the investigation.

Incredulous, Stephen read it again, as though that would make the words change. When they didn't, he pushed the paper away morosely. He stared out the window at the gray clouds that had replaced the beautiful weekend weather. John Demming dead? How could that be? Maybe it was a different John Demming, although the age was about right, and he knew Demming lived in Winchester. It had to be the right one, as much as he was unprepared to believe it. Hadn't they just had lunch together last week? And Demming had even left him a message on his answering machine. Just a couple of days ago—on Saturday. He wasn't home to take the call because he had been away on a quick weekend trip to Hartford to visit friends. Stephen was going to telephone John this very morning to find out what it was all about. Unbelievable!

Stephen didn't know what to do. He certainly didn't feel like going to work. He probably would, but not just yet. He needed to find out more about the accident. Maybe confirm that it really was his colleague and not someone else, although he knew what the answer was going to be. He picked up the wall phone in the kitchen and asked the operator for the number of the Concord police. He dialed it straight away.

"Concord Police Department. Sergeant Dornan speaking. May I help you?"

"Yes. Good morning. I just read an article in today's Boston Globe about a car accident that happened yesterday in Concord. On Route 2. I think I know the victim. I'd like to confirm that it's him and get more information if I could. Am I speaking to the right person?"

"May I have your name and address, sir?"

Stephen provided the requested information. Sergeant Dornan said, "I'll put you in touch with Officer Michael Fitzpatrick. He was one of the investigating officers. Hold on please."

After a few moments, a voice on the other end of the line said, "Good morning, Mr... uh, Blake is it? This is Officer Fitzpatrick. I understand you have some information on the Demming accident?"

"Well, I'm not sure I do or not. I was just explaining that I know a John Demming and I think it must be the same person, but I want to be sure. Did you find anything that would confirm that it's the person I know?" Stephen fidgeted with the curls on the phone wire. He really didn't know if he was ready for what he knew was coming. "I didn't really know his home address, but I do know where he worked."

"And where would that be, sir?"

"The Demming I know worked at a publishing supply house in Boston—Ampex Distributors, on South Street." Stephen held his breath and waited for the inevitable.

"That's the one, sir," confirmed Fitzpatrick. "We found some business cards on his body with that name. Sorry, sir."

Stephen slumped further into his chair. "God, that's awful. I don't know what to say."

"Maybe you can help us out, Mr. Blake. We haven't had much luck so far contacting people who knew Mr. Demming, it being Sunday and all when the accident happened. Can you tell us anything about him?"

"Not really that much, I'm afraid. I'm in publishing too, so we did business from time to time. Saw each other at meetings occasionally. Had lunch now and then. That sort of thing. We didn't really socialize outside of our jobs." Stephen realized he had already made the transition from present tense to past. 'How quickly things change,' he thought. "I do know he lost his wife a few years ago, so he lived alone. I believe he had some family out west—California, as I recall —but I'm not sure about that. Kept pretty much to himself, as far as I know. That's about it, Sergeant." Stephen decided not to mention Demming's call to him on Saturday, especially since he didn't know what it was about. Anyway, he was certain it didn't have anything to do with the accident.

"Well, it's something to start on, Mr. Blake. We can get the rest from his colleagues at work. Thanks for calling. Say, why don't you let me have your home and work numbers. Just in case we need to talk to you again."

Stephen gave him the information, then asked, "Officer, can you tell me anything about the accident? The circumstances, I mean. The paper didn't say much, other than no one else was involved, he hit a pole at high speed, and there weren't any skid marks. Is there anything else you can tell me? I'd appreciate it."

Fitzpatrick hesitated, then decided: What the hell. Maybe giving out a little info would help jog people's memories a little. You never knew

Wicca Codex

where it would lead. Give a little, get a little. That was his philosophy on life in general. And none of the stuff was really that privy anyway. "Well, we don't know a heck of a lot right now. Still investigating, you know. We thought it might be alcohol at first, especially since he didn't hit the brake. But that's been ruled out. There was kind of a strange-looking black mark on the back of his neck, though. And his hair was, well, like it was smoking when we found him, but there wasn't any fire in the car. It was almost like he was...electrocuted. But no electric wires were down. Damnedest thing, really."

If Stephen had been shocked and tongue-tied before, he was doubly so now. His mind was racing to sort out what he had just heard against what was already stored in his memory banks. He just couldn't get a word out.

"Mr. Blake? Are you all right? Are you still there?"

Stephen snapped back to reality. "Yes, officer," he said. "I'm here. That is strange, isn't it?" He was going to end the call, then thought of one other thing. "Oh, by the way, officer, do you know whether Demming's neck was broken in the accident?"

"Not to my knowledge, sir. Why do you ask?"

'Let's play it close to the vest,' thought Stephen. 'For now, anyway.' If he were being honest with himself, he would have admitted he didn't want to get involved. It was more comfortable looking in from outside than getting sucked into the morass. "No special reason. Just wondering. Well, listen, thanks for the info. And if you need anything else, just give me a call. I'll try to help if I can."

"Thanks very much, Mr. Blake. Appreciate it. We'll be in touch if necessary. So long."

Stephen hung up the phone. He couldn't do anything but sit there for the next ten minutes, thinking. Despite his aversion to becoming part of the official inquiry, he was deeply troubled by his friend's death. He was trying to reconstruct the events of the last week that had some connection with his colleague. Make that his former colleague. There was the lunch meeting at Locke-Ober, Demming telling Stephen about the murder in his office building, his phone call and message on Saturday. Why would Demming call him on a Saturday? It must have had something to do with Ernst and the bookstore, judging by the message on Stephen's machine, but what was so all-fired important that it couldn't wait? And what about this black-mark business? Didn't Demming say the murdered guy in his building had a mark like that? And wasn't that the M. O. for those other killings he had read about last week in The Herald? What in God's good name was going on here?

Stephen had an idea. He went into the tiny office he had set up in one corner of his apartment and rummaged around the desk. It was a mess, but he found what he was looking for right away. It was one of last week's Heralds obtained from Jorgensen at work. He found the article on the broken-neck murders and looked at the byline. He thought for a moment, hesitated briefly, then picked up the phone and got the number of The Boston Herald from the operator. He dialed it and asked for Alison Simmons. He was connected with her department, where he was told that Miss Simmons had not yet arrived, but that he could leave a message if he wished. He asked that she call him, giving both his home and work numbers. There was no way he was going to avoid the inevitable. He would go to work and make the best of it. But he needed to talk about all this with someone, and Alison Simmons was as good a starting point as any. He didn't know if she would see him, or exactly what he would say if she did, but he had to try something.

Stephen managed to make his way to the office, walking the two-mile route in a semi-daze. It was still gray, and chilly, too, but the exercise felt good. The crisp air helped him think. As soon as he arrived, he made the rounds of his colleagues, some of whom were just hearing about Demming's death. Most of the other people in Stephen's office knew Demming as well, and they were just as shocked as Stephen had been to find out about the accident.

Stephen heard over the P. A. that he had a call. He rushed back to his office to take it. It was Alison Simmons. "Thanks for returning my call, Miss Simmons," said Stephen, a little out-of-breath. "I appreciate it."

"No problem, Mr. Blake," said Alison. "I tried you at home first, but you'd already left. What is this about? The person who left me the message didn't know."

"Yeah, sorry about that," apologized Stephen, "but I've been kind of upset this morning. Let me get right to the point. A business colleague of mine died in a car accident yesterday. Although I can't say why, for sure, there may be some connection between his death and the series of murders you've been doing those stories on. I've read your articles, and I'd just like to talk to you about what I know and what you know and, well, see if there's something there."

Alison's eyebrows rose a notch. She tightened her grip on the phone and dug for her notebook. "Sorry to hear about your friend, but what makes you think there's a connection?" she asked.

"I just talked to the Concord police this morning—that's where the accident happened, in Concord, Mass.—and they told me a couple of things that made me think of your articles."

"Such as?"

"Such as a black mark on the back of his neck. And his hair looking like it'd been on fire, even though there were no flames at the accident scene."

There was silence for a moment, then Alison said excitedly, "I can be there in a half hour, Mr. Blake. Will that be convenient?"

"Actually, I think I'd rather do it outside of the office, for a couple of reasons. I was wondering if we could postpone it 'til this evening. Would you be available for dinner maybe? Say about six? My treat, of course."

Alison pondered the offer, but only briefly. There was no way she was going to let this first potential lead pass her by. "Well, that's a bit out of the ordinary, but a story's a story. You've got my interest up, so I guess I'm game. And I think I can convince my boss that a free meal isn't a bribe in this case. Or is it?"

Stephen laughed. "No. No bribe, I can assure you of that. So, you agree then?"

"Sure. Why not? Where would you like to meet?"

"How about Chinatown? If you like Chinese, I know a great spot on Tyler Street. 'Shanghai Gardens' it's called. Between Kneeland and Beach. It's about mid-way between us, so it'd be reasonably convenient for us both. What do you say?"

"That sounds good. I love Chinese food. I'll see you there at six, then?"

"Six it is. See you tonight. 'Bye."

Stephen found it hard to get through the rest of the workday. He was dealing with too many emotions, too many uncertainties, too many unexplained events. The hours dragged, especially with the anticipation of meeting the Simmons reporter after work. He left the office at five forty-five and walked the short distance to the restaurant.

He got there right on time and found a young woman waiting just inside the entrance. Her blond hair shimmered in the overhead light. She looked professional, self-assured in her light gray wool skirt and matching jacket over a rose blouse, tiny black leather handbag dangling nonchalantly over her left shoulder. Just a hint of makeup, not overdone. All set off by a single strand of opalescent pearls. He didn't know why, but he wasn't quite prepared for how attractive she was, despite her pleasant voice during their earlier phone conversation. Maybe there was still a hint of gun-shyness left over from his ex. After the painful split with Janet, he had lost interest in women, for the most part. He wasn't a groupie, didn't much care for the singles scene. Perhaps he didn't want to risk further pain. Whatever the reason, he paid little heed to the opposite sex in all but his business dealings, and then it was strictly professional. That's why he was jolted by the attractiveness of this woman. He wasn't anticipating it, didn't really think about anything like that. It was a nice surprise. He hoped it was the right person. It must be. She was looking at him as though she were expecting someone.

Stephen introduced himself. "Hi. I'm Stephen Blake. You must be Miss Simmons from The Herald. Sorry to keep you waiting." He extended his hand.

"Yes, I'm Alison Simmons. Happy to meet you, Mr. Blake." Alison shook Stephen's hand and flashed one of her patented glad-to-be-here smiles. "And you haven't really kept me waiting. I just got here myself. I was a little early, actually. I guess I'm hungry, both for the Chinese food and for what you have to tell me." Alison and Stephen both laughed.

"Well, then we should get right to it, then," said Stephen. They went in, got seated, looked over the lengthy menu, made their selections, and ordered. He went for the Moo Shi Pork, she the Three Delights. They agreed to share a Scallion Pancake appetizer. Each also ordered the Hot-and-Sour Soup. Stephen said it was especially good here, and she went along with the recommendation. Both passed on a drink, preferring to stick with the pot of steaming Chinese tea that had been delivered. It was the real thing, pale green and tangy. It tasted wonderful and helped take the chill out of their bones.

Alison admired the ambiance of the place—multicolored paper lanterns hovering overhead, playful red and gold dragons on the walls and columns, flickering candles in green glass holders on each table, delicate orchids in narrow glass vases, the soft plunking of Oriental strings in the background. It could have been tacky but wasn't. The atmosphere was serene, pleasant, inviting. She liked it. "Nice place," she said. "You come here often?"

"Only when I'm talking to reporters," quipped Stephen. He had only just met her, but felt at home already. 'She has the greenest eyes.' It was yet to be determined, but he knew instinctively he had done the right thing by calling her.

Alison laughed heartily. "Okay, fair enough," she said. "You've probably got this all set up with management, right? A bug under the table? Or maybe in the napkin holder? Movie camera behind the curtain? That sort of thing."

Stephen returned the laugh. "No. Nothing like that, I assure you. But I do feel at ease here," he explained. "It puts me in a good mood, and I need that right now. Things have been a little chaotic lately."

Alison took this as a cue to get down to business. "I'm glad you called me Mr. Blake. I..."

Stephen interrupted. "Look. How about if we dispense with the Mr. Blake routine? Please call me Stephen. And I can reciprocate by calling you Alison, if that's okay."

"Well, since you're providing dinner, I suppose you can dictate the terms of communication. It's a deal. Stephen." She emphasized his name playfully. She was unexpectedly pleased he had taken the initiative to make their contact less formal. That was her preference as well. She felt comfortable with her dinner companion, more so than the guys she went out with on occasion. There were several, but no one in particular raised her interest that much. They were all so...superficial, or serious, or full of themselves, or whatever. Always looking for something she wasn't willing—or able—to give. But this one. There was something different about him that lightened her spirit. It wasn't just physical, although he was certainly good looking. It was something deeper that she couldn't explain. Maybe he was like the rest. After all, she didn't know anything about him. Not yet. But she found him to be a friendly sort, able to smile and laugh easily, despite the problems he had mentioned. Her curiosity was aroused as to what those problems were. They must be formidable for him to talk to a reporter. She got the feeling he didn't do this every day.

The Hot-and-Sour arrived. Each dug into the spicy broth with gusto. Alison agreed it was among the best she'd had in a long time. "So, as I was saying," she said, in between sips, "I was glad to get your call. I can use a little help on my series, actually. My research so far has turned into a dead end and my editor is getting antsy about letting me keep going on this." Alison reached into the minuscule handbag she had snaked over the adjacent empty chair and took out her notebook. Stephen suppressed a smile. It never ceased to amaze him what women could cram into those things. Alison laid the notebook on the table next to her soup bowl and said, "Since this is a business meeting, albeit a tasty one, everything will be on the record. Any objection?"

Stephen thought for a moment, then said, "No, I guess not. That's what this is about, after all. But can you give me some warning if you put me in one of your stories? And maybe give me a chance to check what you said I said?"

"I'll try to do that, Stephen," smiled Alison. "Now, you mentioned something about things being chaotic a moment ago. What is it you wanted to talk to me about exactly?"

"Well, oddly enough, I'm not sure I know," said Stephen. "And I don't really know if I can help you out much. I just thought we could pool our resources. Share what we know with each other. It may lead to something, or it may not. I just thought it was worth a shot." He wasn't at all certain where he was going with this. "I don't even know where to start."

"The beginning is always good," said Alison.

Stephen smiled. She was right. Nothing to do but forge ahead and see what happened. He blew at the steaminess in his soup and took a halting sip, then plunged in. "There were things in your stories that struck a chord when I heard about how my friend John Demming died yesterday. Like the black mark, for example. Then again, there're things about his death different than what you wrote about. Like his smoking hair."

Alison stopped writing and looked up. "That's right. I remember you telling me that on the phone." She tried not to be disbelieving, but it was difficult. "Is that really true?"

"I know it sounds crazy, but that's what the cops told me. His hair looked like it'd been on fire, even though there was no fire in the crash." Alison had resumed taking notes. She was finding it difficult to coordinate eating, listening, and writing simultaneously. Difficult, but not impossible. "Another difference," said Stephen, "was that his neck wasn't broken, at least according to the officer I spoke with on the phone. As I recall, all of the people you wrote about had a broken neck, right?"

"Yep," agreed Alison. "There've been five victims so far, the most recent just a couple of days ago. Friday night. Actually, early Saturday morning, just past midnight. A young high school kid from South Boston. Peter Markis. He was in a car with his girlfriend, parked out at Castle Island watching the submarine races. She was hysterical when they found her, as you can imagine. He had the broken neck and black mark, same as all the others."

"My God, I hadn't heard about that one. I was out of town most of the weekend. That's gruesome."

"Yeah, sure is. It's gotten to the point where everyone's up in arms about the situation. Five horrible deaths, not counting your friend Demming. No suspects. No clues, other than the marks. No real motives that anyone can see right off. The police are going bonkers trying to piece something together. The public's running scared. The victims' families are screaming for justice—or revenge, maybe. Get somebody—anybody—they say. My editor's having a conniption, waiting for a break. It's a mess all around."

"Sounds like it," Stephen said. He refilled their teacups, then went on. "I was intrigued by your story after the police press conference last week, the one where they sprang the occult connection, or at least the possibility of something like that. That must've been a shocker."

Alison didn't mention her earlier suspicions along that line, preferring instead to play it straight for now and see what developed. "And how. I wasn't aware they were into that sort of thing. But I guess when you keep slamming your head against a wall, you've got to try everything. They apparently have had enough experience with cults and the like that it becomes a possible explanation when you run into the unexplainable. God knows that's what we've got here. Even if you buy into the idea of a psycho killer running around loose, the fact that no one's been able to find any physical evidence of any kind is très puzzling. The police may be grasping at straws, but I can understand the need to try a different slant on these cases."

The pancakes arrived, steamy and appetizing. Dishes were beginning to pile up, since they hadn't yet finished their soup. They rearranged things and made space.

"There *is* one other thing that's been bothering me, Alison."

"What's that?"

"When I got back home late yesterday, there was a message on my answering machine from John. He tried calling me on Saturday morning, just before noon. Said he'd just come from a visit to a bookstore I told him about. John and I are both in the publishing business, and I recommended he go see this great collection of old manuscripts and other rarities the shop owner had acquired over the years." Stephen was looking at Alison the whole time, but she didn't return his gaze. She was writing furiously. "John's voice sounded a little strange," continued Stephen, "now that I think of it. It was a shade off, if you know what I mean. In fact, he himself used the word 'strange,' as I recall, when describing the owner of the store. I thought that was odd 'cause I've met him a couple of times now and he seems like a great guy. I can't imagine what John found troubling, but it must've been something serious enough to make him call me, instead of waiting until today. Then he ends up dead right after, with the same kind of black mark on his neck. I have to tell you, Alison. The whole thing is loopy."

"When did you come across this bookstore? And where is it?"

"Beacon Hill. On one of the side streets off Charles. It was a week ago today, actually. I'd just come from one of those yawners, an after-work dinner meeting. John was there too, as a matter of fact. I felt like walking off the doldrums on my way home. I live in Back Bay. On Marlborough Street." Stephen smiled inwardly as he suddenly thought about giving Alison his address. He wouldn't mind if this developed into something. He'd have to work on that. He decided the address thing might seem too blatantly forward. Not to mention inappropriate to the moment. He chose to hold off on that and continue with the narrative instead.

"I wandered into Beacon Hill by chance and came across this quaint little bookstore. It was real late, but the place was still open, which I thought was a little peculiar. Anyway, I went in. I'm a sucker for old books, and it looked like there were tons of 'em in the place. I got to talking to the owner, an old gent with the cutest little accent. He was charming. Invited me to see the private book collection he kept in the back of the shop, which I did. Extraordinary stuff, really. He offered to let me come back any time and see more. To top it off, he secretly threw in a free book I admired when I bought another one. I didn't find out about it 'til I left the shop. I was only a couple blocks away, so I went back to thank him. Then the oddest thing of all happened. Before I got back to the store, I noticed several people going in. They were in groups of twos and threes. The old guy let each group in, then locked the door behind 'em. I didn't know what was going on, so I decided to go home and thank him by phone the next day."

"Wait a minute. You say these people were going in after you left? Do you remember what time that was?"

"It had to be after eleven. Maybe even eleven thirty. I got there before ten. I remember 'cause I was going to watch the Ten O'Clock News at home before I got diverted. Then I kind of lost track of time looking at Ernst's collection. That's the owner—Gustav Ernst."

Alison was still scribbling, but somehow managed to nibble on a pancake. "Okay. Anything else?" she asked.

"Not that night. I called Ernst the next day—to thank him for the free book. I sort of tried to find out indirectly who those late-arriving people were. I told him I came back to the shop when I found the freebie and saw them going in. He said they belonged to a group that met at his place a couple times a week. Talk about books, politics, whatever. They get together late 'cause it's generally the only time they can all fit it in. He said he was even going to ask me to stay for their meeting but decided against it when I told him I had to get home. It seemed to make sense at the time."

The waiter delivered the main meals. He cleared the soup bowls away to make room. Alison said to Stephen, "I'm afraid I've been enjoying the food while you've been doing most of the talking. Why

Wicca Codex

don't you try to catch up? Everything's excellent."

"That's okay," said Stephen, not wanting to make Alison feel guilty. "I've had a little. And you're right. It's the best. That's why I love this place so much. I'll have a couple of pancakes with my Moo Shi."

Despite the seriousness of their discussion, they drifted off to other topics. They spent the next twenty minutes enjoying the good food and chatting about things other than the strange deaths that had drawn them together. They were enjoying each other's company and found they got along well, remarkably so, for two independent souls. Each found it easy to talk to the other. Words flowed naturally, as did laughter. There was no strain, no tension, no discomforting silence. The atoms on one side of the equation balanced those on the other, as they always do when the chemistry is right.

It was toward the end of the meal that Alison turned the conversation back to the main agenda item. "Let me ask you one more thing about John Demming, Stephen. If you don't mind."

"Fire away."

"Can you think of anything that might've caused him to have a different reaction to Ernst and the bookstore than yours? Why would you be so positive toward Ernst while Demming called him strange?"

"That's a good question," said Stephen, "but I'm afraid I can't answer it. I don't know if it means anything, but John and I had lunch together last week, the day after I discovered the bookstore. That's when John mentioned that one of the broken-neck murders happened in his building. Just the night before." Stephen thought back to their lunch meeting less than a week ago. And now his friend was dead. He had to fight to maintain control. "Anyway, I told him about Ernst and the bookstore. He thought it was odd he hadn't heard of either one. And I must admit, if there was anything to know about the book business, especially old books, John Demming was the guy who'd know. He made it his top priority to know those kinds of things. Where books were bought and sold. What kinds of inventory different people carried. Where high-end items were available, things like first editions, rare manuscripts. Everything. That's how he made his living. I talked about it with Ernst late last week when..."

"Hold on," interrupted Alison. "You saw Ernst again last week? After your first meeting on...when was it?...Monday night?" She was filling pages in her notebook at an incredible rate.

"Right. He really wanted me to meet his late-night group, so he invited me to their Friday get-together. Told me to come early so he could show me more of his collection. He was really proud of it, you could tell. Said we'd talk about books and things. I agreed 'cause I really did want to see more of his stuff. I got there about nine, I think, and we had a great time for a couple hours. I'd decided, though, that I didn't want to stay for the meeting, so I made up an excuse to leave. I could see right off he was real disappointed. Almost distraught. Not outwardly, so much. But you could tell he wasn't pleased. He got over it quickly, then insisted I come to the next one. No excuses next time, he said."

"And when is that?" asked Alison.

"Tomorrow night. I'm planning on going. Now I'm more curious than ever about what goes on at those things."

There was silence for a few moments as they finished their meals. Each was thinking about what they had heard from the other during the evening. It was Alison who broke the silence.

"This is probably just sheer coincidence, Stephen—and I have absolutely no basis for saying that what happened is anything other than coincidence—but have you noticed that the last two murders took place right after those meetings you told me about? You first met him on Monday night—when you caught sight of those people going in. The other time was on Friday—the one you didn't stay for. The deaths occurred early Tuesday morning and early Saturday morning. Then your friend Demming calls you right after he visits Ernst. He expresses some kind of concern and ends up dead the next day. No broken neck apparently, but with a black mark. Same as the others. I think you were right to call me, Stephen. There may be something here. It's certainly

Wicca Codex

worth looking into."

"That's all very interesting," said Stephen, "but I'm not quite ready to buy into some clandestine conspiracy at this point." He hesitated before continuing. "I wonder if I should go to the police. What do you think?"

"That's up to you," said Alison, not wanting to foil any police investigation that was going on. But she wanted to be helpful, too. "You could wait for them to find you, if they end up on the right trail. Much of what we've talked about is pure speculation. It's not like you're withholding hard evidence, or anything like that."

Stephen thought about it for a moment. He still wasn't necessarily enthusiastic about getting himself embroiled in the middle of this mess. Not if he could help it. It was a lot different talking to a reporter. Less official, and certainly not as intimidating. Just a friendly exchange of information. "Maybe I'll hold off and wait, like you said."

The waiter returned to clear off the table. There would be no doggy-bags this evening. Each had devoured their meal completely.

There was one other thing Stephen was holding back on. He didn't know whether to bring it up, especially since he had given his word to Ernst that he would keep it to himself. He wavered back and forth, first leaning toward disclosure, then against. He didn't know what to do.

Alison saw his inner turmoil. "What are you not telling me, Stephen?" she asked.

He sat quietly for a few moments and was glad for the temporary relief that came when the waiter delivered the check, along with a small dish filled with pineapple chunks and two fortune cookies. He laid a credit card on the tray and watched the waiter walk toward the kitchen.

Alison picked up the thread of her last question when it was obvious Stephen wasn't going to jump back in with an explanation. "So. What's eating away at you? It must be something."

Stephen still remained silent for several moments, then said, "I don't know whether I should mention it. I promised Ernst I wouldn't say anything about it to anyone."

"I can't help you there," said Alison, even though she desperately wanted to absorb every tidbit of information Stephen could expel. He was the only new connection she had to these cases. Everything could be potentially valuable—another piece of the puzzle. She needed to make him comfortable in deciding to spill the beans. It must be significant, right? Otherwise, why would he hesitate? Come to think of it, why would Ernst bother extracting a no-tell pledge in the first place, if it wasn't something worth knowing? Alison decided to try the direct approach. "I can only tell you we've got some strange goings-on around here. Five deaths, murders most likely. Six, now that your friend Demming is dead, although we don't know his death was anything but an accident yet. If there's anything at all you know that might help break the logjam...well, you know what I mean."

Stephen thought about this. Alison saw his pained expression and knew she was watching a man struggling with a strong personal code of integrity. 'How about that?' she thought. 'An honest man for a change. How refreshing.'

"Okay," said Stephen, somewhat reluctantly. "But you've got to promise me this part is off the record. And that your promise is worth more than mine was to Ernst."

A slight frown wrinkled Alison's forehead. "Well, I don't like it," she said, "but if that's the only way I get to hear about it, I'll agree." She dropped her ballpoint pen on the notebook.

Stephen smiled. "Good," he said. "Here it is. On Friday night, I was talking to Ernst before the meeting. He asks me if I want to see a special book. I say sure. He didn't keep it with the others, though. It was in a separate room, in a safe. He pulls it out and tells me this incredible story of how he found it. It was in Germany, in the ruined house of one of his ancestors. He said he had it checked out and found that it went way back. He then tells me this mysterious tale about the non-initiated—I think that's the term he used—not being able to touch the book without experiencing some kind of unpleasant sensation. He says it's some kind of wizard's manual, full of strange symbols. He shows me the inside. I can't make anything out at all. Anyway, he invites me to touch the book, if I dare, to see if I feel anything."

Alison was completely mesmerized by Stephen's story. She waited for him to go on with it, intrigued by the unknown outcome, but all he did was look at her, playing up the suspense. She couldn't stand it any longer. "Well? Did you?" she blurted, exasperated.

"Did I what?"

"Touch it, for God's sake!"

Stephen was enjoying his little game but was a bit startled at Alison's impatient reaction. He almost felt like laughing but didn't. "Not at first," he said. "I admit he had me psyched about it. I did eventually, though,"—Alison thought she detected a hint of pride in his voice—"and thought I felt something strange. It was probably all in my head. I guess I'd have to call the experience scary, but inconclusive."

"This mysterious book. Does it have a name?"

"Ernst called it The Wicca Codex. That's w-i-c-c-a, Wicca. He said the word means 'wizard.' 'Codex' is what they called an ancient manuscript. Parchment leaves, hand-sewn binding. You get the idea."

Alison took Stephen's spelling of Wicca to mean she was allowed to make a notation of it, which she did. "I'm just writing down the name of the book, that's all. Don't get nervous, it's still off the record." Stephen's expression relaxed somewhat. "Well, that's some tale," said Alison. "I don't know whether I'd've had the courage to touch it. Not after Ernst's story about it."

Stephen started nibbling at the pineapple chunks, as did Alison. They were deliciously cold, with a tinge of sweetness. The perfect end to a perfect dinner. "Yeah, that's the way I felt, too," said Stephen. "But I decided to give it a go, and I'm still here."

Enough of the serious stuff, thought Stephen. "And a good thing, too," he continued. "Otherwise, I wouldn't have had the pleasure of dinner with you at one of the best Chinese restaurants in the city. I'm glad you agreed to come."

"Me too," said Alison. Her pearly whites were showing again. "I really liked the food. You were right about that. And I also enjoyed our conversation. Both the serious side and the lighter side. You certainly provided a more interesting evening than I would've gotten from TV." Alison exhaled a hearty laugh. So did Stephen. She waited a moment, not wanting to break the spell, but there was something bothering her. She had to let it out. "I've got to say this, Stephen. It's your life, of course, but do you really think it's a good idea to go to that meeting tomorrow night? After all we've talked about?"

Stephen smiled. "Why, Alison, I didn't know you cared." He thought he detected a slight blush from across the table. "But seriously," he said, "I want to go out of sheer curiosity." And perhaps for another reason, subconsciously. For five years, Janet's accusation of dullness had grated on him, never really let him enjoy a full measure of peace, of satisfaction. Especially since he knew it was true. Now there was this woman who had suddenly, unexpectedly, rekindled long lost feelings, remembrances. The good ones. Perhaps he had to overcome a few barriers, ones he himself had thrown up. "I didn't much want to last week," he said, "but now it's different. I don't think anything's going to happen, and I might find out something useful, or at least interesting. Then again, there might be absolutely nothing. Like you said, we've just been speculating here. It could all be hogwash. I still think Ernst is a nice guy."

"Well, will you at least promise you'll give me a call at The Herald on Wednesday morning? Just to let me know that you're...that everything is on the up and up?"

"You *do* care," gushed Stephen, who smiled profusely. There was no mistaking the rosy glow on Alison's cheeks now. She raised her hands to her face in embarrassment. "Okay, listen," he said. "I'll call you on Wednesday, first thing. Satisfied? Besides, it's a good way to get your phone number." He made a show of removing a pen from his shirt pocket. He hunted around for something to write on.

"Don't make too much of my interest, Mr. Stephen Blake. It's strictly professional." But Alison couldn't help saying this with a smile that

Wicca Codex

was a little too flirtatious. "And anyway, you already have my office number. You weren't planning on calling me at home, were you?"

"Well, I had given it some thought," grinned Stephen. "Which reminds me. If you want to call me at my office again, you can use my private line if you like. Eliminates one of the firewalls between me and the outside world." Alison jotted it in her notebook.

Stephen was thinking that perhaps he should ask her about those barriers. Maybe this was a good time for that. "Say, uh, mind if I ask you a question?"

"Shoot."

"Well, I was wondering...I, uh, know we just met, and it's hard to know something like this, right off, but...what I mean is, do you think..." It wasn't coming out the way he wanted. Best to let it slide for another time. "Never mind, it's not important." He hated the lie, but it was the only way out.

Alison wondered what it was all about, but instinct told her not to press. "No problem," she said.

The waiter returned with Stephen's credit card. He did the paperwork. They finished the pineapple dessert and left, reluctantly. It had been a terrific evening, and each was sorry it was ending. He hadn't forgotten the little byplay about her home phone number, but he let it go. For now.

Out on the street, Stephen asked, "Would you like a nightcap, Alison? I know this great little..."

Alison was tempted, but said, "No thanks, Stephen. I'm kind of tired. Really." Her voice betrayed the fatigue that had caught up with her.

Don't push, Stephen said to himself. There's time. "Okay, fair enough. Can I walk you somewhere, at least?"

"No need. Thanks anyway. I appreciate the offer, but not tonight."

"'Not tonight' says the little lady. I will take that to mean there is definitely the potential for another night. Let's leave it at that. I'll call you Wednesday."

"I'll look forward to it. Good night, Stephen. And thanks for the dinner. It was great, really."

"My pleasure. Good night, Alison."

Each extended a hand to the other. By handshake standards, the contact of their fingers was just a little too long. The contact of their eyes was longer still.

They parted company under the neon lights that blinked out "Shanghai Gardens" in red and orange. Neither looked back, but Alison and Stephen smiled as they left in different directions. Each was thinking this could turn out to be very interesting.

As fate would have it, that would be the case, in more ways than one.

Chapter 18

Tuesday, October 24

The call came into Boston police headquarters just before noon. The central switchboard routed it to Sergeant Pat Johnson.

"Johnson here."

"This is Officer Fitzpatrick from the Concord police. They told me you're the one to talk to about this."

"About what, officer?"

"My partner and I investigated a car accident in Concord a couple days ago. Guy wrapped himself around a utility pole. Head bashed in. Killed instantly. Anyway, someone here remembered you guys sending out an info request last week in connection with those serial killings you've had in Boston. You know, for similar M.O.'s, and all? Your victims had broken necks and black marks, right? Well, ours didn't have a broken neck, but he did have a black mark. Thought you might want to know."

Sergeant Johnson sat up in his chair. He swiveled around to see if he could catch the Lieutenant's attention, but Mulcahy wasn't in his office. Johnson switched the phone from right ear to left so he could take notes. "Can ya gimme the particulars?"

"Guy's name was Demming, D-e-m-m-i-n-g. First name John. Middle initial J. Lived in Winchester. Worked in Boston. Age 52. Single car involved. No skid marks. No alcohol, according to the M. E. Official cause of death is a crushed skull. No reason to suspect anything but an accident at this point. It's all in a report. I can fax it if you like. Got autopsy photos, too."

"I could use anything ya got—report, pictures, whatever—just as soon as you can get 'em here. We haven't had much of a break on these cases. Maybe this stuff'll help."

"I'll fax the report right away and courier the rest. Good luck, Sergeant. Oh, and by the way. I'd appreciate it if you kept in touch on this and let me know anything you find out. It may change our minds on this one. About it being an accident, I mean."

"I'll do that. Lemme have your number." He wrote it down on a scrap of paper. "Thanks for the call, officer."

Johnson slipped the phone back into its cradle and looked out the bank of windows that lined one wall. Or tried to. Only grudgingly did they permit views out or light in through their accumulated layers of grime. Johnson wondered if Officer Fitzpatrick's call was the break they needed or whether it would just add to their growing list of unexplained mysteries. He noticed Mulcahy returning to his office. Johnson sprang from his chair and scurried after his boss before someone else beat him to it. It paid to be nimble. He leaned on the door jamb. "Guess what, Vin? Just got a call from the Concord cops. They got a dead man with a black mark on his neck. Not broken, though. Killed in his car on Sunday. It's officially an accident for now, but they don't sound convinced. They're sendin' us the info."

Mulcahy hadn't had a chance to sit down yet. He was in a foul mood, having just gotten another earful from the Captain on these damned murders. He rolled out his chair as if he were going to sit, but didn't. Instead, he stood behind his desk and tossed an impatient look at Johnson. "Sunday, you say? Two days ago?" Mulcahy rolled his eyes and said sarcastically, "Nice of 'em to get back to us so fast, don'tcha think, Pat?"

"I wouldn't look a gift horse in the mouth, Vin. It's a wonder they even figured out we was interested. Ya know how things are out there in the boonies."

"Okay. Okay. Just lemme know when the stuff gets here."

Johnson knew the pressure his friend was under to tie up these blasted serial murders, so he cut Mulcahy some slack for his gruffness. Hell, he thought, even calling them "murders" at that point was a bit of a stretch, to be honest about it. No one really knew anymore—if they ever did—what they were dealing with here. Even the new lead from the Markis case was questionable, at best. The young girl swore she saw some kind of light just before her boyfriend's head snapped. Sort of spark-like, she said. Christ. What the hell were they supposed to make of that? Especially from a hysterical teenager. No wonder the Lieutenant was on edge. "Will do," was all Johnson said as he turned and left.

He resisted the urge to grab a bite for lunch. He felt uptight himself. These cases were getting to everybody. He did some busy work for a few minutes, then walked over to the fax machine and asked the operator if anything had come in for him. Nothing had. He spent the next five minutes cleaning off his desk, then went back to the fax. "Anything yet?" he asked nervously.

"Something's coming in now," was the reply. "Maybe it's yours."

It was. Johnson waited impatiently for the pages to scroll out of the machine, then gathered them up and went to his desk to read Officer Fitzpatrick's report. It provided all the details—names, dates, location, facts about the accident, the eyewitness account, road conditions, the medical examiner's report, everything. It even had a section on the unusual circumstances about the case, such as the black mark on the victim's neck, his smoking hair, the lack of skid marks. Johnson didn't see anything earth-shattering that might be of use in their serial killings, though. Then he noticed a list of personal effects found on the victim. In addition to articles of clothing, there was a wallet with some cash, credit cards, business cards, other typical items. Also, a key case, some loose change, a handkerchief, a matched pen and pencil set, a camera, a cellular phone, and a pocket calendar.

Johnson thought maybe this could be a lead. Or at least an opportunity. He picked up the phone and dialed the Concord police. He hoped Officer Fitzpatrick was still there. He was. "Sorry to bother you again, officer, but I was lookin' over your report and noticed the list of Demming's effects. Wonder if I could get a few details on those."

"No problem. What're you interested in?"

"Did anyone inspect his camera? Was the film exposed?"

"Matter of fact, we did look into that. The camera had a new roll of film, but no pictures had been taken yet. Maybe he was gonna see some foliage or something. No way to know."

"What about the cell phone? Did you run a check on it? You know, recent calls, programmed numbers, that sorta thing."

"Yup. Hold on a sec. Got it here somewhere." Johnson heard the sound of papers being shuffled, then Fitzpatrick saying, "Yeah. Here it is. The last number called was on the twenty-first—Saturday morning, eleven thirty-two, to be exact. It went to another number in Boston. Traced it to a Stephen Blake, on Marlborough Street. I also got similar info going further back. There're about a dozen calls last week—in 'n' out. You want all of it?"

"I think it could be useful," said Johnson. Now maybe they were finally getting somewhere. "But don't give it to me now. Summarize it and fax it over later, okay"

"Sure. By the way, Demming had lots of numbers punched into the phone's memory. One of 'em was Blake. It was his business number though. The call..." Johnson interrupted to ask for Blake's work number. Fitzpatrick gave it to him, then continued. "The call Demming made on Saturday went to Blake's residence." Johnson wrote that one down too. "Anything else, Sergeant?" asked Fitzpatrick.

"Yeah. If you could include those programmed numbers from Demming's phone, and who they belonged to, that'd be great. And one more thing. What was in the pocket calendar? Anything interestin'?" Johnson was poised to write. 'C'mon, gimme somethin' good,' he pleaded.

"Well, I guess that's a matter of opinion," said Fitzpatrick. "We did find lots of names, addresses, scribbled notes, you name it. I guess you could say it was interesting that Blake's name shows up for a lunch on Tuesday of last week. That'd be the seventeenth. Place called Locke-Ober's. On the same day, Demming wrote down the name and address of something called 'Ye Olde Booke Nooke.' It's possible he did that at the lunch. Want it?"

Johnson didn't know what any of this meant, if anything, but at least it sounded promising. Hell, anything sounded promising at that point. "Yeah, let's have it. And wouldja mind makin' copies of the entries for, say, September and October, and send those along, too?"

"Get right on it."

"Thanks again. I'll try not to call any more today, officer."

"Not to worry, Sergeant. All part of the job."

No sooner had the last strains of Officer Fitzpatrick's voice evaporated from the phone line than Johnson was dialing Stephen Blake's business number. Johnson's stomach growled noisily for lunch, but he was on a bit of a roll and reluctant to jeopardize it. He knew his luck was holding when he heard: "Hello. Stephen Blake."

"Good afternoon, Mr. Blake. This is Sergeant Patrick Johnson from the Boston Police Department. Homicide. We're conductin' an investigation and wondered if you'd mind answerin' a few questions."

"Why, uh, no, not at all. What's it all about, Sergeant?"

"We got some information from the Concord Police in connection with the death on Sunday of a John Demming. We understand he was a business acquaintance of yours. That right, sir?"

Stephen wondered why the Boston police were calling about an accident in Concord. Then again, given the bizarre stuff going on lately, why not? "Yeah, sure. I knew John. Found out about it yesterday. We're still kind of shocked over here. We did a lot of business together. He was a great guy. It's a shame he had to die like that."

"Yeah. What I wanted to ask, Mr. Blake, is whether you talked to him at all last week." Johnson had decided to find out what Blake would offer and see if it coincided with what he had just found out from Concord.

"As a matter of fact, I did see John last week. A couple times, actually. We were both at a dinner meeting a week ago yesterday. Then we met for a business lunch the following day. Tuesday, it was."

Stephen was debating whether to stop here or mention the Saturday call. He hesitated only briefly, deciding there was no reason to conceal something the cops might know already, or could easily find out. "Oh, and he tried calling me at home on Saturday. I was out of town for the weekend, but he left a message on my answering machine. Said he'd get back to me Monday—yesterday. But, of course, he never did."

"Can you tell me what he said in the message?"

"Well, he was calling to say he'd just paid a visit to an old bookstore I told him about—at our lunch, actually. I guess he wanted to talk to me about it."

There was a brief silence. Johnson's wheels were spinning. "Is there any reason you can think of offhand why he'd go to a bookstore on a Saturday mornin' and call you about it? Sounds like a pretty standard kinda thing to do. Goin' to a store, I mean."

"I wondered about that myself, Sergeant. I can only tell you I just discovered the place last week myself and found it to be kind of a treasure trove of great old stuff, especially for someone who's interested in that kind of thing. John was like me—an old book hound of sorts, and a collector, too. It's possible he found something he just couldn't wait to tell me about. Then again, he did say something in his message that was a little odd."

"What was that?"

"I told him I thought the owner of the place was a terrific old gentleman. Kindly. Humorous. Generous, too. John apparently came away with a slightly different opinion. I remember he used the word 'strange' when referring to him. But I never got the chance to find out exactly why he said that."

'Yeah, and that's what these cases are, too,' thought Johnson. 'Very strange.' "This bookstore. Where is it exactly?" he asked.

Stephen gave him the name and address of the shop, which Johnson noted coincided with the entry recorded in Demming's pocket calendar for last Tuesday. "Okay, thanks, Mr. Blake. I guess that'll be all for now. If I think of anything else, I'll give you another call."

Wicca Codex

"No problem, Sergeant. Anytime. I'll be glad to help in any way I can." He was ready to hang up, then thought of something else. Maybe he could pick up a little more info. "Oh, Sergeant? Can I ask you a question?"

"What?"

"I guess I'm curious as to why the Boston homicide police are calling me about this. From what I heard, it happened in Concord. And they told me it was an accident."

Johnson didn't particularly want to get into anything more at the moment. Blake had caught on to this apparent oddity. Johnson would've preferred that he didn't. Best to leave it alone, though. He and Vinny would have to sort through all this stuff and hopefully make heads or tails out of it. "That's true, Mr. Blake. Let's just say for now there're some things about the incident that got our attention. We're workin' on a string of cases in Boston. There just might be some connection to the death of your friend."

Stephen decided to test deeper waters. All Johnson could say was "shove it," right? In a more polite way, of course. Stephen plunged in, head first. "Does it have anything to do with the black mark they found on John's neck?"

'This guy is somethin' else,' thought Johnson. He let several seconds of silence slip through the line as he shook his head. "So, you know about that, huh? The guys in Concord tell you that?"

"Yup, after I pressed for some details," said Stephen. He was debating whether to volunteer any of the information that he and Alison Simmons had discussed the night before. He decided, for the moment anyway, to let it ride. "I've been following those broken-neck cases in the papers, so naturally I was dumbfounded when they told me John had a black mark similar to the ones your victims had. I can't imagine what sort of connection there could be."

"Well, that's what we're tryin' to figure out, Mr. Blake," said Johnson, just a mite too impatiently. But he really wanted to share all this with the Lieutenant. Got to get cracking. "Look, thanks again.

Appreciate it. We'll be in touch if need be." He broke the connection.

Johnson gathered up his notes, which were scribbled on whatever scraps of paper he could find within the mess on his desk. It turned out to be a formidable pile. He went to see Mulcahy. "Got a sec, Vin?"

"Yeah, come on in, Pat," said Mulcahy, shuffling through a pile of papers as he sat at his desk. He desperately wanted to break these cases, if for no other reason than the paperwork was killing him. The earlier sourness in his voice and demeanor had been submerged under a thin layer of repentance. "Listen, buddy. Sorry I barked at you. I'm afraid I'm losing it a little on these cases."

"Hey, no apology needed. I know how it is, believe me." Johnson did know how it was. He'd been there himself. "Anyway, I may have a little good news on that score."

Johnson reviewed what he had just learned about the apparent connections between Demming, Blake, and the Beacon Hill bookstore. Mulcahy scratched his head and said, "Maybe I'm missing something, Pat, but this is *good* news?"

"Well, maybe I exaggerated a tad," said Johnson. "But at least we got somethin' new to go on."

"Yeah, I guess. Let's be thankful for little things. What say we go look at some books, Pat?"

"Thought you'd never ask, Vin."

* * *

Mulcahy and Johnson pulled up in front of Ye Olde Booke Nooke. Parking was tight, so they left the unmarked car next to a hydrant. They made sure the "Boston P. D., Official Business" placard was visible on the dash, just in case an overzealous meter maid came by. It was one of the nice little perks you got to enjoy as a member of the force.

"This place looks like it's been here since the Stone Age, Vinnie," said Johnson as they strolled up to the front door.

"You got that right," replied Mulcahy. He opened the door, heard the tinkle of the bell, and slipped inside. Johnson was right on his heels.

They noticed an old man working at one of the bookcases. He appeared to be sorting, or cleaning, or something. Whatever it was, he stopped as soon as they came in and turned to see who had entered. There was no one else in the store.

"Excuse me, sir," said Mulcahy. He and Johnson approached the man and showed their badges. The old guy scrutinized them carefully, as though he were inspecting for dirt or smudges or something. "We're with the Boston Police Department. I'm Lieutenant Mulcahy. This here's Sergeant Johnson." Heads nodded. "Mind if we ask you a couple questions?"

"Not at all, Lieutenant. I am Gustav Ernst." He flashed one of his best smiles. "I own the store. Is something wrong?"

Mulcahy ignored the question and said, "We're investigating an auto accident. A man was killed over the weekend in Concord. We're involved 'cause he worked in Boston and had some connections that need to be followed up on. One of those connections is here."

Johnson wandered around to see what he could see, if anything, while Mulcahy did the talking. The sergeant prided himself on being able to listen to extraneous conversation while snooping around. Sort of like patting the top of your head and your stomach at the same time. It was a knack he picked up somewhere along the line. 'This place looks more like a junk shop than a bookstore,' he said to himself. 'Piles of trash everywhere.' He reached for the top book of a stack he picked out at random, but hesitated. It was as if he were considering the risk of contracting some rare tropical disease through contact with the musty object. Admirably, his sense of duty allowed him to overcome his queasiness. He blew a thin layer of dust off the top edge, then turned it to read the title: "The Anatomy of Neoplatonism," by A. C. Lloyd. 'Sheesh! Now there's a fun book!' He dropped it back onto the pile, then bent low to scan some of the titles in an adjacent group. "Reciprocity and Ritual," by Seaford. "Fifteenth-Century Attitudes," edited by Horrox. "Christendom and Christianity in the Middle Ages," by Bredero. 'Holy shit. Ya mean people actually read this crapola? Gimme a good murder mystery any time.' Johnson had had enough culture assimilation for one day. He shook his head and rejoined Mulcahy, who was continuing his interrogation.

"The Concord police found the name of your store in a little appointment book the victim carried around. He also made a phone call that indicated he was in here on Saturday morning. It would've been before noon sometime. Name was Demming. John Demming. Does that ring any kind of bell, Mr. Ernst?"

Ernst massaged his beard with his thumb and index finger. No sense denying anything, he decided. That could be more dangerous than the truth. "Saturday morning? Why...yes, I think I do remember someone who could be the man. He came in perhaps ten-thirty or eleven. We talked a while, and I remember showing him my special book collection. I keep it in the back of the shop. He was a collector himself. I think his name was Demming, now that I am thinking about it." A slight pause. "Wait, he gave me his business card. I think I may still have it here somewhere."

Ernst went over to the counter and rummaged through a couple of drawers, then pulled out something that looked like a business card. He glanced at it. "Yes, here it is. John Demming." He suddenly looked up at Mulcahy, concern etched on his face. "Oh my, you said he was killed? How awful. What happened?"

Johnson had returned from his little tour. He replied to Ernst's question. "Looks like he lost control of his car and hit a pole. Bashed his head in."

"How terrible," said Ernst, sadly. "I am so sorry for him, and his family, of course, even though I only met the gentleman that one time. He seemed like a nice man." Ernst wasn't sure how far he could, or should, probe to find out how much the Boston police knew—and didn't know. He decided not to press.

"Did you notice anything peculiar about Demming?" asked Mulcahy. "Like, was he out of sorts? Did he complain about anything to you?"

"Why no, Lieutenant, I cannot say that he did. On the contrary. He appeared to be in good spirits, especially since we were talking about something we both loved—old books."

"How long did he stay?" asked Johnson.

"Oh, I would say at least half an hour, perhaps forty-five minutes. But I am afraid I cannot say for sure."

"Close enough," said Mulcahy. "Did he happen to say how he came to find out about your store?"

Ernst flicked Demming's business card back into the drawer. "My recollection is he heard about the shop through a mutual acquaintance, a young man who came in early last week. We struck up a conversation and found we both had the same interest. I showed him some of my more interesting books—the ones out back. Perhaps you would like to see?" Ernst extended a hand toward the curtain.

"Another time, maybe," said Mulcahy.

"Anyway," continued Ernst, "it was late, and he said he had to leave. I invited him to come back when he had more time. He must have told Mr. Demming about me."

"Know the guy's name?" asked Johnson. "The one who came in last week?"

"That would be Stephen Blake, Sergeant. He accepted my invitation and returned on Friday evening. We had a most wonderful time." Ernst's eyes lit up at the recollection of it. "It was nice of him to keep an old man company, was it not? Surely you do not have any thought that Mr. Blake is connected in any way with Mr. Demming's death." Ernst tried to read something in Mulcahy's expression, but there was nothing there. Ditto Johnson.

"At the moment we don't have any suspicions about anything, Mr. Ernst," said Mulcahy. "We're just doing a little investigating to help out the Concord Police. Just trying to trace Demming's movements during the time before his accident. See if anything might've happened that could've contributed to it. That's all."

"I see," said Ernst. "I am sorry I was not able to be of more help, Lieutenant."

"You've been quite helpful, Mr. Ernst. I appreciate it. Thanks for your time, and sorry to have bothered you. We'll contact you again if we need anything else. If you don't mind, that is."

"Not at all," said Ernst, enthusiastically. "Anytime, Lieutenant."

Mulcahy and Johnson left and returned to the car. The orange splash of a traffic citation glared from under the windshield. Johnson ripped it out. "What the fuck is this?" he screamed, scowling at the ticket. "Parking at a hydrant? Fifty bucks! Shit!"

Mulcahy grinned. "Must be a new maid on this beat," he surmised. "Hasn't gotten the word yet. Here, lemme have it." He reached for the ticket. "I'll take care of it. It's not a problem." This seemed to appease Johnson. He stopped huffing and calmed down.

They climbed into the car. As Johnson drove off, he turned to Mulcahy and said, "Blake was right. The old man seems like a helluva nice guy."

"Doesn't he, though?" replied Mulcahy.

Chapter 19

Tuesday, October 24

"It was most unfortunate that Demming had to be eliminated," said Lariakin to Gustav Ernst. Both were sitting in the collection room in the back of Ernst's bookstore, the one in which he kept his valuable books and manuscripts. Lariakin's mood was dark. He pressed his elbows into the arms of the chair and clasped his hands before continuing. "That was not in our plans. And unplanned events such as that tend to cause problems. Such as getting the police involved. Then again, they were already involved. And your description of Demming's demeanor indicated we could not afford the risk of his meddling. Blake is too important to us, and Demming could have jeopardized that. Still, it troubles me."

"Yes," agreed Ernst. "It was too bad. Aside from Blake's procrastination in attending one of our meetings, things were progressing satisfactorily. But I was glad you concurred with my judgment on Demming's potential interference. I can assure you I did not make it lightly. It was also fortunate that he provided a personal object when he was here. As it turned out, his business card was most useful."

Ernst knew these meetings with Lariakin were necessary, but he didn't particularly enjoy them. The man's physical presence was imposing, to be sure. Not only his height, which Ernst guessed to be two or three inches above six feet, but also his bulky physique, gruff voice, and penchant for dark, somber clothing. If asked, Ernst would not have been able to identify how old Lariakin was. He could be sixty as easily as thirty, as far as Ernst knew. There was no telling which was closer to the truth. At times it appeared as though he fluctuated from one end of the age spectrum to the other. There wasn't any one feature that permitted a fix. One could normally triangulate on clues from the face, the hair, the eyes. But Ernst construed that Lariakin wasn't anywhere near normal. Consider his face, for example. It did not lend itself to physiognomic interpretation. At times the flesh seemed to twist around his mouth as he spoke. Even when merely listening, Lariakin's sallow skin appeared to be in motion. Ernst would have sworn that it flowed, if that were possible. And his hair. Now there was a feature. A wild crop of scraggly black outcroppings that went this way and that. Ernst doubted Lariakin ever took a comb to it. For that matter, he doubted if a comb would survive even one pass through that twisted wreckage. Then there were the eyes. Ernst could not begin to ascertain their color. For one thing, they were set so deep in their sockets as to be indecipherable. For another, Ernst's stoop, combined with Lariakin's height, made it difficult to match eye levels. However, when the light was right on certain occasions, the hint of a hue was discernible. Trouble was, it never seemed to be the same. Dark gray mostly, lighter occasionally, sparkly never. Yet there was a voracious energy that emanated from within those crevasses. Ernst hardly ever had the audacity—or the courage—to peer into them and decipher the secrets that lay hidden there. It would certainly have been a painful experience, if possible at all. As for demeanor, Lariakin was endowed with a near-permanent scowl that dampened all proceedings in which he was a participant. For Ernst, that meant private meetings such as this one, as well as the occasional coven affair Lariakin chose to attend. They had never met outside of these types of circumstances. In fact, Ernst didn't even know where Lariakin went when he left the shop. That was okay with Ernst. The less contact, the better, as far as he was concerned.

Ernst would have preferred to undertake the conduct of what had come to be called "The Plan" without Lariakin's involvement at all, but in that he was given no choice. He remembered back to their first meeting years ago, when Lariakin had come to offer Ernst the fulfillment of his wishes. The price? His immortal soul, payable at the conclusion of his natural life on this earth. Lariakin had insisted that he be involved directly in the plan's execution. That had been fine with Ernst. He wished it were otherwise now.

It was evident to Ernst that Lariakin was the representative of Satan. What he did not know, and perhaps did not care to know, was whether he was human, or merely a specter, an avatar. He gave it little thought. It mattered only that he was as real as need be. From his early readings and discussions, Ernst had found that Christ was not the answer for him. Rather, he had come full circle. He identified with Satan more and more as the one who could help him complete his life's journey and give it meaning. And substance. And order. It was a pilgrimage that could lead him away from the incorrect path he had initially—and mistakenly—chosen for himself. He often wondered how he could have been so blind. Ernst was not quite certain how that course correction had come about, or even when it began. Only that it did. By the time Ernst had come to America and settled in Boston—earning a modest living much as he now did, as a bookstore owner, something he had done for many years in Germany—the transformation from a devout follower of the Christian orthodoxy to the nether world of darkness was complete. He quietly sought guidance from others on how best to achieve his destiny, but his on-and-off association with others, including Satanists, left him unsatisfied and incomplete.

Then there was the visit one day from the stranger who called himself Lariakin. There was no "Mister" attached to this appellation, nor was there a second name to accompany it. Just Lariakin. No business cards were offered by the man, nor credentials of any kind, for that matter. There was only the formidable knowledge that the visitor had of Gustav Ernst—his past, his present circumstances, his future desires. There was also the imposing presence, exuding authority. Back then, there was no doubting that the visitor was not an apparition, but reality. His timing in approaching Ernst was impeccable. Lariakin's arrival was like a road map given to a lost traveler; like a lighthouse beacon spied by a desperate captain on a storm-tossed ship.

Lariakin's offer to Ernst was a simple one: a long life, unimpeded by the ravages of earthly diseases, the promise of a major role in righting past wrongs against the Dark Prince, and the conferral of extraordinary powers to accomplish that end. It was also made clear that he need no longer be concerned for material things. But this was not important to him. What was critical for Ernst was the promise of a purpose. At long last, he would feel whole. He would have the power to do something meaningful with his puny life. It convinced him he had finally found what he had been seeking. When Lariakin also said that Ernst would find favor in expanding his modest collection of old books and manuscripts, an avocation he had started years earlier, Ernst eagerly agreed to the terms. Indeed, ecstatic would not be overstating his feeling for his sudden good fortune.

Lariakin had described the work Ernst was to be engaged in, as well as the resources that would be provided to him for its accomplishment. First, however, he was to select a site that would serve as the focal point for the necessary activities that would have to be carried out in meeting their objectives. Ernst was given leeway to do this as he saw fit. He chose to maintain ownership in a bookstore, but one that was unobtrusive, modest in size and scope, and equipped with space for meetings between Ernst and the followers of like mind he was to recruit. Such a shop would also serve him well in displaying his growing collection of rare book treasures—his one passion in life, aside from Satan himself. Ernst found a location on Beacon Hill and modified it to suit his needs, which was as presently constituted. Using previous contacts he had established with Satanists and occultists as a starting point, Ernst recruited a contingent of followers and began working with Lariakin to implement The Plan. Aside from the need to interact with Lariakin, he had no regrets to this point. He was in heaven. Or, perhaps in his case, it would be more accurate to say that he was in hell.

"Yes, I agreed with your instinct about Demming," said Lariakin. "He was a threat. However, your implementation was clumsy. You were fortunate to attain the desired outcome. You were instructed in the limits of the power, yet you did not verify the conditions. As you now know from the result, you must be certain that the objective of the force is within the prescribed proximity. Otherwise, *The Codex* may not be able to accomplish all that it is programmed to do. In this case, there was barely enough distance to cause death, but not in the desired manner."

Ernst breathed a muted sigh of relief. There was to be only a mild scolding. Nothing more. "The lesson has been learned," he said. "It will not happen that way again. I can assure you of that."

"Let us not talk of that any further. We must turn our attention to Blake. Will he be here tonight?"

"He will. I have assured his attendance by means of *The Codex*, as I should have done last week. He will be here, without a doubt."

"Very well. And the plan for expansion and escalation—you are prepared to get Blake involved?"

"Again, yes. I am fairly certain that Blake will not participate voluntarily, but the powers of the manuscript will be used to ensure compliance. The plan to duplicate *The Codex* and disseminate it to other areas will begin tonight. We will also discuss the Grand Demonstration planned for All Hallows Eve, one week hence."

"Excellent. I see that you have been conscientious in your preparations."

Ernst said nothing in reply but was pleased with Lariakin's words. It was not often that Ernst was given any indication of satisfaction with his efforts. Apparently, Lariakin knew enough to build up after tearing down.

Ernst remembered a point he wanted to raise. "I should inform you that I exposed Blake to *The Codex* at our last meeting. To test his character, and also his will. I was surprised that he experienced so minor a reaction to it. Apparently, he felt little of the force. Unlike most others, who experience it immediately, with little doubt as to the effects. Perhaps it was due to the short time he was in contact with the book. Only a few seconds. In any event, do you believe there is reason to be concerned?"

Lariakin absorbed this information with interest. It was unusual, but not unprecedented. "I do not think we need be anxious about that, although you must be aware we are dealing with a particularly strong individual in this case. There are some who are able to resist to a certain extent, but all succumb eventually. It is good that you experimented. Having done so, you should now know the importance of taking appropriate precautions when dealing with him."

This second kudo from Lariakin had Ernst almost giddy with delight, although he did not show it. "Will you attend tonight's meeting?" he asked.

"Yes. We are approaching a critical stage, and I want to ensure that things go smoothly. But you will lead, of course, as usual. I assume you have no objection to my attendance?"

"None whatsoever. I am honored to have you anytime." Ernst made sure to say this so it sounded truthful and sincere, even though it was not. "It is also fitting that you be there now that we are ready to advance to the next phase of our work. It is a particularly exciting time."

"Indeed. I cannot emphasize enough how important this is. All those who for so long have cried out for justice have begun to see that their moment is at hand. We have begun the task successfully. We must continue that success. We must not disappoint them."

"And we will not," said Ernst, emphatically. "Most assuredly, we will not."

"I am pleased to hear you say that," said Lariakin, as he rose from the chair and left the shop.

Chapter 20

Tuesday, October 24

The day turned out to be a long one for Stephen Blake, more so than usual. He had gone through the motions at work but, frankly, hadn't gotten an awful lot done. He couldn't help being sidetracked by the hodgepodge of things that filled his head and diverted his attention. There was Ernst's tantalizing tale about *The Codex*. And Demming's death. His phone discussions with the police in Concord and Boston. Dinner last night with Alison Simmons. Not to mention the anticipation of tonight's meeting—just hours away now—with Ernst and his group. An anticipation that was...what?...part curiosity, with a little excitement thrown in? And perhaps...fear? Well, maybe just a tinge, he would admit. He felt himself going through an overload situation at the moment. He was having a hard time handling it all.

Stephen punched the remote to catch the national news as he wolfed down a TV dinner. 'Thank God for the microwave,' he thought. He had neither the energy nor the inclination to prepare anything else tonight. He watched images flash on the screen and heard accompanying voices that spoke of politics and crime and other things, but he wasn't absorbing any of it. 'Maybe Alison was right. Maybe I should skip the meeting. Maybe I should forget about Ernst, and *The Codex*, and everything else. Maybe...'

"No way," he found himself saying aloud. "I'm going."

He finished eating, did a little reading, and watched some more television until it was time to go to the bookstore. He was nervous, fidgety. At about nine o'clock, he left the apartment and walked slowly toward Beacon Hill, arriving at the shop about nine fifteen.

Ernst was in the back, as usual, but came right out when he heard the buzzer indicating that someone had come into the shop. He was glad he had gotten around to fixing the faulty mechanism and that it was operating as it should. Security could depend on it.

"Welcome, Stephen. I am glad you could come," said Ernst, extending a hand in Stephen's direction. "No medical emergencies tonight, I trust."

Stephen laughed while accepting Ernst's handshake, then replied, "I certainly hope not. At least I've decided to stay away from the wine bottle tonight. I think that's what did me in last time. Anyway, I've been looking forward to coming all day. I'm getting more and more curious to find out what you guys do at these meetings." He took off his coat and laid it across the counter, next to the cash register. He was still a bit chilly from the walk, so he kept his sweater on, a dark blue V-neck with a box pattern. It covered a light blue button-down shirt, no tie. The slacks were gray. He saw that Ernst was in his usual baggy pants and flannel shirt. Stephen hoped he wasn't overdressed, but he didn't feel quite right if he dressed down too far. He preferred the casual, sporty look, good for most any occasion.

"I just know you will find it interesting," said Ernst. "But that is for later. In the meantime, how would you like to pass the time? You could look through my regular stock." He slapped a hand on the nearest pile of books. "You have not really had a chance to do that except for a few brief moments during your first visit. Or you could explore more of my collection. Or we could talk. What is your preference, my friend?"

Stephen knew what he wanted to do. He'd been looking forward to it since the last visit. "Actually, I think I'd like to do some more browsing out back, if I could. I saw a few things last time I wanted to check out, but then we got involved with *The Codex*. Is that okay?"

"Certainly. Come." Ernst waved Stephen toward the curtain. "I will get you settled while I attend to a few duties in preparation for the meeting. Afterwards, perhaps we can talk. I have one or two items I would like to discuss with you before the others arrive."

Stephen wondered what Ernst might have on his mind, but it could wait until later, he thought. He and Ernst went to the back of the shop, where Stephen made himself comfortable in the collection room while Ernst busied himself elsewhere. Stephen whiled away the time, examining many of the superior items in the glass-enclosed bookcases.

He was aghast after glancing at his watch and finding almost an hour and a half had ticked by. Ernst had left Stephen alone the entire time, except to stick his head in once or twice to ask if Stephen wanted anything. Stephen declined each time. Just after eleven, Ernst came in and said he hated to interrupt Stephen's enjoyment, but there was something important that required discussion. He asked if Stephen would mind relocating to *The Codex* room. When they had done so, Ernst had Stephen sit in one of the two armchairs while he retrieved *The Codex* from the safe. He set it on the table next to Stephen, then sat in the other chair. Stephen could see he was in a jovial mood.

"Let me say again," said Ernst as he smiled at Stephen, "how happy I am that you came tonight. Then again, I knew you would."

"Well, I could tell how disappointed you were last time, even though you didn't really show it. And anyway, I *am* curious about your meetings. Have been ever since I first saw those people going into the store so late that first night." Now that the moment was almost at hand, Stephen knew he was about to find out the answer to this little puzzle. It made his heart race a little faster.

"Yes, I am sure you were. And tonight, we will satisfy your curiosity." Ernst paused, partly for effect, partly to decide how best to proceed. He continued. "Stephen, when we first met that night, I felt as though I had made a new friend. Sincerely. We have an affinity for the same things—old books and manuscripts. It seemed that we hit it off—is that how you say it?—right away. Then, when you mentioned you were in the publishing business, I knew our friendship was meant to be." Ernst looked deep into Stephen's eyes. "Do you believe in destiny, Stephen?"

"Destiny? To tell you the truth, I've never given it much thought. I honestly don't know whether I do or not."

"I do," said Ernst. "I believe in it with all my heart, Stephen. When you arrived that day, then told me who you were, I knew immediately you were sent to help me with my work. I knew..."

"What work are you talking about, Gustav? I already..."

"All in due time, Stephen. All in due time. Please hear me out, first." Stephen sat back reluctantly, wondering what his friend was getting at. Ernst gathered his thoughts again before going on. "I knew that your being in publishing was a sign to me that my...let me call him a mentor, for the time being...that my mentor had arranged for your arrival in time for the next phase of the plan to be implemented. I will admit to being a trifle overanxious to have you become part of our team, so I may have seemed somewhat demanding in having you get started. Now..."

"Wait a second," said Stephen, leaning forward in his chair and raising the pitch of his voice a degree or two. This was starting to sound a little peculiar. "What plan? What team? Get started with what? What's going on?"

"Please, Stephen," said Ernst, patiently. "As I said, you will be informed of all that you need to know soon. For the moment, it is extremely important that you listen. I promise that things will become clear shortly."

Stephen stared at Ernst and saw something in his face that hadn't been there before—or at least he hadn't noticed. Something unsettling. Stephen leaned back once again, slowly, his hands gripping the fronts of the chair's armrests. He wanted answers—answers to lots of hard, troubling questions—but said nothing. He waited for Ernst to continue.

"Thank you, Stephen," said Ernst. He knew it was important to remain calm. An excessive display of emotion would be counterproductive. He preferred to convince with logic, if possible. "My intent was for you to be groomed slowly to our cause, but now there is no time. We must proceed into the next phases of the plan without delay. And you are to be given a prominent role in that regard." Ernst saw that Stephen was becoming more agitated and was ready to interrupt again. Ernst held up a hand to forestall it, but said nothing.

Stephen remained silent, but his thoughts flashed back to the night before, to Alison's pleas to forego this meeting. Now he wished he had heeded her instincts. He tugged at his shirt collar. It was beginning to feel a little warm in the confines of the tiny room. He thought about removing his sweater, but didn't.

"Normally," continued Ernst, "I would prefer—as would my mentor—that all participants in our endeavor come to it of their own free will. It is much more effective that way, and I must say we have had extraordinary success so far. In fact, in many ways the success of the plan is contingent on voluntary participation. Our leader insists on it. At least up to a point. All of the meeting members have been willingly recruited, and they perform their duties in the same way." This little white lie was required, thought Ernst, to keep things moving along smoothly. No need for complications. "And, of course, I myself am honored to have been selected to lead this effort. I can think of no better way to spend my time on this earth. In your case, however, we have not been able to entice you to join us up to now, so we have had to resort to a different approach. A less desirable one, but necessary nonetheless. When I said earlier that I knew you would come tonight, I was not saying so only from the hope of it, but rather from the absolute knowledge of it. You see, Stephen, we had to be certain you would be here. There could be no doubt. You were, in fact, compelled to come. Compelled by the power of *The Codex* that sits before you."

Stephen had heard enough. He leaped from the chair and was about to bolt for the door, but Ernst merely put his hands on *The Codex* and said calmly, "Come back, my friend, and sit. Listen to the rest of my story."

Stephen could do nothing but comply. He wanted desperately to leave the room, leave the bookstore, but found he was unable to do so. His feet refused to obey the commands to proceed forward. His mind willed it to happen, but the body was being recalcitrant. There was a power failure between the production of the required electrical signals in his brain and their execution into movement down below. A short circuit of some kind. He tried once more, with the same result. That is, there was no result. It was as though his shoes had been bolted to the floor. A fear gripped him such as he had not felt before. He had never experienced such complete and utter failure as this. The lack of control was debilitating. Devastating. He might as well be a robot. He tried movement in the opposite direction and found that he could compel his limbs to obey those directives. He turned and took his place in the chair once again. Or rather, he collapsed into it, crushed by the knowledge that he had been victimized by someone—or something—supremely more powerful than he. He had no idea what he had gotten himself into. Only that it was highly unlikely to be pleasant. His motor skills may have deserted him, but not his anger. Or his courage. "Don't call me your friend anymore. I'm not your friend."

"As you wish, Stephen. I would have preferred that we could continue to be so, but it is not necessary." Ernst shifted positions in his chair but never took his gaze from Stephen. "As I was saying, *The Codex* has assured your attendance tonight, as it can assure your compliance with our wishes for your participation in certain upcoming tasks. You may come to appreciate our efforts in time, but for now, that is secondary. We need your immediate involvement."

Stephen reflected back on what Alison had said the night before about the coincidental timing between Ernst's meetings and the last two murders. He was appalled that she might have been correct. He was gravely concerned—and frightened. "Involvement in what?" he asked, spewing out the words now, outraged at the deception that had duped him. "Are you behind those killings I've been reading about in the papers? I'll bet you had something to do with John Demming's death, too." He raged on, not bothering to wait for answers he already knew. "If you think I'm gonna become part of..."

"Stephen, Stephen," said Ernst, much like a father rebuking an unruly child. "You must keep an open mind. I know that in time you will come to understand what we are doing. And accept it. I will in due course instruct you in the principles of our project. But for now, it is sufficient for you to know that Phase One of the plan requires that we use the power of *The Codex* to undertake acts of cleansing to expiate the accursed wrongs of the past. We cannot undo them, unfortunately, but we can exact a measure of...payment. However, these crimes were so wicked, so widespread, so...heinous, that continuing along the present course is not sufficient." Ernst cleared his throat, pushed up his miniature glasses. "It has been a good start, but it is now time to escalate the cleansing process. There are several ways to accomplish that. One of them—and this is where your involvement is required—is to expand geographically. We must widen the program so that other devotees of our pursuit of justice have the means to assist us. We must train others to become soldiers in this battle."

Stephen couldn't believe what he was hearing. "And what do you want from me? Print up training manuals for your troops?"

"Well, I had not thought of that, but it is not a bad idea. Thank you for sharing that with me. You see, you are being helpful already." Ernst couldn't help broadening his smile, infuriating Stephen all the more. "But your primary effort will be much more significant. The main reason we need your help, Stephen, is to duplicate *The Codex*."

Stephen could do nothing but sit and stare at Ernst—incredulously. He asked himself how he could have allowed himself to be trapped. More importantly, how was he going to get out of it? Nothing came to mind. In fact, he was having a hard time focusing his thoughts on anything. He felt as though he was spinning around in a whirlpool or being sucked into a black hole. He was speechless. After a few moments, he recovered sufficiently to exclaim, "You must be crazy! You can't possibly think I'm gonna help you spread your murdering...program, or whatever you call it. What makes you think I'd help you, you bastard?"

"Please try to remain civil, Stephen," said Ernst, frowning slightly. "You should know the answer to that. It is sitting there next to you. Just as you had no choice but to come tonight, you will have no choice but to do what needs to be done. The very thing to be duplicated is what will make you do it. There is a certain elegance to that, you must admit. *The Codex* will replicate itself through you. You might say you will be the catalyst that will clone the force of the manuscript."

Stephen's mind was struggling to identify the strands of logic in what he was hearing. If he could only focus on them, give them substance, use them to his advantage, maybe he could think his way out of this horror. But first he would have to control his anger, his outrage. They were his enemies, as much as Ernst and his hellish book. He took a deep breath, then nodded at *The Codex* lying menacingly within an arm's length. "Why not just use this one to control everything, no matter where? What's wrong with that?"

"A good question," said Ernst. "But one with a simple answer. *The Codex* is extremely powerful, yes, but its force is effective only within certain limits. As those limits are approached, its power is weakened considerably, until it disappears entirely at some point."

Stephen was startled that Ernst would tell him a thing like that. A limitation of the book's power? Because of distance? Remarkable. He had learned something useful and must store it away. But despite the short-term satisfaction of finding out this potentially crucial nugget of information, he knew it was a manifestation of something much more sinister—Ernst's supreme confidence. Ernst would tell all, if necessary, to satisfy Stephen's curiosity simply because Stephen would never be able to do anything about it. That was the horrible, inescapable truth. Still, knowledge is power, they say, so why not acquire as much of it as possible? Besides, if he was to die resisting this monster, he might as well die a little smarter.

"Let's say for the sake of argument you somehow get more copies of this Codex. They'll still only be books, when you come right down to it. If there really is some kind of force or power inherent in the original, how does it get transferred to the clones?"

Ernst laughed. "Why, that is the easiest part of all. I am surprised you have not guessed it. Think, Stephen. Are you still in the dark? I will give you a hint. It has to do with my mentor."

Wicca Codex

"Your mentor? What the hell are you talking about?"

"I can see that you are not yourself tonight. You are still overwhelmed by all that you have learned. So, I will help you a little. Do you believe in God, Stephen?"

"Do I what? What does that have to do with anything?"

Ernst tapped the table holding *The Codex* impatiently. "Do you believe in God?" he repeated. "Answer the question, please."

"All right. Yes. I do believe in a Supreme Being. Call Him God if you like. So?"

"So, what if I were to say that I also believe, not in God, as I once did, but in His antithesis?"

Stephen was processing information as fast as he could, but this last item acted to slow everything down as though it were frozen in liquid oxygen. A windowpane of thought that would shatter into countless shards if struck. Ernst's last words were like a hammer-blow on Stephen's mind. The electrical impulses that constitute the thought process were still short-circuiting. He didn't know how, but they reconstituted themselves after a while. "Oh, Christ," he bellowed. "You're telling me your mentor is the devil? You worship Satan?"

Ernst clapped his hands with delight. "Good, Stephen. Very good. But more than mere worship. Much more. We have an agreement, an understanding between us. He has let me be his instrument, his tool. I am his. There can be no higher calling. To be in this position is to know the meaning of true joy. The honor is supreme. And you will be part of it. You do not see it now, but you will. Together we can accomplish great things, Stephen."

'This is getting more and more bizarre,' thought Stephen. 'Stay focused. Keep your wits. It may be the only way out. If there is a way. "And how do you communicate with the devil? How does he tell you what to do? Do you get that through *The Codex* too?"

"No, Stephen. That is done through an intermediary who came to me years ago and offered me this extraordinary chance. In fact, you will see him at the meeting. His name is Lariakin."

"That's just great. How do you expect me to copy *The Codex*?"

"Not copy, Stephen. Duplicate. That is for you to determine. You are in the publishing business, so you undoubtedly will know how best to accomplish the task. But there are certain criteria that must be met. For one, it should be obvious to you that *The Codex* is not to leave these premises. You will have to find equipment and materials that can be brought here. Everything is to be accomplished within the bookstore. Another stipulation, which should also be unnecessary to explain, is that no one on the outside is to know the true nature of what you are doing. Only you must be involved in the process, aside from any assistance you may need from me or others in the group. Are those conditions clear?"

"Quite clear. But I don't know why you're even telling me. I'm sure you'd use your friend there..."—he nodded toward *The Codex*—"...to make certain I didn't break any rules."

"Quite so," said Ernst. "But there will be...temptations. I wanted to make sure you knew to resist them. That is very important, Stephen."

"Right. But there's something else I don't get. Why don't you just use a simple copy machine to do the job? Why do you need me?"

Ernst was impressed with Stephen's questions. The young man was clearly upset yet was able to regain his faculties and cut to the heart of what was important. Ernst wanted his clear-thinking mind on their side. He had to be convinced to come. That would be much better than the alternative approach. "A reasonable question, which I will try to answer. You may consider this a fine point, but each Codex must never be thought of as a mere copy of the original. You may have noticed I did not use the word 'copy' to describe the process. It must be a duplication of the original—a regeneration, if you will—right down to its very essence. When complete, each new Codex must be indistinguishable from the first." Ernst laid his hand gently on the manuscript. "Only then will it be worthy of receiving the power of its parent. From the All-powerful One."

"But...that's an impossible task. I can't do it. You don't realize all the skills involved. There're special inks, and...and preparing the parchment leaves, and sewing them up. And laying out imprints for all the symbols. We're not dealing with a standard alphabet here." Stephen's mind raced from one Sisyphean hurdle to the next. "And then there's the binding. And the equipment. How do you expect me to know all there is to know about doing this? It just can't be done. It's as simple as that."

Ernst would not have tolerated such stubbornness and insubordination from a member of the coven. But since Stephen was not in that position—not yet at least—and had been rather abruptly thrust into this situation, he was given much leeway. Besides, Ernst genuinely liked Stephen and wanted to give him every opportunity to join the movement voluntarily, peacefully. "I do not accept that, Stephen. And I am disappointed in your saying it. If there are skills you do not possess, then you must learn. And teach us. If necessary, you can arrange help from outside sources, as long as no one knows what the ultimate goal is. And as long as no one is brought here."

"Look," said Stephen. "Even if I could dredge up all the labor and equipment and knowledge, doing even one new manuscript will take time, and money. This isn't a cheap or easy thing you're talking about. And you certainly won't be able to hide the equipment involved."

"You need not concern yourself with those sorts of things, Stephen. You must only worry about accomplishing the task itself. Funds will be made available to you as required. The time element is of some concern, but I am confident that as you—and we—learn the process, each subsequent document will be produced in a shorter time interval than its predecessor. As for hiding the equipment, there is no need. If anyone inquires, I am printing advertisements, or a newsletter for my club. Or I need it for my book-collecting avocation. That will not be a problem."

"Well," said Stephen, "one thing that *will* be a problem for me is the time involved. Just when am I supposed to do all this? It's not exactly a spare-time thing, you know. This is going to take a major time commitment."

"Yes, it may very well," agreed Ernst. "For the moment, we are hopeful you will be able to do what has to be done without affecting your own work. Your continued involvement with your publishing firm will be useful to us. Also, we would prefer that you lead as close to a normal life as possible, so as not to arouse suspicions. However, if you are not able to do what is required in a timely way, other arrangements will have to be made. This task must be given absolute priority."

"You mean quit my job? You *are* crazy, aren't you, Ernst?"

"You will come to understand that I am not, Stephen."

Stephen could only sigh at the situation he found himself in. "When does all this end? And what becomes of me when it does?"

"Why, there is no end, Stephen. I thought that was clear. And as for you, it is still my hope that as you learn more about us, you will come to understand our mission and the justification for it. If you do, then you will be allowed to assist us in the higher phases of our work. I sincerely hope for that. But, if you do not, you will be compelled through the mysteries of *The Codex* to continue only with the production process. So long as you remain useful, you will participate. If your usefulness ends, for whatever reason, well...let us not even think about that possibility." For the first time since the conversation began, Ernst's eyes left Stephen's. They came to rest briefly on *The Codex*, then found their mark once again. "Neither of us wishes for that to happen. So, you see, Stephen, you have it in your own hands which course is to be followed. There are no other options."

So, thought, Stephen, it's finally been spelled out. Now it was horrifyingly clear. He wasn't sure what his next move should be. He was desperately trying to think how he might extricate himself from this bizarre situation, only he wasn't coming up with anything too promising. It appeared to him that he was at the endgame of a chess match, one in which he had just been checkmated. The only move he had left was to congratulate the winner. He knew this but couldn't bring himself to do it. Not without one last try. "You know, of course, that I'll never agree voluntarily to do what you want. You don't really think I'd go along with being an accessory to your crimes, do you, you madman? You'll have to force me to do anything remotely like what you just described. And what's to prevent me right now from getting up out of this chair and overpowering you?"

"I think you know the answer to that already, Stephen. Just as I took the precaution of guaranteeing your attendance tonight, I also took the liberty of preventing any...let us say unfriendly...behavior on your part. Precautions have been taken to avoid any such unpleasantries. You know the forces contained in *The Codex* from the little demonstration you experienced just a short time ago. You know I am telling you the truth. It is simply not possible for you to leave here as if nothing has happened. Things will never be the same for you, Stephen. It is too late for that. You will either assist us willingly, or under compulsion. It matters little, in the end."

"Except to me. You know that I've got to try to resist you."

"As you wish," said Ernst. It was time to move forward. Ernst had made his case, now Blake must make his choice. The time for discussion was over. He picked up *The Codex* and placed it on his lap. "I must alert you that after you leave here tonight you will come under pressure from outside influences. They will try to deter you from the course that will be set for you momentarily. You must resist those influences. With all of your being, you must resist them. Do you understand, Stephen?"

Stephen knew at this point it was futile to resist. Ernst had asked him to make a choice, but in reality, he had none. The only thing he could hope for was that this nightmare would end and that he would awaken and be in his bed and that the sun would be shining and that he would go to work and that he would see Alison again and...

"I said, 'Do you understand, Stephen?'"

The sound of Ernst's voice brought Stephen out of his momentary trance. He stared at the floor and said meekly, "I understand." Then the sparkle came back into Stephen's eyes for a moment. He raised his head to look directly at Ernst and said, "Just tell me one more thing. What is this supposed injustice you're trying to right? And how do you decide who dies in the process?"

Ernst looked at his watch, which read eleven forty-one. He said, "Those things you will find out soon enough. And when you do, I trust you will come to see the need for our actions and help us with them from the depths of your heart. For now, there is no time to instruct you. You must accept it."

Before Stephen could say anything else, Ernst put his hands on *The Codex* and willed its forces to do their work on the man who sat opposite him. The man who was now gripping both arms of the chair in which he sat tighter than anything he had ever held before. The man whose eyes were bulging from their sockets with the energy he was expending in a vain attempt to counter the powerful elements at work on him. The man whose mind was being reprogrammed at that moment to undertake the tasks required to assist Ernst and Lariakin implement The Plan. The man who slumped back in his chair after a few moments, devoid of his spirit, his enthusiasm, his free will.

Ernst heard the doorbell ring. He glanced again at his watch. Eleven forty-five. "Right on time," he said. Ernst lifted *The Codex* from his lap and placed it on the table. He looked at Stephen and smiled. "Come, Stephen," said Ernst as he rose from the chair, "I would like you to meet my friends."

Chapter 21

Wednesday, October 25

The first thing Alison Simmons wanted to do when she got to work was pick up the phone and call Stephen Blake. She knew the deal was for him to call her, but that was a detail. She had been thinking about him since their dinner two nights ago and, although not quite ready to admit the reason, she was a nervous wreck all day Tuesday. The thought of him going to last night's meeting with Ernst and his buddies troubled her. She hadn't gotten much sleep and was tired this morning, her usual bubbly self nowhere in evidence.

Alison resisted the urge to call right away. For one thing, she wasn't at all sure Stephen was in yet. It was still early. For another, she didn't want to appear overly anxious. One must keep up appearances, after all. Then again, she knew there wasn't going to be much in the way of real work done until she got the scoop on last night. Even so, she forced herself to plunge into an assignment Burgholz had given her the day before. Although still officially on the broken-neck murders, things had slowed down considerably since the initial flurry of activity last week. So much so that she was now being given additional things to do. This kept her occupied for five minutes. Maybe six.

"Oh, what the hell," she muttered under her breath. She just couldn't stand it any longer. She grabbed the phone and dialed Stephen's personal work number—the one he had given her on Monday night. Alison listened as the phone rang once, twice, three times. No answer. The call got bumped to a secretary, who informed her that Mr. Blake had called in sick and wouldn't be in the office today. Perhaps tomorrow. Was there any message? "No. No message," she said. Then she decided to try getting his home phone number. "Wait, it's kind of important and I really need to..." But the line was already dead.

Alison remembered Stephen telling her he lived in Back Bay—on Marlborough Street, she thought. She confirmed that in her notebook, then pulled out the Boston white pages and looked up "Blake." There appeared to be about a hundred entries, but there was only one Stephen Blake, and he had a Marlborough Street address. It had to be him. She called the number, and on the third ring heard a guttural, "Hello?" It sounded like his voice, she thought, only a bit deeper than she remembered.

"Good morning, Stephen" she said merrily. "It's Alison Simmons, from The Herald. I called your office, and they told me you were home sick, so I got your number from the phone book. How're you doing?"

"Good. What's on your mind Miss Simmons?"

There was a hard edge to the voice she was listening to at the other end of the line. Something that wasn't there on Monday night. But it was early in the morning, and he wasn't well either, so she didn't think anything of it. "So, it's back to Miss Simmons already, huh?" she said in a playfully mocking tone. "I thought we had gotten past that point at dinner on Monday. If I remember right, you were the one who insisted on Stephen and Alison. Remember?"

"Alison. Miss Simmons. Whatever. Listen, I'm kinda busy here. Working at home, ya know? Is there anything in particular you wanted to talk about? If not, I'd just as soon get back to work."

Alison didn't know how to react. This wasn't anything like the Stephen Blake she got to know—and like—on Monday. Maybe he was pulling her leg. That must be it, she thought. He knows I was worried about him going to the stupid meeting last night, and he's playing on that. "Okay, Stephen. Cut the baloney. You've managed to get me all in a tizzy, so you can quit clowning around now, buster. I..."

"I don't know what you're talking about, lady. Look, I really can't waste all morning shooting the goddam breeze with you."

Alison was concerned now. She was prepared for a little fooling around, but this had gotten to a point way beyond fun and games.

"Okay, Stephen," she said, a worried cast glazing her face. "Have it your way. I was really just calling to find out how last night's meeting with Ernst went. You did go, didn't you?"

"Yeah, I went. But I don't wanna talk about it. Look, I've gotta go now."

"Wait, Stephen. Don't hang up," she pleaded. There had to be a reason for this, and she wanted desperately to find it. But it wasn't going to come over the phone, she thought. "I don't know what's going on, but I think it'd be a good idea if we could talk about it. Can I come over? I'll bring some sandwiches."

"No," said Stephen quickly, "don't do that. I'm not really feeling that great. And besides, I'm busy, like I said. In fact, I'll be tied up for the rest of the week. And anyway, I don't see that there's anything to talk about. I have nothing to say to the papers."

"Hey, I didn't mean for it to be an interview," said Alison, trying to remain calm but finding it harder and harder to do so. "It would just be between friends. I was concerned. I *am* concerned. Especially now. How about..."

"Forget it, will ya?" Stephen's voice was becoming louder, more agitated. "Didn't you hear me? I don't have anything to say. If I change my mind, I'll give you a call. Okay? So long."

"Stephen? Wait! Stephen!" Alison listened for another moment or two but heard only the emptiness of a broken phone connection. She sat there thinking, holding the receiver in her hand for a long time before replacing it in its cradle. She bounded from her desk and rushed toward Jay Burgholz's office. The other reporters in the newsroom wondered what was happening. She ignored the glances and questions thrust her way and went in through the open door of Burgholz's office without the usual knock on the jamb. "Jay, got a minute?" she blurted, a bit out of breath. "Something's come up and I need your ear right away."

Burgholz was buried in paperwork and grudgingly lifted his head after a moment to meet Alison's eyes. He saw that her normal good-natured manner was AWOL, so he dispensed with the usual joshing around. "Sure, Ali. Sit. What's up?"

Alison walked up to one of the chairs in front of Burgholz's desk, but didn't sit. Instead, she put both hands on the top rail and leaned forward. "Remember yesterday I told you about my dinner meeting with Stephen Blake? He's the one..."

"Yeah, I remember," said Burgholz, somewhat impatiently. "What about 'im?"

"Strangest thing. I just got off the phone with him. I called to find out how his meeting went with that bookstore owner. Ernst, his name is. Anyway, he gives me the royal brush off. And not in a nice way, either. He was really gruff, not at all like he was on Monday. He was home sick, but I don't think it had anything to do with that. I'm worried, Jay. There's something wrong here."

Burgholz couldn't believe Alison was banging on him because of a broken romance. He didn't think she would do that. "S'matter, Ali? You never been shafted by a guy you liked? That's probably what this is all about. You had one dinner and got your hopes up. Maybe he did too. Now he's thinking he doesn't want to get involved with a reporter. Even though he made first contact. He probably just got scared off."

Alison couldn't stand still. She started walking up and down in front of Burgholz's desk, alternating stares between him and the floor. "I think you're wrong about that, Jay. Stephen wasn't anything like what I just heard. Even if he wasn't interested in...well, developing a relationship, I can't picture him acting like he did just now. Sick or not. Something happened at that meeting last night. He admitted to going, but didn't want to say anything about it. Maybe you're right about him getting scared off, but not by me. By someone or something else. He didn't want to meet to talk about it at lunch either or get together anytime soon. Something's not right, Jay."

Burgholz hadn't seen Alison this worked up emotionally since she had been at the paper. He wanted to help, but didn't know how. "Well, I don't know what you can do if he doesn't want to talk to you. You can't force him to, you know."

Alison's anxiety built to a point where she went to the chair she'd been holding onto earlier and actually sat down. She was so absorbed in the situation she didn't notice the discomfort of it. She leaned slightly forward, nervously playing with her hands. "I'm not only concerned professionally, Jay. I'm worried because Stephen is...or at least was...a real nice guy two days ago. Now he's not. I'd like to know why. And there just may be some connection between this and what we've been trying to get to the bottom of for the last week and a half. Longer, if you count when all this started over two months ago. I'd like to do more research, Jay. I think it'll lead somewhere. We've hit a wall lately and this might just loosen things up a bit. What do you think?"

Burgholz said nothing for a moment. He pushed his chair back from the desk, crossed one leg over the other, cupped both hands over the knee. Alison could tell he was pondering how best to deal with the situation. He looked toward the patches of blue sky visible through the window. "I don't like it much, Ali. For one thing, you still owe me a piece on yesterday's assignment. For another, I'm starting to wonder whether it's a good idea for you to be poking around the kinds of characters you've been telling me about. From what I can see, it may be a mite dangerous. No sense taking chances."

Alison inched closer to the desk. Her elbows were leaning on it. "That's rot, Jay, and you know it. Since when do we avoid taking chances to get a story? Things just don't pop onto the page, you know. You've got to go beat the bushes. You know that as well as me. As for that damned article you want me to do, I promise I'll have it finished today. I'll bust my brains out getting it done. Just don't pull me off those murders, Jay. I've...we've got too much invested to quit now, just when things are getting interesting."

Burgholz got out of his chair and walked to the window. He kept his back to Alison. She was passionate, if nothing else, he thought. And passion often begets inspired action, if not an iron-clad guarantee of success. "Okay, okay. You convinced me. Listen. Do the piece I need, then go do your thing. I agree it's gotten a little warmer, so it may be worth another shot." He turned toward Alison and sat on the edge of the windowsill. "Just...you know...be careful. There're ways of finding things out without getting your head chopped off."

Alison popped up out of the chair like a jack-in-the-box, as if she suddenly realized where she was. "You bet, Mr. B. Thanks." She had parlayed her phone call to Stephen into a continued opportunity to do follow-up on the serial murders. Not wanting to jeopardize it, she whizzed out of Burgholz's office without another word before he had a chance to change his mind. No sense in tempting fate.

Alison spent the rest of the morning and the better part of the afternoon researching and writing the article Burgholz wanted for tomorrow morning's edition. It had to do with some political shenanigans about trying to get a world-class convention center built in Boston. They'll never do it, she thought. Too many politicians. Too many egos. But that wasn't for her to worry about. When the article was done and revised to her editor's satisfaction, she picked up her notebook, walked out to the parking lot, got in her car and drove home through the late afternoon traffic. It was only a little after four o'clock and she couldn't wait to get back into the murder cases. But she didn't want to have to deal with any distractions at the office. She needed to concentrate all her energies on the task. Her starting point would be the information she learned at the dinner meeting with Stephen Blake.

As soon as Alison got home, she grabbed a soda out of the refrigerator and fired up the computer. As it was booting, she opened the notebook and started reading some of the jottings from Monday night to refresh her memory. The thing that struck her most was Stephen Blake's description of the old manuscript that Ernst had taken out of the safe. The one he called The Wicca Codex. Despite Stephen's plea for keeping it off the record, Alison had reconstructed his story about it after she got home that night. In deference to Stephen, she intended to honor her commitment to keep it confidential, but considered it an item of extraordinary importance. One certainly worthy of writing down for future reference.

Wicca Codex

When the computer was ready, Alison accessed the Internet and did a search for "Wicca." After a few moments, dozens of references popped onto the screen. She punched up each one in turn, scanning quickly in some cases, reading whole sections in others, making notes as she went along. She was amazed to find so much information on something she had never heard of before. When done with each item, she printed it out, wanting a hard-copy record of everything she came across that might be useful. She went back to several of the references and clicked on various hypertext link buttons to see where they might lead. In many instances, they were dead ends. In others, she found herself going down familiar territory, places she had explored in her research just last week on the supernatural. But she also came across brand new connections that were startlingly interesting. She scanned them all, recording certain facts in her notebook, and printed out what she needed for more-detailed scrutiny later.

When she satisfied herself that there were no additional Internet offerings of relevance, she exited the 'Net and went through her CD-ROM collection to explore the electronic dictionaries and encyclopedias. Some of it was the same or similar to what she had found on the Web, but there was enough new material to make the supplementary search worthwhile. She went through the same note-taking and printing procedure for that information.

When Alison finally shut down the computer, she was surprised to find that several hours had passed. It was almost nine o'clock, which probably accounted for the hunger pangs in her stomach. She had been so absorbed in her meanderings that the thought of dinner never occurred to her. It did now. She was famished. She rummaged through the freezer and found a pepperoni and sausage pizza. She checked the fridge and came across the remains of a noodle casserole. That was pretty much it, so she opted for the pizza. She popped it in the microwave, got another soda, and waited for the ready bell. When it was done, she sliced up the pizza and took her meal, notes, and printouts over to the sofa. She kicked off her shoes and made herself as comfortable as she could, then devoured the pizza and the printouts with equal gusto.

Alison learned that "wicca" derived from Old English. It was the masculine form of the word, defined as "wizard." She saw in her notes this was the same meaning given to Stephen by Ernst. She also found that the feminine form—wicce—meant "witch." Also, the German word "wicken" means "to bewitch." Interesting, she thought. Ernst was German, right? So what?

Alison reread another article she had scanned earlier under the alt.religion.wicca newsgroup. She usually didn't dabble in newsgroups herself, but knew they were essentially collections of people with a common interest in something. There were thousands of groups on every conceivable topic. Participants posted information of relevance, asked and answered questions, and held on-line discussions with each other. In this case, the group's postings indicated that Wicca was very much alive as a bona fide religion, one included in the neo-paganism category. It might not have the same numbers of practitioners as Catholicism, Judaism, Protestantism, or some of the other big "isms," but it seemed to have a rather well-established structure with devotees in many areas of the country, even abroad. They claimed about 200,000 adherents in North America, with a particularly robust and open group in eastern Massachusetts. Alison underlined the last fact and put a big checkmark next to it in the margin.

Then there were the potential ties between the Wiccan religion and Satanism. Alison read that Wiccans professed not to be Satanists, but there could be some connection, she thought. Where there was witchcraft, wasn't there Satanism? One was rooted in the other, she believed. Alison noted that some Wiccans refer to themselves as witches, cast spells, and practice magic—or magick, as they spell it, to distinguish it from cheap parlor tricks. Most also have something called a "Book of Shadows." That sounded kind of menacing. They follow a cyclical calendar and take part in sabbats marking seasonal changes, as well as esbats denoting phases of the moon. Some also meet in groups called covens, another ominous association with the darker side, in many people's minds.

On the other hand, she read that most who took part in the various rites and rituals looked on themselves as healers and admirers of the natural world rather than evildoers. There was a tolerance for the values and opinions and beliefs of others. In fact, their ethic was generally modeled after something called the Wiccan Rede: "An' it harm none, do what you wilt." There were different interpretations as to what this actually meant, especially since there was much latitude available to those who subscribed to Wiccan beliefs. But on the whole, the motto, if you could call it that, didn't sound too aggressive to Alison.

She saw something interesting in one of the printouts: a reference to "the Burning Times." This was the term used by modern-day pagans to describe the medieval witch hunts she remembered hearing about a long time ago. Alison thought back to stories she had heard as a Catholic schoolgirl about people being burned at the stake hundreds of years ago. 'Wasn't Joan of Arc one of those?' she wondered. She now read that many Wiccans considered the victims of these ghastly killings to be martyrs. No wonder, she thought, considering that some Wiccans call themselves witches.

"Okay," Alison said aloud. "So what does all this mean, if anything?" There seemed to be a dichotomy between the relatively harmless-sounding aspects of Wiccan belief and some of the elements that conjured up stereotypical thoughts of witches on broomsticks casting horrible spells. Eye of newt, and all that. She went back and tried to review the material on Satanism she had come across last week. By this time, though, she was having a hard time keeping up a high degree of concentration.

Alison had long since finished her pizza, leaving six crescents of crust on the plate. She never ate the crust. She was still hungry, so she went to the kitchen closet, half of which served as a pantry. She found a bonanza—a full bag of salt-and-vinegar potato chips. She loved the tanginess of the flavors as they competed for attention on her taste buds.

She turned on the TV and polished off half the bag with yet another soda as she watched some nameless sitcom. It didn't matter what she was watching, or even the fact that it wasn't very good. None of them were, really. She just had to clear her brain. And television was the perfect way to do that. She would kill some time until the late news came on, watch some of that, then do a little light reading. She was into a murder mystery at the moment. Had been for the last two months, ever since she did that assignment on what turned out to be the first of the serial killings. She just never seemed to make much progress on it. Maybe tonight.

Alison never even made it to the news. She fell asleep on the sofa with visions of Wiccans and Satanists in her head and pizza crusts on the coffee table.

Chapter 22

Thursday, October 26

"Good morning, Mr. Blake. We missed you yesterday. Hope you're feeling better." The greeting was offered by Connie Parsons, Stephen Blake's secretary, as he passed her workstation on the way into his office. Stephen had felt God-awful on Wednesday and had called in sick. He wasn't feeling particularly chipper today, for that matter, but it wasn't as bad as yesterday. Besides, he felt he couldn't afford to be away for two days at a time, so he had decided to struggle in and put up with whatever was ailing him. Which was a mystery to Stephen. He hardly ever got sick, so the hammer-like pounding in his head and the general overall malaise that had overtaken him were puzzling. He didn't know where it came from. All he knew was that he didn't feel well when he got home from the meeting with Ernst and the others on Tuesday night. In fact, it was all he could do to stagger home, pull his clothes off, and collapse into bed. And on Wednesday morning—well, talk about your splitting headaches! He had never experienced anything quite like that. It was so bad he actually got scared that there was something seriously wrong. He knew he wasn't going to make it into work and thought about going to a doctor. He would have, too, if it hadn't gotten better by noon. But it did let up some after a couple of hours, thank goodness. He didn't know if he could've put up with it had it gone on like that much longer.

"Well, I'm not a helluva lot better, but I'm here anyway," was Stephen's curt reply to Connie. "Too bad for you, right?"

"Why...no. What do you mean, Mr. Blake?" said Connie, a little taken aback by Stephen's hostile reaction to her honest concern for his welfare. "I was just asking, that's all."

"Never mind. Look. Get Sam Peters on the phone, will you? Ask him if he can come to my office right away. I have to talk to him about something...important. Call him now, understand?"

"Certainly, Mr. Blake. I'll call immediately." Connie didn't know what was going on with her boss. He was normally so considerate and mild-mannered. Probably the remnants of whatever was ailing him. Whatever it was, she could see he was in no mood for fooling around, like he usually did. She picked up the phone and dialed Sam Peters down in the print shop as Stephen went into his office and closed the door behind him.

Stephen dropped his briefcase on the floor, plopped down at his desk and stared off into space, as though trying to mentally compute the answer to a complex mathematical problem. In a way, he was. Stephen had spent the better part of yesterday afternoon—after he started to feel a little better—thinking about his problem. He wasn't so sick that he forgot about his problem. How could he? He came away from the meeting knowing he had a difficult task to fulfill. The old TV series, "Mission Impossible," came into his head, especially the show's hero listening to that tape recording at the beginning of every episode, the one that gave him a choice of accepting, or not, some outlandish task involving saving the world, or at least a large part thereof. Then the tape would self-destruct in a puff of smoke—fffffft. If only Stephen had the same choice. But he didn't. He only knew he had to undertake his own personal assignment. And do it successfully, or else. What "or else" meant was never really discussed. It didn't have to be. It seemed clear enough. What wasn't nearly as evident was how he was going to accomplish what was expected.

Stephen thought he heard a familiar voice. "Mr. Blake?" It was Connie. "Mr. Blake, are you okay? Maybe you should..."

"What? Did you say something?" said Stephen, as his mind came crashing back from the twilight zone.

"I knocked, but you didn't answer. So I poked my head in. I was just saying, maybe you should go home. You don't seem to be yourself today."

"That's for me to decide. What about Peters?"

"He said he's finishing something right now but can come up in fifteen minutes or so. Is that all right?"

"No, it's not all right," blurted Stephen, angrily. "But I guess I don't have much choice, huh? Just let me know when he gets here. And close the door on your way out." Connie did as she was instructed, the concerned look on her face growing with every passing moment.

After about twenty minutes, Connie knocked twice and came in to say, "Sam Peters is outside, Mr. Blake. Shall I send him in?"

Stephen looked at his watch. "It's about time, dammit," he said. "Yeah, send him in, why don't you."

Sam Peters was the head of the print shop at HubBooks. He was a top-notch guy who could tackle any impossible assignment on just about any improbable deadline. Stephen knew there wasn't anyone with more knowledge about the printing business than Sam. He had saved Stephen's ass more than once, along with everyone else's in the company. Peters waddled into Stephen's office and sat right down in one of the leather chairs facing the desk. His longevity and quiet competence allowed him that luxury. Peters' blue trousers and white shirt spilled over the chair's edges. He was a big man, not so much in height as in weight. He topped the scales off at about 225 pounds. He was also short, which made him a definite roly-poly type.

"Hi ya, Stephen," said Peters, normally a happy-go-lucky type. He had learned a long time ago it was his best defense against the incredible stresses he was subjected to day in and day out. "Connie tells me you've been feeling under the weather. Hope it's nothing serious."

"No. Nothing serious. Listen, didn't you tell Connie you'd be up here in fifteen minutes? What took you so long?"

"Well, I can see Connie was right. We *are* out of sorts, aren't we? I said *about* fifteen minutes. Not *exactly* fifteen minutes." Peters didn't have the official status to outrank people like Stephen, but he was looked on—unofficially—as their equal. He also didn't like taking any guff from these uppity senior executives. But he decided to give

Stephen the benefit of the doubt. Him being sick and all. And he knew Stephen wasn't normally like that—not before today, anyway. "What can I do for you, Stephen? Connie said it was important."

Stephen felt his head, trying to soothe the slight throbbing that remained from yesterday. He knew he was behaving badly but couldn't figure out why. "Yeah, it is. Listen, Sam, I'm, uh, sorry. I...I guess I still don't feel all that great."

"Forget it," said Peters. "Shit happens."

"Anyway, I'm working on this...project. It's kind of a personal thing, really, and I could use your advice on it. It's also, you know, hush-hush. Wouldn't want anyone else to know what I was doing. It's sort of...well, a surprise. I'd appreciate it if you could keep it to yourself."

"No problem. Mum's the word. What's the deal?"

Stephen waited a moment, searching for the right words. "How would I go about getting the equipment and supplies needed to do my own printing and binding? But not just any job. This would involve an older-type document, with special inks, covers, bindings, the works. I essentially want to reproduce what looks like a medieval manuscript."

Peters sat without saying anything. He straightened his tie and stared at Stephen, looking him dead square in the eyes. Peters could tell a lot about a person when he did that, he found. "We...uh, wouldn't be talking about anything illegal here, would we Stephen? Like making a counterfeit of a rare first edition or something like that?" He said it half tongue-in-cheek, but only half.

Stephen leaned back in his chair and exhaled a strained laugh. "No, Sam, not at all. It's nothing like that. Really." Stephen could see that Peters wasn't smiling. He needed convincing, and the truth be damned in the process. "Look, Sam. It's just that I'm into book collecting. Been doing it for a long time—as a hobby. I was starting to learn more about the production end of things. From John Demming—you knew John, didn't you? He was teaching me everything he knew, which was considerable. Anyway, now that he's gone—sad thing, really—I wanted to keep things moving along. Not let them lapse, you know? I figured I'd set up a little shop so I could do things firsthand. Sort of like the trial-and-error approach. Nothing like the real thing, right?"

Peters got lots of strange requests in his position, but nothing like this before. His curiosity was piqued. "Nope. No substitute for hands-on training, that's for sure. But where would you put all the stuff? We're talking about a lot of materials and equipment here—some of it heavy. Could be expensive, too. Hope you've got a lot of room—and dough."

"I can handle that. Just get me pointed in the right direction. I'll do the rest. Whadaya say?"

"Well, guess I can help you out. Don't know why you'd want to keep it a big secret, though, but it's none of my business. It might take a little time, getting a bead on what you need. Let me give it some thought, make some contacts. I sometimes hear about used presses that companies are looking to get rid of when they upgrade. I'll see what's out on the street. How about if I get back to you by, oh, say, early next week?"

Stephen didn't think he had anywhere near that kind of time. He recalled the pressure put on him by Ernst at the meeting. "Next week? Listen, Sam, I've gotta have something by tomorrow night. It's...well, if you must know, it has something to do with this girl I'm trying to impress. She's into books, too, believe it or not, and I'm afraid I made some promises that're hard to keep. I was gonna get to you yesterday, but I was out sick. How about it? Can you help me out here? I know I owe you a couple already. I'll put this new one on your account. With interest. Please, Sam. You'll be saving my hide." Stephen may have taken a few liberties as he spoke, but Peters had no way of knowing how close to the truth this last statement was.

"I can't make any promises, but I'll see what I can do. That's the best I can offer on short notice. I'll give you a call tomorrow afternoon and at least let you know what I was able to come up with. If anything. Take it or leave it."

"I guess I have no choice, do I? I'll take it, but please get me something, Sam. It's real important."

"Do what I can."

"And remember. You don't know what any of this is about. You're only scrounging info for a friend in need. Got it?"

"Got it. Anything else?"

"No. That's it. Thanks for your help. And I'm sorry I snapped at you before."

"Pay it no mind," said Peters, as he got up to leave. "Just don't let it happen again, good buddy," he said, exiting Stephen's office with a wave and a laugh. That was the great thing about Peters. You could dump on him and he let it slide off. He just wasn't the kind to carry a grudge.

Stephen got up from his desk with some difficulty—he was sore, and his head still ached—and walked to the window. His office overlooked the downtown streets from the twenty-third floor of one of the relatively new high-rises built during the development boom of the 1980s. He wondered why he never noticed before how small the people and cars appeared from up there. 'Just like me,' he thought. 'That's exactly how I feel. Like an ant, ready to be stepped on.'

Stephen went back to his desk and found himself reaching for the phone. He lifted the receiver and held it for a moment, not sure why he had picked it up in the first place. He remembered wanting to call someone, but now, he couldn't remember who. Wasn't he supposed to call...what was the name? Or did he already? Damn! Why couldn't he remember? There were so many conflicting thoughts in his head he was having trouble sorting them all out.

He felt his mind was like an artist's canvas. One moment it was clear, full of vibrant color and form and structure and recognizable images. Images of things he remembered as being real only a short time ago. Those were the best times. Just as quickly, the canvas would revert to a hollow blankness. Then there was nothing but a white void—disturbing but tolerable. The worst was when countless tentacles invaded his brain and filled the canvas with grotesque shapes. There was no form to them, no color. Just black. The shapes kept changing, so he couldn't focus on any one before it transposed itself into another. Then another. And another. There was no stability. Only an agonized search for something that was never quite there.

It reminded him of the bad dreams he used to have as a child. He would start walking down the street, feet touching the pavement securely. Then, with every subsequent step, he found it harder and harder to move his legs forward. And when he did manage it, he wasn't able to keep his feet on the ground. It was as though his body was filling with helium, so that he floated higher and higher as he tried desperately to maintain his forward progress. These episodes were so terrifying that he actually heard himself making noises while still asleep. He was hoping the noises would get loud enough so they would awaken him from his torture. They always did, but not before he had broken out into a cold sweat. Stephen felt that way now, but with the slow-motion, ponderous floating replaced by the awful, jagged configurations on the canvas inside his head.

Reluctantly, Stephen let the receiver slip slowly back into its receptacle. He propped his elbows on the desk and rested his head in his hands. "What's happening to me?" he said into his palms. He rubbed his eyes, trying to erase the bad images, hoping to replace them with good ones. Or at least with the absence of any. That would be an acceptable compromise. After a minute or two, this seemed to work. His mind was returning to some semblance of reality. It wasn't quite clear, though. One small compartment's contents kept alerting him to the need to complete his own personal mission impossible. That thought never went away, it seemed. But he could handle that. It was no big deal. Only one more thing to get done in the long list of things he had to do every day. The only peculiarity about the task was that it was unusually long-term. 'But I can do that,' he thought.

Stephen straightened up in his chair and placed his hands on the desk. He was suddenly feeling better. Much better, in fact, than he had felt in the last couple of days. He pushed himself up and went to the window again, looking down once more at the city and its life-giving activity, much like blood coursing through veins and arteries. "So, Stephen, me lad," he said to himself, "let's get to it. We've got a lot of work to do."

Chapter 23

Thursday, October 26

"Lieutenant Mulcahy speaking. May I help you?"

"Hello, Lieutenant. This is Alison Simmons from The Herald. I'm doing some follow-up on a series of stories we've done on the blackmark murders and wanted to get your side of things. Can you answer a few questions?"

Mulcahy remembered the name from a couple of news articles he read last week. He was getting tired of calls from the press, especially since his continuing investigation wasn't getting anywhere fast. But he knew it was unavoidable, so he was willing to put up with it—for now, anyway. "I will if I can, but we don't really have anything new."

"What about the events of last weekend, Lieutenant? The young high-school boy—Peter Markis, and then John Demming the next day. Two deaths in two days. You must've done some checking on those. Find anything?"

"It's interesting you mentioned Demming. How do you happen to know about him?"

Alison realized she had slipped up. There were only two ways she could have known about Demming and the peculiarities of his death. One was if she had talked to the Concord police. And why would she have done that? Even if she had seen the news brief in The Globe—or even if The Herald had its own little blurb—it gave no indication of any connection to the Boston murders. And as far as she knew, no one else had done an article on it that would have made it common knowledge. The only other way for her to have known was to have gotten it from another source—one close to Demming. Someone like Stephen. She was reluctant to get him involved against his will, so she would have to fudge her way through. 'Dammit,' she thought, 'I've got to be more careful.'

"Let's just say we have our sources," said Alison cryptically. "I'm afraid I can't really go beyond that for now."

Mulcahy didn't feel the need to press the point. Besides, he knew from experience these newshounds had an uncanny knack for ferreting out stuff sometimes even he didn't know. "Okay," he said. "Fair enough. Officially, the Demming death is an accident under the jurisdiction of the Concord Police. You'll have to follow up with them on that one. As for the Markis case, it's pretty much more of the same. I don't mean to sound callous about it, Miss Simmons, but we really haven't been able to come up with anything we didn't already tell you folks at the press conference last week. I believe you were there, right?" He remembered her jabbing the Commissioner with those questions. Ferreting out what nobody wanted to deal with. How could he forget? "So you already know what we know."

"Yeah, I was there, Lieutenant. Actually, since you mentioned it, there's something you talked about at the conference I wanted to ask about." 'Might as well cut right to the chase,' thought Alison. "Has to do with the occult connection. You must admit it was a bit of a surprise, something like that coming from the police. It's not the usual type of thing you guys talk about. What've you done along those lines, Lieutenant? Any leads?"

Still plugging away on that, he thought. "All I can say is, we've put out the info on our cases all around the country, even some foreign departments, trying to find out if anything like this rings a bell anywhere else. So far, no one's rung the bell. But we're still trying. Haven't given up."

Alison was taking it all down in her trusty notebook. "What about the victims' families? Has there been any more follow-up with them? Maybe something was missed the first time around."

"We've actually talked to the families more than once," said Mulcahy. "In some cases, more than twice. Like everything else, we've hit a blank wall."

Alison had to find out more about Demming but didn't want to let on she knew about the black mark on his neck. She tried the indirect approach. "I will contact Concord, Lieutenant, like you suggested, but I have to ask you something about Demming. Are you interested in him because you consider his death to be suspicious, and tied in somehow to your serial killings?" She wrote "Demming" in her notebook, with a big question mark next to it.

Got to be careful, thought Mulcahy. "I don't want to comment on that at the moment, Miss Simmons, other than we've done some investigation on certain connections between Mr. Demming and people or places in Boston with which he may be associated. That's really all I can say right now."

Alison circled the question mark. "Okay," she said, "let's leave it at that. If it's any consolation, Lieutenant, I've done my own checking on these cases and haven't been any more successful at it than you. If I come up with anything, though, I'll let you know."

Mulcahy laughed. "You do that. I wish us both luck."

Alison checked her notes after the call and found she had written "Nothing new" three times. "Well, that was a real eye-opener, wasn't it?" she muttered in the general direction of her desk. It was time for another talk with her editor. Burgholz had asked her to come in this morning anyway to discuss progress. She knew he was getting restless about the cases. Join the club. So was everyone else. She went to his office, and he waved her in. He was on the phone but motioned for her to sit down. She chose to wait standing at the window.

When Burgholz was done with the call, Alison said, "I'm here at the appointed hour as ordered, sir."

"Well, I see you're feeling a little better today, Ali. I'm glad. Have you been able to scout up anything new on our—or should I say your—favorite subject?"

"Funny you should mention that. I was just about to say I've solved all the cases, Mr. B. Every single one of 'em. And I've written a three-page spread exposing all. Shall I go on?"

"Now that you've had some fun, why don't you tell me what you really know."

"I am afraid you have found me out. Damn." Alison noticed that Burgholz sported a slight grin. That was good. She knew she hadn't pushed it too far. They both enjoyed this little give-and-take between them, as long as it was kept within certain boundaries. She came over to his desk and sat on the edge of one of the visitor chairs. It was almost tolerable, she noted. "Okay. Here it is, for real," said Alison.

She proceeded to summarize her computer research of the prior evening, as well as the call just concluded with the Boston Police. Burgholz listened intently and seemed intrigued by the information Alison had found on Wicca. He asked if she had given any of it to the police.

"No, not yet. It could be nothing just as easily as it could be something. And anyway, they said they were into the occult. Let them find out themselves."

"That's the spirit, Ali. Give 'em hell."

Alison ignored Burgholz's joke. "Listen, Jay. I think my next move should be to check out this guy Ernst. You know, the bookstore owner? I'd like to go over to his place this afternoon and see for myself what kind of operation he runs. Snoop around a little. Maybe even buy a novel. I'm only twelve or thirteen books behind in my reading. I'll be needing another one sometime in the next few years. No time like the present."

Burgholz wasn't exactly keen on the plan. He didn't want to tell her outright not to see Ernst, though. "You know what I'd rather have you do?" he said. "Run another series of checks on the families. There's just got to be something we're missing here. I know you've done it, and so have the police, but it seems impossible there isn't some common element to all this. It obviously isn't something that pops up and hits you in the face. It's more subtle. Hard to find. But I'd be willing to bet it's there. If you look in the right places."

"I'm willing to do that, Jay. But let me try the bookstore thing first. If nothing turns up that cracks the case, I'll start getting back to the families tomorrow. How's that?"

"Are you sure you want to get involved with the very same guy you claim put some kind of hex on your friend Blake? You're a mighty brave little lady."

"Brave has nothing to do with it. What's he gonna do in the middle of the day? Abduct me? I don't think so. And anyway, I don't plan on coming right out and asking him if he's a crazed murderer. At least not right away. I'll just see what develops. I think it's worth a shot. Nothing ventured, nothing gained, as they say."

"Well, it's your neck. Before you go, though, maybe you'd better pay up the five bucks you owe me from that bet we made last month. You lost, remember? I think I'd like my winnings now, please."

"Very funny, Jay. Really. It's a scream." Alison got up and started to leave. Before she did, she turned and said, "And by the way, when are you gonna get some decent chairs for your guests in here?" She waved in the general direction of the wooden ones sitting in front of his desk. "Those monstrosities are absolutely atrocious. Ciao."

Chapter 24

Thursday, October 26

After the Simmons call, Lieutenant Mulcahy asked Pat Johnson to come into his office. He needed a little tête-à-tête with his partner. Although the press had backed off some over the last few days, the call was a little jab-in-the-side reminder they were still out there. It also hit home that he hadn't made much progress either, or any, to be honest about it. Johnson trundled in wearing the shade of brown du jour and parked himself in a chair.

Mulcahy wasted no time getting to the point. It may be October on the calendar, but there was no relief in the summer-sizzler heat wave being generated by the Commissioner. "Just got another tweak from the press, Pat. You remember those folks, don't you? The ones with the notebooks and cameras and the adoring public who end up calling the Commissioner's office when they don't get solutions to big crime cases? I think you know what I was able to offer the lady, right? Zippo. Nada. Zilch. We aren't coming off looking too good, Pat. That press conference last week bought us a little time, but we've long since used that up. We're running on fumes here. We've got to come up with something. Fast."

"Like to help ya out, Vinny. Really would. But I'm fresh outta ideas. Don't have to tell ya we been over all of it every which way but loose. The stuff from last weekend on Demming and Blake and Ernst looked..."

"What did you say?" interjected Mulcahy.

"Huh? What'd I say about what?"

"Just now. Something about Demming and Blake. That must be it."

"Must be what, Vin? Christ! What the hell are ya talkin' about?"

It was like a lightbulb snapping on over Mulcahy's head. "I was just wondering how our Herald reporter friend knew about Demming. Maybe Blake is the secret source she can't tell us about. Maybe we should have a little chat with him. What do you think, bunky?"

"Yeah, I guess. If ya say so, Vinnie."

"Okay. Let's keep that in mind for future reference. Now, what were you saying?"

"Jeez. I forget." Pat scratched his head and tried to recall his earlier train of thought. "Guess it was just that all the hot info we dredged up last weekend ended like everything else. In other words, el blanko."

"Well, when the Commissioner barges in here later on, Pat, I'll tell him you said that. I surely will."

Johnson spotted the certificates in cheap frames on the wall behind Mulcahy's desk. It jogged his memory. "Man, we been on the force, how long? Don't tell me, I don't wanna know. A lotta years, though. We had some toughies, but never like this, huh? I don't like this feelin' of bein' completely and totally bummed out. I just wish I had the answer, Vin. But I don't. I know you're frustrated. The Commissioner's frustrated. The public's frustrated. The press, the families, me, everybody. We need some kinda break, Vinnie. Unfortunately, the way things are goin', I don't see anything droppin' in our laps any time soon."

"Well, we've got to do something," said Mulcahy, exasperated. "I think we should lock ourselves in a room with what we've got and go over it again. Every last friggin' thing. With a fine-tooth comb. At least we'll be able to say we're doing something. Instead of sitting on our asses waiting for a miracle. Which is probably what it's gonna take. And if that doesn't work, we'll go see Blake. How does that sound?"

"I'm game," said Johnson. "How ya wanna handle it?"

"I've got something to wrap up that'll take the rest of the morning. What say we have some sandwiches brought in and sequester ourselves in here for the duration?"

"Why not? Can't think of anything better to do. See ya 'round noonish. Your treat, right?"

"Absolutely. Peanut butter and jelly sandwiches all around. Nothing but the best for you, pal."

Chapter 25

Thursday, October 26

The "previously-owned" Chevy Nova snaked its way up Charles Street through the mid-afternoon traffic. The Public Garden was on the left, the Common on the right. Alison Simmons was on her way to Ye Olde Booke Nooke. She liked this section of downtown, one of the few with a significant swath of green breaking up the urban topography. She made a left onto Beacon and—miracle of miracles—there it was. A metered parking space, just being vacated. Her immediate thought was on the order of 'I must be living right'. She swung over to the left and waited for the car to extricate itself from the cramped space. Alison managed to maneuver her way in, despite her antipathy for parallel parking. 'Good thing I paid attention during that particular driver's ed lesson,' she thought. 'And that I can't afford a bigger car.'

From Stephen Blake's description and Alison's perusal of the Yellow Pages, she knew Ernst's bookstore was somewhere in the general vicinity, another reason the parking space was so valuable. She fed the meter, dodged her way across Beacon Street, and made her way into the innards of the Beacon Hill community. She managed to locate the shop without too much hassle. As a matter of fact, she wished it was always this easy when she was out on her search-and-destroy missions, as she liked to call her field trips. Alison spent a few moments eyeing the store from afar before going in. Nothing unusual, she noticed. No obvious gremlins lurking about.

She walked up to the front door, paused briefly, overcame whatever reluctance she had, and opened the door. The sound of the little bell above her head as she entered reminded her of the word "tintinnabulation" in the poem "The Bells" by Edgar Allan Poe. She had always liked the rhythm and sonority of it.

Alison saw there was no one else in the shop, at least in the part she could see. The owner was probably out back, she guessed. Sure enough, no sooner had she completed her visual inventory than a stoop-shouldered, gray-haired old gentleman came out. 'Has to be Ernst,' she thought.

"Good afternoon, young lady. And what can I do for you today?"

'Yup. German accent. It's him, all right.' "Nothing right now, thanks," said Alison. "Just thought I'd browse a little." Her eyes were taking in the stacks of books balanced precariously wherever she looked.

"Of course. Take your time. I will be in the back if you need help. Just call out. My name is Gustav Ernst." He started to make his way toward the back.

"Actually, I *am* interested in something," said Alison, not wanting to lose his attention. "I've been looking to buy a gift for a friend and haven't been able to find anything good. He's into magic and the supernatural. Stuff like that. I don't really know anything about it at all, I'm afraid. Could you point me in the right direction? Or give me any recommendations you might have?"

"A most interesting topic, indeed. I think I do have some material on that, if I recall. It should be over this way." Ernst raised his arm in the general direction of one of the shop's corners. He walked that way, stepping around stacks of books on the floor, beckoning Alison to follow. "Is there something specific your friend is interested in?"

Alison's eyes were taking it all in. Not that there was that much to see, unless you liked old, older, and oldest, that is. "Not really. He just seems to like the topic in general. I've never gotten into it myself. I find it kind of spooky actually, if you know what I mean." She grinned.

"Yes, some people do find it so. Like you, I myself have never taken to it. But let us see what we have here for you to look at." Ernst rummaged through several book stacks sitting on a table and others lining one of the bookcases along the wall. Alison read the titles she could make out on a few of the books in her vicinity. They were as dry as the dust accumulating on most of them. Ernst picked out three or four volumes and passed them to Alison. "See if you find these enlightening."

She feigned perusing each one while Ernst looked for other possibilities. Eventually she said, "I just don't know if he'd like any of these. Do you have anything else?"

"I do not believe I have anything in my regular inventory, other than these few volumes. None that I can see, anyway. However, I think I have a few items in the back, but they are quite expensive. Most are in the category of rare manuscripts and first editions. Things of that nature. They are part of my special collection, but I do sell them if an interested buyer comes along. If you are in that price range, I can show them to you."

"Gee, I don't know. I don't really think I can spend more than a few dollars. I'm not exactly a high-powered executive." Alison paused a moment. She was dying to catch a glimpse of what it was like out back. It was where Stephen had gone to the meeting, most likely. But she knew she didn't look like the type of person who could spring for big bucks. She smiled and said, "Just out of curiosity, though, do you think I could see what the fancy ones look like? I'd love to see something like that. The closest I've come has been in a museum. And they're always under glass, or in a special case."

"Yes, I know what you mean. But I am afraid that my special books are no different. Their value requires me to keep them secure. However, I am always willing to let people see them, if they are really interested. That is what they are for, after all. It gives me pleasure to show them off every so often. If you like, I will take you inside so you can see them."

"Great. I really appreciate it."

Ernst had Alison follow him through the curtain to the back rooms. She took note of everything her eyes could see in the relatively dim light. Stairs leading up just opposite the curtain. 'He must live up there,' she thought. Three doors—all closed—along the corridor. 'I'll bet the meetings take place behind one of those. And *The Codex* Stephen told me about has to be around somewhere, too.' They stopped at the collection room door. Ernst unlocked it—'he does keep them secure, doesn't he?'—and ushered Alison inside.

"This is where I keep my old treasures, miss, or as I am fond of saying to people, my old friends. I have been collecting for many years, as you can see."

"Wow, this is awesome," exclaimed Alison, as her eyes roamed over the various volumes in the display cases. They didn't especially mean anything to her, but they certainly looked impressive. "I can see why you'd be proud of them."

"As for the topic you are interested in, I have one or two, I think, that may be in the right category. They will be over here." Ernst led Alison to one of the cases and identified the volumes with a point of his finger. "Do you wish to see them up close?"

"Gee, I don't know. As I said, I couldn't possibly afford to buy anything like this. I really just wanted to see what valuable books looked like."

"Certainly. There is no need to feel uncomfortable about that. As I said, you have given me an opportunity to show them, so I am grateful for that."

"Thanks. I feel better, now that you said that." 'Gotta go for it,' she thought. "By the way, is this the only place you keep your collection, or are there other rooms, too? I noticed a couple of other doors in the corridor. Do you have more books hidden away?"

'This is a particularly inquisitive one,' thought Ernst. "No, not really. There's a small office for my administrative duties—none of us can escape paperwork, after all—as well as supplies and other necessities of the business. Everything of interest is in here, or out front."

"I didn't mean to pry," tittered Alison. "I'm just naturally curious. I'm always asking people about everything."

"No need to explain, miss. I understand."

At that moment, Alison heard the soft tinkling of the bell over the front door, along with a raspy buzz that went off somewhere nearby. Ernst said, "Will you excuse me while I see who it is? I do not get many customers, and I would not want to lose one." He laughed.

"Not at all," said Alison, looking around at the room full of assorted rarities. "Are you sure you trust me with your valuable friends in here, though?"

Ernst smiled. "I will guess I do not have anything to worry about in that regard. Look around some more if you like. Or make yourself comfortable in one of the chairs. I should not be too long."

Alison ambled over to one of the bookcases. "Thanks. I'd like to check out some more of your collection, I think. I'll keep myself occupied."

Ernst left. He didn't close the door to the collection room, she noticed. She had to make an instantaneous decision, and she did. She walked toward the open door and listened. There were voices coming from the shop—Ernst's and someone else's. It sounded like a customer asking for help in finding a book, just as Alison had done a few minutes ago. She thought there would be enough time.

She peeked outside the door and saw what she expected to see—nothing. She stepped into the corridor and immediately turned right toward the furthest of the other two doors, the one at end of the corridor. She hurried to it and tried the knob. It squeaked slightly as she turned it—not enough to hear out front, she was certain—but the door didn't open. It was locked. She stooped to see if anything could be seen through the keyhole, but there was only darkness. 'No windows,' she thought. 'Too bad.'

She quickly went to the other door, the one along the wall opposite the collection room. She went through the same procedure, with the same result. She silently cursed her bad luck. She wondered why, if one of these other rooms was his office, as he had said, both doors were locked. Wouldn't he keep an office open and functioning in the middle of a business day? For a moment she considered the idea of trying to see what was upstairs but decided that would be foolhardy in the extreme. The risk was too great. Ernst could return at any moment.

Disappointed but not surprised by her lack of success, Alison scampered back to the collection room and immediately fell into one of the easy chairs. Despite the limited scope of her daring mission, her mouth was a little dry. She felt her heart pounding and noticed her palms were sweaty from the exhilaration of it. She hoped she could compose herself before Ernst came back. She did, since Ernst was preoccupied with his customer for several more minutes.

When he did finally return, he apologized profusely for keeping Alison waiting. "No problem," she said. "It isn't often I get a chance to relax in the middle of the day like this. I actually enjoyed it."

"I think I know what you mean," laughed Ernst, "although I myself have plenty of time to relax. It is usually very quiet, so I do not have the same stresses you young people experience."

"I'm envious," said Alison, only half-jokingly. "Well, I guess I'll be going. I hope you'll forgive me if I don't buy anything. I didn't really see what I was looking for, so I think I'll keep searching." Alison almost smiled at the double meaning of her last statement. "Thanks for showing me your special books. It was really interesting. You've made my day, actually."

"I am glad to have done so. Perhaps you will come back another time and look through some of the other items I have out front. I am sure you could find something of interest for yourself—or your friend."

"I'll do that, now that I know you're here."

They left the collection room, which Alison noted was locked again by Ernst. She glanced down the corridor once more. 'I'd love to know what's behind those doors,' she thought. Ernst held the curtain aside for Alison, and both returned to the front of the shop, where they exchanged goodbyes.

Once outside, Alison went around the corner to see if she could identify whether the bookstore fronted on a yard or alleyway, but it didn't appear that there was any way in or out other than the main

Wicca Codex

entrance. The conclusion she had reached a few minutes ago about there being no windows in the back rooms seemed to be correct, as far as she could tell. The bookstore must be surrounded by buildings on all sides, except the street. One way in, one way out, she surmised. She spent another moment or two reconnoitering the area but came up with nothing new or interesting.

She made her way back to Beacon Street and saw there was still a little time left on the meter. She hadn't used up the full hour. She unlocked the car and got in, but didn't start the engine. She sat there, looking straight ahead as she thought about Ernst and the bookstore. He certainly seemed like a nice enough fellow, all right. Very pleasant. Helpful. Polite. Great little accent. The kind of guy you could never say anything bad about. No wonder Stephen took to him so readily. 'I would too,' she said to herself. 'If I didn't know there was something wrong with all of it.' She didn't know what the problem was exactly, only that there was one. After all, there was the business of the locked and darkened office, right? Wasn't that a clue that something was amiss? And why did nice-guy Stephen suddenly turn into an ogre right after supposedly going to a meeting here, a meeting he admitted attending? What about that? And if there was a meeting room, and that's really what it was used for, why was it locked? It's possible, she thought, but why? It seemed as though there was something funny going on back there. Something that had to be kept hidden from prying eyes. "There's got to be," she said aloud to the windshield. "Doesn't there?"

Chapter 26

Friday, October 27

The last day of the workweek always made Alison feel good, even though she enjoyed her job a lot. She liked it so much, in fact, that having to work on a story after hours or on a weekend didn't phase her at all. It was the price she paid for doing what she wanted to be doing. She wouldn't have it any other way. Nevertheless, a full weekend off was something to look forward to. And this weekend promised to be one of those. A chance to do some of the things that Saturdays and Sundays were made for.

But there was still Friday to get through before she could think about that. All of Friday, for that matter. It was only just after nine A. M. She wondered if it was too early, in fact, to be paying an unscheduled call on one of the black-mark murder victim's family members. But she had told Jay Burgholz yesterday that this is what she'd be doing today, and she wanted to get an early start. If the first one didn't pan out, she'd try the next one on her list. Then the next. In fact, morning was probably the best time to catch some of them, before they got into the swing of their daily routines. She'd talked to just about all of these same people before and hated to bother them again. But she knew Burgholz was right about this. They had hit a brick wall, and there was little else that could be done. That was even more true today, now that she had gone and snooped around Ernst's place yesterday afternoon. And found nothing. Nothing, that is, except more questions. The options were diminishing rapidly. It was back to the grind-it-out-and-hope-for-something approach.

Alison had thought about taking the easy way out and doing the follow-ups by phone, as she had done for the original interviews, but she wanted to see everyone face-to-face. You could tell a lot from looking people in the eye and reading body language, and right now she needed every advantage she could get. So, the decision had been made to take the extra time to search them out. She hoped it would be worth it.

She was on her way to talk to the parents of Mary Clark, the first victim. Alison knew from a previous interview with Mary's widowed husband that he was likely to be at work by now after having dropped off his two motherless kids at a day-care center. The parents were the better option, although they lived in Canton—a Boston suburb south of downtown. She could reach him by phone later, if she needed to.

Alison fought her way through the remnants of the morning rush hour traffic and settled the Nova in front of the Clark house. She rang the bell and heard voices inside. The door was cracked open about a foot by a lady whom Alison recognized as Mrs. Clark from their first meeting about two months ago. "Yes?" said the lady.

"Excuse me for intruding, Mrs. Clark, but I'm Alison Simmons, from The Boston Herald. I did an article on your daughter a while back. We spoke then, and also by phone last week." Alison was referring to the recent article she had put together for Burgholz. She'd had to contact a few of the family members again for additional information. "I was wondering if you'd mind my asking a few more questions."

The door opened wider. Mrs. Clark was a pleasant-looking lady in her mid-fifties. She said, "I remember you, Miss Simmons. I wouldn't mind except my husband, and I will be going out shortly. I could only spare a few minutes."

"That'll be fine, Mrs. Clark. It won't take long. I promise."

"Well, in that case, please come in."

Alison greeted Mr. Clark as they went into the living room. He excused himself and went off to do something while the two women chatted. Alison went over some of the things they had discussed earlier, hoping for a new angle or the recollection of some forgotten piece of minutiae. But there was nothing new. She didn't really think there would be. She felt she had been there long enough and prepared to leave. She put on her coat and said, "I want to say again how sorry I am about the loss of your daughter, Mrs. Clark. The pain of it must be very great for you and your husband."

"Yes, of course. I'm not sure we'll ever get over it. We were fortunate that Mary's uncle was able to bring special comfort to us during a very difficult time."

"Mary's uncle?"

"Yes, her Uncle Ed. My husband's brother. Father Edward, from St. Christine's parish in Dorchester. Didn't I mention him before? He said the funeral mass and did the services at the burial. He helped us so much, just being around at a time like that. And since, of course."

"Yes, that must make it a little easier to bear," Alison offered in sympathy. "Well, I've taken too much of your time already, Mrs. Clark. Thank you for seeing me." Alison got up, said goodbye, and left. She went to her car and pulled out her notebook, not wanting to take notes inside. She didn't think it would be seemly. She wrote: "Clark—Catholic. Uncle a priest—Father Edward, St. Christine's, Dorchester." 'Well, it wasn't a total loss,' she thought. 'At least I learned one new thing, even though it wasn't much.'

Next on Alison's list was the sister of the second murder victim, Elizabeth Walters. Ms. Walters had been unmarried, and the parents lived out-of-state. The only local relative was a younger sister, a housewife, married name Karen Bratton. Alison located the house out in Newton and lucked out again. She was home.

"Hello, Mrs. Bratton. I don't know if you remember me. I'm Alison Simmons, from The Herald." Alison could hear the screams of at least two kids inside the house. One of them—a boy of about three—came running up to his mother and grabbed her around the leg. Alison smiled at the child, then said to Mrs. Bratton, "We spoke earlier about your sister Elizabeth."

"Oh, yes. Hello. How are you?"

"Fine, thanks. I'm sorry to bother you, but I'm doing some follow-up on the stories The Herald ran last week. I wonder if I could have just a few minutes of your time. I know you're busy, but it shouldn't take long."

"Sure. Come on in. The kids are keeping themselves occupied, as you can hear. We should be able to sneak a couple of minutes to ourselves."

Once inside, Alison said, "I have to admit I'm groping for new information on all of these terrible crimes. We just haven't been able to come up with anything new that might help to shed light on what happened, or why."

"It seems the same is true of the police," said Mrs. Bratton. "They've been by a couple of times. They keep asking the same questions, and all I can do is give the same answers. I wish they could find out something more. The worst part is not knowing why Beth died. It was just so very strange, the whole affair."

Alison had a hunch. It was probably nothing, but at this point she might as well go for it. What was there to lose? "Mrs. Bratton, I hope you don't mind me asking, but could you tell me what your family's religious affiliation is?"

Mrs. Bratton seemed surprised by the question. "Why, we're Catholics. Born and raised. Why do you ask? Is that important?"

"I can't say for sure, Mrs. Bratton. I know this is out of the blue, but like I said, I'm just trying different angles." Alison felt a little funny pursuing this line of questioning, but she was fresh out of alternatives. "And one more thing, if I may. Are any members of your family in the religious community? You know, priests, brothers, nuns?"

Mrs. Bratton let several seconds slip by, merely staring at Alison. "That's really quite remarkable, Miss Simmons. How did you know that? One of my brothers is in the priesthood."

* * *

Alison wasn't sure what she was feeling at the moment. She had started the day with nothing. Now, back at The Herald, she felt she was on the verge of a potential breakthrough. When she left the Bratton house that morning, she was mildly excited, but with a sense of restraint. After all, two priests in two victim's families could be nothing more than coincidence. But her discipline melted away after interviews with members from the other three families. All were Catholics, and all had someone who wore the black cloth and white collar of the priesthood! Every one! Surely it couldn't be mere coincidence for all those victimized by the black-mark killings to have a Catholic priest as a son, a brother, a nephew, whatever. Alison figured the odds against it must be astounding. That *must* be the connection they were looking for.

There was only one problem: John Demming's death didn't fit the pattern.

It was true he wasn't officially a murder victim like the others. His case was still considered an accident. But what about the black mark? Just like the other five. He didn't have a broken neck, but there *had* to be a link. The only thing was, Demming wasn't a Catholic. He was Protestant. A WASP. And obviously, no priest in the family. Not even a minister. No one remotely religious. Alison had some trouble finding this out, there being no relative in the area, but she got a lead on a brother living on the west coast and managed to reach him by phone. She was glad to get the information but was disappointed in it, nonetheless. Why was that one different? It was somewhat troubling, but did not detract significantly from the euphoria she felt about the other cases.

Alison brought all of this to Jay Burgholz, who was optimistic that this might be the break they needed. The question of how Catholic priests in the families resulted in bizarre murders still had to be resolved, but they had as good a direction in which to proceed as ever before. In fact, prior to this, there was no direction. The first thing Burgholz suggested Alison do was contact the police and give them what she had, a decision Alison agreed with wholeheartedly. Alison called Lieutenant Mulcahy immediately, but he was unavailable.

Instead, she was put in touch with Sergeant Johnson, Mulcahy's partner on the investigating team.

"What can I do for ya, Miss Simmons?" asked Johnson.

"I've just been doing some follow-up on our stories on those black-mark murders and may have come up with something. It's just too strange to be coincidental."

"What is?"

"The fact that all five murder victims were Catholics."

"I'll admit that's interesting, Miss Simmons, but hardly..."

"And that all five had a priest for a relative."

There was silence on the line for a moment as Johnson absorbed this little bombshell. Alison couldn't tell, but the sergeant was smiling when he said, "Why don't you tell me the details, Miss Simmons."

Alison went through her notebook and told Johnson what she had discovered that morning, primarily the names and residence locations of the various clergy members. Two were in the Boston metro area, one in the western part of the state, one elsewhere in New England, and one out in the mid-west. She also provided each priest's relation to the victims. She mentioned her confusion about Demming's not being a Catholic. Johnson took it all down and said, "Thank you very much, Miss Simmons. We appreciate your help on this. Obviously, we may need to talk to you further about this at a later time."

"Certainly, Sergeant. I'll be available if you need anything else."

After the call, Alison chafed to do more research on the Internet. Her desk terminal wasn't hooked up for it, but there were several other computers with that capability in the newsroom, including one right outside Burgholz's office for general staff use. No one was on it at the moment, so she quickly grabbed her notebook and scampered over. In no time at all she was into the Web, specifically one of the search mechanisms used to find things in the huge conglomeration of infojunk floating around in cyberspace. She typed various entries into the "Search For What?" box and waited impatiently while electronic tentacles were disseminated to pull back anything they found on the requested topics. Depending on how you searched, you either got nothing or too much. Through trial and error, Alison had learned how to be masterful at it. As a result, she retrieved a manageable number of articles that included the key words she had specified. She scanned these to find ones of particular relevance and printed them out. She took the haul over to her desk and began reading.

About thirty minutes later, she closed her eyes. "My God," she said aloud. "I'll bet that's what this is all about!"

She immediately picked up the phone and called Sergeant Johnson again to tell him what she had found. She admitted it was only a theory, that there was no proof, but it seemed to fit. In any event, she thought he should know. It was up to him to follow up as he wished. Johnson asked Alison if The Herald planned to do a story on what she had just told him. She said she didn't know. She hadn't even talked about any of this yet with her editor. Johnson said he couldn't force them not to, but it would be best not to spread this around just yet. It might alert those involved and close up opportunities this new information might afford them in their investigation. Besides, Johnson emphasized, most of what Alison had offered was just speculation at this point, unsupported by facts. Alison had to admit that was true. She said she would raise the issue with her boss.

Alison immediately placed a call to Stephen Blake at his office. She reached his secretary, who said he was out of the office and wasn't expected back until late in the afternoon, if at all. Alison said she had talked to him a couple of days ago and that he seemed to be feeling poorly. She asked if he was better. The secretary said he was a little improved but seemed to be out of sorts most of the week. Alison left a message for Stephen to call her if he got back in time.

After the call, Alison went to see Burgholz. He saw her coming down the aisle, walking fast but not smiling as usual. "What's wrong, Ali?" he asked, as she sauntered into his office.

Alison came right up to his desk and sat down. "I was going crazy not knowing what this whole thing was about, Jay. And now that I

Wicca Codex

know, or think I do, I'm not sure I want to."

"Know what, Ali? Spill it."

Alison rubbed her eyes. The strain of the last few days was getting to her, especially now that she was inching closer to a horrible truth. "You know about how all the victims were Catholics, and had priests in the family, right? Well, I just did more research and found a key link. It seems to make sense when put together with facts I discovered earlier. Like for instance...The Burning Times."

"The burning what?"

"Burning Times. The witch hunts from the medieval period. They'd always been persecuted, but it really picked up in intensity around the fifteenth century and kept going for two or three hundred years. Most of Europe was affected by the craze. Modern-day witches call it "The Burning Times" 'cause many of those condemned and put to death were burned at the stake. It's what most of us know as the Inquisition."

Burgholz still had a puzzled look on his face. All he could manage was, "So?"

"So, bear with me while I give you a little history lesson," said Alison. She was still excited but starting to calm down a little. "The Inquisition," she began, "was brought about by the Church to consolidate its power and authority over those who were seen as a potential threat. These were mostly just town and country folk, simple people, really, but ones who generally catered to the old-style pagan religions. I found out that 'pagan' comes from a Latin word—'paganus." It means country dweller. Anyway, the old religions were fairly safe when the Church was relatively young and growing and not yet too powerful. When it got bigger, it started to flex its muscles. Anyone who got in the way of that...well, all of a sudden, he or she was a 'heretic,' or a 'witch.'

Alison was listening to herself, and it seemed to be coming out okay. Burgholz seemed caught up in the tale. Keep going, she told herself.

"Things got out of hand when some of the early popes decided to put the squeeze on. Inquisitions were set up in Spain, France, Germany, all over. Scads of people died as a result. Some say millions. Others say hundreds of thousands. In any event, it was a lot. There are actually lists of names you can read. Most who died were women, but there were men too. Most of the killings involved peasants and farmers and the like. But again, not exclusively. Horrible tortures were sanctioned by the highest Church authority. Most of those killed weren't witches, of course, or anything other than people who wanted to practice their own beliefs in their own way. But the fanatics wouldn't allow it. Let's teach 'em a lesson, they said. Besides, it was profitable too. The condemned had their property confiscated, so The Church's coffers were kept filled. Not a bad deal all around, it seemed. Except for the victims. It was a pretty sorry time. And scary. After the worst of it ended, there were some who admitted to being witches. People who practiced healing and magic. Some of their descendants have been persecuted even into relatively modern times. That's pretty much over today. Now there are religions based on the old witch tradition. I came across one the other day on the Internet. It's called Wicca. It even sounds like 'witch.'"

Burgholz couldn't help himself any longer. He wanted Alison to get to the bottom line. "So how does all this tie together? What are you saying?"

Alison took a deep breath. This would be the first time she expressed her thoughts on this to anyone. She hesitated, not wanting to jump in and get it all muddled up. She wanted this to sound as convincing in the telling as it did in her mind. She didn't have it all worked out yet, but there was enough to hang your hat on. 'Take your time,' she thought. 'Get it right.' "What I'm saying is that those who died during the Inquisition are seen as martyrs by modern-day witches, and it's possible that someone is out to avenge those horrible deaths. Although the witch craze involved more than just The Catholic Church—Protestants weren't exactly standing idly by—The Inquisition was an institution created by some of the early popes. So, it stands to reason that whoever is out for western justice would see Catholics as culpable. In particular, the clergy. What I don't understand is why it's not the clergy themselves who are the victims. And I don't see a strong connection between the modern Wiccan belief code and this kind of destructive behavior. Wiccans tend not even to associate themselves with Satanism, although there are elements of witchcraft—and I guess Satanism, by extension—in some of the things I've read. Also, Wiccans tend to emphasize individual beliefs and initiative, so what we could have here is someone accepting the general overall concept of witch martyrdom, then going off to do his or her own thing as a revenge kick. Essentially, it could be a blend of Wicca and witchcraft and Satanism. Wicca run amok, you might say."

Burgholz leaned back and was silent for a moment. All of a sudden, his glasses seemed looser than normal. He made the usual adjustment, then said, "Wow. Some theory. But tell me this. What is this black-mark business? Why is the murderer doing that? And how?"

"Those are harder questions, and I admit to not having the answers. But try this on for size, as long as we're theorizing." Alison paused to gather her thoughts. Until then, she had been sitting on the edge of her chair. Now she followed Burgholz's lead and leaned back onto the chair's hard wooden surface. She was so engrossed in her own tale that she took no notice of her discomfort. "Stephen Blake—you remember him—told me about a book Ernst had in his shop, a really ancient manuscript. He promised Ernst not to tell anyone about it, but he thought it was important for me to know. Stephen likewise asked me not to mention it, and I did say I wouldn't, but I think we're beyond the point of worrying about broken promises. Anyway, Ernst has this weird book called, of all things, The Wicca Codex."

Burgholz eyebrows clicked up and his eyeballs increased in diameter. "Say again?"

"That's right. The Wicca Codex. Translate it as 'The Witch Book,' if you like. So, Ernst tells Stephen it has this funny effect on people. Gives them the creepies when they touch it, if they're not supposed to. Stephen tries it and thinks he feels something strange. The following night he goes to one of Ernst's meetings, and the next time I talk to him he sounds like he flunked out of charm school. I already told you about that. So, what if there really is something to this Codex? What if it has some kind of power? What if Ernst has found a way to harness some kind of awful energy through *The Codex* to control people, like Stephen? And to kill if necessary"

Once again, Burgholz's fingers went up to his eyeglasses, which seemed to have been sprayed with silicon or graphite or some other incredibly slippery substance. "Lord in Heaven. I don't believe I'm hearing you right. You're saying the bookstore guy is doing all this? With some magic book? Are you serious?"

"I know it's crazy, Jay, but think about it. Let's say, just for the sake of argument, that I'm right about this. It accounts for so many things. Like the fact that the police have never found any clues at any of the murder scenes. There just wasn't any evidence of human intervention, when you think about it. *The Codex* force fits that. It also could account for the black mark. Some kind of magical ray comes out of *The Codex*, searches out its victim, and strikes, leaving only the tell-tale mark on the back of the neck. And it's a burn mark, which could represent the burning of the witches. How fitting, really. You people burned our ancestors at the stake. Now it's your turn. And then there're the late-night meetings at Ernst's place. Saying they're coven meetings is probably just as plausible an explanation as getting your best friends together at midnight to talk about books and politics. Covens generally do meet at midnight, as I recall. How about it?"

"You've got an answer for everything, I see."

"Not quite," said Alison, shaking her head. "Like why those particular victims? Why not avenge the witch deaths by killing priests rather than their relatives? And why get Stephen involved in this grisly business? And why doesn't Demming fit the theory about Catholics, even though he died with a black mark?"

"What you're really saying here, I think, is that we're dealing with ritual killings perpetrated by a little old man who owns a bookstore using some unearthly force that he somehow has acquired and learned to control." Now it was Burgholz's turn to shake his head. "Is that about right?"

Alison grasped the sarcasm in Burgholz's voice but stuck to her guns. "I guess that's a fair assessment of the situation, as I see it."

"What about the police? Have you apprised them of any of this fantastic story?"

"I just got off the phone with one of the lead investigators. As a matter of fact, I talked to him twice this morning. The first time I mentioned the Catholic priest connection. The second was to tell him about the Inquisition and the possibility of a revenge motive. He asked me not to do any stories on any of it. Not yet anyway. Can we accommodate him?"

Burgholz thought about that one long and hard. "I certainly wouldn't do anything on the theory end of it. It's just too speculative and sensational. Just right for The Enquirer, but not us. The part about priests and Catholics is powerful stuff, and my first inclination would be to go ahead and write it up but hold off on publication for now. Why don't you do something on that? Just to have it available. I'll raise the issue with the big guys in our next editors meeting and see what the consensus is, but I'll support the police position to withhold—temporarily anyway."

"Okay. Done. I'll get right on it."

Burgholz saw that Alison remained seated and fidgeted with her hands. He said, "What's wrong, Ali? Is there something else bothering you?"

She hesitated. "I guess you could say that."

"You're worried about Stephen Blake?"

"That's part of it."

"What else?"

"I'm Catholic. And my uncle's a priest."

Chapter 27

Friday, October 27

"Now what exactly is it that makes you so happy in the midst of all this chaos, Pat?"

Lieutenant Vincent Mulcahy was sitting at his desk at the Boston P. D. He was addressing his friend and partner, Sergeant Patrick Johnson, who was just entering Mulcahy's office. Johnson was smiling, a facial feature that was decidedly uncharacteristic around these parts. Especially recently.

Johnson blew into the room and pulled up a chair at the lieutenant's desk. "Funny you should ask, Vinnie, but we may just've gotten a bit of a break in our quest for truth and justice. Actually, I got some good news and some bad. Your preference?"

It was no contest, as far as Mulcahy was concerned. "Not sure I can take any more bad news. Give me something to soften the blow."

"Thought so," said Johnson. "Then chew on this. It's been brought to my attention that every one of our black-mark murder cases involves a Catholic victim. Better yet, all five—count 'em—had a priest in the family as a relative. We're in the process of verifyin' all this directly, but I don't have any doubt it's true."

Mulcahy put both hands on the desk and pushed himself out of the chair. "Damn," was all he could say. He stood leaning out over the desk toward Johnson. "Where'd you get this from?"

"That's the bad news. It took a young whippersnapper reporter to turn it up. That Simmons gal from The Herald. Just got off the phone with her. Says it was a stroke of luck to uncover the first one. The others fell into place after that. Luck or no, she dug it out and gave it to us. On a platter. We just goddam missed it, Vinnie."

"Double damn," said Mulcahy, collapsing back into the chair.

"Couldn't have said it better myself, old buddy," said Johnson. "Only fly in the ointment is Demming. He's Protestant, and there doesn't appear to be any hidden Catholic wing in the family harborin' a priest in residence, so he doesn't fit the pattern. Then again, he's not officially a murder victim. Yet."

Mulcahy was still hot about the gaff in their investigation but starting to cool down a bit. "That's nice, Pat. Really. But it doesn't exactly resolve our problem, does it? Like, for instance, who's responsible, and why?"

"Well, no, not exactly," agreed Johnson, "but, uh, you'll wanna hear the second part of this, Vin. It seems our Miss Simmons has been doin' some more checkin'. She's come up with what you might call an interestin' theory about that."

Mulcahy ran his fingers through his hair, or what was left of it. No wonder it was going the way of the dinosaur. "No shit. Seems she's been a busy little bee, hasn't she?"

"Ya don't know the half of it, Vinnie. Listen to this. She thinks this could have somethin' to do with revenge for all those witch deaths what took place durin' the, uh, Inquisition. Ya know those religious massacres? Like hundreds of years ago? And get this. The guy doin' the avengin' is none other than our friendly little bookstore owner, one Mister G. Ernst."

"Holy Christ, Pat." Mulcahy was like a microwave in a house full of kids, heating up all over again. This was getting to be gut-wrenching in the extreme. "That's a bit much, isn't it? An eighty-year-old guy is going around breaking people's necks? Or maybe he's hiring someone else to do it. Simmons happen to say which?"

"Uh, none of the above, Vin. She, well, she thinks it may have somethin' to do with a force that Ernst conjures up from this old book she found out he had. Supposed to have somethin' to do with witchcraft. She called it...wait, she spelled it for me...The Wicca Codex."

Mulcahy closed his eyes for a moment and just sat there, silent. He didn't know what to say, which was quite uncharacteristic. Lieutenant Vincent Mulcahy, Boston P. D., always found something to say. Except now.

"Listen, Vinnie," said Johnson, mostly just to break the silence, "I know this is out of the blue and all, and prob'ly off the wall..."

"Probably off the wall?" screeched Mulcahy.

"Okay. Look. Why don't we keep an open mind on this? It was us, remember, who brought this kind of thing up in the first place, didn't we? At last week's press conference? The occult connection, it got called in the papers. And we're supposed to be the experts in this weirdo stuff, right? Me and you, with our fancy courses and all." He eyed his partner, who didn't seem to be buying it. He plowed ahead anyway. "It's true no one's ever had any experience like this—as far as we know, anyway—but why not go on the assumption for the time bein' that this could be possible? Check it out, ya know? If it don't wash, we don't lose nothin', right?" Johnson's raised both hands, palms up, and shrugged his shoulders. "What's our choice, Vin? We been stymied up 'til now. Spent nearly the whole damn afternoon yesterday goin' over every lousy scrap we had. I don't have to remind ya what we came up with. At least now we got somethin' to check on, even if it is crazy. Instead of sittin' on our hands, with the Commish screamin' at us from down the hall."

Mulcahy thought about countering this with logic but gave up without a fight. Or at least made known the real reason he was on this emotional roller coaster. "What the hell, Pat. You're right. Maybe it's just that it busts my balls we didn't come up with something like this, you know? We sit here on our asses and some girl reporter hears us talk about the occult and comes up with a theory. Maybe it sucks and maybe it doesn't. But it's something. Serves us right, huh?"

"I'm pissed about it too, Vinnie. You betcha. But it's what we got. Let's run with it."

It was back to business for the team of Vee and Pee. Gut-check time had come and gone, and they had passed muster. Next on the agenda: action.

"So. Okay," said Mulcahy, springing up out of the chair and rubbing his chin. He was suddenly chock full of ideas. "Here's what we do. First, get on the horn and call the Boston Archdiocese. Tell 'em about the Catholic thing and the priest connection, but don't mention the other stuff. Not yet. Pick their brain about what they think it could mean. There've been lots of stories lately about priests gone bad in one way or another. Maybe our victims' relatives fit that mold. Who knows? Check it out." He was rolling now. Fired up. "Second. I'll call our friend Miss Simmons and get her in here. Later today, if possible. I'd like to go over everything she knows—and I mean every last friggin' thing—in detail. Soup to nuts. Seems she's done a ton of research. I'd like to compare notes. We may be able to fill in some gaps. Maybe she can convince me her fantasy story...excuse me...her theory, holds water. We can punch holes in it and see if she can plug up the leaks." Mulcahy's pacing was quickening, his stride increasing. "Third, I want a stakeout on the bookstore. Round the clock. And Pat, put someone on it who knows how to keep from being made, fer Chrissake. If this guy can zap unfriendlies from long distance, we don't need anyone taking unnecessary chances. I don't think we should go out there again. It may spook 'im. If there's anything to this at all, we've got to ease our way in rather than do a power move. Otherwise, we may end up with a crash landing—with us in the wreckage Anything else you can think of?"

"How about another press conference announcin' a solution to all of these damn murder cases?"

"Maybe tomorrow."

* * *

An hour later, Mulcahy and Johnson reconvened and filled each other in on progress. Mulcahy said that Simmons had agreed to come in, but it would have to be after work. She'd try to be there between 5:30 and 6:00. "You weren't doing anything tonight, anyway, were you, Pat?"

"Hell no, Vin. And anyway, what could possibly be more entertainin' than hearin' how our most productive informant came up with her stuff."

"You got that right. What about the stakeout?"

"All set. Evans and Merrill will handle it. They're good. They'll stay out of sight—guaranteed. And I asked 'em to take photos—if circumstances permit, of course. Light conditions and all. They know how to do that, too. They'll be on early this evenin' and see what develops." Johnson waited a second to see if his partner had caught the pun, but it sailed way over his overstressed head. Johnson didn't press it. "Weather's supposed to be mild, so they'll do tonight in a car. If we need 'em to go longer term, they'll try and get a spot in a buildin' nearby, one with good sightlines to the store. Wherever it is, it'll be un-ob-tru-sive." This was one of Johnson's favorite words. He used it every chance he got. He drew it out now, emphasizing each syllable, milking it to the max.

Mulcahy rubbed his hands together. After so many days of blind alleys and excuses, he was psyched. It almost didn't matter if it led anywhere or nowhere. It just felt energizing to be on the move again. "Okay, good. What else?"

"I talked to someone over at the archdiocesan office," said Johnson. "Turns out he couldn't tell me much about the priests in question. They'll dig into it, but they need some time. Did tell me one interestin' thing, though. We got to talkin', and he happened to mention there's this big bishops' conference scheduled for Boston next week. On Wednesday. That's November 1. Ya notice anythin' peculiar about that date, Vin?"

"November 1? No, not really. Other than it's the first day of the month."

"Which follows the last day of October, which is what?"

Mulcahy thought for several seconds. "Which is Halloween. Which is when little witches and goblins play dirty little tricks on their friends and neighbors. Especially if they don't like their friends and neighbors for some reason."

"Maybe I should get back to the Archdiocese and tell 'em about this, Vin."

"You read my mind, Pat."

Chapter 28

Friday, October 27/Saturday, October 28

Ten minutes to midnight.

The watch on Stephen's wrist informed him there were only those few minutes before Ernst would walk into the room and begin what could be the most important meeting Stephen had ever attended. To say it was a matter of life and death would not be overstating the situation, he thought. Life and death for people he didn't even know. Perhaps for him as well. The possibility was very real, he felt. At that moment, he would have given anything to trade this meeting for even one of those horrendously boring industry affairs he went to on a regular basis. He vowed that if he ever got out of this, he would never complain again about having to attend those dreary nighttime events with his business colleagues. Everything was relative.

Stephen had arrived only about ten minutes ago. He may have been compelled to come tonight, but there was no way he was going to spend any more time with these murdering monsters than he absolutely had to. And compelled he was, by his own verification. Stephen desired not to be there, willed himself not to be there, yet found that he was powerless to resist. It appeared that Ernst's pronouncement made to him on Tuesday night was true. He could not fight *The Codex*.

Stephen himself wore one of the dark robes common to the other members, having been instructed to do so by Ernst prior to the meeting. He was told that all attendees, whether full-fledged members, initiates, or invited visitors, had to be properly attired. Apparently, they kept extras available for special occasions such as this. How thoughtful, Stephen muttered to himself.

He took note of the rather simple layout as he sat in the bookstore's meeting room: the circular table on the center platform, two candles gracing its cloth-covered surface; several tables along the walls, all festooned with candles, now being lit by some of the membership; the circle of chairs surrounding the center platform. He counted fourteen. Stephen didn't know it, but two extra chairs had been placed in the circle on this night. One for him. Another for Lariakin, who had informed Ernst he would be attending due to the singular importance of this particular meeting. Several of the chairs already had robed occupants in place.

There were also the cryptic symbols and quotations painted on the walls. Stephen thought they might be in Latin, but their crude script made them somewhat hard to read. Even if he could make out the words, he certainly would not be able to discern their meaning, although he could probably guess at the gist of it.

Then there was the mesmerizing, almost overpowering presence of the dark Satanic image hanging on the far wall, facing Stephen squarely. This came about because he had deliberately seated himself as close to the door as possible. He knew he wasn't going to be carrying out any daring escape, but he thought he might feel better nearer the exit than buried more deeply in the room's interior. In so locating himself, he did not realize he would be facing that awful image for the meeting's full duration. He thought briefly about changing his position but decided against it. Stephen didn't want to call any more attention to himself than was absolutely necessary. He chose instead to endure the penetrating stare of the hellish eyes looking down at the circle. Looking down at him.

Stephen sat silently for several more minutes. He spoke to no one, and no one spoke to him. In fact, he saw there was very little discussion taking place among those in the room. A quiet word was exchanged now and then, but it was not what you would call a social gathering on a festive occasion.

Now the chair to his right had just been taken, as indeed had all the others, except for the one to his immediate left. That remained unoccupied. Stephen stole one final glance at his watch: eleven fifty-nine. The others must have sensed the proximity of the sacred hour—twelve o'clock midnight, straight up—for what little murmuring there had been suddenly ceased. One of the members rose, walked to the door, and turned off the lights, leaving only the soft glow of dozens of candles to illuminate the surreal scene. It was time!

At exactly twelve o'clock, Ernst entered the room, accompanied by Lariakin. Both wore a dark robe, similar to the other attendees. Theirs bore no special designation to indicate any difference in rank, except that Ernst wore a pentacle suspended from his neck on a gold chain. Despite this sameness, Ernst exuded a presence and demeanor that left no doubt as to who was in charge. He proceeded to the center platform, stepped onto it and stood next to the circular table. Lariakin sat in the last available chair next to Stephen, who shivered as he felt a strange coldness run through him. The room remained deathly quiet. Stephen felt the eyes of the devil boring into him. He dared not look anywhere but straight ahead at the figure of Gustav Ernst as he paced around the edge of the platform. 'Just like an actor on a stage,' thought Stephen. 'Only this is a deadly drama.'

After a few moments, Ernst broke the eerie silence. He spoke slowly, but with an assurance of unchallenged authority. This was what he lived for. He was in complete control, speaking to his minions, performing for the representative of his idol. Another might say he was in heaven. Ernst would say he was in hell.

"I welcome you, my brothers and sisters," said Ernst, "to this special meeting of our glorious coven. Special because we have two honored guests with us tonight. You all know Lariakin, of course, and we are most pleased he has joined us. In addition, we have the honor of a return engagement from our good friend, Mr. Stephen Blake, who you will recall from our last meeting has agreed to participate in our endeavor in a most important way. He has joined us as an initiate..."

'I have?' thought Stephen. 'I don't remember doing that.'

"...and so we will not yet refer to him as Brother Stephen. But we

Wicca Codex

look forward to the day when we will all call him 'brother.' In any event, we will hear from him later as he reports on his progress."

Stephen could feel sets of eyes peering at him from within dark hooded recesses. His normal reaction would have been to squirm, but he felt the need to remain perfectly still. Stephen bristled at Ernst's use of the word "friend" in his remarks, but he dared not object. In fact, he didn't know that he could, even if he wanted to. But he wasn't about to test *The Codex*'s effect on him in that regard. As for reporting to the group, Stephen was not surprised since Ernst had alerted him to it just before the meeting. In any event, Stephen had expected to say something about the terrible task Ernst had assigned to him only three nights ago, so he was prepared to do so.

"Now, however," continued Ernst, "we will hear from Lariakin, who has requested the opportunity to speak to us tonight. Let us heed his words."

Ernst and Lariakin exchanged places, Lariakin climbing onto the raised platform, Ernst seating himself in the chair next to Stephen. As Lariakin was preparing to speak, Ernst leaned toward Stephen and put a hand on his knee. He said, in the barest whisper, "Do not be nervous, Stephen. You will do fine." Stephen abhorred the feel of Ernst's touch and the sound of his voice but did nothing and said nothing in response. He merely fixed his gaze on the mysterious Lariakin, whose tallness was enhanced by the platform's elevation, causing his large frame to tower over them. He was about to say the first words Stephen had heard from him.

"I am most pleased," said Lariakin, in a deep voice that reverberated off the walls, "to be among you tonight. I first want to say I am here with all of you at every meeting. If not in physical form, in spirit. Your doings are known to me, and I commend you for your steadfastness in adhering to the principles established by your leader, Brother Ernst. I wish to congratulate him for his devotion in establishing and leading this group. He has chosen well, and you have performed well."

Stephen could not see Ernst's face, and certainly would not look over, but knew he was enjoying this immensely.

Lariakin went on, keeping his hands buried in the large folds of his robe. "As you are aware, we are engaged in a most important struggle. The attainment of lost justice is always difficult. Yet the plan we have identified and carried out to this point has been successful, and for that I am most grateful. You are all to be congratulated. Now, however, we are at an important crossroad. We must proceed to the next level of implementation. This involves two significant elements. The first is the need to expand the operation from this venue to many others. In that we are to be assisted by Stephen Blake, as you have just heard. We thank you, Mr. Blake, for your help." Lariakin opened both arms to Stephen in a gesture of appreciation, looking straight into his eyes. Stephen remained motionless and returned the stare but had to avert his gaze after only a few seconds. He could not maintain eye contact. Lariakin paused briefly as he took note of Stephen's reaction, then continued his monologue as he paced around the table. "Mr. Blake will develop the means to duplicate that which allows us to carry out our mission. He will work with us to ensure that we will all be able to join in the effort to expand our limited base of operation."

Stephen noticed that Lariakin's voice rose in pitch slightly. He was becoming more animated, more enthusiastic, more forceful. He was getting ready to whip the troops into shape. Lariakin was gesturing repeatedly now. His pace picked up as he circled the table.

"*The Codex*," continued Lariakin, "is the mechanism by which all is accomplished. But we can affect only a very small area at present. The cleansing fires must be dispersed elsewhere so that additional slayers of our martyrs can be expunged. And, of course, we must prepare for the other phase of our work. We have experimented with individual members of the Catholic cohort. One here, one there. A mere trifle. But we have shown what can be done, given the will, and the means. We have both. There is no doubt we have both."

Stephen heard nothing from the membership, but sensed they were getting into the spirit of Lariakin's words. There was more movement of arms and legs and heads from the audience.

"Yes, my compatriots, we must now move ahead toward a grander design. Until this point, we have spared the hated clergy from our powers, knowing that they would be hurt more by the loss of their loved ones than by their own deaths. And it has been most satisfactory to see that such has been the case. But now, my friends, it is the moment to pass judgment directly on the purveyors of past crimes. They must experience the devastation that can be thrust on them and their profane institution. The Church and its practitioners are now at risk. We will demonstrate to them their mistakes, as well as their failure to take responsibility for them. Also, the futility of resistance to those of us who would re-establish equilibrium in the world order. The balance of things has been out of scale for too long. It is time to remedy this unfortunate situation."

Lariakin was into it now. His voice boomed. His arms waved wildly. His routine pacing had turned into hurried movements from one spot on the platform to the next. He leaned in toward one member, then another, exhorting them with his rhetoric. And it was effective. Now there were audible cries of agreement and support from the audience. Their normal staid demeanor was replaced by a frenzy of passion and enthusiasm for the grand design that was being set before them. They were about to participate in no less than the expiation of some of the most heinous crimes in the entire span of human civilization, and they reveled in their role in that marvelous endeavor. Ernst himself had gotten into the spirit of things and was clapping his hands and yelling along with the others. Stephen did not know if this was part of the predetermined strategy that Ernst and Lariakin had devised or if Ernst was really becoming affected like the others. Stephen himself sat without any display of emotion. He glanced up once or twice at the picture of Satan on the wall and could swear he saw the eyes move. 'It's got to be my imagination,' he thought.

Lariakin started again, "And do you know how we will do that, my friends? Do you know how we will regain order? There is only one way. The way of fire! The flames of the past have never been quenched, brothers and sisters. No. Not at all. They have remained smoldering in the burned bodies of our departed ancestors. Those who gave their lives in worship to The Prince. But he has returned! Yes, he has. He is here among you, urging that you carry out his will. You can see him! You can hear him! You can feel his presence! He is here! Do not disappoint him. Do not let his coming be in vain. Do not deny him the measure of justice that has eluded him for so many years."

There were now screams and shouts from the circled members. Most were on their feet, waving their arms, swaying from side to side. Others were stomping on the old wooden floor, sending up booming waves of sound that lingered after the deep bass tones of Lariakin's voice had disintegrated.

Lariakin stepped from the platform and walked up to Ernst. Each man grabbed the arms of the other and exulted in the moment. They exchanged a few words, although Stephen could not hear what was said due to the continuing cacophony. After a minute or so, Ernst made his way back to the platform while Lariakin sat once again next to Stephen. As before, Stephen sat quietly, observing the spectacle. It was clear to him that *The Codex* could compel him to be here, but not to participate in the wild chanting and breast-beating. Another limitation on its power? Ernst let the members whoop and holler a while longer, then held up both arms to restore order. The revelers gradually calmed themselves and took their seats. Ultimately, the quiet and serenity of the early part of the meeting took over.

Stephen waited nervously for Ernst to begin speaking. He hoped Ernst wouldn't call on him just yet. Lariakin was a tough act to follow. Stephen was grateful when it became evident it wasn't his turn. Grateful, that is, until he heard Ernst's next words.

"Thank you, Lariakin," said Ernst, "for those inspiring thoughts. It is good to be refreshed from time to time on the reason for our mission. And who better to provide that to us than you, sir." Ernst glanced in Lariakin's direction and nodded slightly. Lariakin returned the gesture but said nothing. Ernst continued: "And now that we have been educated once again on 'why,' I will attempt to enlighten you on 'how.' We have spoken in the past of the eventual need to escalate the scope of our efforts. That time has come, my friends. We will now carry the struggle to our antagonists, the criminal Catholic clergy. In fact, we have been given an extraordinary opportunity to begin this phase. Given to us, ironically, by our most hated enemies themselves. They have seen fit to schedule a conference of bishops in this very city. Scores of black-suited clerics, those carrying the miter and staff, will be in attendance. But the very best part is the timing of it. It is so delightfully appropriate as to be beyond belief. The good fortune of it convinces me that our work is truly sanctioned by the highest authority we honor here. You see, my friends, the conference is to be held on Wednesday next. On the first day of November. The day after our sacred celebration of All Hallows Eve. We will be able to undertake the special celebration we had planned for the occasion, and conclude it with a truly memorable event: the destruction of all Catholic bishops attending the conference!"

There were a few cries of thanks and exultation from the audience, who could not contain their joy at this turn of events, and their good fortune at being permitted to participate. Normally, such a breach of discipline while Ernst was speaking would have been reprimanded. Today's announcement, however, was of special significance, and he permitted them their little demonstration. How could he object, after Lariakin had inspired them so? Ernst merely held up his hands and urged them to desist.

After order was restored, Ernst went on. "Of course, we will have to extend our celebration beyond the time normally allocated. We expect that all of you will arrange your schedules so that you can be in attendance. Conference events are planned to be underway beginning at nine o'clock Wednesday morning. But we will wait until ten to make certain we have most, if not all, of the attendees present. We will then unleash our powers on them. Powers such as they have never seen.

Until now, we have been restrained, cleansing only family members of the clergy. It has been a symbolic act, a representative one. There was no need for a more elaborate display. We were, after all, carrying out the judgment on lay victims, not totally innocent of the wrongs of the past, but yet not quite at the same level of responsibility as their priests. We must not be so kind any longer." Ernst's ire was rising within him, and he struggled mightily to keep it under control. But it was no easy task to restrain the hatred that had been accumulating for so long. "We must turn our attention to the primary criminals and bring the same fiery destruction to the bishops they rained down on our martyred ancestors. They must be totally extinguished by the flames. It will be the perfect way to celebrate so great an event on our calendar." Ernst's demeanor and tone lightened somewhat as he contemplated the neat juxtaposition of unfolding events. Symbolism was important to him and served to enhance his sense of accomplishment and satisfaction. Actions without meaning were hollow. "As a bonus, you might say, the first day of November is referred to as All Saints Day in their liturgy. It is a happy occasion for them; their priests wear white at mass. The following day—the second—is All Souls Day, when The Church commemorates all the faithful departed. Dark robes and emblems of mourning are worn to indicate the sympathy of Mother Church for her children. Well, my friends, we will ensure that many new souls are available on that day for them to mourn."

'So,' thought Stephen, shaken and dismayed by what he had just heard, 'this is their grand plan. The plan in which I'm now involved, in a small way. Actually, not so small, if you think about it.' He was waging titanic battles in his mind. One side of him recognized the horror of it all. That he was being called upon to have a role in this scheme—large or small—was anathema to that facet of his character. On the other hand, there was the part that had been programmed to ward off the sanctimonious babblings of those who would deter him from accepting this role. Deter him from taking his rightful place in the hierarchy that had been established to correct past crimes against humanity. Enormous crimes. Horrific crimes. Such a role seemed reasonable to his darker side. The forces at work to keep this latter element uppermost were powerful. Yet there was that other component, the one that might be called his innermost conscience. It was definitely down, but not quite out. Suppressed, you might say. Below the surface.

Stephen thought he heard his name being called. "Stephen, are you ready to give us your report?" asked Ernst.

"Uh, yes, I am," muttered Stephen, somewhat half-heartedly. He fought against the Mr. Hyde within him and tried to restore Dr. Jekyll. He may not be calling all the shots when it came to his head, but he needed to snatch whatever control he could for the immediate task at hand. He rose from the chair but remained in place to make his remarks. As Ernst had told him beforehand, he was not to use the platform. Ernst hadn't said it in so many words, but the clear implication was that no one other than Ernst—and Lariakin, obviously—had that privilege. Stephen felt fourteen sets of eyes focus on him in anticipation of his message. Another set, not human, was the most discomfiting to him, though. They belonged to the hideous image dominating the far wall, shrouded in dark hues. Stephen would have sworn the evil creature was about to leap out of the frame and devour him, such was the ferocity of its aspect and the feeling of reality it instilled.

"I, uh, am pleased to tell the group," began Stephen, somewhat shakily, his voice one notch higher than he would have liked, "that I've had some success in identifying the means to carry out my assignment, which is to duplicate *The Codex*." Stephen noticed for the first time that the manuscript was not in the room. 'No need for it today, I guess,' he thought. 'Thank goodness.' "As you know, I believe, I'm employed at a large publishing firm in downtown Boston, and so, I have some knowledge of the process. However, it's a rather complex one, especially for a document like *The Codex*. I'll need quite a lot of help in learning all the elements involved. Fortunately, the means to do so are available, and I've begun arrangements to work with a knowledgeable person at my firm, who has agreed to help. Of course, he's not aware of the reason for my request. Nor will he be informed of it."

These last remarks were not quite one hundred percent true. Stephen did talk to Sam Peters about it the day before, and Sam had agreed to help him find equipment and supplies but was not necessarily aware that he would be asked to help in other ways. There was enough truth in what Stephen said, however, to make him comfortable. He could only hope there was no way for Ernst or Lariakin to find out about this tiny untruth. Stephen cleared his throat and went on, warming a little to the task. "In addition, we'll need to get hold of a rather formidable array of printing and binding equipment, as well as related supplies. The source I mentioned has already begun to do some research to find suitable items, hopefully second-hand or surplus to keep the cost down. Only this afternoon he informed me he has one or two leads that may bear fruit. He promised to follow-up on it and let me know by early next week. Obtaining all the necessary items, though, will take a little time. But the process has begun, and it looks promising. That's all for now. I'll have more to report, hopefully, at the next meeting."

Stephen sat down and felt a hot flash run through him. He didn't look at anyone but sensed Lariakin peering his way from the chair just to the left. There were a few murmurs of what seemed to be approval from several of the members, but otherwise there was little reaction. He realized now that everyone took their cues from Ernst, and the old man hadn't initiated any outburst's of applause or cheers. Not that Stephen had expected any.

Ernst, still up on the platform, said, "Thank you, Stephen. We are truly pleased with your work, and with the progress you have made in a short time. We reiterate, however, that time is of the essence, and ask that you redouble your efforts so that we may expand our operation without delay. I am sure you will do what is required to accomplish that."

Ernst did not ask for a response, and Stephen gave none. He merely sat and silently acknowledged the dark side of him that agreed with

Wicca Codex

Ernst on the need for getting the job done in a timely way. If not sooner.

"And so, with that, my friends, all scheduled activities on the agenda have been concluded. Are there any questions among the members about anything we have discussed here tonight?"

There were none.

"Very well," said Ernst. "In closing, I urge you once again to prepare yourselves for the great celebration that will take place here beginning on All Hallows Eve. It will be a truly momentous occasion. One that is not to be missed. With that, brothers and sisters, I declare the meeting closed."

Ernst stepped down from the platform and walked toward the door, followed by Lariakin. The others had risen from their seats but remained standing, dispersing only after the two leaders had left the room.

As Stephen disrobed and prepared to leave the shop with the others, he felt a tug at his elbow. He turned and saw Ernst facing him. There was a broad smile on the old man's face. Ernst pulled Stephen aside and said, "Thank you for coming, Stephen. I hope you enjoyed it. I want to say that you did a fine job. A very fine job. And I know that Lariakin thinks the same. I wanted to let you know that. And to say that I believe you will do well for us in your continuing work."

Stephen said the only thing that came into his head. He spoke slowly and without emotion, almost in a monotone. It was as though his mouth were being operated by a puppeteer. Words were coming out, but they were not really his. "Thank you. It was quite an experience. I was glad to have the chance to come. I'll try to justify your faith in me. I look forward to the next meeting." That said, he turned, put on his coat, waited for the next group to leave the shop, and quietly departed.

The usual precautions were taken by those leaving: use no lights, check the street for passersby, exit in small groups, maintain total silence, disperse quickly. These measures were sufficient to avoid detection by anyone. Anyone, that is, except two super sleuths of the Boston Police Department—Officers Evans and Merrill, who were ensconced in their unmarked cruiser a discreet distance from the shop, hidden by the shadows.

* * *

With everyone else gone, Ernst and Lariakin let the evening's success sweep over them. They were seated in *The Codex* room. Lariakin spoke first. "It went quite well," he said. He wore a satisfied expression, one that Ernst had never experienced before.

"Yes," said Ernst, "I thought so too."

Lariakin looked at Ernst, who noticed a brief flicker of something dark that marred the top layer of celebration on his younger companion. "And what do you think of Blake?" asked Lariakin.

Ernst hesitated momentarily, then said, "I believe he will be with us for the duration. He has a strong will and is not yet fully engaged, but we will overcome whatever...misgivings...he still maintains about The Plan. The force is too strong. He will come to accept us. At the very least, he will do what is required."

"Let us hope what you say is true. I myself am not yet fully convinced of his total commitment. It was not in his actions, nor in his eyes. I will look to you to ensure his compliance."

"You need have no concern about that."

"Excellent," said Lariakin. "Now, let us enjoy the moment. And in particular, that which awaits us in but a few days. Our time is almost at hand, my friend. It has been long in the making. Much too long. But I believe that it will have been worth the wait. Can there be any doubt of that?"

"No doubt," said Ernst. "None whatsoever."

Chapter 29

Saturday, October 28

The start of another weekend was not having the desired stress-releasing effect on Alison Simmons. Since yesterday, when she'd put two and two together and it came up odd, Alison had been deeply troubled. On the one hand, she was gratified that progress had been made on the murder cases—primarily through her initiative. After so much frustration, that was a good thing. Then again, her dire suppositions could prove true, meaning that people she cared for were either now in serious danger or could end up that way. This overshadowed any feeling of accomplishment she may have been feeling. Stephen Blake was most affected. Then there was her Uncle Mike, a Catholic priest. Although clergy were not among the victims in these killings, that they were involved at all was an ominous thing. Finally, she had to be concerned for her own safety. She knew Burgholz was right about the risks. Not only was she exposing herself as a reporter to dangerous individuals and circumstances, but she was, after all, the relative of a priest. The very same category targeted during the last two and a half months. The idea made her shudder.

These contemplations turned Alison's breakfast into a rather forgettable affair. She hardly knew what she was eating. Enjoying it was out of the question. She had timed it so she would be on her way to Cambridge by nine thirty to make her meeting with Father Mike at ten. She had called her uncle the day before and asked if she could see him this morning, giving him only the barest of reasons for the visit. He was available, he said, and would be happy to see his "favorite niece" again. This favored status must be true, she thought. Priests don't lie, right?

Traffic was light, so it did not take long to cross the Charles River and maneuver her way out to St. Brendan's parish church. It was a gray stone building, nicely landscaped, with the obligatory bell tower. Alison thought the best part about it was the little parking lot next to the rectory. Trying to locate a legal—and available—spot anywhere in Cambridge was usually not a user-friendly experience.

Alison pulled into the lot, then sat in the car for a minute or two, wondering whether this was really a good idea. She went over all the pros and cons again, the advantages and disadvantages, the good, the bad, and the ugly. After coming to the same conclusion that had bubbled to the surface after all the other titanic mind games of the last twenty-four hours, she trotted up to the wooden door of the rectory. She had been here only once or twice before but remembered the front entrance. It was something you didn't forget—sort of medieval-looking, like the entrance to a castle or a fort, though not quite as large. She didn't know why, but it gave her a positive feeling. Perhaps that was a good omen, she thought. Alison rang the bell, stated her business to the frocked cleric who answered, and was ushered into a small sitting area.

While waiting, she took comfort in the quietude of the place, as well as the homey atmosphere of the tiny room. She didn't hear a single phone clanging in the background, nor was there one computer terminal in sight. It was a relief to be away from the fast-paced environment that had become her world. She wanted to close her eyes, throw her head back, and suck in the silence. She would have had not Father Mike interrupted her peaceful contemplation. He came bounding into the room with a quick gait and an enormously happy smile on his face.

"My Lord," gushed the priest, "if it isn't little Alison." He grabbed her in a huge bear hug. Alison tried to return the favor, but she was significantly overmatched. Her uncle was a large man—tall, and strong, but not the least bit rotund. He looked as though he could play power forward for the Celtics. He was in his late forties and had what most would call ruggedly handsome features. These included curly brown hair, blue eyes, and smile marks that betrayed his propensity for making friends and enjoying life, at least to the limits allowed by his chosen profession. "I haven't seen you in...what?...nearly a year," he said, pushing Alison away and examining her at arm's length. The voice was a hearty baritone, tight and crisp. "It was last Christmas, I think. Wasn't it? How have you been, my dear?"

"Oh, the usual," said Alison, as she got caught up in his beaming smile and returned the same. "Busy, and stressed out, and living life in the fast lane. You know how it is. But otherwise, no complaints. And how are you, uncle?"

"Never better, Ali, I'm happy to say. The Lord has treated me well. Better than I deserve. My health remains good, and He's seen fit to let me stay in this fine parish for a good long while—it'll be four years next month—so I consider myself fortunate, indeed. No doubt about it."

Alison removed her coat. She was dressed somewhat more sedately than she might have normally, snatching a blue corduroy jumper out of the closet this morning, followed by a frilly little high-necked blouse, the whitest one she owned. She wasn't quite sure if she chose the conservative wardrobe because of the rectory visit or because it matched her mood.

They sat and exchanged the talk of relatives who haven't seen each other for many months. After an appropriate interval had passed, the priest felt he could indulge his curiosity. "Well, you know, Ali," he said, "I must say your call yesterday intrigued me. You've had me wondering what is so all-fired important that you need to see your Uncle Mike. I hope it's nothing ominous." 'Funny he should use that word,' thought Alison. She said nothing, and he caught the meaning of her silence. He said, "But why don't we go make ourselves comfortable in one of the offices down the hall. We can have a little chat and keep it between ourselves, so to speak."

He escorted her along a carpeted corridor with photographs of various religious figures adorning the wall, including the current pontiff, John Paul II. As they walked, he asked, "Can I get you some liquid refreshment? Coffee or tea? Or something else, perhaps?"

"No thanks, uncle. I just finished breakfast before I came. I'm fine."

They arrived at a room just off the hallway. Father Mike stopped at the open door and waved Alison inside. It was a mini-office, used for purposes much like this one—private meetings, consultations, keep-it-to-yourself discussions. There was a small desk and two softly upholstered armchairs covered in a flower pattern. A lace-curtained window let in lots of light, and two or three small pictures with non-religious subjects graced the walls, mostly flowers and landscapes. "I hope you don't get claustrophobia," said the priest. "We keep the conference rooms small for a reason. We like to say conversations that take place here never go beyond these walls, and since the walls aren't that far away, the words don't have far to travel before they slip into oblivion."

Alison smiled and said, "That sounds like a pretty good rationalization." She took one of the chairs, her uncle the other, after first closing the door behind him.

The priest saw her outward smile, but also her troubled eyes. It was a look he knew well. You became adept at reading faces in his business. "Now, what can I do for you, Ali?" he asked.

Alison said nothing for a moment, trying to decide how to begin. Best to come right to the point, she decided. "Have you heard anything about those deaths that've occurred under mysterious circumstances the last two or three months? The ones they call the broken-neck murders, or the black-mark murders?"

The priest maintained his happy expression, but it was the smile of one who was used to keeping a positive outward appearance in the midst of the chaos and confusion of the modern world. He focused on his niece, then answered slowly. "I have read a little about those, yes. In fact, you yourself did a few stories on them, didn't you?"

Alison looked out the window, then at her uncle. "Yeah, I did. I covered the first one, then got into it again after the fourth. I've been involved with these cases almost exclusively over the last couple of weeks. The pace has picked up, and it's been quite troubling and frustrating dealing with it. The horrible circumstances, the lack of leads, everything about them, really."

"So how can I help?" He didn't want this to seem as though he was impatient, just trying to ease whatever pain was bothering her. It came out right from years of practice.

"I'm not sure," said Alison. She was groping, not at all certain where she was going with this. "What I do know is I had to come see you. Up until yesterday, I was in the dark about the whole mess, just like everyone else. But over the last twenty-four hours or so, I've come across some things that make it look like that word you used a moment ago—ominous."

The priest was used to this sort of thing. Difficult issues to talk about make for endless false starts. Sometimes it required a little gentle prodding to move things off dead center. "Forgive me, my dear, but that still doesn't explain why you're here."

"Yeah, you're right," she said, wondering why she didn't just come to grips with it. She took a deep breath. "So, here's the story, or the way I see it, anyway. I found out yesterday that all five of the victims of these crimes were Catholic. And that..."—she found it hard to go on with the rest of it—"and that every one of them had a priest in the family."

Father Mike raised an eyebrow and tapped the fingers of one hand on the arm of his chair. His early smile had faded almost to extinction, though not quite. "That *is* interesting, isn't it?" he said. "You're absolutely sure about that, are you?"

"I don't have any reason to doubt it, uncle. The information comes straight from relatives of the victims."

"I see," said the priest. He paused a moment, then said, "Is that the reason you came to see me? The only reason?"

Despite her subdued feelings, Alison couldn't suppress a laugh. This loosened her up enough to feel more at ease. More comfortable. More willing to let it all out. "You are a sharp one, aren't you, Uncle Mike? As a matter of fact, it's not. There's more. A lot more. And it's easily the scariest thing I've ever had to deal with before. Are you up to hearing it?"

"You wouldn't believe what I hear in the confessional, my dear," said Father Mike, his smile returning for the moment. "I think I'll be able to handle it. Why don't you give me a try."

"Okay, you asked for it." Alison spent the better part of the next hour going over everything she knew about the murders. She held nothing back. Ernst, Blake, Demming, the police—it all came out. She also related the results of her research on Satanism, Wicca, the Inquisition, witchcraft, everything. Then came the upshot—her theory on the why and how of it all. Although she had brought her notebook along, she didn't need it. All of it was done from memory. The facts were permanently embedded in her brain. She wasn't sure she could ever get rid of them. At the end of her narrative, which was for the most part uninterrupted by the priest, she felt emotionally drained and exhausted. She slumped back in her chair and said, "That's it, Uncle Mike. Every last thing I know or am guessing at."

There was no reaction from Father Mike for what seemed to Alison like an incredibly long time, although it was less than a minute. At the end of the interval the priest took in a long pull of air followed by a slow exhaling. He finally said, "My, my, my. You do have one heck of a story on your hands, don't you?"

"That's the question," said Alison, as she tried to bring herself back to some semblance of reality. "Whether it's just a story, or whether it's real. I just don't know. Everything seems to fit, but the whole thing is so bizarre, so impossibly unbelievable, it's hard to imagine anyone in their right mind could ever buy into it. I guess what I really came for is your reaction to it. As you can see, I'm whistling in the dark. I need a guiding beacon."

Alison had come to her uncle not only because he was a priest, who normally might be expected to know about these things, but also because of his background. Father Mike was somewhat of an expert in this area, having studied at Georgetown University's history department, both as an undergraduate and graduate. She knew his major concentration had been Modern Europe but remembered speaking to him on past occasions about several courses he'd taken that delved further back into medieval times. Things like an analysis of the writings of Dante, and others in the context of the political and religious upheavals of the times. Also, an exploration of monasticism in western Europe. He eventually went on to secure a master's degree, with an emphasis on medieval religious history. In fact, he had told her it was this experience that led him into priesthood. She felt there shouldn't be much he didn't know about the topic.

Because of that background, Father Mike was well aware there were troubling issues here. Issues that were difficult to raise, to discuss, to understand. He wasn't sure he himself had a firm grip on it all, despite his past immersion in these topics. Above all, he knew there were things that simply defied imagination. He felt he had to proceed with caution. "Well, okay," he said, measuring his words carefully. "You said you needed a beacon. I'm willing to play the role of lighthouse. Let's give it a go and see where it leads."

Alison hesitated, then pulled out her notebook and a pen. She saw the look of consternation on her uncle's face. "Don't get nervous," she said. "This isn't an interview. I just need to jot down the essentials, so I don't forget anything crucial. This is too important to rely on memory, especially mine."

"Fair enough," said the priest. He paused briefly, then said, "Let me start by saying that your historical context is pretty much correct in terms of the roles of paganism and Catholicism: the early posture of the Church, the growth of its influence, real or perceived threats to its power, and, I'm sorry to say, the Church's response to those threats in the form of the Inquisition. It was something that happened that shouldn't have. I think that's pretty much a given these days. But it did. No question. There are still some who would deny it, or condone it, or explain it. But, more and more, the consensus is that it was…let's call it an overreaction to a problem."

Alison liked her uncle a lot, but this representation of what she had come to feel was a horrendous event was just too much for her to accept. She almost screamed out, "An overreaction to a problem? God, Uncle Mike, what an awful thing to say. I can't believe you'd be that self-serving. I..."

Father Mike raised both hands, indicating time-out. "Whoa, Alison. Hold on. I see you haven't given up your old habit of jumping to conclusions. I used the phrase to describe what some others think about it. Not necessarily me. I personally think it was the sorriest era in our long history. It was a disgrace, as far as I'm concerned. Does that make you feel any better?"

Alison felt badly about jumping all over her uncle. She had, in fact, succumbed to her penchant for concluding things before hearing all sides, getting all the facts. "I'm sorry, Uncle Mike. You're right. I'm still incorrigible. Please forgive me."

The priest laughed good-naturedly. "So many people ask my forgiveness over the course of a week, I guess I can pass along one more absolution. Especially to my favorite niece." He made the sign of the cross over her as he would at the conclusion of a confession, throwing in a few choice Latin phrases to make it sound more official. Alison burst out laughing at the gesture.

"I deserve that, I guess," said Alison, trying to regain her composure and restore the seriousness of the matter at hand. "Anyway, please continue. I promise not to interrupt again. At least not in such an obnoxious way."

"Okee-dokee," said the priest, as he and Alison shared one last smile before going on to darker things. Father Mike said, "Now, where was I? Oh, yeah. I was about to say that the rest of your story leaves me a bit numb. In spite of your creativity in coming up with a potential explanation for what amounts to some very strange happenings, I'm afraid I'm having a hard time buying into the theory part of it. You must admit it isn't exactly your standard everyday situation."

"Of course I admit it. Then again, if it was ordinary, I wouldn't be here," said Alison, starting to get a little frustrated. "How about if we take it one step at a time?" she asked, groping for a way out of the morass. "What about the identification of the victims? Suppose there was someone intent on hurting priests by knocking off their relatives. How would they go about getting names?"

"That wouldn't be too difficult, really. There are ways. Especially for someone familiar with Catholic administrative procedures. Anyone like that on your list of characters?"

"Not that I know of."

"Even so. Let's just say it can be done. Priests' names are available from seminary yearbooks, things like that. Someone intent on doing what they're doing will be resourceful enough to make the connection between a particular priest and his relatives. It's a solvable problem."

Alison was happy to scratch at least that item off her mental checklist of theory busters. "Okay, so we've taken care of that one. Now what about the Satan connection?"

"That's not too far-fetched, actually. I'm sure you remember your Catechism lessons as a youngster, right?" said Father Mike, hopefully. Getting no response from Alison, he continued. "Then again, maybe not. Anyway, the Church teaches that there is a Satan, that he's a fallen angel cast out of paradise by God—you must've heard of Lucifer—and that he's the epitome of evil, intent on tempting all of us into acts that'd cause us to lose our souls and join him in hell after we die. That's the basic stuff. Then there's a higher plane, meaning there're documented cases of demonic possession, many accompanied by unexplained phenomena. Levitations, speaking in tongues, unusual feelings of extreme heat and cold, extrasensory incidents, movement of objects and people, sometimes violently. Strange things have been known to happen."

"There, you see?" said Alison, feeling more upbeat now. "You admit it's not impossible then. C'mon, fess up."

Father Mike did not want to close completely the little opening he had given Alison yet hesitated to widen it to Grand Canyon proportions either. He wanted to force her to build a case—convincingly, logically, unerringly. He was not interested in something that would stand up in a court of law—this was not exactly that kind of case—but there needed to be a continuous thread running through it. It was either going to withstand intense scrutiny or collapse of its own weight. His help and support would be contingent on that. "All I admit is that there've been unexplained incidents. I've never heard of anything like your Satan book. You called it some kind of codex?"

"The Wicca Codex," said Alison. "That's what Stephen Blake said Gustav Ernst called it. Which brings me to Wicca and the witchcraft connection. What about those aspects? *The Codex* could be Ernst's 'Book of Shadows,' but how do you reconcile the evil destructive tendencies of Satanism with the nature-loving and healing elements inherent in Wicca? It doesn't seem to fit."

"I'm not an expert on that," said Father Mike, truthfully. He had dabbled in those things on the periphery of his studies, but had never concentrated in that area at Georgetown, or elsewhere. "I've heard a little here and there, plus what you just told me. I know that some Satanists have been known to subscribe to what they call 'selective culling,' a sort of weeding out, survival-of-the-fittest concept. Scary stuff. But I'm afraid I don't have any strong opinions. You probably know more about those things than I do."

"Okay. Let's talk about Stephen Blake's behavior pattern? Doesn't it strike you as odd that a perfect gentleman turns into an ogre overnight?"

Father Mike tried to look more deeply into Alison's eyes for a clue to her innermost feelings on all this, but there was nothing in particular he could read. At least nothing different than the vibrations he was receiving from her voice and body language. "Odd, yes," said the priest. "But it's quite a leap to say the change was caused by a Satanic book. He could've been affected by any number of things. Work stress, a serious illness in his family, a financial setback, maybe even the death of his friend Demming. Didn't you also tell me Blake was feeling poorly; that he was out sick? That could've had something to do with it, too."

"Those are all perfectly rational explanations," said Alison, with the flicker of a smile starting to emerge. "And it's just like you to come up with them. You always do." Any trace of a grin that had been there vanished as her thoughts became serious again. "But I don't think they wash," she continued. "Not from the way Stephen sounded and acted when I spoke to him on the phone. This just wasn't the same person, Uncle Mike. I'm willing to bet on that." Father Mike was picking up conviction here. There was no waffling. None at all. "And what about the timing?" inquired Alison. "Was it just sheer coincidence he got sick and turned sour immediately after that meeting at the bookstore? I don't buy it. And how about the fact that his friend Demming died one day after paying a visit to Ernst? And Demming trying to call Stephen on a Saturday morning and leaving a message to the effect that he thought Ernst was strange? No way is all that pure chance. There's just got to be something kooky going on."

"It does seem like you've got some strong circumstantial evidence," conceded the priest. "But why not just let the police handle it, now that you've given them everything you know?"

"They can, but I'm still worried about Stephen. I can't just let him go without a fight." She had had the germ of an idea earlier, but wasn't sure she should broach it before. Until now. "Look, would you be willing to meet him, talk to him, if I can arrange it? See for yourself what I'm talking about?"

'So that's it,' thought Father Mike. 'We're down to crunch time. That's what this is all about.' He considered his options. First, not helping Alison was not one of them. She was troubled, apparently very much so, and it was his business to assist troubled souls and comfort them. Besides, she really was his favorite niece, wasn't she? Second, he could suggest that her young man seek assistance of a more professional nature, with someone who had a slew of graduate degrees hanging on his or her office wall denoting expertise in psychology, psychiatry, sociology, or whatever. But that would be a cop out, he told himself. The easy way out. Don't get directly involved. Pass the buck. Besides, this sounded like it had at least as many religious angles as others, and wasn't he the "expert" in that category? He had his own wall-hung credentials, and they might mean more in this particular case. Third, he could agree to meet this fellow Blake and check out for himself whether Alison's contentions about him were accurate or perhaps a bit exaggerated. Love—he didn't doubt that's what he was dealing with here—tends to do that, he knew. If there was nothing there, or less than what Alison was intimating...well, he wasn't making any commitments just by meeting him once. Beyond that, he would see. In fact, beyond that, he would almost surely have to get the Church authorities involved, if Alison's musings were anywhere near the truth. But he would worry about it later, if it came to that. He turned his gaze from Alison to the window and peered out at the world beyond its panes, as if that would help him decide how to proceed. But he had already made up his mind. There really was no doubt.

"Okay," said Father Mike, "here's what we'll do. You call your friend Stephen and talk to him. If he'll agree to see me, I'll be glad to meet him. Try for tomorrow afternoon at his place. I'll be through with my Sunday morning masses, and we'll keep it entirely comfortable for him if it's in his own home. Things should work better that way. I'll go civilian so as not to intimidate him. You can call me later and let me know if he agrees to it, and where he lives. I'll meet you there, we'll discuss the situation and see what develops. What happens after that depends on how it goes. But I have to be honest with you. If I don't see a problem, or if he isn't a willing participant, then I may not be able to continue past that point. If you can accept that possibility, then I'm willing to get the process started. Is it a deal?"

"I can live with that," said Alison, more than happy with her uncle's offer, qualified though it was. "Especially since I wasn't sure you'd do it at all. Thanks, Uncle Mike. I appreciate it. I know you'll end up seeing it the same way I do. I'm sure of it. And I also know you'll be able to help Stephen."

"Well, let's reserve judgment on that for the moment," said Father Mike as he rose from the chair, inviting Alison with an offer of his hand to do the same. She accepted his hand and stood. They left the room and walked slowly toward the front door of the rectory, exchanging more family talk as they went. Before leaving, Alison gave her uncle a hug, a tight one. He couldn't see her face but sensed she was on the verge of tears, something he was not accustomed to in her. She almost always managed to keep her emotions in check. He gently moved her away so he could hold her by the elbows. He said in as comforting a tone as he could manage, "Now Alison, I don't want you to worry about this. I'm here to help in any way I can. I want you to know I'll be there for you. You're not alone. Do you understand?"

Alison was having a hard time with words at the moment. "Yes, Uncle Mike. I understand," was all she could croak out.

She turned toward the door to leave, but was stopped by the priest. "You like this young man, Alison?" he asked.

There was only a slight hesitation, not because of any embarrassment on Alison's part, but rather because she wanted to be sure her answer made sense to her uncle, someone she admired and respected greatly. "Yes. I do," said Alison. "I only met him once, but sometimes you don't need lots of time to tell these things. I think I learned more about him during that short time than I know about some people I've dealt with for many years. It's a funny thing, and maybe it sounds dumb, but that's the way I feel about it."

"Nothing dumb about it, my dear," said Father Mike. He took both her hands into his. "And do you have reason to believe he feels the same way towards you? Or at least did that night, before his...predicament?"

Again, a momentary pause, followed by a twinkling in her eye as Alison recalled that look from him, the gentleness of their parting touch. "Yes, I think I...I know I do."

Father Mike said, "Now come on, dear girl. How about letting me have one of those big toothy grins I've been used to seeing all these years? Can you manage that?" He brightened his face considerably to encourage his niece to do the same. Seeing his smile and hearing his soothing words immediately made Alison feel better. She broke into a hearty laugh. "That's more like it," said the priest. "Now, you go on home and make that call. Let me know how it turns out and we'll go from there. Okay?"

"Okay," laughed Alison, who couldn't leave without one last hug, which she imparted most energetically. "I love you, Uncle Mike. You're the greatest."

* * *

"Hello?"

"Hi, Stephen. This is Alison Simmons. I've...been thinking about you and wanted to find out if you were feeling any better. How're you doing?"

"Alison Simmons? From The Herald? I think I remember you. Didn't we meet last week, or the week before?"

Alison could see that things hadn't changed much from their last conversation. 'At least he's not yelling at me,' she thought. "As a matter of fact, it was last Monday. After work? Chinese food? Remember?"

"I, uh, seem to recall something like that," said Stephen, struggling to bring his store of memories into focus. A shadow emerged of what the person on the other end of the line was talking about, but it was only a dull, amorphous image. Smoke curling up from a dying ember. He waited for it to coalesce into something concrete. It started to, then he lost it again. He had only the vaguest sense of who Alison Simmons was. He was torn between hanging up, as one might do on an unwanted call from a sleazeball telemarketer, and listening to what she had to say in the hope it would provide structure to the storm clouds. "How did you know I was sick?" he asked.

"You told me when I called you at home on Wednesday, remember?

On Monday we spoke about you going to the meeting at the bookstore the next night. I didn't like the idea much, but you said you wanted to. I called on Wednesday to find out how it went. You..."

"You know about the bookstore?" asked Stephen. Alison heard agitation in his voice and a heaviness in his breathing.

"Sure. We talked about it on Monday. It seemed to be the connection between..." She started to mention the strange occurrences and coincidences they had discussed at dinner, then thought better of it. They might trigger a hostile reaction in him, or at least further memory lapses that would make him more uncomfortable and distant. Short of Stephen admitting everything—which he wasn't about to do, of course—she was as certain as she could possibly be that her worst fears had been realized. The only thing that mattered was to play out the scenario she and her uncle had worked out. "Anyway, I really did call to find out how you were. And to ask if I could come over to see you, maybe tomorrow." Alison had decided not to say anything about her uncle. It was going to be hard enough getting Stephen to open up to her, let alone someone else, and a complete stranger at that. He might see it as a conspiracy against him, or something equally devious. "Are you doing anything tomorrow afternoon?" she asked. "I could come over after lunch. How's one o'clock?" She hoped she wasn't pushing too hard.

Stephen was still in a semi-daze and confused by what was happening. "Huh? Tomorrow? Well, I don't know. I'm not sure this is a good idea. I...I hardly know you, really. What is there to talk about?"

Alison knew she couldn't tell the truth. That would be a disaster. She tried to be as jovial and light-hearted as she could—under the circumstances—to take away any hint of intimidation or coercion. "It'd just be a little get-together between friends. Just to make sure you're okay, maybe cheer you up a little. And whether you admit it or not, we *did* have a good time last Monday night. That must be worth at least one visit, don't you think?" She didn't give him a chance to respond. "C'mon. Say yes. I promise not to bite your head off."

Alison listened for what seemed like an eternity. She could almost feel him debating with himself through the line. Alison had the fingers of one hand crossed and raised in the air. Finally, he said, "Well, okay. I guess it can't hurt any. One o'clock, did you say?"

Alison was elated. This was one large hurdle she had vaulted, but only the first of many, she was certain. "That's great, Stephen," she crackled. "I'll be there at one. I remember you live in the Back Bay, but tell me again what the address is, just to be sure." He gave her the information. She said, "I'll look forward to tomorrow then." He didn't say anything. She concluded the call with, "Hang in there, Stephen."

He couldn't imagine why in the world she said that.

Chapter 30

Saturday, October 28

After Alison left the rectory, Father Mike strolled back to the room where they had met and reclaimed the same chair he had occupied a moment ago. He sat there for a long time, thinking, staring out the window at the clouds that had turned the day from blue to gray. When Alison had called and asked to see him, he had no idea what it was all about. Now that he knew, he wished it had been something else, anything else. He wasn't sure he could deal with another one of these cases. Not enough time had passed since the last one. He wasn't sure there could ever be enough time. A hundred years, a thousand, ten thousand. It would still be too soon.

He rubbed his eyes, as if that could erase the thoughts, the fears, the longings for peace that had never really gone away. When that didn't work, he instinctively clasped his hands in front of his chest, closed his eyes, and prayed silently that he should be spared this ordeal. It wasn't exactly the same context, but he couldn't help thinking about the line in that great Bogart movie "Casablanca"—his favorite film of all time—where Bogie speaks bitterly of his recently returned lost love, Ingrid Bergman: "Of all the gin joints in all the towns in all the world, she walks into mine." It was exactly how he felt at that moment. He knew he would have to ask forgiveness for the thought, but he couldn't help himself. It was almost too much to bear.

It was even harder knowing the situation could not be avoided. This was his niece. She was family, dammit. 'Forgive me, Father.' He asked himself how he could do anything but come to her aid, regardless of the potential consequences. The answer was: There is no alternative. You're it.

It was time to see the Monsignor.

He reluctantly peeled himself from the comfort of the chair and walked down the hallway to the rear of the rectory, where Monsignor Ryan presided over his domain from a corner office. Father Mike paused in front of the closed door, summoned his courage, and knocked softly. He knew "the boss" would be there. He always was, especially in the afternoon, even on weekends, dealing with mountains of paperwork, exploring ideas for future homilies, pondering where he'd get the money to keep the operation from collapsing—this last item despite the well-worn maxim from on high, admonishing one and all not to be concerned over material things. After all, are not the birds in the air and lilies of the field amply provided for?

"Enter," heard Father Mike. It wasn't so much a command as an invitation. The Monsignor had a knack for doing that, even through a wooden door. It was as though a hand of greeting had been extended through the partition to lead the visitor into the promised land of milk and honey. Father Mike swung the door aside and walked into a space familiar from his having occupied it so many times before. It was a large, well-tended room, functional, comfortable, not ostentatious. Light and airy. Lots of wood and books and papers. Pictures of the Monsignor's family and friends in little frames scattered about. A well-worn, low-pile rug on the floor. An orange-shaded banker's lamp on the desk. A couple of green leather chairs, dimpled from extensive use, extending an invitation to join the Monsignor in conversation.

"Father Michael, welcome, come in," boomed the Monsignor, as he popped up out of his chair and waved his guest to sit. Father Mike was used to the formality. He rather liked the sound of "Michael" better than "Mike," actually. He also marveled every time he heard the Monsignor's voice. He couldn't figure out how such a huge sound came from such a little man. Monsignor Ryan was a full eight inches under six feet, yet he sounded as though he stood eight feet tall. He always told everyone that God had to skimp on his height because He used up so much material on his vocal cords. This was usually good as an ice-breaker.

"What brings you to my humble abode?" inquired the Monsignor. He ran his fingers through what was left of his silvery hair, about the only thing that gave any indication of his sixty some odd years. Otherwise, he was in fighting trim, as they say.

Father Mike settled himself into the soft leather and said, without any preliminaries, "I have reason to believe that Lariakin is back."

Monsignor Ryan sat down slowly, not saying anything for some time. He steepled his fingers and looked at Father Mike. "Are you certain?" he asked solemnly.

"Not totally, but the indications are there, I'm afraid."

"What makes you suspect it?"

"My niece was just here," said Father Mike. He did not look at his older colleague but sat staring blankly at the papers lying on the Monsignor's desk. "She came to talk about some rather bizarre circumstances involving people she knows, and the series of strange killings in Boston over the last several months. She has surmised some rather vivid explanations for these events in her mind, which are beginning to affect her adversely. Her descriptions are reminiscent of my previous experiences. It could be otherwise, but I fear the worst."

Father Mike was propelled back some six years, before his tenure at St. Brendan's. He had been assigned to a parish in Boston's South End, doing good work with the local community, involved in its affairs; he was enthusiastic, committed, and a leader. He was admired, respected, well-liked by his pastor, fellow priests, and the parishioners. Then the visions began.

They started right after he headed a committee formed to defuse a local hate group operating in the neighborhood. He and the committee suspected there was something sinister about the group. They seemed to have an air of evil about them. Witchcraft was mentioned, but nothing was ever proven. Things got nasty for a while—confrontations, accusations, threats of physical violence—then died down. But it was too late for Father Mike.

The visions were subtle at first. Almost like someone trying to implant subliminal messages in his brain. 'Stop. It's wrong. You'll be sorry.' That sort of thing. The words were usually in frames, hung on a wall as if in a museum. Then they became more disturbing. 'Death to the heretic priest. You'll burn in Hell.' These were accompanied by horrific images. Abominable things he could never accurately describe to any of the analysts. And a voice. An awful, eerie, grating voice that gnarled words and spit them out with such hatred that they were barely comprehensible. 'Do not fool with Larry Ah-kin,' the voice would sometimes say. Father Mike would grab hold of his pounding head and try to answer. 'Who are you? I don't know a Larry Ah-kin. Leave me alone.' The images became so real they drove him nearly insane. The final straw was the jagged message scrawled onto the steamy mirror in his bathroom one day after his morning shower: "You are dead, priest." Under it was what looked like a signature: "Lariakin." The drip marks from each letter oozed venom.

Father Mike's torment forced him to leave the parish and rehabilitate for nearly a year at a facility out west. After he was deemed to be cured, he was assigned to St. Brendan's, mainly because of the overabundance of patience and compassion characteristic of Monsignor Ryan. The elderly priest was told what had happened and had agreed to take Father Mike on and watch him carefully. The young priest had done well. Up until now.

"Did you discuss anything about those times with her," asked the Monsignor.

"No," said Father Mike. "She was quite troubled and seeking comfort. It didn't seem wise to do so."

"Yes, of course. And how did you counsel her."

"I offered my assistance, at least for now. She believes an acquaintance of hers, a young man she just recently met, has gotten himself involved involuntarily with questionable individuals and has been adversely affected by the experience. She thinks he's in serious trouble as a result and has asked me to meet him, then decide how to proceed, assuming he's under the influence of the evildoers. I said I would, under the condition the young man agrees to see me. She'll try to arrange it for tomorrow afternoon. Judging by my niece's descriptions and my own prior experiences, I'm fairly certain of what I'll find. I suspect I'll return to you for permission to undertake a deprogramming, and to discuss the proper means to do so."

The Monsignor looked at his young assistant, trying to assess the struggles taking place within him, yet wanting to show support and encouragement. The gravity of the situation was evident, and difficult times might lie ahead for his friend. Whether he was ready for it was the question. "I trust your judgment, Father," said Monsignor Ryan. "If you think that will be the case, then I would want to discuss it with the archdiocese right away and get them to agree to the procedure, although I wouldn't expect any problem in that regard. This way, you—or whoever it is—can go fully prepared to do what has to be done." Father Mike squirmed but said nothing. Monsignor Ryan, noticing his colleague's discomfort, hastened to add: "I only hesitate on the question of who, Father Michael, because, given your...past experience, they'll want to know if...I'm sorry, Father, but I don't know how else to put it... if you..."

"If I'm the right man for the job." Father Mike completed the Monsignor's thought, mostly to relieve him of the need to express it. "Yes, it's a fair question. I gave it some thought myself when it became clear what my niece was asking me to get involved in. Aside from the normal apprehensions, I can honestly say I'm prepared for it. In fact, having gone through it once before—although on the other end of it—there's probably no one better suited to it than I am. Add the fact that my family's involved, and I don't see how it can be anyone other than me. I pray that you and the archdiocese will see it that way, too."

Monsignor Ryan had been watching his young friend closely for the last several minutes, watching him for any sign that would foretell Father Mike's reaction to what was coming. Had there been any indication of reluctance, of doubt, of fear, he would not have hesitated to restrain Father Mike from this ordeal. He was pleased that he saw none. "Your assurance is sufficient for me, my son. I'll make that my recommendation to the archdiocese. I'm certain they'll go along with it."

"Thank you, Monsignor," said Father Mike, relieved in one respect, though remaining apprehensive in another.

"Now," said the Monsignor, "on the matter of approach, have you given any thought to what might be appropriate? The archdiocese will ask when I call."

There was no hesitation. "Yes, Monsignor. I'd like to use the Voynich, if it can be acquired in time. Or at all." Father Mike remembered back to the earlier incident. He knew that the priest who had been assigned to deprogram him had used the Church's standard prescribed prayer ritual to perform the rite. It was not the same as an exorcism, of course, which deals with Satanic possession of the body. In his case, it was the mind they had to deal with. Brainwashing, some called it. The best that could be said for the ritual was that, in the end, it worked. The road to the final destination, however, was a long, difficult, and painful one, strewn with huge potholes and boulders. It was, in short, a horrendous experience. The year he spent in rehab was something he would not want to go through again, nor would he wish it on anyone else. In this case, Stephen Blake. If the young man survived at all—surely no guarantee—he could end up requiring a long recovery period like he himself had to endure. He knew Alison would be devastated by that, as would Blake himself, of course. Given that potential scenario, the time appeared to be propitious to give the Voynich Manuscript a try.

Father Mike had learned of the Voynich during his Georgetown studies. It was an old book that had come to be called "the most mysterious manuscript in the world." Father Mike had been intrigued by it from the first. He did a paper on it while at school, even going to study it firsthand, since it was available for serious research, not to mention being relatively close by. It was located at Yale University in New Haven, at their rare book and manuscript library—the Beinecke, he recalled. Father Mike wasn't able to solve its mysteries. Not that he expected to, since countless numbers of formidable scholars had tried before him, unsuccessfully. But he was convinced there was a real secret buried in the manuscript's ancient leaves and in its indecipherable script. If only he, or someone, could unleash it.

He frequently thought of the book during his student days, then less often afterwards, but he could never completely eliminate it from his innermost being. It was always there in the deepest recesses of his soul, nearly forgotten, yet crying out to be exhumed from the darkness and thrust into the light. He had never followed up on this desire, never fleshed out his thoughts on the manuscript, its meaning, its possibilities. Yet he felt the book had been created—and remained in mankind's possession—to fulfill some good purpose, to honor the surreal beauty of its somewhat bizarre illustrations and delicate swirls of text. He had no evidence for this, only a blind faith. Much like his – and every Christian's – acceptance of the mysteries of God. You could never hope to actually know these things. You simply had to believe.

Monsignor Ryan's words brought Father Mike out of his dream state. "Yes, time is of the essence," said the old priest, who was no conservative theologian, despite his years. He was always willing to try something new, quick to embrace the innovative approach or idea. He never pushed Father Mike, but when the young priest was in the mood, they spoke about the past, including the younger man's speculations about the Voynich Manuscript. The Monsignor may not have had the same predilection towards its hidden secrets, but nonetheless respected the possibilities mentioned by Father Mike.

"I'll see what I can do," said the Monsignor. "It so happens I'm acquainted with one or two higher-ups at Yale. I'll put on my best Irish charm and see what can be arranged. Failing that, I'll beg." The smile from both men temporarily lifted the heaviness that had permeated the room for the last several minutes. It was welcome relief. The Monsignor continued, "If I'm successful, I'm sure they'll insist on having the manuscript in our personal care and possession while it's away from Yale. That means you should plan on driving down this evening. I'll arrange for you to stay overnight. You can bring it back in the morning. Father Julian and I will cover your masses tomorrow. All this presupposes I can convince them of the urgency of the matter, however. Let me get on the phone with the archdiocese first, then follow up with Yale. I'll let you know how it goes."

"Bless you, Monsignor, for your understanding," said Father Mike. "And for your help. I think I'll go to the chapel and pray for even higher-level assistance. I have a feeling I'm going to need all I can get over the next couple of days."

* * *

Coleen, the rectory housekeeper, was always reluctant to disturb any of the priests in the chapel as they communed with God. However, the telephone caller insisted it was important. She tapped Father Mike on the shoulder as he knelt in the front pew, head bowed.

"I'm very sorry, Father," she whispered in her Irish brogue, "but you've a phone call. It's your niece, Miss Simmons. Said it was quite urgent."

"Thank you, Coleen," said Father Mike, as he blessed himself hurriedly and rose from the pew. "I was expecting the call. Thanks for getting me."

He rushed up to his room on the second floor, picked up the receiver, and punched the blinking light where the call was parked. "Hello, Alison," gasped the priest, somewhat out of breath. "Sorry I sound like I just ran the Boston Marathon, but they had to snatch me out of the chapel. I just ran up the stairs. How did you make out with Mr. Blake?"

"It wasn't easy, but he's willing to meet. I set it up for tomorrow afternoon, like you said. One fifteen." Alison didn't want her uncle to arrive when she did, at one. She felt she would need a little time to get to know Stephen again. Maybe more importantly, get him to know her again. And since he wouldn't be expecting anyone else, she thought she'd have to prepare Stephen for her uncle's visit. That might take some doing.

"Okay, good. So he's agreed to see me, right?"

Just the briefest hesitation from Alison. "He'll see you," she said. It wasn't exactly a lie, and it wasn't exactly the truth. It was a statement with elements of both. It was what was necessary at the moment. Then, before her uncle could explore that area, she gave him Stephen's address and said, "That's in the Back Bay. You know where it is?"

"No problem. I'll find it okay." Father Mike sensed it was time for another hug, this one through the phone line. "And don't worry, Ali. I have a feeling everything's going to be all right. Trust me on that." It was more selective truth-telling. It was what was necessary at the moment.

"Thanks, Uncle Mike. I hope you're right."

"When have I ever been wrong before? Don't answer that," he bellowed, before Alison had a chance to say anything. He heard a feeble attempt at a laugh from Alison. "See you tomorrow," said the priest. "One fifteen. Hang in there."

"I will. 'Bye, Uncle Mike."

"Atta girl. 'Bye."

Chapter 31

Sunday, October 29

It was already a most unusual Sunday for Father Mike, and what promised to be the most interesting part hadn't even happened yet. Here it was late morning and, instead of saying mass for his parishioners, he was sitting in his room at St. Brendan's rectory with one of the world's most significant old manuscripts on his desk. He had just gotten back from Yale, about a three-hour drive up I-95, after an early morning mass in New Haven, a speedy breakfast with one of Monsignor Ryan's old university friends—the one he had somehow cajoled into borrowing the precious Voynich Manuscript—and a hasty departure with the prize book securely packaged in its special protective container for the trip north.

Judging by the looks of it as it sat on the little wooden desk in his cramped quarters, the Monsignor must have pulled a harp's worth of strings, or called in some humongous favors. This just wasn't something that made the rounds every day. It was a valuable historic treasure. If he didn't know it before, he certainly was made aware of it during his brief visit to Yale. He hoped they had an appropriate amount of insurance coverage for it, not that that would do much good if it was lost or damaged. It was irreplaceable. He was extremely nervous to be its temporary curator.

He remembered the Voynich fondly from his earlier study of the volume, when he wrote that paper on it at Georgetown. He sat at his desk and put his hand on the book. He was surprised by its small size—about seven inches wide by ten tall, only slightly larger than his hand. It didn't even have a cover. And he was told that some of its pages were missing. For such an important volume, he thought, it wasn't much to look at, and in somewhat seedy shape, at that. Yet he let his hand rest on it for a minute or two, feeling its coolness, its importance, its mystery. So many people had tried to decipher it, using some of the most sophisticated tools of the twentieth century. All had failed. What was it about the book that resisted every attempt to reveal its meaning? He had no answer to that.

What he did know from his previous research, or from having just been told by his Eli hosts, was that it had been discovered in 1912 by an American antique book dealer and collector, Wilfrid M. Voynich. It was found among a collection of ancient manuscripts in the villa Mondragone in Frascati, near Rome. The villa was then a Jesuit College, which had since been closed in 1953. Voynich estimated the manuscript to date from the thirteenth century, based on the calligraphy, pigments, drawings, and vellum used for its leaves. Its two hundred plus pages gave it a hefty girth for its rather modest dimensions. Its strange script, found to exist nowhere else in the world, to anyone's knowledge, filled page after page, along with awkward drawings, rendered in color. Drawings of plants, tiny nude women, strange zodiacal signs, mysterious charts, and other obscure elements.

Its history could be traced to the court of Rudolph II of Bohemia in 1586, one of the most eccentric European monarchs of that or any other period. He was said to have acquired the book from an unknown source. Whoever it was had come to the court and presented the manuscript, along with a letter stating that it was the work of the Englishman Roger Bacon, a noted pre-Copernican astronomer who lived in the thirteenth century. Rudolph's collection was dismantled with the passage of time, with several rare manuscripts, including the Voynich, making their way to the venerable and famous Jorge's library in Italy. It survived the fire that destroyed Jorge's abbey and took his life and came to be stored at a Jesuit college for many years afterwards.

Some thought the volume to be a coded work, a special cipher, yet Father Mike knew it had been fairly reliably shown not to be such. Others surmised that it was an elaborate hoax, merely gibberish. This theory, too, had been quashed, to the satisfaction of most. After an inordinate amount of study by a strikingly large number of impressive intellectuals, the consensus interpretation is that the manuscript appears to be genuine, and that it has a real meaning, yet that meaning eludes interpretation and understanding.

Father Mike was drawn to a particular line of thinking by one of the document's many researchers. It had to do with the Endura. He was intrigued by the concept's simplicity and elegance, knowing that complex theories oftentimes give way in favor of more straightforward explanations. He remembered taking notes on the topic and vowed one day to look into it more deeply, though he never did. No better time than the present, he thought.

The priest had dug out his student writings in anticipation of borrowing the manuscript. He now reviewed their content. The speculation that had caught his interest years ago centered on the activity depicted in the puzzling drawings of those nude female characters in what appear to be tubs used for bathing. The researcher had surmised that the women are taking part in a Cathar sacrament called the Endura, or death by venesection. This involves cutting a vein and bleeding to death in a warm bath. Now, on the face of it, this may appear to be a gruesome thing. However, there was another way to look at it. The priest read what he had written years ago:

"The person who is knowledgeable about aid knows there is only one way to treat agonizing pain. He treats each one by putting them through the Endura. It is the one way that helps Death. Not everyone knows how to assist the one with pain. The one who is with Death and does not die will have pain. But those who have such pain of Death need his help. He understands the need. He is also aware that the person who needs help does not know that he needs it. We all know that everyone of them needs help and each of us will be available to help."

From his studies, Father Mike knew that the Cathars—also known as Albigensians—called themselves Christians and based their teaching on the parts of the Bible they recognized. But they differed from Christians on a fundamental point: they believed not in one God, but in two. All their life and teaching was derived from one premise of overwhelming importance: that creation was a dual process; there was a kingdom of good, which was immaterial, and a kingdom of evil—the material world. They subscribed to a blend of Gnosticism, which claimed to have access to a secret source of religious knowledge, and Manichaeanism, which claimed all matter is evil. In every material body a soul was immured. Salvation consisted of escape from the flesh.

Father Mike recalled one story he had read about the Cathars back at Georgetown. It had always stayed with him. He even remembered the name of the book: *The Holy Blood and the Holy Grail*. He learned that the Albigensian Crusade was essentially one against Manichaeanism. In 1209 an army of some 30,000 knights and foot-soldiers from northern Europe descended like a whirlwind on the Languedoc, the mountainous northeastern foothills of the Pyrenees in what is now southern France. In the ensuing war the whole territory was ravaged, crops were destroyed, towns and cities were razed, a whole population was put to the sword. This extermination occurred on so vast and terrible a scale that it may well constitute the first case of genocide in modern European history. In the town of Beziers alone, at least 15,000 men, women, and children were slaughtered wholesale, many of them in the sanctuary of the church itself. When an officer inquired of the pope's representative how he might distinguish heretics from true believers, the reply was, "Kill them all. God will recognize His own."

Was all of this part of history? Was any of it? There was no way to know for certain, but Father Mike felt there could very well be something profoundly powerful in the manuscript. Whether it was used for good or ill would depend on the user. In any event, it seemed to him that Stephen Blake's situation was much like that described in his notes. The young man was in pain, even potentially near death, and in dire need of assistance, but was unaware of it. Could the manuscript hold the answer? Father Mike didn't know. What he did know, for sure, was that it sat now in his possession, and that he would try to summon whatever powers it held to his benefit.

He glanced over at the little digital clock with its red numerals announcing the time. Twelve thirty. Time to go. He had been so absorbed in the manuscript that he hadn't remembered to eat lunch. Then again, he found he wasn't the least bit hungry. He gathered up the book, placed it in its protective cover, and headed for the door. "Here goes nothing," he said to himself.

* * *

Stephen Blake was munching on a ham and Swiss sandwich—hold the mayo—while reading the Sunday Globe in his third-floor apartment. He heard the buzzer and snatched a look at the clock: one oh two. 'Who the hell could that be?' he wondered. Annoyed at the interruption to what he thought would be a quiet afternoon, he slinked over to the intercom. "Who is it?" he barked.

"It's me. Alison."

Alison? he thought. Alison who? He was drawing a blank, then had a vague recollection of speaking with someone named Alison yesterday—he thought it was yesterday—about some kind of meeting. Why was it so hard to remember things? he asked himself.

"Stephen? Are you there?" said Alison.

"Yeah, I'm here. Wait a second." He closed his eyes and thought hard but couldn't make the connection. He was going to say the hell with it and forget the whole thing when he heard another ring. He didn't know why, exactly, but he buzzed her in. In a minute, there were footsteps in the hall, then a light knock. He fumbled with the lock and swung the door open. He saw her standing there. Fabulous smile, hair done up just so, pretty face, nice outfit. A flash of recollection swept over him. He was almost sure he had seen this person recently. He just couldn't think where, or when. Then the familiarity of her vanished just as quickly as it had come.

Alison decided not to wait for an invitation to enter. She came in like a breeze and took off her coat, laying it on a chair near the door. She turned to Stephen and said with a big smile, "Well, I'm glad to see you looking good. You must be feeling better."

"I'm...I'm feeling fine. Much better." He did remember being sick most of last week. It was good he could recall that, he thought. "I'm sorry. You'll have to forgive me. I don't seem to be able to remember things like I used to. Did we arrange this for today?"

Alison had steeled herself for this. She had decided not to get unduly alarmed when he exhibited these symptoms. She walked up to him and gently took one of his hands into both of hers, saying, "Yes, Stephen. We did. Yesterday. I know you've been having these problems. I'm here to help you. Me and my uncle, that is. He'll be here in a few minutes. I hope you're not angry that I invited someone else to come. He has special training with...your kind of problem, and I think he'll be able to make you better. Is that okay?"

Someone else coming? Stephen didn't think anything of it, one way or the other. "I guess so," he said, lamely.

Alison stole a quick look around the apartment. It was small, but comfy looking. They were in an open space separating the living room on one side from a combination kitchen-dining area on the other. One corner of the dining space sported a small desk with papers, books, a computer, and a wicker chair. It looked like a mini office. There was a tile-top table tucked against the wall nearby, presumably used for meals. Three wood and leather chairs were pushed under it. A nearby door led to a closet, Alison guessed. The living room had a small sofa and armchair, both upholstered in a boxy pattern. A glass coffee table separated the two. There was a large teak bookcase on one wall stuffed with books, stereo, TV, and ceramic and wood bric-a-brac. A couple of tall potted plants sat on the floor in rust-colored pottery vases. A more distant door off the living room most likely led to a bedroom. The furniture was contemporary. Area rugs broke up the parquet flooring. Everything was in various shades of white or pastel. The only windows were those in the living room, two large ones that looked out onto the street behind beige mini-blinds.

Wanting to retain the initiative, Alison said, "Why don't we sit on the sofa while we wait for my uncle. We can talk in the meantime." She led him to the couch and tried to engage him in conversation, but she could tell he wasn't there. One moment it seemed as though he was pulling out of it. The next, he was back in the depths. He alternated between looking out the window and reading the paper. She didn't know what else to do, so she just sat there with him, praying that her uncle would come soon. And that he would be able to do something. Anything.

At one twenty, she was almost beside herself with worry. What if her uncle didn't come? What if he's been in an accident? What if he's decided this whole thing is a crock? What if...?

She heard the buzzer. Alison didn't wait for Stephen to answer it but sprang up herself. She went to the intercom and confirmed that it was her uncle, then buzzed him in. When he arrived, she noticed he was carrying a small package but couldn't tell what it was. They exchanged greetings. Alison saw he was in civvies, as he had said he would be. He wore a Boston Red Sox jacket and cap, jeans, and sneakers.

Alison introduced the two men to each other. Father Mike noted she didn't refer to him as a priest, but merely as her "Uncle Mike."

Stephen asked, "Have we met before?"

"No, Mr. Blake, we haven't, but Alison has told me a great deal about you, so I probably have an unfair advantage. I'm sure Alison has mentioned that I'm a priest at St. Brendan's parish in Cambridge, and that I... "

Stephen's demeanor changed instantly. It was as if something snapped inside him. His face became darker. He developed a menacing scowl. His voice changed also, from meek, uncertain ramblings to a vigorous, deep-throated growl. Alison was taken aback. As much as she was disturbed by his episodes of amnesia and lack of familiarity with her, this was infinitely worse. This was scary. She was glad her uncle was here. Yet it seemed to be her uncle who brought this change on.

Stephen's mind swirled as it churned over what Ernst and Lariakin had told him during the past week or so: there were those who would try to dissuade him from his objective, turn him from his mission, cast aspersions against them. And who better than a priest to do the evil work of their enemies? The look in Stephen's eyes was a fierce hatred. He pointed at Father Mike and literally spat out his words. "Ah, now it becomes clear," he said. "They warned me about you and your kind. Evildoers. I curse you, damn priest. You can't change what I have to do. Your cause is futile. Get out. GET OUT! And take this bitch with you." He glared in Alison's direction and waved an angry fist at her. She cringed from the viciousness of the attack and half hid behind her uncle. It was all she could do to keep from crying. She would have, if she hadn't been so frightened.

Father Mike turned to Alison and whispered, "I have to assume from this reaction that you didn't tell him about me being a priest. Or perhaps you didn't mention me at all." He didn't say this as a reproach, but rather to make sure he knew what conditions he was dealing with.

Alison looked pained. "I'm sorry, Uncle Mike. You're right. I didn't. I..."

"No need to explain," said Father Mike. He quickly turned to Stephen to try to gain control of the situation. Right now, there was nothing resembling control, certainly not on his part. "Now Mr. Blake...Stephen, if I may call you that...I'd appreciate it if you'd let me say something before I go."

Alison, still clutching her uncle's arm, squeezed harder as if to protest his words. Go? Surely, he wasn't thinking about leaving. Not now! He couldn't!

Father Mike half turned toward his niece and gave her a quick wink and a slight nod, as if to reassure her he knew what he was doing and that she shouldn't worry. Her face betrayed her apprehension, but she said nothing. Father Mike turned back to Stephen and continued:

"That's right, Stephen. I promise to leave, if you want me to, but I'd like you to hear me out first. Just give me a few minutes to say what I have to say. Then you can decide if I'm your friend or your enemy. Will you do that?"

The priest's words had been spoken so soothingly and in such contrast to Stephen's harsh diatribe that Stephen was momentarily silenced, almost stunned. He had fully expected a fierce rebuttal from the cleric. When it didn't come, he was caught off guard. All he could say was, "Go ahead, then. Have your say. Then you can both go."

Stephen's words weren't friendly, by any means, but at least they were an invitation rather than an expulsion. Father Mike had to take advantage of the temporary lull and consolidate his tentative toehold as best he could. He felt as though he were on a high wire at the top of a circus tent, teetering delicately, the slightest imbalance set to throw him off. He reminded himself to keep his tone and gestures non-threatening, non-menacing. If there was a benefit to be gained from Stephen's outburst, it was to convince him that Alison's assessment of her friend was an accurate one. There was no way she ever would have been attracted to someone with his current personality traits. He knew beyond a doubt there was a problem—a major one. The only issue now was how to resolve it.

"Thank you, Stephen," said Father Mike. He waved an arm gently in the direction of the sofa and said, "Would you mind if we sat down to talk? That'll make it easier all around. Please?" The last word was spoken as a question, though intended to reinforce his invitation to sit. He walked slowly toward the two-person sofa. The combination of his movement, comforting gesture, and soft words seemed to work. Stephen said nothing, hesitated briefly, then turned and walked slowly toward the couch, taking a place at the near end. Father Mike said, "Thank you, Stephen." He turned and took Alison by the hand, then escorted her to the position next to Stephen. He wanted her there on the chance that her proximity might cause him to recall some spark of their developing relationship before his troubles. It was worth a try. Father

Mike wanted to sit facing Stephen, so he selected the chair opposite the sofa. The coffee table between the two would act as a buffer, both physically and psychologically. Stephen might feel less threatened with his priest antagonist on the other side of it. Father Mike removed his jacket and hat, draping the former over the back of his chair and setting the latter on the table in front of him. He sat down and put the package containing the Voynich Manuscript next to the cap. He had placed the actors and props into position. All he had to do now was write the play. He said a quick, silent prayer for guidance. He stole a quick glance at Alison, who sat with her hands in her lap, looking quite uncomfortable. He gave her the most imperceptible of smiles.

"Let me begin," said the priest, turning back to Stephen, "by saying that I'm on your side. You may not believe that yet, but I hope to convince you it's true. Not only that, but Alison here is, too. She told me about how you got sick. She was concerned about you all week. When you didn't get better, she thought you might be seriously ill, so she came to see me. She thought I might be able to help. I don't know if I can or not, but I told her I was willing to try."

Father Mike never took his eyes off Stephen's. He saw no change deep inside them. The young man merely sat passively, arms folded across his chest, shifting his gaze between the priest, the coffee table, and the opposite wall. At least he was calm, thought Father Mike, who went on with his monologue.

"You may wonder why Alison would ask a priest to help you rather than a doctor. That'd be a logical question. The answer is that she, and I"—he glanced briefly over at Alison to let her know he had come over to her point of view—"both believe that your illness isn't physical, but psychological. What I mean is, someone, or something, has been trying to get control of your mind and plant thoughts that aren't your own. They want you to do things against your will, things that you normally wouldn't do, if given a choice. Your illness is caused by your inner conflict about this."

There was still no softening in Stephen's eyes, yet Father Mike thought there was the barest hint of change on his face. A line or two on his forehead seemed to have lessened in intensity. There was no doubt he was listening—intently. But was he understanding? Father Mike would try to find out in a moment.

Alison also seemed to have emerged slightly from her desperation. She had barely moved since her uncle had begun, yet she started to feel slightly better with each word. She began to see her uncle as a snake charmer, squatting before a deadly King Cobra, endeavoring to render it harmless. It was a fascinating, yet dangerous, game that was unfolding.

"You see," Father Mike continued, "your inner core is good, and so it rebels violently against what it sees as a threat to its well-being. It doesn't want to comply with what the other side, the dark side, is telling it to do, so it struggles vehemently. That fight is what makes you feel like you do sometimes. You want to do the right thing, yet you can't control the dark side. This sense of confusion results in psychological rebellion. Can you understand that, Stephen?"

Stephen's arms were still folded, his eyes still impenetrable. Yet there was something inside him that felt soothed by the words of this man. What he said seemed to make sense. Yet Ernst had warned him that that would be so. They would come at him expertly, logically, furtively. Yes, they would seem to be his friends, yet they would cause him pain and anguish if he succumbed to their wiles. The turmoil welled up in him, ate at him, wrenched his insides. He closed his eyes. The pain was coming now. Strong, sharp twinges. He grabbed his head with both hands. His body rocked back and forth. He screamed out, "I don't know what I understand anymore! It hurts so much! Help me! Please help me!"

Alison raised her hands to her mouth to stifle a sob. All she could do was stare at the tortured person next to her in disbelief. She felt utterly helpless.

Father Mike rose quickly from his chair and went to stand next to Stephen, placing a hand gently on the young man's head as it bobbed up and down, up and down. The priest said, "I hear you, my son, and feel your pain. I'm here to help you. Will you let me?"

Silence, then: "I don't know! Yes! Please, do something!" pleaded Stephen. He still clutched his head but stopped the rocking motion.

Father Mike kept a gentle pressure on Stephen's head, then said, "Okay, Stephen. Here's what we'll do. We'll wait a moment until the worst of this pain goes away and you feel a little better. Then, I'm going to ask you to sit quietly with your eyes closed and listen while I say some words. I'll be asking for help from my 'boss'—the One in whom I have absolute faith—to allow us to overcome what has taken hold of you. I'll also go through a ritual using a special book I brought with me. I want you to know these things so you're not surprised by anything I do. I have to tell you, though, that it may be frightening for you. And painful. You may feel a recurrence of your aching-head symptoms as your inner struggle builds. To be completely truthful, there may be other effects I can't anticipate. Some of this is experimental, and there are no guarantees. But it's very important that you try to understand what's going on and resist with every fiber of your being the evil forces at work on you. They're very powerful. As strong as they are, though, they're less potent than what we have on our side. But you'll have to fight, Stephen. Now, take a minute to rest before we start."

As Stephen prepared himself, Father Mike turned his attention to Alison, still sitting beside her tormented friend. "I don't expect that you'd agree to walk around the block a few times, would you?" he whispered.

Alison was shocked he would even suggest anything like that. "Absolutely not," she said, firmly. "There's no way I'm leaving."

"That's what I thought," said the priest, not surprised by her reaction. "But I will insist that you move away from Stephen. Anywhere behind me will be fine." Father Mike looked around and examined the layout of the apartment. "Why don't you sit at the kitchen table?" he said, calmly. "You can watch from there. But you must promise that no matter what happens, you won't say or do anything. You must stay in your place. Okay?"

Alison wasn't used to being dictated to like this, even by her editor at the Herald. She didn't much like it, even though it was her uncle, and a priest at that, but what choice did she have? Besides, she was feeling intimidated by this whole situation. All she could do was mutter a weak "Okay" in reply.

While Alison moved away from the sofa and Stephen waited for his pains to subside, Father Mike sat back and took a prayer book out of his jacket pocket. He placed it on the table. It was small and black, with red edging around the pages. He then picked up the package he had brought with him, opened it, and removed the Voynich Manuscript. He set it next to the prayer book. He gazed at the two volumes, his arsenal of weapons. He hoped they would be sufficient. They would have to be. He looked up at Stephen and saw he still had his eyes closed but was no longer holding his head. Father Mike said, "If you're ready, Stephen, we can begin." Stephen replied with a slight nod, but did not open his eyes.

The priest swung around toward Alison and gave her a quick smile and a thumbs-up signal, then turned back to Stephen. He took a deep breath and closed his own eyes for a moment while he silently implored God for the help he knew he would need. When he was done, he picked up the prayer book, kissed it, and opened it to a spot he had marked in advance. He held it with both hands directly in front of his chest, then proceeded to read.

"Almighty Father," he began, saying the words slowly and distinctly in a strong, confident voice, "we implore You to look with favor on this Your earthly son, who comes before You and asks for Your assistance. He has been afflicted by the evil of Satan. We ask on his behalf for Your intervention. Take the pain from his body and the beast from his mind. Open his heart to Your teachings, O Lord."

Father Mike looked up at Stephen to see if there was any noticeable change. There was none. He waited a moment, then said the words a second time, again with no result. After another repetition, he began to see an agitation developing in Stephen. There was a marked change in his facial expression, the buildup of an unmistakable tension. The lines tightened on his forehead. His mouth started to curl up, almost as though he was about to whistle a tune. A low, intermittent moaning sound issued from his mouth. Father Mike tightened his grip on the prayer book and said the words again.

Halfway through the recitation, Stephen opened his mouth wide and uttered a wild animal cry. It was one of fierce pain, agonizing turmoil, incredible torment. Stephen reached down and gripped the edge of the seat cushion as tightly as he could with both hands, so tight, in fact, that his knuckles turned white and the cushion was compressed into nothingness. Father Mike heard Alison stifle a shriek at the ferocity of Stephen's cry, but he did not turn to look at her. He focused his entire attention on the anguished man before him.

It seemed to the priest that Stephen was trying to form a word, or words, but nothing that came out was comprehensible. Just the same wild bleating sound. Father Mike decided to recite the ritual once again. This time, he barely started when Stephen emitted another piercing yell and started thrashing his head from side to side, violently, still latched onto the seat cushion in a death-like grip. Father Mike stopped speaking and observed Stephen's behavior, listening intently to see if there was any sense to be made from what seemed like random noises. Father Mike put the prayer book down on the table and leaned toward Stephen. He spoke to him loudly, trying to make himself heard. "Stephen, I want you to listen to me. You must listen to what I say, not to the voices inside you. You must focus all of your energy on trying to hear my words. Tell me..."

"NO! NO! NOOARGH!" screamed Stephen, his hands leaping to his head once again, compressing it, trying to crush his agony. It was clear to Father Mike that whatever dwelled therein was causing him excruciating pain, so much so that the words coming out of his mouth were gnarled and twisted. The inner force was powerful and wouldn't let Stephen listen to the priest. "NOOOWARRGHHH!" growled Stephen. "SIIIII—LLLLENNNCE." Suddenly, Stephen let go of his head and uttered a wild, shrieking laugh. High pitched. Unearthly. It reminded Father Mike of the Wicked Witch of the West in The Wizard of Oz. Just as suddenly, the weird cackling stopped and Stephen spoke in a near natural voice, although his eyes were still shut and he began gesturing wildly, pointing fingers and waving arms. He said, "You must not continue talking to me, you know. It is bad for me and bad for you. Larry Ah-kin says to cease and desist. He wants you to know that if you don't, some rather unpleasant things will befall the both of us. And we don't want that, do we? No, we don't. We don't. We don't."

Father Mike said, "Tell Lariakin that I hear him but reject his words. Tell him..."

"Tell him yourself, damn priest," said Stephen. "He hears you. Yes, he does. He does."

"Then I tell you directly, Lariakin, and I tell you plain. Release your grip on this man. You can't have him. We will not allow it. You..."

There was more wild laughter from Stephen, then another voice—bizarre and strident and ear-piercing—came from Stephen's mouth, but it was not him speaking. The voice said, "YOU are telling ME to let go? You DARE to order ME to give him up? I almost had you once, didn't I? But you escaped, damn you. DAMN YOU! If I couldn't have YOU then, I shall have HIM now. Fair trade, don't you think? DON'T YOU THINK? Do you hear me, you decrepit mound of rotten flesh? You think your puny words are enough to save him? Not today, my putrescent priest. Not ever. Do you hear me? NOT EVER!" There was more blood-curdling laughter from Stephen, who clapped his hands with delight, as though he were a three-year old at a birthday party. But Stephen's happy frolic turned to pain as he clutched his head and screamed. "NOOO! HELLLPPPPP MEEEEE!"

"See what your interference is doing to this fine, upstanding specimen of a man, priest?" said the voice inside Stephen. "Now why don't you lift yourself up and take yourself away from here. And take the stupid hussy back there with you. You'll be saving Mr. Stephen Blake here lots of pain. Yes, you will, you will. Then again, maybe you should stay and watch him suffer. I'm having a hell of a time. Get it? HELL OF A TIME!" More peals of laughter from Stephen's inner voice.

Father Mike decided that bandying words about with Lariakin wasn't going to get him anywhere. And in the meantime, Stephen was, literally, going through hell. Father Mike wasn't sure how much more of it Stephen would be able to take before his mind cracked open like a walnut. It was time to expand the game plan. The priest put the prayer book down on the table and reached for the Voynich Manuscript. He did so deliberately, slowly, as if contemplating the boldness of this act. 'Is this going to save Stephen or kill him?' thought Father Mike. 'And what of Alison, and me? What's going to happen to us? No time to think about that now.'

Despite his having no prior experience with what he was about to do, he had a high degree of confidence in himself and, especially, in the power of the Lord to overcome the black forces he was contending with. He believed strongly that it is implacable faith, more so than anything else, that moves mountains and produces the power to outduel seemingly impregnable foes. Blind faith. He had it—in God, in the manuscript, in himself—and he would need to summon it now.

Father Mike held the volume in both hands and felt the weight of it. He hoped it was heavy with the powers he would need. He brought it up to eye level, then raised it further so that it came to rest against his forehead. There was no need to open the book, he surmised. He couldn't possibly know what any of it meant, anyway. He closed his eyes and remained silent for a moment, then began speaking quietly. It was totally extemporaneous. There was no prescribed ritual here. It was completely from his heart.

"Lord God," he began, "we need Your help as never before. Here sits one of Your servants, Stephen Blake, whom tragedy has overtaken at the hands of Your bitterest enemy. This young man has been enslaved through the evil power of Satan. He has fought against it with all of his will, Lord, but is unable to drive away the dark forces and regain his life. He has asked for Your help through me, Merciful Father. We have employed what we know, but without success. Now we must employ what we do not know but only believe to be Your instrument. If we are right in this, Lord God, we pray that You will send Your spirit down to this man and release him from the mighty grip of the devil. His torment is real, as You can see. His anguish is debilitating, and we fear that without Your intervention he will succumb, not only in mind, but in body as well. And so, we ask You to aid us in this effort. We believe in Your almighty power, and in Your compassion for the downtrodden. Father in Heaven, please help us, and him."

Father Mike opened his eyes and brought the manuscript from his forehead down to his lap. He fixed his eyes on Stephen, who continued to writhe in agony, still clutching his head. If this was going to work, it wasn't going to be instantaneous, it seemed. If anything, Stephen's moaning became more intense, the words and sounds exiting his mouth harder to identify. This continued for another minute, perhaps two. The priest debated what his next action was going to be. Alison looked on in horror at the spectacle.

Suddenly, and without warning, Stephen leaped across the table, throwing himself at Father Mike and grabbing at the priest's throat with his hands. The force of the assault caused the priest's chair to fall over backwards and crash to the floor. During Stephen's attack, he railed loudly against the priest, utterings oaths and curses with the foulest of language.

Stephen and Father Mike ended up in a heap on the floor, with Stephen on top, struggling to gain control. He did, straddling the priest with both knees on the floor and hands around his throat. Stephen kept a powerful stranglehold with one hand, raising the other high into the air, forming it into a deadly fisted instrument, ready to bring it down on his victim in a crushing blow. Alison screamed and started to run toward them. Father Mike caught her movement out of the corner of his eye and gasped through Stephen's death grip for her to stay away. She stopped before reaching them and merely stood there, able neither to advance nor retreat. Father Mike had somehow managed to retain his grasp on the manuscript throughout this turmoil, though he remained pinned under Stephen. The priest extricated one hand from under Stephen's body and raised it and the manuscript upward. As Stephen was about to strike, Father Mike yelled out, "The power of the Lord is great. He will not allow it."

Stephen's fist remained above his head, as though frozen. Try as he might, he was unable to bring it crashing down into the priest's face, which he was fully committed to doing. Father Mike kept his own hand—still clutching the manuscript—pointed toward Stephen. He repeated his prayer once more. The two men remained in their respective positions for some time, seemingly turned into a stone sculpture, each unable to move, each unable to speak.

After what seemed like an eternity, Father Mike felt the grip on his throat relax as Stephen's entire body went limp and collapsed onto the floor next to the priest. The young man's face was an ashen white. It was covered in beads of sweat, and he didn't appear to be breathing. Father Mike laid the manuscript on the floor and quickly lifted himself so that he knelt over Stephen's body. He shifted Stephen onto his back, then grabbed his wrist and checked for a pulse. It was weak, but at least there was one. He put a finger under Stephen's nose to locate any hint of a breath. Again, weak, but detectable. Stephen was alive! He had survived the ordeal. The question was, which Stephen had survived?

Father Mike looked up at Alison and asked her to bring one of the cushions from the sofa to place under Stephen's head. The priest didn't want to risk moving him for the moment. Not until his condition stabilized somewhat.

They knelt there next to him for some time, not speaking, emotionally drained, just letting the quiet settle over them and start what they could only hope would be a healing process. Father Mike realized for the first time how much his own throat hurt from the force of Stephen's—or was it the devil's—potent grip. He tried to rub the soreness from it. It was hard to swallow. They stayed that way for several more minutes, neither saying a word.

It was Alison who broke the silence. "Is he going to be all right, Uncle Mike?" she asked.

"I think so," said the priest, not knowing for sure one way or the other. "I hope so. We'll have to wait and see."

Alison saw how worn out her uncle was. And there was a nasty looking redness around his neck. She placed a hand on his shoulder and said, "Are you okay?"

He coughed a couple of times and rubbed his neck again. "Yeah, I think so. A bit tapped out, maybe, but otherwise fine. But I don't think I'd want to do that again. Not for a while, anyway." He lifted a hand to his shoulder and placed it on Alison's. "How about you?" he asked.

Alison looked down at Stephen as he lay between them. She let out a long sigh and said, "I don't know yet. I guess I'm okay, but I'll let you know for sure when I see what happens to Stephen." There was no need for any more words. There would be time for talk later. Alison's hand moved from under her uncle's to cover one of Stephen's, which rested on his stomach. They remained that way for a long while. The sounds of Sunday filtered in from outside: children's voices, the whoosh of traffic, the distant bark of a dog. Alison could see tree limbs doing a gentle dance through the window. A cloud drifted by, marking the passage of time.

Then, a twitch. There, in Stephen's hand, under hers. Again. Yes, it was unmistakable. She removed her hand from his and looked at Stephen's face. It was still pale, but his head was moving from side to side. He was regaining consciousness. She glanced over at her uncle, who was sitting on the floor, arms propped on his knees, head resting on his arms. He looked totally exhausted. "Uncle Mike," said Alison, excited. "I think he's coming around."

"Huh? What'd ya say?" mumbled the priest.

Alison moved away a bit to give Stephen some room. His eyes opened. He blinked a few times, seemingly not able to focus on anything. Then they remained open. He swung his head from one side to the other and fixed his gaze on the face looking down on him. "Alison?" he said weakly. "What are you doing here? Why am I on the floor?"

Alison couldn't say anything for a moment. She ignored his questions but took his hand again and broke into a smile. "Oh, Stephen. Thank God. I think you're going to be all right. And thank you, Uncle Mike." She reached out and squeezed her uncle's hand as he offered it to her.

Stephen had recovered sufficiently to try lifting himself off the floor, but all he could manage was to lean on one elbow and cry out in pain. "My God," he said, bringing his hand to his forehead, "what a headache. What happened?"

"Maybe you'd better rest another minute or two before trying to get up, Stephen," said Father Mike, now fully awake himself. He whispered a silent prayer of thanks.

"Who are you?" asked Stephen, turning toward Father Mike with a puzzled look.

Alison laughed. "We'll explain everything, Stephen," she said. "Just rest a minute."

Stephen closed his eyes and jerked his head from side to side once or twice. After a while he said, "I...I think I'm okay now. I...feel a little better. My head doesn't hurt as much. Maybe you can help me get up."

Alison and Father Mike got up off the floor and helped Stephen do the same. They led him to the sofa and helped him sit down. Alison sat next to him while Father Mike righted the chair that had been knocked over in the scuffle. He replaced it in its former position, then retrieved the Voynich Manuscript and prayer book from the floor, along with his jacket and cap. He walked back to the chair, threw the jacket over the back, sat down, and placed the manuscript, prayer book, and cap on the table. The scene looked much like it did when they started, but it was clear that much had changed in the interim.

"You look much better," said Alison, as she turned toward Stephen. "How do you feel?"

Instinctively, Stephen's hand went back up to his head. "Okay, I think. Head still hurts a little, though. Feels like someone gave me quite a knock on the noggin."

Alison laughed again, along with Father Mike. "You might say that, in a manner of speaking," she said. "Now, I think we owe you an explanation. Have you got an hour or two?"

Alison proceeded to review the events of the past week, beginning with their dinner meeting. She mentioned their subsequent phone conversation, his strange behavior during his illness, and her discussions with relatives of the murder victims. Also, how this had led her to learn about all of them being Catholics and having a priest somewhere in the family. She explained the theory she had formulated about Ernst and *The Codex* and the Burning Times, then went on to say how she became concerned for Stephen's safety, fearing he had been brainwashed at his meeting with Ernst. This led to the visit to her uncle for help, which in turn led to today's events. She described everything in detail, saying it was her uncle, and whatever it was in those books sitting on the table, that had saved him. Her uncle interjected a disclaimer, saying it was the power of God, not anything he had done, that led to the happy resolution.

At the end of the summary, Stephen said he recalled many of the events Alison had described. At least the ones he was aware of beforehand. He knew nothing of her latest research, and certainly not her theory about Ernst. To these he expressed incredulity, shock, dismay, anger. A swarm of sensations washed over him and made him feel like a wet rag. Limp, dripping with emotion. As for today, he had no recollection of any of it.

"That's probably for the best," said Father Mike. "You went through a pretty traumatic experience. It's just as well you don't recall it. In a way, you're a very fortunate young man. If it hadn't been for Alison's persistence and her faith in your character, I don't think we'd be sitting here with smiles on our faces."

"Yeah, you're right," said Stephen, as he turned to look at Alison, who met his gaze. He extended a hand toward her. She accepted it, their fingers intertwining. "Thanks," he said. "I appreciate what you did for me." He turned toward the priest. "And I also want to thank you. The two of you make quite a team. I'm just glad you're on my side."

They exchanged more pleasantries and chit-chat. Then it was Stephen who turned serious. "We've got to do something about Ernst. He's a madman, along with his cohorts. They sure as hell killed those people. I know that now. And they've cooked up a crazy scheme to turn up the heat. I'm supposed to figure out a way to produce more codexes, so they can expand operations. Not only that, but they're planning a massacre for this coming week. It seems there's a big bishops' conference on Wednesday. Ernst and this other fellow—Lariakin, I think he called him, or something like that—(Yes. That's who it is, thought Father Mike)—talked about celebrating All Hallows Eve by killing them all. We've got to warn the police about this. Ernst has to be stopped."

"My God," said Alison, "he is crazy. We should call the police right away. Let me see if I can reach one of the investigating officers on the case. I've talked to them before. They may not be there on a Sunday, but maybe headquarters can reach them if I explain the situation. I think this qualifies as a bona fide emergency."

"Good idea," said Stephen. "And while you're at it, why don't you see if they'd be interested in meeting us here later on to discuss what we can do to nail Ernst. I have an idea or two on that. Maybe we can work out a plan."

Having witnessed Stephen's narrow escape from a potentially fatal confrontation, Alison was reluctant for him to reenter the fray. "Why not just let the police handle it?" she hinted. "Ernst and those other crazies are too dangerous to fool around with."

"Ordinarily, I'd agree with you. In this case, though, I think we can be helpful. In fact, there may be no other way to do it. What do you say, Father Mike? Would you be willing to see this through?"

"What do you mean, 'See this through?'" asked Alison. The worried look on her face betrayed her feelings. "What are you getting at?"

Before Stephen could answer, Father Mike turned toward him and said, "If you're planning what I think you're planning, count me in." He was starting to get excited. "I haven't had this much fun since my college days. Let's go for it."

"What in God's name are you two talking about?" asked Alison. "We just brought one of you back from the brink of a cliff, and the other almost fell over, too. Have you both relapsed into insanity?"

"On the contrary, my dear," said Stephen, smiling. "I don't think I've ever been saner. How about you, Father Mike?"

"Ditto," said the priest.

"Now why don't you make that call to the police and get them over here?" Stephen said to Alison. "Then I'll explain what we're going to do."

"I can't wait," said Alison.

Chapter 32

Sunday, October 29

Ernst never opened the bookstore on a Sunday. He considered it a day of rest, a notion most likely left over from his early years as a Christian. It was quite an oddity, given his current situation. He certainly didn't do it to honor the Lord. In any event, it was a long-standing habit to keep the shop closed and do other things. It was the only day of the week he indulged himself.

He wasn't quite alone, however. With him in the meeting room was Lariakin, who had expressed a desire to "discuss things" with Ernst. They were approaching a critical point and could not afford a foul-up. Hence, their little get-together.

"Are you certain everything is under control?" asked Lariakin, sitting in one of the folding chairs. He faced Ernst, who sat in another.

"As certain as we can be," said Ernst. "We have prepared well, and it appears that all is going according to plan. Still, there have been one or two unsettling signs that remind us to remain on guard. I told you about the police coming by. Then there was that young lady who was here the other day. She seemed just a little too eager to see my book collection. I suspect it was a rather clumsy attempt to snoop around the shop. She found nothing, of course. But we must be alert to the possibility that others are a danger to us and our cause." As he spoke these last words, Ernst cast a glance up at the picture of Satan hanging on the wall. That was what they were fighting for, he thought. That's what made it all worthwhile.

"Yes," said Lariakin in his deep, raspy voice, taking note of Ernst's look at the picture. He was always pleased to be reminded how devoted Ernst was to him. "That is always something we must be vigilant against. It would not do for someone to create difficulties, just when things are going well, and we are preparing to proceed to the next level."

"Perhaps a little display of power—a minor demonstration—would be appropriate to discourage anyone intent on thwarting us." The lines around Ernst's mouth twisted themselves into a smile as he thought about such a delightful diversion.

"Tempting," said Lariakin, who was seldom averse to the use of such measures, as long as they had a purpose, "but I would caution against it. It would make for good theatrics and some amusement, but it might draw attention to ourselves when there may be no cause to do so. It is entirely possible that these anomalies we worry about are innocent and harmless. It may have been the same with Demming, yet we chose to eliminate what could have been a potential threat. It may have been so, but his...deletion...did bring the police to your door. Nothing seems to have come of it, thankfully. Yet it would not be wise to duplicate that experience needlessly."

"You have convinced me," said Ernst. "Let us not create a problem where none exists."

Having disposed of topic number one, Lariakin turned his attention to the next item on the agenda. "Now, I must ask you again about Blake," he said. "I am still concerned about his commitment. His demeanor at the last meeting was somewhat unsettling. I sat next to him to gauge his attitude, and I must say I did not come away feeling he was entirely ours. During my oration, he appeared to be somewhere else entirely. He spoke the right words when the time came, yet I saw something troubling there as well. He is a key element in our plans, as you are aware. It would be a major setback to us if he faltered."

"I agree, yet I do not see how he can resist the power of *The Codex*," said Ernst. "He may continue to struggle against it, but it is futile. He showed no ability to counter it prior to the last meeting. He was compelled to come, and he came. He was also prevented from leaving beforehand, and he succumbed. No, I do not believe we have anything to fear in that regard. He may not be unswervingly committed just yet, as the others are, but I believe that, given time, he will be. Even if he never reaches that level, I do not have any doubt he will always be under *The Codex*'s control."

"I hope you are correct," said Lariakin. "Yet I had strange sensations but a short time ago. It was as if there was...turmoil, or struggle, some unexplained disturbance. I experienced unsettling vibrations. I cannot be certain as to their source, but I am troubled by them. I would urge you to watch Blake carefully. Caution is always preferred to misplaced trust."

"No doubt."

Lariakin considered pressing the point, so unnerved was he by whatever had caused this...misconnection, this...unbalance. He hesitated, then decided to move forward. "So now, tell me about your plans for this week's celebration. Have you completed the preparations? Are things progressing satisfactorily?" Lariakin knew what had been taking place. He just liked to have it reinforced for him. He appreciated Ernst's attention to detail in such matters.

"They are" confirmed Ernst. "Our dedicated coven members continue to serve unstintingly to achieve what all of us crave. We were indeed fortunate to find so many with the right backgrounds and the fierce determination to ensure success."

"That is your doing, my friend," said Lariakin, who thought it might be time to bolster Ernst's ego once again. He never ceased to be amazed at how much mileage he got from little things like that. "It was through your efforts that our ranks were filled with such stalwarts. You are to be commended for it."

"Thank you, indeed," gushed Ernst. "It was difficult work, but well worth the effort. And as you yourself know, their dedication is assured, so I cannot take all of the credit for it."

"Even so, you were the catalyst for what we now have. The fact that *The Codex* compels them to obey is but a minute detail."

"Yes," said Ernst. "Their hearts followed nicely, once we had control of their minds."

Chapter 33

Sunday, October 29

The buzzer sounded in Stephen Blake's apartment. "That must be the police," said Alison. Stephen heard the names Mulcahy and Johnson through the intercom speaker, rang them in, and waited at the door for them to climb the stairs. He let in two officers Alison recognized from the press conference. Stephen remembered the name Johnson from his phone conversation right after Demming's death, but didn't know Mulcahy. Introductions were exchanged, chairs pulled into a circle, coffee offered and accepted.

"So," said Mulcahy, "what exactly is this all about? Miss Simmons here said something about new information involving the murders. I assume this must be top-shelf stuff." There was no rancor in his words, just enough of a bite to let them all know this had better be good to roust him and Pat away from their families on a Sunday. He had gotten the call from headquarters that the Simmons reporter wanted to talk to him, that it was urgent, that she would appreciate a call back at such and such a number. When he called, she told him there was a new lead in the case and that it was extremely important he meet her at Stephen Blake's apartment on Marlborough Street that afternoon. If he could make it, that is. He had asked what it was all about, but she preferred to hold off on that until they met. It would be worth it, she said. He told her he'd be there in about an hour, somewhere around three thirty. Mulcahy managed to reach Pat, give him the scoop, and ask if he could join him. He could. Wouldn't miss it, in fact. And so here they were.

"I think you'll find this interesting, Lieutenant," said Stephen, "and worth the trip. Let me start by saying flat out that I know who's been doing those murders—and how they're being done. It's that guy Ernst, the one who owns that bookstore on Beacon Hill."

"You don't say," said Mulcahy, perhaps a little too sarcastically. "And how did you come upon this information?" Johnson had taken out his notebook and was already starting to write.

"I got myself sucked into his group—involuntarily—and happened to be at one of his meetings when they talked about it. They're a bunch of murdering witches, or Satanists, or something. I'll give you all the details, everything you wanna know, but right now we've gotta come up with a plan to stop these nuts. They're getting ready for a big display on Wednesday, right after All Hallows Eve. A lot more people are gonna get killed if we don't do something."

All of this sounded familiar to Mulcahy. Hadn't he just heard this stuff recently? Maybe the whole crazy scheme was true after all. He said, "If you're referring to the bishops' conference, we already got wind of that. We took the precaution of alerting the archdiocese that things could get nasty there. We talked about canceling but they wanted to go ahead with it so's not to lose a chance to get the bad guys. In light of what you're telling me, though, we'll give 'em another ring and tell 'em it's a firm plan we're dealing with now, not just idle speculation. They'll probably still wanna stick with it, but we'll call anyway. Make a note of that, will ya Pat?"

"Sure thing," said Johnson, scribbling in his notebook.

"Maybe you wouldn't mind telling me something, Mr. Blake," said Mulcahy. "I'm a mite puzzled by how you just happened to get involved in all this. What the hell...uh, sorry Father... were you doing at one of their meetings?"

Stephen looked at Alison, then at Father Mike. "I was brainwashed. Or programmed. Or whatever you want to call it. They got to me through this book Ernst calls The Wicca Codex. It's powerful, and it works. I can vouch for that. Their plan was for me to dupe *The Codex* so they could carry out similar plans elsewhere. Speed up operations. I bang out the book's chassis, Ernst takes care of the power train, so to speak. And it might've worked, too, if it hadn't been for Alison and her uncle."

"No shit," said Mulcahy. "Oops, did it again, didn't I?"

Father Mike couldn't help laughing. "Don't worry yourself about it, Lieutenant. If that were the worst I ever experienced in my line of work, I'd be a happy man."

"Yeah, I guess," said Mulcahy. "That's quite a tale, Mr. Blake. Brainwashing, huh?" He looked toward Alison and the priest. "Can either of you verify any of this?"

It was Father Mike who spoke first. "We both can, Lieutenant. This man is telling the truth. It was only a short time ago that we experienced the compelling power of *The Codex* over Stephen. Right here in his apartment. We were able to overcome it through prayer, faith in God, and the Lord's own power. It happened just as Stephen said it did. On my honor and word as a priest."

Mulcahy didn't looked convinced. "And you, Miss Simmons," he said. "What do you have to say about all this? This isn't just some made-up story to give credence to your little theory, now is it?"

Alison said, somewhat pointedly, "I won't take offense at that, Lieutenant, because I know how unbelievable the whole thing seems. But it's just as Stephen and my uncle have described it. I know it boggles the mind. I may not have believed it myself if I hadn't witnessed it with my own eyes and ears, theory or no theory. But now that we know it's true, the important thing is, what are we going to do about it?"

"That's another thing," said the Lieutenant. "You all keep talking about 'we' doing something about all this. There ain't any 'we,' folks. It's me, and Pat here, and the rest of the police. We're in. You're out. I think we can handle it from here on."

"Wait a minute, Lieutenant," said Stephen. "We're not trying to steal your thunder or anything. We're not heroes. Not by a long shot." Stephen thought back to Janet, and being dull. Is that why he was doing this? "But it just seems your best chance at getting these guys is through me. All you've got now is my say-so on all this. And Alison's theory. We know it's right, but there's no proof. I can get it for you. They think

Wicca Codex

I'm still under their control. All I have to do is go to their next meeting on Tuesday night. You put a wire on me, and I get what you need to nail these bastards. When you've heard enough, you come in and nab 'em. End of problem. But you can't do it without me."

Mulcahy thought for a moment. He shook his head. "I don't know," he said. "It's too damn dangerous. The whole thing could blow up in your face."

"Look," said Stephen, "you're not asking me. I'm volunteering. It's okay. I want in. No repercussions if it doesn't work. But it will. It's foolproof."

"Wait, I don't understand," said Alison, respecting Stephen for his courage, but fearing he'd be exposing himself to tremendous danger. "We've gotta think this through," she said. "How can you possibly believe you can get away with anything like that? Won't this guy Lariakin, or whatever his name is—the one whose voice we heard—be on to you? My uncle just drove him out, didn't he? He knows what happened. How can you hope to fool him?"

"Let me take that one," said the priest. "Lariakin was never in Stephen's body. He was in his mind. It's a fine distinction, perhaps, but a crucial one. Stephen was not possessed, at least not in our sense of the word. Yet his mind was very much under the control of evil forces. Lariakin was never present per se, just his will. You might say his thoughts were juxtaposed on Stephen's brain. When they were expunged, Stephen was freed from his control. But Lariakin himself was never aware of what was going on. It was all in the power of *The Codex*, not Lariakin's possession. As smart and wily as he is, he still believes Stephen is programmed to do his bidding."

"Would someone like to tell me who Larry Ah-kin is?" asked Mulcahy.

"How do ya spell that?" interjected Johnson, who up until then had been trying to absorb all of this and record it at the same time.

"It's one name, not two," said Father Mike. "Lariakin is actually the driving force behind all this. Ernst is just his tool. Lariakin is Satan, plain and simple. He's given Ernst powers through *The Codex* in return for his soul."

"Holy Christ," exclaimed Mulcahy, incredulously.

Johnson's head whipped up. He stopped writing and nearly dropped his pen. "Uh, pardon the expression, Father," he said, "but are you loco, or what?"

"You are forgiven, my son," said the priest. "I've been accused in the past of being a little daft on occasion, but I'm afraid this is all too real."

Alison reminded the policemen they were supposed to be the department's liaison with the occult and supernatural, that they should keep an open mind on such matters. "Maybe so," said Johnson, "but no one's ever dealt with the real thing before, far as I know. It's hard enough fightin' the bad guys without havin' to overcome the devil himself."

"Look," said Mulcahy, impatiently, "I still say this thing's too dangerous for Mr. Blake to get involved. We'll come up with another way. We can't have civilians on the front line, especially in a bizarre case like this."

"Listen, Lieutenant," said Stephen, becoming a little frustrated. "Ernst expects me to be there on Tuesday. If I'm not, he's gonna get suspicious. Especially since he's programmed me to do what he wants. It's just like the archdiocese told you about the bishops' conference. If they cancel, you don't get Ernst. If I don't show up, he's gonna wonder how I was able to overcome his damn Codex. It's too risky for me not to go. How dangerous can it be if I just play along with 'em? Let 'em think I'm still in their grasp. You get your evidence, then go in and bust 'em up. It's neat and clean. Besides, you've got to give me a chance to do something to get back at those scumbags. Especially after what they did to me, and especially those other people. It's an offer you can't refuse."

Mulcahy thought about it for a moment, then said, reluctantly, "I still don't like it, but I'll agree. Under certain conditions, which are…"

"Uh, Lieutenant," said Father Mike, "you're going to need me there, too. Not inside, but outside, with you."

"What? Absolutely not," yelled Mulcahy. "Listen, it's bad enough I'm gonna have one civilian involved as it is. I'm not gonna have you there, too, gumming up the works."

"With all due respect, Lieutenant, I won't be in your way. In fact, from what I witnessed here today, I think it'll be very desirable to have my knowledge and experience available to you. Those guys have some rather powerful forces at their disposal. I don't think police firepower is going to do much good against it, if it comes to that. You're going to need something even more powerful than their Codex. Something I've got here." He held up the prayer book and the Voynich.

"Oh, yeah?" said Mulcahy, getting somewhat flustered. He felt outnumbered and outranked. How could he not, what with God lined up on the opposing side? "And just what the hell are those?"

"One's a simple prayer book," said the priest, "the other's a very special volume called the Voynich Manuscript."

"How do ya spell that?" asked Johnson.

"V-o-y-n-i-c-h," said Father Mike. "Listen, Lieutenant. We just witnessed the power of these documents. Stephen was literally withering away from the onslaught of the vile forces within him. We were able to overcome them, through these." He waved toward the books on the table. "We have our own weapons, you know. They may not be high tech, but they're effective."

"I can vouch for that," said Stephen.

"Me too," said Alison.

"Okay, okay," said the exasperated Mulcahy. "Two down and one to go." He turned his attention to Alison. "I suppose you've got your own story as to why it's absolutely essential you be there too. Right?"

"That's correct, Lieutenant," said Alison. "I've got a right to cover this story. I've been on it from the beginning. Besides, I think I've been instrumental in breaking this thing wide open, if you'll excuse my immodesty. Where would you be without my help? And one more thing. Father Mike's my uncle. I got him into this and there's no way I'm gonna let him be there without me. We're a team."

Mulcahy looked over at Father Mike. "She's got a point," said the priest. He tried not to smile but it was impossible.

Lieutenant Mulcahy could only shake his head. "Man, I'm getting it from all angles here." He thought for a moment. "Okay, look. You can all be there. Blake'll be inside. The rest of you, outside. Way outside. Behind our guys. We'll post men all around the place. When we hear what we need, we go in. Got it? Any questions?"

"Not a question, Lieutenant," said Alison. "Just an observation. There's only one way in or out of the bookstore, and that's through the front door. You won't need to surround the place. Covering the front will suffice. I've been there. I know the layout."

"You've been there," said Mulcahy. "Of course you have. I should've known that. How stupid of me."

"And another thing," said Stephen. "The front door'll be locked, but I'll find a way to open it for you. That's another reason you need me inside. Also, Ernst has a warning signal attached to the front door. It buzzes in the back when the door opens. I'll have to find a way to disable that, too. But I don't think it'll be a problem."

"I'm very glad to hear that, Mr. Blake," said Mulcahy. "I surely am. This is getting to be complicated, isn't if folks?"

"Nothing we can't handle, Lieutenant," said Alison.

"I'll bet," said Mulcahy.

WICCA CODEX

Chapter 34

Monday, October 30

"Did you have a nice, relaxing weekend, Alison?" asked Jay Burgholz, offering his typical Monday morning greeting as he passed through the newsroom on the way to his office.

"Oh yeah. Just super. Top notch," retorted Alison, who had arrived bright and early. She had gotten hardly any sleep last night, what with the excitement of the previous day and the anticipation of tomorrow night's planned rendezvous at the bookstore. "Listen, Jay. We've got to talk. Right away. Sooner if possible."

"Now why am I not surprised by that?" asked Burgholz, looking for some clue on Alison's face as to what was going on this time. Not finding any, he said, "Okay. How about if we squeeze you in right now, before I get involved with the editors."

She followed him into his office. He sat down at his desk. She stood, too excited to sit. She wouldn't have anyway, not after casting a glance in the direction of the two wooden devices awaiting their next victims. 'Might as well be a bed of nails,' she thought.

"What's on your mind, Ali?" Burgholz was good at identifying when lighthearted back-and-forth was appropriate and when it wasn't. He estimated, correctly, that this was definitely one of the "wasn't" cases.

Alison took the cue and jumped right in. "You know how you pooh-poohed my theory the other day on Ernst and the murders and the Inquisition? And how I was worried about there being some kind of hanky-panky between Ernst and Stephen Blake? Well, guess what? It's true. All of it. Without a doubt. I just had a weekend you wouldn't believe. Better than bungee jumping. If we don't get the Pulitzer Prize with this material, I don't know what it'll take."

Intrigued but impatient, all Burgholz could offer was, "I assume you're going to fill me in now on the details. Anytime is fine. Preferably before my meeting."

"I was getting to it," said Alison. "Besides, it's worth waiting for." Alison saw Burgholz roll his eyes. "Okay, here it is," she said.

Alison proceeded to fill Burgholz in on everything that transpired over the weekend, from the visit to her uncle to their confrontation with Stephen to the subsequent meeting at his apartment with the police. She described the plan they had devised for tomorrow night, and said she'd have the story to end all stories when it was over. It would be a Herald exclusive, she said.

After Alison's presentation, all Burgholz could do was sit. He was speechless. Finally, he said, "If you're alive to write it. Listen, don't get me wrong. I'd be thrilled to put this one in a box and wrap it up with ribbons and bows, especially after all the work you've put in on it. You deserve it. Hell, *we* deserve it. Wouldn't it make The B.G. cringe to know we beat 'em out on a big one for a change? As much as I'd like to get this done, I'm concerned about the safety aspect. The whole thing sounds awfully risky."

"Why is this any riskier than anything else?" asked Alison, determined not to lose this fantastic opportunity to be involved with THE major story of the year, maybe the decade, maybe...well, it was BIG, no matter how you looked at it. "How can I be any safer than being behind a phalanx of police? They're going to have the equivalent of a couple of armored divisions there, the way I hear them tell it. If anyone's taking a risk, it's Stephen Blake. And my uncle. I'm not about to take a back seat while they put their lives on the line."

"I'm not saying you shouldn't go," said Burgholz. "I'm just thinking out loud, that's all. This is strange stuff we're dealing with here. You don't have to be face to face with these psychos to end up terminal. You of all people should know that."

"I know, I know," said Alison. "But just think, Jay, if we can put these guys away for keeps, and maybe get *The Codex* as a bonus to stick away in a museum someplace. What a great thing that'd be. I'm part of it, Jay. I've got to be there. Story or no story. It's either going to be on The Herald's time or my own."

Burgholz thought for a second, then said, "Okay, listen. I'll authorize it, on the condition you take every possible precaution. I'll discuss it with the editors and get the go-ahead from the big kahuna."

"Great," said Alison. "But Jay. Tell 'em to keep this buttoned up. There can't be any leaks. Otherwise there just may be some adverse repercussions if anything gets out that shouldn't."

"I'll stress that," said Burgholz. He leaned way back in his swivel chair and rubbed his hands together. It was usually a sign to Alison he was thinking hard about something. "Oh, Alison," he said, "as long as you're going, why...uh, don't you take along a photog. You may be able to get some great pictures to go with your story."

"Why, you big fraud," chided Alison, good-naturedly. She had a huge smile on her face as she turned and left his office.

"Yes, I am," said Burgholz, to no one in particular.

Chapter 35

Tuesday, October 31—All Hallows Eve

It was the day most kids looked forward to all year: Halloween. This was their chance to be whatever they wanted, as long as a suitable costume could be begged, bought, borrowed, or built that effected the desired transformation. Ghosts, goblins, and ghouls were big, of course, along with just about anything else that was "in" with the younger set that particular year. Not only that, but they got to threaten their elders with "tricks" and get special "treats" for their trouble. What could be better?

Despite the good times they would have, it was doubtful that any of the youngsters who would traverse their neighborhood streets this night knew anything about the origin of the events and festivities they would take part in. The same was probably true for most of their parents, for that matter. It was not exactly common knowledge that Halloween was a corruption of All Hallows Eve, the day before one of the most important milestones on the calendar. But others knew. Only too well. Some reveled in what they called the most magical night of the year. The veil separating now and before was at its thinnest. Therefore, the dead could, if they wished, return to the land of the living for this one night, to celebrate with their former family, tribe, or clan. Equally sheer was the veil between now and later, and so it was also the night par excellence for peering into the future.

Many ancient—and unconnected—cultures celebrated this festival of the dead. But those who knew of such things traced the majority of today's traditions to the British Isles. The Celts called it Samhain, or "summer's end," according to their ancient two-fold division of the year, when summer ran from Beltane to Samhain and winter from

Samhain to Beltane. Some modern covens echoed this structure by letting a High Priest rule the group beginning on Samhain, with governance shifted to a High Priestess at Beltane. To witches, Halloween was one of the four High Holidays, or Greater Sabbats, or cross-quarter days. Because it was the most significant holiday of the year, it was sometimes called "THE Great Sabbat." Apple bobbing, the jack-o-lantern, dressing in costume, and other Halloween rituals all harkened back to various pagan or religious activities, practiced so long ago in so many lands. Yes, there were those who knew these things, and others who did not. Some who celebrated them, and others who did not.

This year promised to be a good one for the trick-or-treat crowd. The evening forecast called for mild and dry weather, perfect for parading around and scaring folks. And so, depending on their ages, the kiddies were either at home getting ready, or in school and thinking about it. All were sure they were going to have a great time.

Others were preparing in other ways, conjuring up tricks of their own. Tricks of a much more serious nature. Deadly serious.

Gustav Ernst, owner and sole operator of Ye Olde Booke Nooke, was looking forward to a night of fun and frolic such as few had seen before. He was preparing to orchestrate a magnificent celebratory scenario on this grand night, the night of the living dead, culminated by tomorrow's denouement. It would be unbearably difficult to endure the anticipation of it, but the outcome promised to make it more than worthwhile. It would be absolute ecstasy.

Then there were Vincent Mulcahy and Patrick Johnson, long-standing members of the Boston Police Department, who were charged with pulling off one of tonight's neater tricks: preventing Gustav Ernst and his cohorts from carrying out their sordid plan. That would be a treat, indeed, if they could manage it.

There were also Stephen Blake, Alison Simmons, and Father Mike, protagonists in the deadly game that was unfolding, sucked into the morass and unable—or unwilling—to avoid it. Odysseus may have survived the perils of the deadly whirlpool Charybdis, but would

Stephen and Alison and Father Mike be so fortunate? They knew they had better have a few tricks up their sleeves if they were to get through the night without mishap.

* * *

Stephen was spending the day at home. There was no way, he had decided, he was going to go to work today. Not with what was planned for tonight and the preparations leading up to it. There were no ill effects left over from Sunday, so he had gone in on Monday—yesterday—mainly to explain to Frank Newell, his boss, what was going on, at least enough to make things credible. He also wanted to apologize for his recent behavior and lack of productivity. He figured it was the least he could do. He promised to make it up to him and the company. But for now, he would need one more day to square things away. He found Mr. Newell to be very understanding and accommodating. Stephen thought that would have been the case even if he hadn't mentioned the possibility of ending up with The Wicca Codex to publish—a non-lethal version, of course.

Sergeant Johnson had called Stephen to say they would be coming by this morning to bring the recording device he was to wear, show him how to use it, and go over any final arrangements before tonight's meeting. Johnson had also called Alison and Father Mike and asked them to be there as well. They needed the entire team to be in sync on this. They weren't leaving anything to chance. Not if they could help it.

Alison and Father Mike arrived at Stephen's place before the police. They were sipping coffee and chatting at the kitchen table. Mulcahy and Johnson got there shortly afterwards. They had come with a third member of the force—Ed Benning, an expert on electronic surveillance. Mulcahy introduced Benning to the group, calling him the department's "bug boy," which drew a laugh or two, including a smile from Benning himself. He apparently was used to the slightly

Wicca Codex

ignominious title. Stephen offered coffee, filled the acceptances, and got everyone settled in. He had to scrounge a few folding chairs out of the closet to accommodate the crowd.

"Glad to see everyone's here," said Mulcahy. "We've got lots to go over, but we'll try to be quick about it. Let's start with the bug. Ed?"

Benning pulled out a tiny listening device from his jacket pocket. "This here's one of our latest models," he said in his matter-of-fact style. He seemingly had given this spiel many times before and was bored with the process. "Ultra small and light. High quality reception. Very sensitive. It'll sit right here." Benning touched the index and middle fingers of his right hand to Stephen's chest. "You don't have to get nose-to-nose for us to hear what's goin' on, either. This'll pick up normal conversation real clear within about twenty-five, thirty feet. Less if it's coming from behind you. So, what you wanna try to do is keep the talker in front."

"Shouldn't be a problem," said Stephen. "The meeting room at the bookstore is arranged in a circle, with the main stuff taking place in the middle of everything. It'll be well within range."

"That's good," said Benning. "Sounds like you should be okay. As long as you don't take your shirt off, that is." Benning's dead-pan presentation made this lame attempt at a joke go over like a lead balloon.

"I think I can handle that," said Stephen, smiling thinly so as not to make Benning feel like a total nebbish. "If anything, I'll have an extra layer of clothing on. The uniform includes a heavy robe for everyone. Will that affect the mike at all?"

"Not really," said Benning. "Like I said, it's very sensitive, even under a couple layers of clothing. Just to be sure, though, we'll turn up the power a notch when we're listening in. It'll be okay. Oh, by the way, just in case you don't know, this is a one-way job only. We can hear you, but not vice versa. It's just too risky to try planting an earpiece on you. Copeesh?"

"Got it," said Stephen.

Johnson said, "Ed'll be back with us tonight before ya leave. He'll hook it up and get everything set. Make sure it's workin' and all. You won't have to do anything except show up at the meetin'."

"Wouldn't miss it," said Stephen.

"Thought not," said Mulcahy. "Okay. Item Two is the front door. You said it'll be locked, but that you'd find a way to leave it open for us. We can save you the trouble, if need be, as long as Ernst doesn't have an alarm system hooked up to the door. Our crack cat burglars can punch out a circle in the glass and hold it with a suction. No noise. Only thing is, we wouldn't want it to trigger anything out back. Whadaya think?"

"Don't know for sure," replied Stephen. "I don't remember seeing any wiring other than for the buzzer I told you about. I would think that with one device he wouldn't have need for another system. He lives over the shop, so the buzzer acts just like an alarm. He'd hear the door opening even if someone managed to break the glass and open the lock. I'd guess he doesn't have a dual system, but I don't think you want to take the chance. I've got to disable the buzzer, so why not take out the lock at the same time?"

"Except ya could do the buzzer out back and not have to find an excuse to get into the front of the shop," said Johnson.

"Not so," explained Stephen. "I noticed on an earlier visit that Ernst has the wire running way up high near the ceiling on its way out back. The only place it's down low where I can get at it easily is at the front door."

Mulcahy thought about it for a few seconds. "How do you propose to disable it?" he asked.

Stephen reached into his pants pocket and pulled out a small wire cutter. "With this," he said, as he plunked the device down on the table. "I pulled it out of my toolbox this morning."

Mulcahy smiled. "Thought of everything, huh?" he said. "How about this? Does Ernst keep a lookout in the shop during the meetings? If he does, that could put a crimp in your plan."

"Not that I know of," said Stephen. "At least he didn't during the meetings I attended. I don't think that'll be a problem."

"Let's hope not," said Mulcahy. "What about weapons? Do you know if they have any firepower back there?"

"The only firepower I know about is *The Codex*. That's plenty. I'd worry about that sooner than I'd worry about guns, Lieutenant."

"Thing really works, huh?" said Mulcahy.

"Better believe it," said Stephen. "Which reminds me. You'd best bring along some kind of container to put the damn thing in when you recover it. You don't wanna go around handling it. That could cause some problems."

Mulcahy and Johnson looked at each other. "Whadaya mean 'problems'?" asked Johnson.

"You didn't hear about that, huh?" said Stephen. "Well, *The Codex* doesn't like to be handled by just anyone, apparently. If you or I touch it, it'll cause an uncomfortable feeling. Nothing destructive. Just unpleasant. Numbing. At least short term. Longer term could be much worse. Who knows? I experienced it in the shop. Ernst just about dared me to lay a hand on it. I gave it a quick try. Very quick. Didn't much enjoy it. Like I said, no sense fooling with it."

Mulcahy shook his head. "Make a note of that, will ya Pat?" was all he could think of in reply. He turned back to Stephen and said, "Now you know why we're having this little talk. Anything else we need to know about?"

Stephen again: "Just that you'd better get inside fast. If Ernst gets wind of you and has ready access to *The Codex*, he won't hesitate to use it. That could be murder, if you'll excuse the expression."

"I'll keep that in mind," said Mulcahy. "Look, if worse comes to worst and you can't unlock the door or take out the buzzer, we're gonna bust through the front and come crashing in. If everyone's in the back like you say, they probably won't hear us until we're right on top of 'em anyway. We'd gain maybe a few extra seconds of surprise if you're successful on your end, which'd be nice, but it's probably not critical."

"Let's hope not," said Stephen.

Mulcahy had an idea. "I think it'd be a good thing, actually, if we set up some kind of password. If you're really in a hole and don't see a way out without us, just use the word and we'll be in faster than you can say 'wicca.' What would you like it to be, Mr. Blake?"

Stephen thought for a second. "How about 'Alison?'"

Everyone turned to look at the red-faced reporter. All she could do was bury her face in her hands and shake her head.

"Hearing no objection, it is so ordered," said Mulcahy. "Make a note..."

"I got it. I got it," said Johnson.

"Now, since you mentioned this Codex thing," said Mulcahy, turning his attention to Father Mike, "maybe now'd be a good time to talk about how the reverend here fits in. I thought you might stay outside the shop, with Miss Simmons. No sense taking any chances. If we need you, we'll holler."

"Begging your pardon, Lieutenant," said the priest, "but you just heard Stephen tell us what a threat *The Codex* is. If I'm outside and Ernst sics *The Codex* on you, there may not be time to react. I think I should go in with you. Just in case. I'll have my own weapons for protection." Father Mike patted the prayer book and the Voynich Manuscript sitting on the table in front of him.

"Begging *your* pardon, Father, but I prefer my own," said Mulcahy as he patted the bulge under his jacket.

"My uncle's right," chimed in Alison, who had been taking all of this in. "And I should be there right behind him. For moral support."

"Absolutely not," said Mulcahy, emphatically. "That's a no-brainer. I'll go along with the priest, but you're out. You're lucky to be tagging along, young lady. Don't push it, or I may change my mind even on that. You'll have to get your story long distance."

"But Lieutenant...," complained Alison.

It was Father Mike who acted as peacemaker, mainly because he knew the police were right on this one. He didn't want his niece inside any more than they did. He thought he should be the one to tell her the real reason she shouldn't go in. It would probably be slightly more palatable to her, coming from him. "Hold on, Ali. You really can't help inside the store, you know. If anything, you'd be in the way."

"In the way?" shouted Alison, indignantly. She looked at Stephen and started to protest to her last line of defense. But he anticipated her plea. He shook his head and threw up his arms as if to fend her off. "Whoa. I really don't want to get in the middle of this, but I'm afraid I agree with the others. There'll be enough of us in there as it is. It's liable to be pretty cramped. And..."

"All right! All right!" said Alison, dejectedly. "Call off the dogs. You're just all too logical. I surrender." Under the circumstances, she thought it best not to mention she'd be bringing a photographer along.

"Now that that's settled," said Mulcahy, "let's talk about timing. What's the scoop on that, Mr. Blake?"

"All meetings start at midnight," explained Stephen. "Ernst likes everyone there early. Most arrive between eleven thirty and eleven forty-five to help set the room up, get their robes on, etcetera. I'd like to get there about eleven thirty myself. That'll give me a little time to work on taking out the lock and the buzzer. You've got to keep your people clear of the place until there's no chance of anyone else coming. As unlikely as it is that there may be a straggler, I'd advise staying away until midnight, or just before. I assume you'll be in the vicinity somewhere, ready to get in position before then. Just don't make it obvious."

"We'll be as obvious as our stakeout last Friday night," said Johnson, a hint of pride on his face and in his voice. "Guess ya missed it, huh?"

"Really?" said Stephen, surprised. "You guys were there?"

"Not us personally," said Johnson. "A couple of our people. They were set up all evenin'. Saw everyone go in and come back out after the festivities. Includin' you."

"I'll be damned," said Stephen.

"Oh, I hope not," said Father Mike. That broke the layer of tension that had settled over the scene, which is what the priest intended.

"Okay," said Mulcahy. "We'll set it up to have our people come in just before midnight. Anyone comes late to the meeting, we nab 'im. As far as Ernst is concerned, the guy's a no-show. I recommend we all reassemble here around nine-ish. Get Blake hooked up. Go over everything one more time. Is that all right with everyone?"

There were nods and okays around the table.

"Good. I guess we're done for now, then," said Mulcahy. "You should all try and get some rest before tonight. I wouldn't recommend any of you stay out late trick-or-treating."

"Darn it," joked Alison. "Wouldn't you know. I've been working on my costume for the last month and a half."

Chapter 36

Tuesday, October 31—All Hallows Eve

As the weather forecasters predicted, it had been a great night for all the little ghosts and goblins who scampered around their neighborhoods collecting treats. They were home now and tucked in bed, having sampled as much of their loot as they could convince their parents to part with. In fact, some of their mothers and fathers were asleep as well or perhaps watching the tail end of the late news.

For all his bravado earlier in the day, Stephen Blake was wishing he was home in bed as well. Instead, he was sitting in the back seat of an unmarked police cruiser on the way to what promised to be a most interesting meeting. Much more interesting, he assumed, than those horrendous industry affairs he was always complaining about. Given the circumstances, he would have traded tonight's extravaganza for one of those boring dinners. No question. In fact, he told himself if he ever made it past tonight, he'd never complain about them again. He would enjoy going to every last one of them.

Stephen was having second thoughts, or even third thoughts, about this latest and perhaps most exciting chapter in his life. Was it to be the last chapter? he wondered. He would probably know in an hour or two, however long it took Ernst and his buddies to say enough for the police to charge in and bag the whole lot. Then he could get on with his life and maybe convince Alison to share it with him. He'd been thinking so hard about all this that he completely forgot she was sitting there next to him, holding his hand for comfort (his comfort, and hers, she would admit), but staying silent so as not to intrude on his private thoughts. She pressed down on the hand gently, just enough to let him know she was there for support. He acknowledged the gesture with a slight squeeze of his own, as well as a quick smile in her direction.

Alison, for her part, wasn't quite sure what she was feeling at that moment. There were too many layers for her to identify. Excitement? Exhilaration? Fear? Pride? Concern? All of those, and more. Some were in conflict, tugging at her in different directions to add further complications to the already complex situation. She was personally involved with these two men—Stephen to her right, Uncle Mike on the left. But this was also a professional assignment. It was a story. A big one. A potential career-maker. She relished the chance to be part of it yet had enough of a head on her shoulders to keep it in perspective, even accepting Mulcahy's prohibition against her bringing along a staff photographer. The Lieutenant had absolutely held the line on that one, and she had abided by it without complaint. This story was important to her, for sure, but not more so than the safety of these men. Her men, as she had come to think of them. Two of the three in her life—along with Jay Burgholz—whom she had come to think the world of, each in his own way. She loved and respected all three, and didn't want to lose any.

Alison acknowledged Stephen's smile, then turned toward her uncle. She noticed how authoritative he looked in his black tunic and white collar visible under his opened and equally black coat. He and the police had decided it would be appropriate for him to wear his "work clothes." Perhaps it would even give him a kind of psychological edge. Every little bit would help tonight. He caught her glance and winked in the dim light filtering through the windows of the cruiser.

Father Mike was involved in his own thoughts, as multi-faceted as those of his companions. His personal faith in God and in his Church was strong, and this gave him the courage and conviction he might need to call upon shortly. Then again, he was troubled by the potential for danger and violence inherent in the upcoming confrontation. Success, he knew, was far from certain. As usual, his greatest concern was for others. For Alison, his niece—a lovely, smart, hard-working girl he was proud to have as a member of his family. He was glad she would not be on the front line going into the battle zone. Still, she was here, and you never knew what could happen. Concern as well for Stephen Blake, the young man Alison had come to know only recently yet had already developed an affection for. It was obvious how deep that affection reached. Father Mike had to admit there was a lot to admire and respect in the young man. Stephen had put himself right in the middle of things, so he would be in the greatest danger. Especially if something went awry. He prayed for that not to happen. And finally, concern for the police, in particular the two men sitting up front, Lieutenant Mulcahy and Sergeant Johnson. Hard-working and honest public servants, as far as he could tell, and he was a pretty fair judge of character. They put their lives on the line day in and day out, almost without thinking about it, it seemed. All the more reason to include them in his prayers, along with all of their colleagues on the force who would be there tonight.

It was true that Father Mike's greatest concern was for others. But it was not his only concern. He could not help it this time. He was apprehensive for his own safety, based on his prior experience. A frightening one that had almost done him in. He knew his nemesis would be there tonight. The one he came up against last time. Lariakin. Satan. But he was a priest. He confronted the devil every day, didn't he? So what made this any different? Only that the evil would be there to see, in the flesh. And maybe, God forbid, to touch, and to hear. It was bad enough to know that your arch enemy was pitted against you in mind and spirit, ready to tear away at your will. It was quite another to bring the other senses into play. The addition of each one would serve only to intensify an already frightening encounter, much like he had gone through two days earlier, hearing that awful, rasping voice emerging from the depths of Stephen's inner self. He thought it was like trying to acquire knowledge of electricity by reading about it in a book. It was a powerful force, but harmless enough, so it seemed, alive only in words and letters. Then you decide you need to experience the force for yourself, so you stick your finger in the nearest electric outlet. You feel the surge of power and pain rip through your body. You hear the crackling of the electrons as they work to break you down into elemental particles. You see the sparks and smell the burning of your flesh, and perhaps even taste the dry, acrid, vaporized fumes as they consume you. It would be a foolish thing to do, indeed. Yet that was just what he was about to do: plug himself into Lariakin and hope the experience did not destroy him.

Alison, Stephen, and Father Mike were yanked abruptly back to reality from their private thoughts by Lieutenant Mulcahy, who half turned toward them as they drove along Boston's nearly deserted streets. "Awfully quiet back there," he said. "Everyone okay?"

"Just getting ready mentally, I guess, for whatever adventures are about to befall us," said the priest. Alison and Stephen each thought that was a sufficiently lucid explanation to preclude having to add anything.

"Guess you're entitled to that," said Mulcahy, as he turned back toward the front. He stole a quick look over in the direction of his partner, who had opted to drive. Pat was being strangely silent, Mulcahy thought. He usually had something to say. Guess everyone's a little up tight on this one, he thought. "Well, almost there," said the Lieutenant. "We'll get within a couple blocks, then drop you off, Stephen." The last few hours had changed "Mr. Blake" into "Stephen." Mulcahy figured there was no need for formality any longer. "Best to go the rest of the way on foot, like we said." They had all heard this numerous times already, but Mulcahy wanted to go over it once more. It couldn't hurt, he thought. Or perhaps it was just his nervousness. After so many years, you'd think he'd have been used to the routine. Except this one wasn't exactly routine. "We'll get in preliminary position, then move in closer when we're sure things are settled down inside the shop. Around midnight or so. Reinforcements'll be there by then. Any last-minute questions?"

The common, unexpressed feeling among the occupants of the back seat was: Let's just get on with it. There was no need for any more talk. It was time for action. There were no questions.

"Good," said Mulcahy. "My feelings exactly. Let's do it."

Johnson eased the cruiser over to the curb on Charles Street, near Beacon. "Show time," said Mulcahy. He turned again toward the back, this time fully, so he could see Stephen. "Hey, listen, buddy. No hero stuff, okay? Let's do it just like we said." He extended his hand and said, "Good luck."

Stephen took it and said, "Thanks. Piece o' cake."

Alison and Father Mike also offered their best wishes. As Stephen started to leave the car, Alison put a hand on his shoulder and said, "Be careful." He merely smiled back at her, then was gone, walking swiftly up Charles in the glow of its old streetlamps.

Alison turned to her uncle and said, "I don't know if I'm going to be able to wait this out, Uncle Mike. Please say your very best prayer for him. And for me."

"I'm way ahead of you, Ali," responded the priest.

* * *

"Welcome, Stephen. I am glad to see you," said Ernst. "Are you ready for a memorable night?" Stephen had just entered the bookstore and found Ernst ready to greet the arriving members. It was clear that disabling the buzzer would have to wait, but he had anticipated that.

Before coming, Stephen had tried to reconstruct in his mind how he acted and sounded the last time he was here—last Friday night—so he would not raise a red flag with uncharacteristic behavior, now that he was free of the influence of *The Codex*. The success of tonight's plan would depend on his ability to blend in, stay in the background, not do anything that might arouse the curiosity of Ernst or Lariakin. He wasn't certain but thought he had been direct and to the point, not overly enthusiastic about things, yet not aggressively antagonistic in any way. Neutral, you might say. He tried to take on the same demeanor now. "Yes, I suppose I am," he said. "It should be interesting, from your description last week."

"'Interesting' will be an understatement if all goes according to plan tonight," replied Ernst. "I appreciate your coming early. In fact, you are the first one. That is a good sign." Ernst did not elaborate on what he meant by that. Stephen thought it might refer to his coming around to Ernst's way of thinking, but he did not pursue it. "By the way," said Ernst, "are you prepared to give us an updated report on your mission to duplicate *The Codex*? We are most anxious to hear about that. You know how important it is to the success of our plans."

Stephen hadn't given this any thought at all and was, in fact, not ready to say anything about it. He thought he would be at the tail end of the business part of the agenda, like last time. Everything should be over by then, or so he hoped. If not, he would just have to wing it. "Yes, I am," lied Stephen. "I think you'll like what I have to say. But no sneak previews, I'm afraid. You'll have to wait along with everyone else."

Ernst laughed, clearly enjoying himself on his night-of-nights, and buoyed by Stephen's hint of good news about *The Codex*. "Excellent," he said. "But you do not have to worry. I will not pressure you for advance information." Ernst saw two or three faces appear at the door. "Ah. Pardon me while I greet our new arrivals. Why not go on back to the meeting room and get ready?"

"Thanks. I will. See you there," said Stephen. He took his coat off and deliberately left it in this part of the shop rather than take it to the meeting room. He thought this would afford him an opportunity to return here after all the members had arrived, but before the meeting started. While Ernst's attention was diverted to the front door, Stephen laid his coat across the counter. While doing so, he glanced toward the entry as if to see who was arriving, but his real aim was to check on the wire leading from the door to the back buzzer. He was gratified to see that things were as he had remembered them. He stifled an urge to feel for the wire cutters in his pants pocket, as well as for the listening mechanism attached to his chest. Despite the small size of each device, they felt enormous to him. He didn't know how anyone could help but notice them sticking out, like cancerous tumors. Or miniature bombs,

Wicca Codex

ready to explode. He started to feel hot and wanted to gag. He wasn't sure he was going to be able to pull this off. He had to move, get away from Ernst.

He turned and went through the curtain to the back of the shop, then walked along the dim hallway on the way to the meeting room at its far end. He passed the door on the right, the one leading to the collection room. It was closed. The door on the left—the one to *The Codex* room—was open a crack. A thin shaft of jaundiced light created a geometric pattern on the dark wooden floor and the opposite wall. As Stephen passed, he caught a side glimpse of Lariakin, clad in black as usual, sitting in one of the chairs. Stephen tried to resist the urge to stop but couldn't. He edged closer to the opening and peered intently into the light. Lariakin was leaning over a book on the table and holding it by its edges. Stephen couldn't be certain, but guessed it was *The Codex*. Lariakin's eyes were closed. He appeared to be murmuring something, but the words—if that's what they were—were unintelligible. He seemed to be in a trance, almost as if he were extracting energy from the document. Or perhaps transferring energy *to* it. In any event, there was something strange and mysterious occurring just a few feet away. Was this person, this...thing, really the devil? thought Stephen. He shuddered, almost violently. Just as he was about to turn away and scurry for the relative safety of the meeting room, he saw Lariakin's head whip around toward the door. He glared at Stephen through the cracked opening. There was no emotion on Lariakin's face. No grimace, no scowl, no smile—nothing. Yet Stephen saw something in it that was utterly terrifying. Stephen couldn't move. He was rooted as if in cement. Lariakin did not remove his grasp on the book but continued looking in his direction. Stephen couldn't tell if Lariakin knew who it was since there was not much to be seen through the narrow crack. Then, just as suddenly as he had turned toward Stephen, Lariakin looked away and closed his eyes once again. It was as if nothing had happened to interrupt his concentration.

Stephen let out a huge sigh of relief and found—thankfully—that his motor skills in general, and legs in particular, were still intact. He slowly pulled back from the door and hastened toward the meeting room. It was all he could do to make it to the nearest chair encircling the center platform before collapsing in a heap from fright. He was thankful no one else had arrived yet. He could feel the heart pounding in his chest and wondered if the rhythmic thump...thump...thump was being picked up by the police through the microphone. He hoped not.

After a minute or two Stephen recovered sufficiently to get up—cautiously—and walk to the nearby closet for a robe. His legs were still a little wobbly, but he managed to make it without mishap. He heard voices out in the hallway and wanted to pull himself together before anyone else arrived. He knew there was little time to waste. He maneuvered into one of the black robes and noticed for the first time how thick and heavy it was. He hoped it wouldn't interfere significantly with the quality or range of his mike. The police had told him not to worry about it, so he tried not to. 'You've got to relax,' he told himself. 'Yeah, easier said than done.'

He didn't want to sit down. Not just yet. He thought he would have an easier time getting out to the front part of the shop if he kept on his feet. He walked around and found that his legs felt sturdier. He wasn't afraid of falling over any longer. At least he had gotten over that little problem. The first of the early arrivals were just now starting to filter into the room. He had never really spoken to any of the members before, so he casually ambled over in their direction and exchanged greetings with two or three of them. Nothing elaborate, just a nod or a few words here and there. He found this helped take his mind off the encounter with Lariakin a few moments ago and actually gave him a small degree of confidence that things would turn out all right.

The brief sojourns with other members, fleeting though they were, drove home that there were faces under the hoods at these meetings. It made him curious about who the faces belonged to. What their names were. What kind of lives they led. What drove them to Ernst and his grisly plan of revenge. If things went well tonight, perhaps he would

Wicca Codex

find out. If not, he might not be around, and none of it would matter.

Others were coming in now. He wandered over to the newcomers and exchanged pleasantries. There was no clock in the room, so he surreptitiously checked his watch. Eleven forty-seven. He counted the people in the room, trying hard not to bob his head as he did so. Seven. Five to go, not counting Ernst and Lariakin. Two more coming in now. That leaves three. Eleven fifty. 'C'mon, where are the rest?' He was getting nervous about the lock. He would have to get out there in the next five minutes at most, he figured, to do what needed to be done and still have time to get back for the meeting, which he knew would start promptly at midnight. Ernst and Lariakin would probably stay in *The Codex* room until the last moment, so he would have to get past them somehow.

Eleven fifty-two. 'God, this is almost too much to bear. Where the hell are...Wait. Here come two more. One to go.' Eleven fifty-three. Most of the members were in their seats now. He'd have to chance it. He left the room and headed down the hallway toward the front of the shop. He passed *The Codex* room, door still slightly ajar. Just as he reached the curtain, Ernst and the last member came through.

"Stephen," said Ernst in a surprised tone, "where are you going?"

'Easy does it. Stay cool.' "I think I may've left something I need for the meeting in my coat. It's got some facts I wanted to present to the group. It'll only take me a minute."

"You must hurry. It is almost time to start the meeting."

Stephen nodded in reply. He sped toward the curtain; then, he brushed through it into the front of the shop. He went straight to his coat, just in case Ernst might be curious and follow him. The room was dark, Ernst having doused the lights after the last arrival. It was illuminated only by a sickly glow creeping in through the front window from outside. Stephen didn't know why he hadn't thought of that. It was difficult to see. The only thing he could hear was his own breathing. When it seemed certain that Ernst was not following him, Stephen didn't hesitate. He moved quickly to the front door and felt for the lock. He flicked it to the open position. He then reached under the robe into his pants pocket and pulled out the wire cutters. Good thing he had checked for the buzzer wire when he first came in, he thought. He couldn't see it now in the darkness. Stephen groped for it with his fingers, found it, then wedged the cutters to fit around the leathery strands. When he judged it to be in position, he squeezed the handle and heard a faint 'snip'. Done. He slipped the cutters back into his pocket and started for the curtain. Suddenly he remembered the tiny bell over the door, the one that tinkled when the door opened. Something else he hadn't thought of. *Damn.* No time to do anything about it now. But maybe he should try to warn the police. He hurried back to the door to get as far away from the curtain as possible. He lowered his chin to direct his voice toward the listening device on his chest and whispered, emphasizing each word: "Lock open. Buzzer out. Bell over door still in place. Careful." He hoped it got through—and was understood.

Stephen dared not take any more time. He rushed back to the curtain and halted for a few seconds, trying to calm himself. He stepped into the hallway and passed *The Codex* room. He could see through the narrow opening that Ernst and Lariakin were still inside. 'Thank God.' The light spilling out allowed him to steal a quick glance at his watch: eleven fifty-eight. 'Too close.' Ernst and Lariakin were discussing something, but he couldn't make out what they were saying. Their gestures were not argumentative, but animated, purposeful. No time to worry about it. Stephen continued into the meeting room, which by now had been darkened as well, and made his way to one of the two remaining vacant chairs. He felt rather than saw pairs of eyes follow him in. He had done it!

Within a minute or so, Ernst and Lariakin entered. Ernst carried *The Codex*. He walked to the center platform, stepped up, and laid the book on the table. Lariakin took the last seat in the circle. Stephen was glad it wasn't next to him this time. He felt an itch where the listening device was attached, but resisted the urge to scratch, lest he somehow call attention to the tiny microphone, or even work it loose. He felt beads of sweat ooze from his forehead. He wanted desperately to wipe them away but did not. He made a concerted effort not to look up at the Satanic image glaring out at the room from within its framed rectangle. Even though he did not look, he could feel the eyes. Those damned eyes.

Ernst waited dramatically before beginning his remarks, pacing slowly around the platform, as if trying to decide what to say. But there was no indecision. Everything had been orchestrated in advance. Nothing was left to chance in the world of Gustav Ernst. After several moments, he began. "Welcome, brothers and sisters, to what portends to be an auspicious celebration of one of the most noteworthy days of the year. All Hallows Eve has just concluded, and we will mark its passing with appropriate festivities throughout the night. I trust you have all come prepared to stay for the duration. I know it will be worth it, because we have given special attention to preparations for this night. The advent of the morning will be the culmination of our struggle to this point, worthy of all our efforts."

Stephen was hoping against hope that Ernst would reveal everything right off the bat. He wanted the police to get what they needed and invade the place as soon as possible. Stephen wanted this nightmare to end—now, this minute. He inched closer to Ernst, the better to pick up his words. It was frustrating not knowing whether this was getting through. It had to. He was disappointed when it became clear that Ernst's opening monologue would not go into specifics on what was planned, or the killings that had led to this point. He realized it was too much to hope for. In retrospect, it would have been downright amazing if the old man had come right out and said, "We took great delight in killing those five people and look forward with relish to terminating a hall full of bishops tomorrow morning." End of story. Case closed. C'mon in and round 'em up, Mulcahy. They're all yours.

'Back to reality,' Stephen thought. 'Let's deal with that.' He heard Ernst go through the agenda for tonight. There was to be another exhortation from Lariakin, then a series of presentations by individual members on research they had each been assigned on various elements of implementing The Plan. The last of those was to be by Stephen on his efforts with respect to duplicating *The Codex*. He hoped—prayed—it wouldn't get that far. This would be followed by a long ritual designed to celebrate All Hallows Eve. 'That's probably why they have *The Codex* out here.' Afterwards, because of the all-night nature of this special event, there would be light refreshments and an extended period of social encounter, or rest, or private contemplation, whatever the members wanted to do. Finally, everyone would reassemble for festivities leading up to the main event—the bishops' conference. 'Finally. Something useful. Hope you're getting this, Mulcahy.'

* * *

"Are you getting anything, Lieutenant?" asked Alison. "What's going on?" Alison and her uncle were huddled in the back of the cruiser, elbows propped up on the front seat, trying to get any information they could out of Mulcahy and Johnson. Both policemen were listening to the goings-on at the meeting. Johnson had relocated the vehicle to within a half block of the bookstore, with several other cars full of police arrayed within a block or two, ready to act on Mulcahy's radio signal.

Mulcahy held up his hand in a silent "Quiet, please" gesture. He was trying to catch the end of what Ernst was saying. After a moment, he turned toward the back and said, "I'm reading them loud and clear. Meeting's underway. Nothing incriminating so far. Got a quick report from Stephen a few minutes ago. He did the lock and buzzer okay. Said something about a bell over the door."

"That's right," remembered Alison. "There's a little bell Ernst has that tinkles when the front door opens. I heard it when I was there."

"How loud is it?" asked Mulcahy.

"Not very. I think you can only hear it as far back as the hallway behind the curtain. I doubt if it'd be audible where they're meeting."

Mulcahy held up his hand again and said, "Hold on. That Lariakin guy is about to say something."

* * *

As Lariakin exchanged places with Ernst and stepped onto the center platform, it seemed to Stephen that Lariakin was strangely troubled by something. On this night in particular, so close to success in attaining one of their primary objectives, as well as celebrating what for them was the most important milestone of the year, he should be pleased. Things had gone well so far. There was the promise of much greater things to come. What was wrong? Why was he brooding? Stephen watched as Lariakin circled the platform ever so slowly, stopping occasionally to gaze straight into the eyes of each member encircling him. He was searching for something. But what? When he came over to Stephen's side, Lariakin's eyes drilled into his and lingered for an extra moment. It was all Stephen could do to maintain eye contact. He told himself not to look away, but he didn't know how long he could hold it. Finally, after an eternity, Lariakin passed. 'Dear God,' prayed Stephen, 'please let this be over soon.' Lariakin continued in this way until all around the circle were...what?...evaluated? Intimidated? Stephen did not know what was going on. Even Ernst was not immune from this little exercise, Stephen noticed.

When he completed his tour around the perimeter, Lariakin moved to the center of the platform and put his hands on the table as if to steady himself. 'Ready Mulcahy?' thought Stephen. 'Here it comes. Assuming you guys can hear anything at all, that is.'

"I spoke to you," began Lariakin in a low, almost sad, voice, "only a few days ago." Stephen noticed in the candlelight a slight twitch on Ernst's face. It was as if Ernst knew, just by means of these few introductory words, the tone of voice, the demeanor, that Lariakin was about to proceed on a course that would deviate from what had been planned. Perhaps that is what they had been talking about a moment ago in *The Codex* room, thought Stephen. If this was unsettling to Ernst, what would it mean for Stephen and the others?

Lariakin continued: "I spoke about our glorious mission, and how each of you had assisted in its fulfillment to this point. All have played a useful role, and it is appreciated." There was a slight pause, during which Lariakin moved away from the table and started circling once again, his eyes switching between the floor and *The Codex* lying in the center of the table. "We have shown our ability to right the wrongs of the past by means of selective cleansing." 'Good. Keep going.' "We have befuddled the tormentors of our ancestors and have demonstrated to them the power that lies in our hands..."—he raised his arms above his head—"... and in *this*." Lariakin slammed a fist down hard on *The Codex*. The sound reverberated through the room like a clap of thunder. Stephen jumped reflexively, then listened for the rest of Lariakin's words. "Here lies your power. Here, in this ancient manuscript. Its mysteries provide the means to do incredible things. It has been delivered to you for use in glorifying your leader...our leader..."— Lariakin spun on his heels and pointed to the picture of Satan high above them— "...and attaining for him that which he has commanded be done." He whirled around once more, facing Stephen as he shouted as loudly as he could, "Is that not so, Mr. Blake?"

Stephen was stunned. He was taken completely by surprise. He had absolutely no idea what was happening. As much as he felt a need to respond, he was unable to do so. He was, quite literally, speechless.

"I see that you have lost your tongue," screamed Lariakin. "Perhaps I can help you find it." He paused, then said, more calmly, "Let us try a little experiment, shall we?" He paused again, then said, "Blake is the Duplicator," while staring straight into Stephen's eyes.

Stephen sat motionless. He was still befuddled, but had recovered just enough to mutter weakly, "I...I don't know what you mean."

"I believe you do," said Lariakin. "If you were still under the power of *The Codex*, Mr. Blake, you would have automatically repeated that phrase. Just a little precaution we build into the process. It gives us somewhat of an edge, you see. Now, the question is, how did you manage to divest yourself of that influence, Mr. Blake? Would you like to tell us about that?"

Stephen's mind raced. He didn't know whether to deny knowledge of what Lariakin was talking about or accept the fact that he had been found out and go from there. Following the first course was his initial reaction. It was a defensive posture, and he felt as though he needed some sort of defense mechanism at the moment. Big time. On the other hand, denial could turn out to be more dangerous than the alternative. It was not likely he was going to fool anyone, so why play dumb and create further antagonism? If he confronted Ernst and Lariakin—try playing a strong hand, essentially—it might throw them off guard, maybe even delay any retribution against him long enough for the police to swoop in and save his hide. 'God, I hope they're hearing this,' he prayed. Not only that, but he realized there had not been much in the way of hard evidence yet. Maybe he could elicit some incriminating statements before the whole thing came crashing down. But to do that, he'd have to get Mulcahy to wait. Hold off just a little longer. One thing Stephen knew for sure. There'd be no use of the "Alison" password to deliver him from this mess. It wouldn't solve anything. Not yet, anyway. Stephen made up his mind to go for broke.

"Well, I guess you fellows are smarter than I figured," said Stephen. He rose slowly...oh, so slowly...out of his seat, trying to regain some control and speak in an evenhanded tone. He was still reeling inside and did not think he was succeeding, although to the others his voice had a certain strength of conviction. He went on, hoping Mulcahy would understand. "But wait," said Stephen. "Don't do anything rash. Just let me say what's in my heart first." As he said these last words, he thumped his chest with his fist twice, as if emphasizing what he was saying. His hope was that Mulcahy would interpret it as a signal to stay away, at least for the moment. "Then you can do with me what you will," concluded Stephen.

By now, Ernst had joined Lariakin on the platform. It was he who spoke next, without malice, but with a profound sadness. He looked down at Stephen, still standing at his place in the circle. All the others remained seated and silent, only now starting to understand that something of enormous import was unfolding before them. "Stephen, Stephen," said Ernst, "you foolish man. There was such a glorious opportunity for you here. Yet you threw it away, as though it were nothing but...but a scrap of waste. You could have been such an integral part of our plan, particularly at this critical time. I gave you my friendship and trust, and you rejected me—and us—in this hour of need. I see now that I was wrong about you. Perhaps you can explain what turned you against us."

He realized instantly he had been given the opening he needed. 'Got to seize it.' He dug down into his innermost soul for whatever courage lay there. It would be now, or it would be never. "What turned me?" he said indignantly. "How about the deaths of all those innocent people? At least five lives snuffed out as though they were nothing but...scraps of waste, to use your own phrase. Six, if you add my friend John Demming to the list, since you were probably responsible for him, too. I'll have to live with the guilt of sending him to you. Then there's the hideous plan you've cooked up to exterminate all those Catholic bishops in a few hours. And you ask why I turned against you? Surely you don't deny any of this."

"Deny it?" roared Ernst. "On the contrary. We proclaim it with the greatest pride and honor. Those deaths do not begin to expiate the wrongs of The Inquisition against our brothers and sisters. But it is a good start. And I can assure you we will continue, so that we eradicate as many of the perpetrators of these crimes as possible."

'There. He said it. He admitted all of it.' Stephen had what he – and the police—wanted. Ernst had incriminated himself and the others. Beyond question. Stephen could now play for time. But he was incensed at the callousness of these criminals. It infuriated him that they had so little regard for human life. "How can you call them perpetrators?" he asked. "They've done nothing, except perhaps be born as Catholics. None of them had anything to do with whatever atrocities may have been committed in the past."

Ernst took up the gauntlet. "That is easy to say, but it is meaningless. No one is devoid of culpability. Time does not erase it. The guilt is a permanent blot on the soul of every member of The Catholic Church, particularly the clergy. Just like your original sin, it stains the soul of everyone who comes after."

"That's too simplistic," said Stephen. He was no religious zealot. He wasn't even a Catholic. Then again, he didn't feel as though he were arguing theology, just morality. "It's awfully easy to cast a net over everyone, even though they may deplore the atrocities of an earlier time, and hundreds of years ago, at that."

"The crimes were too great. They cannot be escaped merely by the passage of time. Or a convenient change of heart." Ernst was growing impatient. Stephen had never seen him do that before, even to the slightest degree. "In any event, the matter is not open to debate. There is no alternative to our course of action. It is irrevocable."

Lariakin stood next to Ernst throughout this dialog. His face carried the faint trace of a smile, as though he were proud of his chief follower. It was clear to Lariakin that Ernst had done his work well, so strong was his commitment to the cause of justice that had been set out, and so eloquent his elucidation of it. He was content to let his student play the role of teacher.

Ernst continued: "Further discussion would be a waste of time. I have said enough. It is unfortunate that you will have to join your meddling friend Demming. I had hoped we could avoid such an unpleasant end for you. You had such...potential."

Stephen realized he was not going to be able to delay the proceedings any longer, and that he himself was in extreme danger. He had to get Mulcahy inside—now. Maybe it was time for that password after all. Then again, it could be suicide for anyone barging in, especially with *The Codex* so accessible to Ernst and Lariakin. He had to find a way to even the odds. Stephen's gaze turned to *The Codex* lying on the table.

It was only a few feet away. He wondered if he could spring onto the platform and grab it before they realized what was happening. He didn't expect to be able to escape with it. Hell, he didn't even know what effect the book would have on him. But at least he might be able to keep it out of their hands at the critical moment. Trouble was, how could he know when that was going to be? He couldn't afford to dwell on it. The time for action was now. He would simply have to trust that things would work out, or he would die trying. He was going to die anyway, wasn't he? What did he have to lose? He thumped his chest once more and yelled, "Now would be a good time, Alison."

"What are you talking about," asked Ernst, puzzled. "Now would be a good time for what? Who is Alison?"

Lariakin understood immediately. "It's a signal, you fool. He's warning someone, he's..."

In the blink of an eye, Stephen seized the chance to spring for *The Codex*. He leaped for the platform but stumbled as he tried to jump onto it. He ended up on his knees at its edge. The mishap was just enough for Ernst to react. He grabbed the manuscript and, as he did so, lashed out at Stephen, yelling, "Get back! You're no better than the rest! I'll show you what happens to your kind!" Ernst held the book in both hands and thrust it at Stephen, who was trying to scramble back to his feet. Too late. A flash of blinding light slashed through the darkness toward Stephen. He felt a burning sensation tear into his left shoulder. He screamed in reaction to its hotness, its debilitating sharpness. The force of it threw him backward violently, causing him to crash through the circle of chairs and land hard on the floor. Two or three members tumbled over with him, but quickly jumped up and moved away. They knew what was coming next. The others, though awestruck by this turn of events, remained seated, fascinated by the unplanned deviation from the course that had been set out for the evening.

The pain in Stephen's arm and shoulder was intolerable. He could do nothing but lie there and await the next thrust, which was sure to be a fatal one.

At that moment, the door to the meeting room burst open. Mulcahy and Johnson, crouching low, lunged in with guns drawn. Mulcahy shouted, "Police! No one move! I want all hands where we can see 'em! Now!" Right behind them, standing in the doorway, was Father Mike, holding the Voynich Manuscript straight out over the heads of Mulcahy and Johnson, extended at Ernst and Lariakin, still standing on the center platform. The priest said nothing. He merely stood erect, pointing the document. Mulcahy and Johnson stayed down but moved a short distance into the room, trailed by the priest, who in turn was followed by several other uniformed police officers, all with guns in hand, ready for instant use. All this happened so swiftly that Ernst, despite holding *The Codex*, was momentarily stunned by the surprise entry. Lariakin, although hearing Stephen's earlier warning, was also unprepared for the intrusion. He stood next to Ernst, watching. The other members remained transfixed, able only to turn their heads toward the invading force, unaware of what they might do to counter it.

After a few moments, Mulcahy made his way to where Stephen lay, still writhing in pain and grasping at his shoulder. Mulcahy never took his eyes—or his gun—off Ernst but directed his words at Stephen. "How bad?" he asked. "Can you walk?"

"Dunno," mumbled Stephen, his speech garbled. "I'll try." He made a move to get up but fell back onto the floor. The pain was too great.

As Mulcahy dealt with Stephen, Ernst and Lariakin were recovering from their initial shock. Lariakin was the first to regain his function. He spoke at Ernst without looking at him. "*The Codex*," he said softly. "Use *The Codex*." Ernst heard. He started to raise the book. All guns in the room were trained on him, ready to fire.

"Wait!" shouted Father Mike, as much at the police as at Ernst. The priest continued to point his own weapon—the manuscript—toward the center of the room, sighting along it as though he himself were aiming a handgun at a bullseye target. In a real sense, he was. "Don't shoot. I don't think he can do anything." Father Mike was anything but certain that his bold statement was accurate. But, for the moment, it was a standoff. Ernst and Lariakin versus Father Mike and the police. No one moving. No one quite sure what to do next. Approximately a quarter of a minute ticked off the clock, each second seemingly drawn out far beyond the normal concept of earthly time for everyone in the room.

It was Ernst who broke the spell. He directed his words at Father Mike, noticing for the first time his religious collar, eyes penetrating into his adversary as a laser beam plows through all in its path.

"I see you are a member of the murdering priesthood," said Ernst, laughing contemptuously. "Do you think that qualifies you to counter our power?"

"It is not me, but the Lord God, who will do it," responded Father Mike.

"Of course," said Ernst. "I had forgotten how arrogant you all are. So certain of everything, so long as it is done in God's name. Just as our ancestors were tormented. Nothing has changed."

"And how are you familiar with us that you can judge us all?"

"That is a fair question, but one with an easy answer," said Ernst. "I am sorry to say that I once wore the collar of Rome. I was a priest. Just like you."

The room fell into a stunned silence. This shocking revelation had been known to no one. No one except Lariakin, of course. He was not only aware of it, but it had been a prime consideration in Ernst's recruitment. To the other members of the coven, however, it was beyond comprehension that their leader had had anything to do with the institution they each despised with a vengeance. In fact, it was Ernst himself who had increased their hatred of it tenfold.

'So that's how he got the names of his victims, those with a connection to the clergy,' thought Mulcahy. 'Or at least it made it easier, knowing where to look.'

Father Mike was as taken aback by this news as anyone. It took him a while to recover from it sufficiently to respond. "Well, that's quite interesting. But not all that surprising, I guess, when you think about it. You would have studied about The Inquisition during your training and somehow became disenchanted with The Church's response to those terrible times. After that, you became easy fodder for your friend there. There's nothing he likes better than to bring a priest into his fold, even a fallen one. He couldn't get me, so he settled for you."

Ernst was puzzled by Father Mike's words and was about to ask what he meant, but it was Lariakin who spoke next. "Yes, of course," he said, drawing out the words while staring intently at Father Mike, still holding onto the Voynich Manuscript and pointing it toward the middle of the room. The book, though small, was becoming heavy, but he dared not lower it. "I thought there was something familiar about you, priest." Lariakin almost spat as he spoke. "I almost had you back then, didn't I?"

"I'll admit it was a close call," said Father Mike. "But, as you learned, there was a higher power than yours back then, just as there is now. You may control the weak and faithless, but to those whose belief in the Lord is strong, you are nothing. Your work is finished here, Lariakin."

"You speak boldly for someone who almost succumbed in body, in mind, and in spirit."

"That was a long time ago. I was young, and inexperienced. My faith was not yet...fully developed. Yes, you almost won that time, but you didn't. In fact, you did me a favor. I learned many things from our encounter, not the least of which is that you can be controlled by sheer force of will, if it's based on the sacrifice of our Lord Jesus Christ."

Ernst continued to hold *The Codex*, looking for an opening to use it. He and Lariakin saw that Father Mike was finding it harder and harder to hold his own manuscript up. They did not know what they were dealing with but sensed that it should not be taken lightly. His force, whatever it was, had to be disengaged. If they could keep him talking and distract him for an instant, it might be the opening they needed.

Mulcahy and Johnson remained in a crouch. They straddled the door, Mulcahy up near Stephen, Johnson pulled further back and off to the side. The other police who had come in with them were arrayed along the back wall near the door, others in the doorway itself or in the hallway beyond. The line of armed police extended back into the bookstore. All were alert for any provocation, but for now we're content to let the main protagonists play out their deadly game. Stephen remained on the floor, holding his throbbing shoulder. He listened along with the others.

"What little toy do you have there, priest?" snarled Lariakin. "You think that puny book will save you from me a second time?"

"Books are only collections of symbols," said Father Mike. "They have no power in themselves. But the messages they contain can be forceful on the mind. If you believe that something is so, very often you find that it is. And, of course, if the book has inherent in it the message of God, as this one does, it only serves to reinforce the feeling of invincibility against your forces of darkness, death, and destruction. I wouldn't advise you to test me on this."

Father Mike turned his attention to Ernst. Perhaps there was still a remote chance he could be diverted from his evil course. Perhaps all the way back to the Church. Christ accepted the most grievous of sinners to the fold. "Even for you, it isn't too late. Your 'god' is one of hatred and violence and contempt; mine, one of love and compassion and forgiveness. If you renounce Satan and forsake his evil works, you can achieve redemption and find what you lost long ago. You'll have to atone for your sins, as we all do, here on earth and later in purgatory, but you can avoid the hellish fires for which you have sold your soul. I pledge to do all I can to remove you from that terrible bondage, if you'll only express remorse and let me help you."

"You waste your time with me," said Ernst, contemptuously. "There is nothing you can say that will deter me from my mission. Remorse? Yes, I have it, but only because I was so blinded to the truth that I became one of you long ago. For that I am truly sorrowful. Bondage? The links that bind you to the crimes of your Church are as heavy as those I wear. I carry mine willingly. Yours are a horrendous burden from which you are still trying to free yourself. Death and destruction?

Wicca Codex

That is laughable. How easily you forget the armies of men, women, and children your pompous popes caused to be destroyed." Ernst had to pause for a moment to keep the hatred that was rising within him under control. At least for a while longer, until he and Lariakin could exact their revenge on this upstart priest and his lackeys.

"Before we deal with you," continued Ernst, "you may find interesting one more thing. It amuses me to tell it to you before you die. The fact is, I found more than *The Codex* on my last trip to Germany. I learned who I really was. Many go through an entire lifetime without finding their true identity. I was fortunate, indeed. You see, in researching my ancestry, I discovered my correct family name. It is not Ernst, but Faust."

If those in the room were shocked into silence by Ernst's revelation about his prior association with the priesthood, they were doubly so now. All remained in their places, frozen in time, listening for what would follow.

"Yes," said Ernst, "the very same whose activities are engraved in history. Faulty record keeping over the years modified the name to Ernst, but there is no changing the facts. My lineage extends in an unbroken line back to the fifteenth century. To the one whose life and endeavors so many have taken such delight in extolling for hundreds of years. Art, music, literature. The record is there for all to see. I am proud to be able to say I am part of that. So you see, priest...and Blake, and all of you...there is no possibility you will change what I am. I will not dishonor my heritage."

Those who heard could only wonder. Was it possible this could be true? Could this old man be a direct descendant of the original Dr. Johann Fausten—sorcerer, magician, conjurer—one of the most enigmatic figures in history? Was the similarity of Ernst and Faust just a coincidence, or was it possible that a careless transcriber or a smudge of ink had caused "F" to become "E," "a" to turn itself into "r," "u" to transmute into "n"? It was no secret this kind of thing had happened to others. Even in the same family, relatives' names were changed, spelled differently. Could he be telling the truth? It was beyond belief.

Except to Father Mike. Suddenly, it all fit. The pieces of the puzzle had assembled themselves into a mosaic that made sense. Save for one thing. "So that's the source of your Codex," he said. "But how did you come to call it 'Wicca?' My understanding of the sect is one of healing."

"Exactly so," said Ernst. "After I forswore the priesthood, I gravitated to the Wiccan religion, only to find it did not fulfill my needs. It honored our fallen ancestry, but there was reluctance to...let us say...redress past grievances. Satan was to be my savior, not nature. I retained the Wiccan name for *The Codex* simply because it was appropriate. Witchcraft is what the book, and our mission, is about." He paused. "I am pleased to enlighten you in these matters at the hour of your death. But now, enough."

The enormity of Ernst's disclosures jolted everyone to inattention. Father Mike, in particular, let Ernst's words and the increasing weight of the Voynich Manuscript cause the book to fall slowly to his side. It was just enough. Lariakin whispered to Ernst: "Take the policeman. The priest is mine."

Ernst sprang into action. He quickly raised *The Codex* to eye level to bring its powers to bear against their enemies. Father Mike realized his mistake a moment too late, but Mulcahy and Johnson caught themselves in time. They each shouted a loud warning to Ernst, who ignored them. He rushed at Mulcahy, pointing the manuscript and uttering words that were incomprehensible. At the same time, Lariakin lunged toward Father Mike, who by now had recovered sufficiently to raise the Voynich Manuscript at the on-rushing demon. The room erupted in gunfire, first from Mulcahy, then from Johnson and the other police officers. Mulcahy saw three of his shots rip into Ernst just before the old man could reach him, huddled on the floor near Stephen. Ernst's momentum caused him to fall across Stephen and onto Mulcahy, toppling him over. The lieutenant struggled to free himself from under Ernst's weight, managing to move him off to one side. Mulcahy saw the bright red stain expand on Ernst's robe. He was dead.

Wicca Codex

Pandemonium ensued. The coven members, who had been seated throughout, except for those knocked over by Stephen, panicked in the loud uproar and started running about the room, some trying to get out the only doorway, even though it was blocked by police. Others simply tried to save themselves from the flying bullets, but did not know where to go. Some crouched on the floor. Others tried hiding under the tables along the walls. It was hard to see what was happening in the gunsmoke and dim candlelight.

In a flash, fires erupted all around the room from the many candles used to illuminate the proceedings. Most had been knocked over in the confusion, and before long had caught hold of papers scattered about, the room's old wooden floors and walls, even the robes and clothing of a few of the coven members. The rapidity with which the fire spread in both extent and intensity was unbelievable. Smoke from the flames further obscured what was going on in the room. It was becoming hard to breathe.

Mulcahy thought about trying to kill the flames with a coat, but it was too far gone. It was difficult to see but he turned in Johnson's direction and yelled, "Get everybody out! Now! Get someone to call the damn fire department! And alert the neighbors! This place is goin' up!"

Johnson got up off the floor and told the nearest patrolman to warn everyone about the fire. He started rounding up the coven members still inside, herding them toward the door. Mulcahy grabbed Stephen by the arms and managed to get him seated upright. Stephen howled from the pain of the movement. Mulcahy had no choice but to ignore the protest. He crouched and leaned into Stephen's body, raising himself and Stephen up to a standing position. More yells and curses from Stephen. They limped toward the door, where Mulcahy turned his burden over to another patrolman, with instructions to get him outside to safety, then call an ambulance.

Mulcahy turned back into the room, which by now was almost totally obscured by smoke and flames. He bent low to escape the worst of it and headed back to his previous position, or at least where he estimated it to be. He stumbled into Ernst's body a few seconds later. He felt for the arms, latched onto them, and dragged him out the door and down the hallway into the outer shop. He left him there and ran back into the meeting room. He got as far as the doorway. "Anyone in there?" he shouted. "Anyone left?" He listened hard for a few seconds but heard nothing. The heat was getting too intense to remain much longer.

He was about to turn away when he heard a faint voice: "Over here, hurry," followed by a fit of coughing.

Mulcahy shouted into the flames, "I can't see anything. Where are you?" He got on hands and knees and started crawling toward where he thought the voice had been. "Say something," he said, frantically. "Keep talking, dammit."

For a moment, nothing. Then: "Here, this way, over here." More coughing. Deep, hacking coughs. Mulcahy changed his direction slightly to the left and bumped into a figure lying on its stomach, face twisted toward Mulcahy. It was Father Mike.

"Jesus H. Christ," said Mulcahy. "It's you. We've gotta get the hell outta here. Now! Can you move?"

The flames were starting to lick up against the priest's clothing. "I...I don't think so," he said weakly. Coughs.

"Never mind. I'll drag you out."

"W-wait," stammered the priest. He fumbled around with his hands, first to his right—nothing there—then his left. Yes. There it was! He grabbed what he had been seeking and thrust it at Mulcahy. "Here. T-take this," he mumbled.

Mulcahy grabbed what Father Mike offered and thrust it impatiently into the slack of his belt next to his stomach. "Let's go! Let's go!" he said. There was no time to do anything other than grab the priest's arms and pull him toward the doorway, almost totally obscured. He was starting to feel lightheaded from the heat and smoke but fought it off. He navigated toward where he thought the opening was and managed to find it through the swirling mix of colors all around him. Grays and blacks and browns and yellows and reds and oranges. Wild, fantastic shapes everywhere. And the heat! It felt as though he were inside an oven. 'God,' he thought, 'lemme outta here! Just give me a little more strength. Please.'

He managed to get the priest into the hallway, then stopped to close the door. He thought he might impede the spread of the flames as much as possible, but he could tell from the looks of the place that it was not going to take long for it to turn into a torch. He hoped the firemen would get there soon or the whole area could be lost. He turned to look at Father Mike lying on the floor. The priest was saying something to him, but he couldn't tell what. He could hear a faint voice, but it seemed as though it was miles away. The sound was coming to him in slow motion, the words suspended in midair, trying to reach him, failing. He was having trouble staying on his feet now. 'Got to rest,' he thought. 'Got to close my eyes. Just for a minute. Just for...'

Mulcahy fainted dead away, falling onto the sprawled body of Father Mike.

Chapter 37

Wednesday, November 1

The early morning news reports being broadcast to Boston's rivers of commuters included a piece about a multiple-alarm fire in the Back Bay. It had started sometime during the early morning hours. Details were sketchy, the reports said, but firefighters were still on the scene, trying to bring the stubborn flames under control. Many buildings—almost an entire city block—had already been destroyed, but the hope was that further damage could be contained. The cause of the blaze was unknown at this time. Several casualties were reported so far, including at least one known death—the elderly owner of a bookstore located in one of the buildings—and a handful of injuries, mostly suffered by fire and police personnel on the scene. They were being treated at nearby Massachusetts General Hospital. Additional injuries had been miraculously prevented by quick action in awakening startled residents of adjoining buildings. Despite the one fatality, officials said they had been extremely fortunate that no one else had died. Things could have been much worse, given the circumstances, one fire official said. Several residents who were evacuated reported hearing strange noises just before the fire, sort of like a car backfiring, or gunshots, but those reports remained unconfirmed by police, who were refusing to talk to the media at this time. The scene around Charles and Beacon streets was reported to be chaotic this morning, and things were not expected to improve for at least several more hours, at best. Motorists were advised to avoid the area. Further details would be forthcoming as soon as they were known.

Alison Simmons was listening to these reports as she sat at her desk at The Herald. She had spent the better part of the night at Mass

General, keeping tabs on three survivors in particular—Stephen Blake, her Uncle Mike, and Lieutenant Mulcahy. When she was satisfied that all three had miraculously sustained only relatively minor injuries and would likely recover quickly—all were scheduled for release that morning—she was driven home by Sergeant Johnson and managed to catch a little sleep. Just enough to ward off the worst of the fatigue and anxiety and the other debilitating effects of the previous hours.

Stephen, she was told, had burn marks on his left shoulder. He would have to keep his arm in a sling for a few days to keep it immobilized, but he was otherwise all right and was expected to recover fully. As was Lieutenant Mulcahy, who had succumbed to smoke inhalation, the extraordinary heat of the flames, and the effort involved in dragging others to safety. A little oxygen, not to mention a few hours of bed rest, was all that was needed to set things back in order for him.

As for her uncle, Father Mike, his ailment was a bit more difficult to diagnose. He complained of limpness in his arms and legs, although doctors were unable to find anything in particular that might cause such symptoms. Thankfully, he had started to regain the use of his limbs as the hours passed and was soon walking around and eating. Welcome signs, they said. His problem was surmised to have been more psychological than physical, given his quick recovery, although they could not begin to speculate on what might have caused his difficulty. They would keep him a while longer for observation, but he was expected to be okay.

As she sat at her desk, Alison recalled what an extraordinary night it had been for her, forced to stay in the background and not knowing what was going on mere yards from where she sat in the police cruiser. She had promised to stay put as the others went about their dangerous business, but it was unbelievably difficult sitting on the sidelines. It was totally against her character. When they dragged Stephen out, looking as though he were dead, she almost passed out from fright. Then they couldn't find her uncle for the longest time. It appeared everyone else had made it out, but he and Lieutenant Mulcahy were missing. God, if anything happened to Uncle Mike, she thought, she would never be able to forgive herself. His involvement was her doing. Sergeant Johnson and another officer had gone in after the lieutenant and the priest. They found both huddled outside the meeting room, about to be overtaken by the advancing flames. Even though they managed to pull them outside to safety, it was just about all she could bear. All of the emotions bottled inside her welled up and flowed out in a torrent of tears. She simply could not contain them any longer.

When all were on the way to Mass General, Johnson wanted to take her home, but she insisted on going to the hospital and wait it out there. She started to feel better only after it became clear that one, then another, then all three would recover, and fairly quickly at that. Only then did she consent to go home herself and get some much-needed rest, although there was some reluctance even then. Her desire to start telling this unbelievable story was almost overwhelming. She felt the need to begin immediately. But reason prevailed, not to mention the cajoling influence of Sergeant Johnson. She finally had agreed she needed to recover from the events of the past few hours as much as those lying in hospital beds at MGH. Besides, she knew it was too late to make even the last edition of this morning's paper, so it was really an academic issue. Otherwise, ...

Alison's mind snapped back to the present. She had been staring for some time at the blank computer screen in front of her. Now the blinking cursor brought home the fact that a story needed to be written. Words had to be formed and strung together. It was an act of creation, she felt, much like the birth of a child. A story was given life and nurtured. It grew from infancy to adulthood, taking advantage, hopefully, of the experiences of youth. Sometimes there was struggle and conflict and pain along the way, but these only served to make the attainment of success more pleasing and enduring, more satisfying, more meaningful. Like people, a story could live a long life or a short one. The span was unpredictable, but the objective was a good life, no matter what the duration. Alison felt this story would enjoy a lengthy existence, if only because of its nature. This was not your everyday murder mystery, precipitated by a drug deal gone bad, or the misplaced passion of domestic dysfunction, or the retribution of a disgruntled former employee, or a sick political statement, or even the random violence of a deranged serial killer. It had all of these, to be sure, but it also had so much more. And she had lived it, been a key player in it. No one else would be able to give it the perspective she could. She would try hard to do it justice. But the most important thing now was for the story to be born. Better get to work, she thought.

Alison had seen Burgholz when she came into the office that morning. She had started to fill him in on the events of the previous day and night, wanting to make him part of it and draw him into the web of intrigue and violence that had been spun. He was professionally interested, of course, and wanted to hear it all. But he was also personally concerned for Alison's well-being. He could not believe she was in the office, not after the night she had experienced. He insisted she take the day off and go home, but she demurred. She was fine, she said. A bit tired, but otherwise okay. And raring to go on the story.

When it became clear to Burgholz that Alison was not going to be deterred, he sat down with her and sketched out the approach that seemed best. Others—radio, TV, and press—would be giving the world the details on the events of the past few weeks, facts that anyone could get by talking to the police and fire departments, as well as the families of the murder victims. Alison would present these as well, but wrap them in her own mélange, especially the "why" and "how" of it all. It would be an enthralling story, not just an article. They would put it out as a series spanning the better part of a week. It had the potential to be a blockbuster. Burgholz gave Alison free rein to do it up as she saw fit. He had faith in her ability and wanted to use this as a springboard to launch her career into a new, uncharted area. Which was exactly what Alison had in mind.

Sometime later—Alison had lost track of time as she plunged into her work—she got a call from Sergeant Johnson. He had just come from the hospital and was happy to report that her uncle, his boss Vinnie, and her friend Stephen had all been released from the hospital. He thought she'd like to know. But he was also calling to ask if she could stop by the station later on that afternoon—say about three o'clock. The Lieutenant had asked Father Mike and Stephen to be there as well, and they had enthusiastically agreed, although both were still hobbling around some. It was sort of a combination debriefing/celebration/thank you get-together that Lieutenant Mulcahy wanted to arrange with the principals involved. Could she make it, by any chance? What a terrific idea, she said. She'd be there, assuming it wasn't a problem with her boss, but she didn't think it would be. Part of the job, really. Great, said Johnson, he'd see her then.

* * *

At about three fifteen, Alison strolled into the Berkeley Street headquarters of the Boston Police Department and asked for Lieutenant Mulcahy. She was ushered into the same room where the news conference had taken place a couple of weeks earlier—it seemed to her such a long time ago—only now there were no lights, cameras, or microphones. The place was set up for a small party. There was a long table with soft drinks, sandwiches, cookies. Several folding chairs were scattered about in case anyone felt the need to sit, although no one was so inclined at the moment. The small gathering included Lieutenant Mulcahy, Sergeant Johnson, Father Mike, and Stephen Blake. There was a possibility that Assistant Commissioner Westerman might drop by later, maybe even the Big Cheese—Commissioner Rizzotto. There were lots of smiles, animated discussion, toasting with cans of Diet Coke and Sprite. The scene wasn't exactly reminiscent of the Ritz ballroom, but it was, after all, the idea that counted, Alison thought. Best of all, no one looked the worse for wear.

"Well, well, our honored guest has finally arrived," said Mulcahy happily, as he caught a glimpse of Alison. "C'mon in, join the party.

Wicca Codex

You've got a little catching up to do." The others turned in her direction and supported Mulcahy's words with clapping and cheers. Alison exchanged emotional hugs with everyone, including the two police officers. She had to fight back the tears that threatened to well up in her eyes.

"I'm so glad you're all okay," said Alison, as she surveyed each of the men in turn. "I was worried about all of you last night, and this morning in the hospital, but you seem to have survived to fight another day."

"Hey, it takes more than a few Satan worshippers to get the best of *this* group," laughed Mulcahy.

"Hear, hear," said Father Mike.

"I'll drink to that," said Stephen, raising a can of soda with his good arm. The other remained in a sling.

Picking up on Stephen's remark, Mulcahy said, "Yes, we—Pat and I—want to drink a toast to all of you. To thank you for your help and cooperation. There was no way we could have done this without you. But I especially want to acknowledge the real hero—or should I say heroine?—of this whole episode, our intrepid reporter from The Herald, Miss Alison Simmons." More cheers and huzzahs all around.

Alison was embarrassed by the attention and tried to deflect it. "Why, thank you, gentlemen. But I think there was enough heroism by everyone in this room over the last few days to warrant a million toasts. Stephen here"—she went over to him and tucked an arm around his waist, as he did the same to her—"had to endure Ernst's and Lariakin's mind control, then volunteered to expose himself to them after he was released from their evil hold." Cheers once again.

"And my uncle,"—she looked at him with such devotion that he could not meet her gaze—"he had to console a dejected niece who had some cockamamie story and who thrust herself on him mercilessly. He got involved without hesitation and put himself in harm's way to help me and Stephen. Thank you, Uncle Mike." Another round of shouts and clapping.

"And let's not forget the Lieutenant here. He'll probably say he was just doing his job, but it was still something special when he pulled Stephen out of that burning building, then went back in to find my uncle, even though he himself was feeling the effects of the smoke and flames. Cheers to you, sir." Everyone joined Alison as she toasted the lieutenant.

"And finally—last but not least, as they say—there's Sergeant Johnson, who goes into a raging conflagration to find his missing partner and my uncle, and helps drag them out just before they..."—she started to tear up again and couldn't say the words—"well, let's just say it was in the nick of time." There was a final set of congratulatory thank-yous and toasting. "So you see," concluded Alison, "there're more than enough kudos to go around. We can all pat ourselves on the back."

"I guess you're right," said Mulcahy. "But I did want to acknowledge all of your efforts in some way. So did Pat. This little shindig is a start, but I'll also be sending out letters to your respective employers citing your contributions. It may come in handy someday." Everyone said it wasn't necessary, but thanked him nonetheless.

"In addition," added Mulcahy, "I want to publicly thank my partner here for saving my life. We've been together a long time, and I guess I'll have a few more years on the force, thanks to him." He turned toward Johnson and shook his hand. "Thank you, Pat, very much. I mean that."

"Anytime, Vinny," replied Johnson, sheepishly.

"Oh, and one more thing," said Mulcahy, still holding onto Johnson's hand. "I'll be submitting your name to the promotions board tomorrow, pal. If I have anything to say about it, it'll be Lieutenant Johnson in the not-too-distant future. You'll have to pass the test, but that shouldn't be a problem, not with me coaching you. I may regret it, but, what the hell, I think it's worth a shot. Whadaya think, Pat?"

Johnson couldn't say anything for a moment. He merely hung onto his friend's hand and pumped it once again after regaining a little of his composure. The room erupted into the loudest cries and screams yet. Everyone was happy for Johnson. All he could offer was, "Thanks, Vinnie. Thanks a lot."

Father Mike asked Mulcahy about what was likely to happen to the members of Ernst's coven, the ones who had been rounded up the previous night. "They've all been booked on Murder One charges," explained Mulcahy. "Every last one of 'em took part willingly in those meetings, so they all had a hand in the killings. They're all professing innocence, of course, and there may be some question as to whether they may've been coerced to a certain extent—maybe the same way Stephen was—so I guess it'll be up to a jury to decide their fate. They'll have a court full of lawyers and self-proclaimed experts on this and that, duking it out. But I can't imagine any of these kooks being let go. In this crazy day and age, though, I suppose insanity pleas are possible. But either way—jail or the psychiatric ward—I'd be willing to bet the whole lot'll be put away for a good long time. Good riddance, too."

"Amen to that," said Father Mike. Everyone laughed.

"And what about Ernst?" asked Stephen. "I heard shots and saw him go down, but I wasn't sure if he survived or not."

"Unfortunately not," said Mulcahy. "He's dead. Don't get me wrong. He deserved to die—excuse me for saying so, Father—but it would've been nice to have him around to interrogate. I'm sure he was chock full of fascinating information about lots of things we may never get to know anything about now. Like that weirdo book—what was it called? The Wicca Codex, or something like that? I'm afraid it was lost in the fire. The last I saw of it, Ernst had it when he rushed at me. But it was gone when I dragged him out. At least I didn't see it. I assume he dropped the damn thing when he landed on top of me and we hit the floor. The flames didn't take very long reaching that spot, as I recall. Maybe it's just as well it's gone, given the evil powers it was supposed to have had."

"Oh, it did, all right," said Stephen. "I can vouch for that. All those poor victims were killed through its force, including my friend John.

Ernst and Lariakin admitted as much. I had first-hand experience with what it could do."

"I guess so," said Mulcahy. "By the way, speaking of books..."—he walked over to the table, picked up a package, and brought it over to Father Mike—"you'll want to hang onto this. It's that Voynich thing you had last night. You gave it to me for safe keeping just before we made it out. Someone must've put it with my other things at the hospital last night. I brought it in this morning."

Father Mike was relieved beyond belief. "Bless you, Lieutenant. I wondered what happened to it. I honestly thought it was gone. That would have been devastating. Now I can get it back down to Yale where it belongs. Thanks so much."

"No problem," said Mulcahy. He turned to Stephen. "How's the arm?"

"Stings a bit, but much better than last night. They tell me it'll be okay in a few days. Just needs time. I talked to my boss a little while ago and told him I'd be back in the office tomorrow. He wanted me to take a couple more days, but I told him there was no need. I feel fine."

"Glad to hear it," said Mulcahy.

"What about Lariakin?" asked Stephen.

"Don't know," replied Mulcahy. "No one saw him get out last night, that's for sure. I heard several police officers talking this morning. They swear they shot him as he lunged at Father Mike, but he didn't turn up anywhere. We may find a body buried in the rubble, once it cools down."

"Not so, Vinnie," said Johnson. "I checked with the fire boys before we got here. They've been in there already and didn't find anyone. Not a trace."

"Excuse me, Lieutenant," said Father Mike, "but I don't think anyone will be finding any evidence of Lariakin."

"What do you mean, Father?" asked Mulcahy.

"You're forgetting what I told you a few days ago, back at Stephen's apartment, right after we were able to free him from Lariakin's grip.

I'm convinced that Lariakin was—is—the earthly representation of Satan. He's the devil, as sure as we're standing here. When he came at me last night, I was lucky to still have control of the Voynich Manuscript. Just enough, apparently, to ward him off. I'm sure his intention was to get inside me and take what he couldn't get so many years ago. He'd gotten Ernst, a fallen priest, but now he was on the verge of getting a real one. It would've been a triumph for him, salvaging a prize on his night of defeat. Despite the manuscript, he managed to get close enough to affect my arms and legs. They became numb, useless really, before the Voynich did its work. When it did, Lariakin just...well, disappeared. One second, he was on me. The next, he was gone. Just...not there. I think I passed out at that point, 'cause the next thing I remember, the Lieutenant was leaning over me, with the fire all around. I thought it was all over and Lariakin had gotten me after all. But, thanks to you, Lieutenant, my ugly mug is still around. Just don't expect to find any evidence of Lariakin."

"So you weren't kidding about that, huh?" said Mulcahy. "I remember you saying it, but it just didn't register back then. I'm not sure I wanted to believe it, I guess." He paused, then added, "It looks like Pat and me'll be able to provide lots of new material for that police course on the occult. The one we took a while back? They may even ask us to teach it, for that matter."

Alison wanted to tie up the only loose end she could see. She spoke to Mulcahy. "Now that we know what this was all about, it seems odd that John Demming's death didn't fit the pattern. He wasn't Catholic, and obviously didn't have any clergy in the family. Any ideas on that?"

"I think it was as simple as Demming stumbling onto Ernst's operation and not liking what he saw. He wanted to warn Stephen about his concerns. That was the reason for his Saturday call, not to mention his calling Ernst a 'strange' dude. Ernst got suspicious and...well, unfortunately, Demming got in the way." Mulcahy paused. There was an awkward silence. "The important thing," continued Mulcahy, speaking directly to Stephen, "is that you shouldn't feel that it's your fault. You can't blame yourself. It's just something that happened. It's Ernst's doing, not yours."

"I hear you, Lieutenant," said Stephen. "But I think it'll take a little while for me to get over it. Time heals all wounds, they say. I expect the same will be true for me." Stephen wanted to change the subject. He remembered something he had been meaning to ask Mulcahy about. "Say, Lieutenant, guess that mike I wore last night did the trick, huh? I assume you got everything you needed on tape, right?"

"Yep, for the most part," replied Mulcahy.

"You guys came right in on cue," said Stephen. "Good thing, too. Things were getting a bit dicey right about then. Glad you deciphered my message."

"Yeah, well..." stammered Mulcahy. "Been meaning to tell you about that. We heard everything up to their admission of guilt about the killings. The mike went dead after that. Didn't hear a thing, so Pat and I decided not to chance it. We went in as soon as we lost contact. Luckily, we heard your message about the door and buzzer, so we knew we could go in quietly. We wanted to be inside just in case things got hot, which we assumed could happen any moment, so we positioned ourselves just outside the meeting room and listened at the door."

Stephen turned a little pale at this news. "Christ," he said, "good thing I didn't know that. I would've been even more frightened than I was." He turned toward Alison and said, "Did you know what was going on the whole time?"

"I did," she answered. "At least up until the mike blew and Lieutenant Mulcahy and Sergeant Johnson left the cruiser to go inside. After that, I was in the dark. That was the worst part, not knowing what was happening. The last fifteen minutes were pure hell. I felt so useless. I wanted to help but couldn't."

"It must've been awful for you," said Stephen, squeezing Alison's hand. "I hope you'll let me make it up to you. How about dinner tonight? Any place you like, as long as it's in Boston, that is. Whadaya say?"

Everyone whooped and hollered at Stephen's invitation. Father Mike said, only half in jest, "Now, if you youngsters decide you need my services at some point, I'm available," then whistled and clapped as loudly as the others.

Alison blushed, then said, "Well now, Mister Blake, how can I possibly refuse an offer as public as that?" She hesitated a moment, then joined in the laughter. "It's a date," she said.

* * *

Jay Burgholz picked up the phone on his desk and dialed Alison's extension. He could see she was back and asked her to come into his office. He had a little surprise for her, he said. Be right in, she said.

When she got to Burgholz's office, she expected him to ask her about the little party at police headquarters. Instead, he merely sat there behind his desk, grinning. She was so taken aback by his odd behavior she almost missed the surprise. Then she saw it. There, in front of the desk, sat two brand spanking new chairs, replacements for the relics she had so long endured. They were upholstered in brown leather and looked quite elegant.

Burgholz saw Alison's gaze focus on the chairs. "Well, what do you think?" he asked. "Swank, huh?"

Alison didn't answer. Rather, she walked slowly over to the new additions and sat down in one of them. She leaned back and grasped the arms, basking in the luxurious leather and feeling its coolness on her legs and arms. She pushed her head back until it touched the top of the chair, then closed her eyes. She remained in that position for some time. Finally, she opened her eyes, looked at Burgholz, and smiled. All she could say was, "Why, Jay?"

"Funny you should ask," he said. "I decided, when you win the Pulitzer Prize for your story on *The Codex* murders, people are gonna want to talk to your editor. I just thought I'd better make my office a bit more homey looking."

Those in the newsroom had to turn their heads at the sounds emanating from Burgholz's office. It was Alison, roaring away in fits of uncontrollable laughter.

Chapter 38

Wednesday, November 1

The evening promised to be a wonderful experience. Gone were the troubles that Alison and Stephen had been dealing with for what seemed like an eternity. The murders were solved, Ernst was dead, *The Codex* was destroyed, and justice would be done with respect to the remaining perpetrators. Alison could now work on the story of the year, if not the decade, and Stephen looked forward to resuming his career in publishing. The only thing that would have made it better is if the victims could have somehow been brought back. Although this was not to be, at least their deaths would not go unpunished. Perhaps the best part, as far as Alison and Stephen were concerned, was that they could now get back to living their mundane lives. Well, maybe not so mundane, after all. Only now there was no doubt they would do so together. And tonight would be the first step toward that end.

Stephen had offered to take Alison anywhere she wanted for dinner, but was surprised to learn her choice was Shanghai Gardens. "What better way to celebrate than to return to where it all started for us?" she asked. Stephen couldn't disagree with that logic. Besides, it *did* have great food. From now on, this would be their special place.

They were working on their hot-and-sour soup course when Stephen said, "By the way, Ali, that was quite a bombshell Ernst dropped when he said his real name was Faust. I'm still amazed that such a little old man with gray hair and stooped shoulders turns out to be not only a mass murderer, but also the descendant of one of the most mysterious figures in the occult world."

"That *was* quite a revelation, wasn't it?" agreed Alison. "Then again, it seems to fit, really. What's one more bizarre twist to an already strange tale?"

"Yeah, I guess," said Stephen, somewhat nervously.

Alison sensed his unease. "What?" she asked.

Stephen hesitated. "It's nothing, really. Forget it."

"C'mon? What're you talking about?"

"Well, I was more than a little curious about the Faust legend, so I did a little research of my own after we left police headquarters. What I found was just a bit disconcerting."

"Tell me," said Alison. Her jovial smile had given way to a strained grin.

"It seems that rather odd things have befallen some of those who have delved into the life of Faust, real or imagined, over the years. Lots of artists, writers, composers, whatever, found him to be a fascinating subject for their works. Some of them have paid the price, it seems."

"For instance."

Stephen pulled out a piece of paper he had tucked into his pants pocket. "Took some notes as I was reading," he said. He glanced at the paper. "Item number one: Goethe. *Faust* was arguably his greatest work. He finished it in 1831. In a year, he was dead."

"Not very compelling," said Alison.

"Maybe not, but perhaps just a little coincidental, all the same. Then there was Eugene Delacroix, one of the greatest and most influential of French painters in the nineteenth century. He did a series of lithographs illustrating a French edition of Goethe's *Faust*. Eventually, his health suffered, and he died. Next on the list is an Austrian poet named Nikolaus Lenau. He used Faust as the subject of one of his poems. Died insane in 1850. Christopher Marlowe, the English dramatist, wrote *The Tragicall History of Dr. Faustus* in the sixteenth century based on an English translation of the German *Faustbuch* of 1587. He lived less than thirty years, killed in a quarrel over a tavern bill. Want more? How about Gerard de Nerval, another nineteenth century French writer? He adapted Goethe's *Faust* into French, also wrote about ancient and folk mythology, symbols, religion, and supernatural events. He was afflicted with severe mental disorders and was institutionalized about eight times."

"My, you *have* been busy, haven't you?" said Alison, her smile returning.

"C'mon, Ali. It's not funny. There's this long record of strange happenings associated with those who've been connected with Faust in some way, and now you're writing about him. It just makes me a little nervous, that's all."

"That's sweet, Stephen, but I don't think anything's going to happen to me. Really. Don't worry about it. It's not like I'm doing a major artistic work about the guy. I'm just reporting a story. And besides, I've got my Uncle Mike in my corner, just in case."

"That's true," laughed Stephen. "That does make me feel a little better. But I can still worry about it if I want."

"Fine. You go ahead and worry. But not tonight. Let's not spoil the evening and what it means for us. We've survived a horrible ordeal and have nothing but good things ahead. I think that deserves an upbeat mood. Don't you?"

Stephen looked into Alison's eyes and saw things he hadn't seen in a long time. Things like love, and support, and happiness, and confidence in what lay ahead. Things that had been missing in his own life for many years. They could now be restored to him, he realized. They were within his grasp. And he didn't even have to ask her about barriers anymore. He was glad he hadn't at the first dinner here. 'What barriers?' he thought. "You're absolutely right," he said, raising his teacup in a toast. "I'll drink to the future, on one condition."

"And what's that?" asked Alison.

"That you share it with me."

Alison looked into his eyes. "I'll definitely drink to that," she said.

* * *

As Alison and Stephen enjoyed their meal and looked forward to the promise of a bright future, the figure of a small boy walked the back streets of Boston, little more than a half-mile away. He was haggard looking, with unruly dark hair and penetrating eyes that cut through the darkness. He appeared to be no more than ten years of age, though he seemed unaffected by the chilly air and his lack of protective clothing. What he did wear was dark in color. The boy's path favored shadowy areas, and he darted from one to the other with considerable ease and without hesitation, as though he knew exactly where he was going and would not be deterred by any impediment.

His destination that night was the Beacon Hill fire scene. The blaze had been brought under control that morning and had since been picked over by the fire department. They had stayed most of the day, wetting it down to prevent a new flareup, then departed late in the afternoon. The site was a complete ruin, but no longer in need of professional attention. The boy, on nearing the scene, surveyed it cautiously to verify that there were no fire or police personnel lurking about. He saw none, only an occasional curious passerby. He waited until the street was deserted, then moved quickly into the debris left by the fire.

Almost an entire block had been destroyed, but the boy ignored all but one area. He went immediately to the spot where the bookstore had been located and stopped. He turned rapidly, examining the charred ruins in all directions. The remains were a sodden mess, still wet from the firemen's hosing. At first, he saw nothing. Then, after no more than a minute had elapsed, the boy noticed something. It was faint, at first, then progressed in intensity until there was no mistaking it. There, less than ten feet from where he stood, came a glowing light. It was an odd color, not green, not purple, but rather a mixture of the two. The boy moved quickly toward it. The light came from somewhere beneath the rubble. He immediately bent down and started to work his hands into the wet mass of ash and charred wood. About a foot down, he found what he was seeking. Still bent low, he pulled it from its resting place and held it so that it caught the faint light of a nearby streetlamp. He knew it would be undamaged but was nevertheless pleased to confirm it.

Wicca Codex

The boy smiled, then whispered as he held the object in both hands and looked at it with reverence. "Thank you, my prince. I shall use this well," he said.

He rose, tucked *The Codex* under his arm, and disappeared into the night.